CLAIMING DARKNESS

CLAIMING DARKNESS

NELLY ALIKYAN

To my Maderjan Baderjan.
Thanks for always supporting me.

ALSO BY N. ALIKYAN

Buttercup Baby

Promise of A Lifetime

At the young age of thirteen, he'd taken the powers of seven different people. One after another after another. As his first attempt to steal.

Ever.

At nineteen, he took the power of nine different people.

At twenty-nine, another five almost directly one after another.

And in between it all, he'd taken more and more and more.

He was an anomaly that didn't come about every century, but luck was with them this time.

Yes, some of these powers weren't strong.

Yes, some of them were dormant, uselessly sitting in his system.

Yes, that was the one little problem in this entire equation.

But he was exactly what was needed. He was exactly what could bring together all the supernatural and create one super creature.

Completely unstoppable.

Wholly unbeatable.

Entirely in control.

Now all that was needed was to get him to bow down in order to take over his form and possess the power. But that would be easy. He hadn't exactly hidden his weakness from the world.

_I_t really was a wonder that Harry had never realized the amount of neglect he'd shown to his old friend. Sure, Harry had always been closer to the man's wife, but it didn't change the fact that they'd also been friends and he was the father of Harry's charges. He was the father of the woman Harry had fallen for.

And they'd never come to see Bishop.

With Harry's porting ability, he would've been able to bring the girls to this cemetery two towns over easily. And Bishop deserved at least that much.

But he hadn't thought to do so. None of them had.

Until Maya.

It made him feel utterly like garbage.

He should've brought Vera at some point. Bishop had been her best friend.

Point one to Maya for making him feel like a wanker.

The cemetery Bishop was in was much smaller than the one Loretta had been buried in. Harry still wondered how they hadn't arranged for both of them to be buried together. They could've chosen one of the two cemeteries, or just met in the middle and both been buried in the town that separated them.

Harry had come to this grave about a week after he'd found out about Bishop's death. But only that once. To say goodbye to his friend and fellow warlock, so few and far between they were. Both friends and warlocks alike.

Harry landed them right in front of the stone that marked Bishop's final resting place, and Vera's hand tightened around his. He didn't have to look at her to know her heart hurt at missing her father.

"Wow, Vera," Maya started. "I hadn't realized how weird it must've been to visit Mom's grave without ever meeting her until now."

Vera crouched before the stone and took out a water bottle and towelette she'd brought with her to clean it. "Hey, Pops. Sorry I've been gone for so long." She wiped away the little bit that had stained the stone in the months she'd been gone, and again, Harry felt like a total arse for not bringing her. "But I'm back, and I've brought some company."

There was a caw that stiffened his back. Harry's gaze immediately jumped from Vera crouched before the headstone to the branch on the other side of the cemetery and the crow that was flying away. He was being ridiculous, but he swore he'd seen that crow before.

Twenty-six years ago. Right around the time Loretta took the deal to stay away from her daughter for a quarter of a century.

Harry looked back to their little group in time to notice Maya's gaze on the bird. When her eyes turned back, Harry caught the bit of recognition there.

He must be making it up.

She couldn't recognize that bird. Harry was sure *he* didn't even recognize it.

"You remember Harry." Vera's still crouched position pointed up. "You guys are nothing alike, I hope you know that. I guess warlocks are all very different, huh."

"Of course the old man remembers me. I was the best of friends they could've asked for," Harry joked.

Vera rolled her eyes and turned back to the stone, gently wiping it down a final time. "He didn't mean that, Pops. You're not old."

Harry scoffed, and Vera turned to whip his leg, a knowing grin trying not to cross her face.

Then she was facing the stone again. "And your other daughters. I'm sorry you never got to meet them."

Because of me.

That's the part Vera didn't say, but Harry knew she felt. He hadn't gotten to meet his two other daughters, after being there for their births, because Vera couldn't be near Loretta. Harry still didn't know how to make her believe that it wasn't her fault as she stepped back beside him again and took his hand.

He was still getting used to the feeling of her fingers clasped around his, the tingling it shot up his chest. The rightness of it all.

Camilla was the first to step up between the two younger Whittles. "Hey...Dad? It feels weird saying that."

Harry had told Camilla and Maya that Bishop truly was their father, but he could imagine it was just as weird for them to call Bishop 'Dad' as it had been at the beginning for Vera to call Loretta 'Mom.'

But it did bring up the question Harry would ask the two if he could—why hadn't Loretta told Maya and Camilla about their father? At least a little bit, the way Bishop had told Vera about 'Lore.'

Camilla unwrapped and placed a small bouquet of red roses before the stone. "Honestly, I don't know what to say. I think it sucks that we never grew up with you, but Mom was so good to us that I can't be mad about the life I had. And I know a lot more now. Like why you couldn't be there. You were raising my beautiful big sister for us, and I have to be thankful to you for that. And I have to be thankful to you for loving Mom so much that you continued to see her even knowing you two couldn't have a normal, real relationship for a quarter of a century."

Harry knew Camilla wasn't saying that because her parent's continued relationship brought her along. She truly meant it.

But hearing her speak those words made Harry truly consider their situation for the first time. Well, the first time he'd be able to better understand their decisions. How difficult it would be.

Thinking of it now, Harry couldn't imagine doing as they'd done. Having to leave Vera's side for twenty-five years.

If they fell into the same situation, he'd do it. Of course he would. But he couldn't even begin to imagine the pain of not being beside her every day.

And up until a week ago, he'd thought Hunter had felt the same way about Maya. Even with his hundred plus years of existence, Harry had fallen for the trap Hunter had so beautifully executed. Even though a nagging feeling in him told him that Hunter wouldn't have done that to Maya.

Maybe Harry had been fooled better than he'd thought if his heart was even fighting for Hunter's defense.

Harry glanced at Maya as she stared down at the stone. There wasn't much emotion on her features, but Harry knew she must be hurting. He tried, twice now, to go to her for a little potion lesson and to talk to her about everything that had happened, but she was always disappearing. Harry had to assume she was going on her habitual jogs in order to sweat her feelings away, because even though she'd never said it aloud, she'd fallen in love with the demon.

And he'd betrayed her.

Camilla brought her fingers to her lips and kissed them before sending her love to her father. "I know I didn't know you, but I also know I would've loved you so much. Part of me thinks I would've been a daddy's girl."

She looked lovingly at the stone for another few moments, then stepped back.

Vera's hand tightened again in his hold, and Harry looked over to find water lightly lining her eyes. He soothed a thumb over the top of her hand and stared. She was so beautiful, Harry couldn't believe it sometimes.

Finally, Maya moved to crouch before the stone, her flowers already unwrapped. She'd gotten an array of colored tulips, and mixed them in with her sister's roses.

Her fingers grazed over Bishop's name, and a small smile rose. "I know you're still here, Dad."

Harry's heart constricted. It was the first time he'd heard Maya call Bishop 'Dad,' and he didn't know why, but he felt a happiness for his friend that he hadn't realized was missing.

"Sucks that you're not here here though," Maya continued, the small smile turning into a knowing smirk. "I'd give anything to see your reaction at your little girl and your old friend going at it like a couple of teenagers."

The laughter bubbled up, but Harry didn't let it come out as he glanced over to Vera to find her turning redder by the moment.

"I don't know what you gave her growing up, but your daughter's bits are act-ive." Maya's wide smirk said she knew Vera was burning up without having to turn in her direction.

And she was.

Maya was so crude sometimes, even childish in moments like these, but in instances where Harry got to enjoy Vera's flushed skin, he was thankful for it.

Vera's eyes moved to meet his, and Harry was shocked by what he saw there. Because it wasn't embarrassment.

It was need.

His pupils grew darker, and he wanted more than anything to cover his hips from the younger Whittles because they did *not* need to see him so affected.

He could bring them back another time, possibly individually so they each had time with their father to talk it out. But now? Now he needed to get home. Needed especially to get a certain Whittle home.

Vera had wondered since she'd found out about Maya and Hunter what it was that always sent her body back to him.

Now she knew.

Her back slammed into the window of the piano room —*their* room— and Harry's hands ripped open the button up she had on.

She moaned as Harry's mouth nibbled at her collarbone. "Harry, we can't…my…sisters…" *What were their names?*

He licked up her throat to her lips, and she couldn't remember her arguments. "I have a feeling they won't be staying home." He nibbled at her ear. "But even if they do, Maya's already charmed every room in the house. They won't hear."

Her body arched into him, and she knew it would be a losing fight to try not to moan as his hands skimmed up her body and cupped her bra-covered breasts.

Then he was between them.

Up until Harry, motor boating had sounded so weird to Vera. But now, she loved every time his face found its way between her breasts. And he loved doing it.

Vera squirmed at the feeling of his tongue in the valley as his hands played with her nipples through the laced bra. She'd also come to learn, with Harry's help, that she wasn't very patient.

And he annoyingly loved wearing three-piece suits.

She threw his jacket off his shoulders as one cup fell to expose a brown nipple. It was exhilaratingly dirty the way Harry grinned up at her before taking it into his mouth.

"Harry." She clawed at the jacket. "Take it off."

His teeth tweaked her nipple, causing her hips to buck forward in need as he stripped the jacket off. She had the buttons of the vest ripped off and was shoving it down as he switched to the other nipple. His breath teased her before his mouth went to work.

The buttons of his shirt followed those of the vest, and finally, after scraping the shirt down with unsteady fingers, he was bare from the waist up.

He licked from her nipple to her mouth. "Your turn, love."

His tongue slipped into her mouth as he pulled her shirt off and unhooked her bra. They both moaned as their naked chests met.

But Vera wasn't very patient. And she was very, very wet. "Harry, would you please stop messing around and just get your cock inside me?"

He chuckled against her lips as he unbuttoned her jeans and slipped his hand inside, his fingers sliding over her folds. He always loved when she spoke to him like that. "Lords, Vera. So primed already."

She stopped waiting for him. Instead, she pulled on his belt to loosen, then unfastened his trousers. "Stupid expensive suit. Just get off."

He pulled away. "Take your clothes off, Vera. I want to watch."

Vera pulled off of the window and moved shaking hands to the waistband of her jeans and hooked her underwear too as she slowly pushed the pieces down. As much as she wanted him, she also still wanted to look sexy for him, so she kept the speed controlled.

She stepped out in the most seductive way she knew how and slipped the two pieces of clothing to the side, then watched his gaze eat her up. She had to squeeze her legs closer together in order to relieve some of the pressure while indulging in the feeling of having his eyes on her. It was both thrilling and torturous to not command him to get his ass back to her.

His trousers were undone but still hanging from his waist

when he walked over to her again and slammed her into the window.

The most beautiful part of this room was definitely the floor-to-ceiling windows two of the walls were covered in that looked out over their mazed garden. Hopefully her sisters hadn't decided on a morning stroll.

His hands gripped her bare ass and lifted her up, his tongue finding it's way from the back of her ear to her mouth. He hooked her legs around his back and Vera pushed his trousers down just low enough for his cock to jut out. She was tired of waiting for him.

He pulled on her bottom lip as he angled himself and pushed into her.

Vera's back arched into him as her hands slammed into the window behind her to find balance. She knew—and loved—that there would be handprints afterward.

"That's right, love. Spread that cunt for my cock," he groaned into her ear, making her insides squeeze in the way that drove him crazy. But she couldn't help it, the sounds he made drove her crazy.

Then it was the sounds she made. That they made.

"I want to watch you come apart for me, Vera," he gasped into her mouth.

"Keep talking like that and I will," she muttered, unable to say anything clever back. She was too filled with…everything. Too filled and too close to care. The sound of their bodies coming together over and over and his breath mixing with hers was all too much.

She knew she was calling out his name, but her mind was fizzling into such oblivion, she couldn't concentrate on it. All she knew was that she was about to come and she wanted—no, needed—him to come with her.

Her fingers pulled on his hair and she bit his bottom lip. "Come with me, Harry. Fuck, come with me."

His tone was both guttural and cocky. "I thought you'd never beg, sweetheart."

That little nickname, mixed with the way he said it, sent her over the edge. He had a way of controlling her with the little things he said.

"Milk me, love," he moaned into her ear. "Let me fill you."

She spasmed in his hold as she rode the orgasm, feeling like it would never end as he watched her.

He was so fucking handsome.

When she came back from her high and could feel him dripping down her leg as he slowly pulled out of her, he leaned in closer. "I think I'll ward this room so no one else can enter. I want to fuck you on every inch."

A way with fucking words.

2

Oddly enough, just the simple act of shadowing made Maya feel that little bit closer to Hunter while he was gone.

And shadowing into the house that he'd been raised in? The office he still came to often to discuss Delvaux family matters? He was all around her and yet, nowhere near her.

Augustine Delvaux, head of the family and father of her demon, stood with his back to her as he fixed himself a drink. He stiffened at her arrival, but she saw his shoulders relax after only a second, like he knew it was her.

He turned, cup of brandy in hand and smirk wide on his features. "That's a nifty trick. Especially considering that *one* in particular is a specifically demon, and *not* dark, power. I'd have to wonder how you acquired it."

Her smirk matched his own. "Your son is a bad influence."

He shook his head in her direction, but there was pride booming in him. "I bet."

Maya moved to take her seat—the green leather armchair by the fireplace that had apparently been Hunter's go-to. It was hers now.

Her legs wrapped beneath her butt as she sat and stared at

the fire.

Augustine took the leather chair across from her. "How are you today, Daughter?"

Her breath blew out. "I went to my father's grave."

He sat back and took a sip of his drink. "Ah, Bishop Whittle."

This was her third time over in the past week, and the first two times they'd only spoken of Hunter. But now? The way he said her father's name… "What?"

"What?" His act was poorly done and he knew it.

"Augustine." Her eyes narrowed on him.

He scoffed through a hidden laugh. "It's Father to you, darling."

Her eyes fell to slits, but didn't waver.

"You know, even if my son's cock didn't beg for you, I cannot fathom him denying you anything."

"We're not talking about your son right now." Plus, Maya knew he couldn't deny her anything.

But she wouldn't deny, it was still nice to hear his father say so. Even if he did so in such a crude manner.

He finished off his drink and moved to refill it. With his back to her, he said, "When I found out you had high-level dark powers to match powerful demons, I wasn't too surprised. Bishop's line would have been the one."

She froze in her spot and watched his back. "I thought it was my mother's line that had dark-power witches."

He moved back to his seat. "It is. Even without Bishop, I wouldn't have been surprised, but with Bishop, I have to wonder if fire control is all the true darkness you have."

Tell him about the portal.

No. She'd tell him when Hunter was around.

No real reason why—it wasn't that she didn't trust Augustine. She did. But she wanted Hunter with her when she told such a big secret.

"What about my father makes that so?" she asked.

"From what I understand, he comes from a long line of dark

witches. You know the way warlocks are born. If a male is born into a witch family, they either come out a warlock, or the more likely case, completely human. Bishop's line before the Whittles, I believe it was the African coven with the most dark witches in it. And before that even, I've heard rumor of it's descendants from Europe before mixing."

Maya loved that like his son, Augustine never lied to her. It made conversations so much simpler with him.

"It makes one wonder, with Europe's coven of the most dark witches and Africa's coven of the most dark witches, what is the true darkness lingering inside you?" He smirked. "Or your sisters, though I'm less convinced about them."

He never lied to her, so she wouldn't lie to him.

But that didn't mean she'd tell him. Yet.

"Have you heard from him?" She knew her voice grew somber and almost weak as she asked, but she couldn't help the pain that echoed through her.

Augustine's knowing look told her he knew she was holding something back, but she didn't care. She would wait to tell him, even though she desperately wanted to hear his theories on why her portal power went away.

He finished off his drink again, his gaze never leaving hers, then placed his cup on the arm of the chair to balance and inter-locked his fingers. "I still do not understand why you would think he would ever come here before coming to you."

She shrugged. *Fear.*

That he never truly loved her.

She stared at the fire and let the memories of their flames mixing envelop her to drive away that nagging feeling.

"You're his mate, Daughter. He will come to you." Augustine's tone was almost soothing.

Her eyes shot to his. "Why are you comforting me? Demons aren't supposed to care for others. Hunter still doesn't care about most of the people he grew up with. I imagine you're the same."

"I am." He wore a slight grin now. "But I have always cared for my boys, and now I have the daughter I have always wanted."

"So because you like the advantages I can bring to the family," she dumbed down.

"Partly. And partly because I truly do understand the fascination my son has with you. You're intriguing in the most delightful ways, Daughter. But also because as his mate, you were made to be my daughter as much as you were made to be his. I cannot help but feel the need to protect you at all costs. I imagine this is what it would've felt like had I had Colette with a witch less distasteful."

Maya rolled her eyes and tried to hide the small smile. "Be careful, Delvaux, your bleeding heart is showing."

He barked a laugh because they both knew he didn't have a heart, even for his children. But Maya enjoyed being there, in the presence of the man who had raised her future.

He leaned over so his elbows rested on his knees. "Trust me, darling, he'll be back to you, and soon enough you two can bring me grandchildren. I cannot fathom the power you two reproducing will bring to this world."

Maya shook her head, but felt a lightness in her soul. "You mean to this family."

"Potato, potato."

***

Camilla sat on the Persian rug in the middle of the attic with the Book opened between her legs. She wanted to speak to it again and hoped that it would work since she would no longer be asking it for that spell it had been trying to hide from the halfies.

She tried something simple—a spell she already knew was in the Book and could flip to on her own.

And was surprised when it worked. Instantly.

"Ooo!" She clapped with excitement. "Okay, Book, now be good to me. Show me something you haven't shown us before."

Again, Camilla was shocked by how easily it flipped. Like not having the threat of the halfies trying to resurrect Grandmama completely opened the Book up to her.

It opened to a page with a short paragraph about the oldest witch-demon romance in history—Miradora and Adramalech.

There was no spell to accompany it, just a short paragraph about the couple. Camilla had found that a few times, a short paragraph to tell them about different people or couples. They were usually about animal demons, but she'd seen the odd history story within too.

She wondered if the importance here was the relationship between the enemy species. The one Maya's relationship would have greatly mirrored, being that these two were in love and Adramalech was a full demon.

Though the difference was glaring to Camilla since Hunter had obviously not been in love with Maya.

"Thank you for that little history, Book. Now, another!"

This time it flipped to a page, seemed to think about it again and changed its mind, then flipped to another. It was amusing watching it make these decisions like it was a real person.

"What's this, Book?" she questioned it like it would begin narrating. Then she wondered if there *was* a way she could get the Book to narrate to her.

It was a two-page spread she hadn't seen before. Camilla still couldn't believe how many pages there were that they had yet to see, all these pages that were hidden half the time. Incredible magic.

The two-page spread showed a pentagram with a dagger going down the middle, and the edges looked to be bleeding out in black. There were small sentences around the edges of the pages describing this design as a dark magic used over a millennia ago.

One of the sentences also told of the lasting effects of the dark magic used for this spell and that the design was mostly a depiction that dark magic had been in use and not indicative of any harm itself. Useful to know as a witch when you're dealing with so many people who wanted power.

"I wonder if this was around Grandmama's time?" Camilla whispered to herself. "Is that why you're showing this to me, Book?"

No answer. Of course not. All the Book could do was flip pages for her.

Camilla sighed and pushed the psychopath out of her mind. She smiled at the Book again. "Thanks for the interesting information. Now show me another, my friend."

The pages all stood up like the Book was thinking about it, then flipped quickly like it was excited to show her the next page.

It came to a page with a dog-eared corner Camilla was shocked she hadn't seen before, and on the dog-eared section in a heart was a 'B+L.' Camilla laughed at the sight, then looked down at the page to find a spell to enhance sexual pleasures.

"Oh my god...Book, why would you show me what spells my parents used!" But she laughed along with the outburst because it was nice to see any rememberings of her parents.

<hr>

She wasn't home.

She wasn't in her bedroom or her office, at her mother's grave or that gelato shop Mario's that she loved so much. She wasn't on her favorite jogging route or in the shower, out to any of the shops she'd mentioned before or on a walk.

She wasn't home.

He shadowed into the grand entrance of his manor—which was really just a wide open space of black marble with the grand staircases on either side—and thought about any other place he may be able to find her.

Hunter looked down to the ring he wore on his left hand.

He'd begun the process of making the rings right around the time Colette had showed back up in his life. When she'd threatened what was his.

And since they'd finished cooling the night before Grandmama was resurrected, Hunter had worn his. Now, he wanted to present Maya with hers. And she was nowhere to be found.

The last thing he wanted was to be in this enormous manor without her. Every square inch of the place reminded him of her. The way she commanded him around like it were hers.

It *was* her manor. Everything he had was hers. He was ready to give it all to her.

But first, he needed to find her and make her believe he hadn't betrayed her. Make her understand that every breath he took was in order to keep her safe. Show her that he was at her disposal, that any way she needed him to prove it, he'd do it.

He looked back up from the ring and froze.

Maya was standing beneath a grand staircase at the other end of the room. In only his large shirt. Her dark hair tumbled around her form and her lips slightly parted.

And she just stared at him. Like *she* couldn't believe it.

Hunter's heart raced in a way he hadn't ever experienced before.

"I checked for you everywhere," he spoke, but didn't feel his lips moving. "You weren't home."

"I am home," Maya breathed out.

She *was* home.

Home.

She broke first and ran into his arms.

Her body broke his frozen stance and his arms wrapped tightly around her as he stumbled but didn't fall. Her legs wrapped around his waist as her arms tightened around his neck, and all he could think was that finally *he* was home.

He breathed her in, and when he finally convinced himself he wasn't dreaming this, he let his arms loosen just enough to graze over every bit of her. Almost like another confirmation that she was here with him.

He could feel her breathing him in at his neck like she was trying to convince herself of the same thing. "You're home," she mumbled into his skin.

Home. Because outside of her, this was his home. And the Whittle house wasn't hers anymore, this manor was. This was theirs, and every bit of his uncaring demon soul loved the sound of that.

He couldn't process how lucky he was. How much faith she'd had in him. He didn't understand how she wasn't making him beg forgiveness.

His hands moved to the end of the shirt she wore and slid beneath the fabric, finding it was *all* she was wearing. "I'm home, love."

She kissed his neck, then pulled away just enough to look at him, water brimming her eyes. "I hate you so much, Hunter Delvaux. If you ever think you could leave me like that again, I'll burn this world down just to find and kill you."

A chuckle left him as one hand reached out from the shirt and stroked her hair, stopping at the back of her neck. "Good, love. So fucking good."

He pulled her in by the neck so that their lips pressed and every fiber of his body finally felt alive again. Because she was his life. These lips were his life force.

And the passion with which she kissed him back? His entire reason for being.

Hunter felt a wetness touch his cheek and pulled away to find a single tear sliding down Maya's cheek. His thumb immediately reached out to wipe it away as those brown eyes that were his favorite sight in the world stared back at him. "Thank you for coming back to me."

"Eternally, love."

3

The air moved around Maya, and she knew he was shadowing them to another room, but didn't care enough to focus anywhere but on him. Everything about this very moment made her whole again.

His hand cradling her face as that thumb skimmed her cheek lest she cry again.

The light caressing of his fingertips beneath the shirt she wore.

His body pressed against hers, and those eyes that told her he felt exactly as she did. Those black, depthless eyes that showed her more emotion than any other pair ever could.

Then his hands moved so that they were at her thighs and pulling away the tight hold she had around his waist. Maya was ready to complain when she realized he was only trying to adjust their positions as he took a seat at the armchair before the fireplace in their room. Maya's legs fell over his lap as most of her weight landed on one thigh.

Then he was kissing her again, and it was a taste she'd never get tired of.

This time, his tongue joined in on the fun.

It darted out to lick its way around her lips, both getting an initial taste and asking for entrance, and Maya didn't even try to hold back the whimper. Their tongues clashed as a chuckle rattled out of him, and Maya felt his cock twitch behind his trousers.

She bucked her hips and felt him grow harder beneath her, the need to have him inside her sending her body on overdrive.

Then he pulled away, and her whimper grew more wanton.

And his chuckle sexier. "Don't worry. We'll continue, love." His fingers played with her swollen lips as she tried to kiss him again. "But first, I want to give you something. Then we're going to move to the bed and you're going to sit on my face because I've been craving your taste like crazy. Then, and only then, will I fuck you. Got that, love?"

She wasn't wearing underwear so she knew the scent of her arousal was stronger than normal, and he was enjoying every single—large—inhalation.

And she really didn't care.

She was so wet that she'd be dripping onto his trousers soon anyway.

She raked her hands up and down his chest to sate her need to touch him and calm her nerves. Waiting would be its own form of pleasurable torture. "Make it quick, Hunt."

He didn't say anything in return as he stared at her. His thumb continued to brush her bottom lip, but all he did was stare at her as if he couldn't believe life. Maya took those minutes to watch him and feel whole again.

When he finally spoke, there was a heaviness to his tone. "You were here. Waiting for me. After I'd betrayed your family. Betrayed you."

Maya pushed her jitteriness aside as her brows furrowed, and she softly held his face between her hands. "You never betrayed me, Hunter."

"You don't know that," he said softly.

Her lips tipped up as her thumb mirrored his and brushed

his bottom lip. "You're right. I don't *know* it. But I didn't care. I need you."

His eyes shined like he was about to test her. "And if I asked you to betray your family for me?"

She took in everything about him. His black eyes. His cunning lips. His light stubble. His slicked back brown hair. All of it created the one thing she could not live without.

"I might hate you extra for it, but all that means is hate sex, and we both know that's fun."

She pushed her ass into him for affect.

The grin he gave her in response had her hips moving again, this time in the mere hopes of relieving some of the tension.

He stayed her with both hands. "Behave, Maya."

She closed her eyes because she wanted to listen to him, but he knew what it did to her when he said her name.

His hands were no longer on her. "Open your eyes, love."

She breathed in to control her urges and opened her eyes only to find his beautiful black button up peeled apart to bare his chest to her.

Her breath hitched and the desperation was there, not a single care in her trying to hide it. "Please stop teasing me, Hunt."

His thumb played with her bottom lip again before bringing her in for a kiss.

A light, barely touching kiss.

Maya felt the irritation bubbling inside her, but tried to fight it. "Hunter."

Then his hands were moving to unclasp the chain around his neck and it was the first time Maya noticed he was wearing one. He never wore jewelry.

So the ring on his finger also became apparent.

Her breath hitched again when she noticed a ring of the exact likeness on the chain.

He will give you his mated ring, Daughter. And soon. Trust me.

Hunter held the chain up so the ring was eye level, and

before he could say anything, Maya whispered through controlled breaths. "A mated ring."

He seemed almost shocked that she knew what it was, but didn't ask. Instead, he grabbed her hand and opened it palm facing up to catch the ring as he placed the chain down. "Werewolves aren't the only ones that mate, love. We just have a different way of showing it."

The analogy worked because werewolves couldn't choose their mates. It was merely meant to be, like it was meant to be between Felix and Juliette.

Demons didn't get to choose either. Their uncaring forms didn't allow it. But for a mate, they'd let down the barrier no other being was allowed. Like Augustine had mentioned before —as much as he may care for his sons, it would be nowhere near the love a mated demon would give.

Maya's eyes latched to the ring resting in her hand as Hunter continued, "I guess the rings work in the same way as humans in letting everyone else know you're taken, but the important part of it is what happens when they're both worn."

Maya looked up to him, wanting to watch him as he spoke.

"Each one is specifically made for the pair, with only yours and my blood in it. It means that magic isn't needed, technology isn't needed, no advancement past our beating hearts is needed."

She didn't want to breathe lest she break this amazing spell, but she had to know. "For what?"

"For the way back to each other. No technology or magic, I'll feel your presence no matter where you are."

Maya's gaze fell back to the ring in her palm, the matching one on his left ring finger on her thigh. "That's what you came back to the manor to get? Before we left with Colette and everything happened last week?"

He nodded. "I would've given it to you then, but the moment hadn't been right. Then everything happened, and I was glad I hadn't given it to you yet. If you'd chosen to wear it, you would've been able to find me and come after me and gotten yourself hurt."

Her eyes flickered up to his for only a moment. "Oh, we're going to talk about that later." She ignored his laugh as she looked back down at her palm. "How long does it take to make?"

"Ten days. It had just finished when I came to get it." After a moment, he added, "It only works if we're both wearing them. If you don't put it on your finger, it'll be null. It also needs to be a self-made decision. Any forced application will null them too. It's why they're called mated rings. Mates won't need to force."

You're his mate, Daughter. He will come to you.

"Hunter…"

He brushed her hair back. "You were right, love. I would never betray you." That hand cradled her jaw. "I'm just glad you had the faith in me to trust in that."

Maya looked back up at him and saw the pure honesty in his eyes. She tried to speak again, but nothing was coming. Nothing able to articulate what she was feeling. "Hunter…"

"You don't have to make your decision now," he interrupted. "I've had time to think about it. Decided before making the rings. I knew what this meant the entire time I was making them. I had my time to prepare. But it's yours whenever you're ready."

She may not have been a demon, but Maya had a feeling, she felt the mating as strongly as he did. Because it wasn't even a consideration. She'd known she'd wear the ring the moment Augustine had mentioned it.

Maya finally moved.

She picked up the chain and brought it up so the ring swung in the air between them. The light hints of deep crimson mixed in with the black marked the meeting of their bloods as one.

She looked back to him, his black eyes watching her every movement, and let one end of the chain fall. The ring slid off and fell into her waiting palm.

Her other hand moved to drop the chain on the ground

beside them. "I don't need to think about it." She didn't break eye contact as she moved to place the ring on her finger. "I've known from the very beginning, no matter how much I wanted to fight it, that you were mine."

She settled the ring at the base of her finger and immediately felt the tingling run up her entire body, then vanish. But there was still a presence in her that hadn't been there before.

His presence.

He didn't move as he watched her finish placing the ring, every bit of his features telling her how much he enjoyed the sight.

She dropped her head so their foreheads touched as her hand went to cradle his cheek the way his cradled hers. And she knew he was feeling the same sensation of excitement at the feeling of the cold metal of the ring touching cheek as she was.

"You're officially mine, love." His tone was guttural and possessive.

"Eternally, love." She copied what he'd said not too long ago and watched his entire demeanor break.

Their lips pressed together again and Maya felt both the exhilaration of the moment and the sense of peace fill her.

And her flames weren't too far behind.

It'd only been a week, but her body needed this. Though if their relationship was anything like a wolf's, as mates, a week was a *long* time.

Her flames couldn't wait to join the party. And his flames seemed equally as eager.

Hunter's hands dropped for her waist and pulled her in closer so their chests pressed together. Maya's peaked nipples craved to touch his skin, almost like they were begging her to rip his shirt off.

Then he was standing and her legs were once more wrapped around his waist. Her hips didn't wait for permission to ride against his cock and they both moaned at the sensation.

Hunter didn't drop her on the bed when he finally stepped

up to it. Instead, he dropped himself so she fell over him and broke the kiss. Straddling him, Maya watched him slither farther up the bed, then pause, waiting.

Then we're going to move to the bed and you're going to sit on my face.

Maya's eyes filled to a black to rival his.

This wasn't new to her; they'd done it before. Hunter had insisted she sit on his face only the second time they'd ever been together, but there was something different about it now. Something about the past week of not knowing what had happened to him until moments before when she'd received the mated rings. Something that made the shivers run through her like this was her first sexual experience.

She crawled to him, a panther slowly moving towards its prey.

His shirt still lay open so she enjoyed the taste on the way up, her tongue coating him like she were laying a claim.

She sucked at his throat for a moment, then bit his jaw like she was playing with her meal.

"Now who's teasing, My?" He smiled at her. One of those smiles that would send species straight down to Hell's Gate. Cunning and delicious.

But his voice dripped with need.

She licked the way up to his lips and bit down on the bottom one. "I forgot. What was it you wanted to do?"

He growled. "I want every last drop of your cum dripping down my face."

Her giggle was more possessive than cute as her tongue darted into his mouth, taking a final taste, before she pulled away with furrowed brows. "Well, I need to make sure my mate is properly fed, don't I?"

She purposefully didn't move again and acted as if she were waiting for an answer.

The command in his tone was lethal as he gripped her. His

hands held her thighs so tight, Maya was sure they'd leave bruises. "Sit. Now."

Maya didn't respond, just let her body skim over his mouth as she lifted herself up. His mouth latched onto her shirt clad nipple as she rose and suckled so hard, her hips bucking against his chest. With how wet she was, Maya was sure she'd coated him with her arousal with that simple movement.

Finally, she was situated atop him, and her flames danced around her, mixing with his where they touched.

His tongue impatiently tasted for her before she could fully sit, and she jerked against his face so he had to wrap his arms around her thighs to hold her down. Fuck, she'd missed this.

"Be a good girl and don't move, love," he purred against her sex and she clenched at the feeling.

Then his tongue was on her, tasting her, devouring her.

And she'd never been a good girl so her hips didn't even bother trying not to move. Instead, they bucked against his mouth, and she felt the bruising pressure of his arms keeping her still above him.

She moaned as she tried to hold herself up by the headboard as his tongue found its way to her clit and circled it like it were a game. When her hips fought against his arms in order to move so he was sucking right where she wanted him, he finally gave in.

One little suckle on her clit had her back arching as her grip on the headboard tightened. They'd broken this bed twice already. She wondered if it'd happen a third time tonight.

Another suckle had her stiffening like her body was preparing for the crescendo.

The final suckle had her coming over his face, and his moans told her he basked in every moment of it.

But he wasn't done.

He circled her clit before she could come down from her high, then licked down to her opening and thrust his tongue into her like he was fucking her already. But like the master to her body that he was, he didn't stay long. She barely had time to think between one thrust of his tongue into her opening to another suckle of her clit, this one hard and demanding.

She'd never particularly cared about being careful when she sat on his face, so she didn't consider anything but her own pleasure creeping closer as she thrashed over his face.

The knowledge of how much this was affecting him pushed her to climax so soon after her first. Because even though she had her back to his hips, she felt the way he bucked against the bed. Like he was fucking the air to get some relief.

Between sucking on her clit to licking down her folds to thrusting his tongue inside her, Maya could barely hold herself up with both arms, one falling into his hair and pulling for dear life.

He chuckled beneath her. "Your cunt is perfect, Maya," he mumbled into her folds before giving her another lick. "Now I need you to come in my mouth again, love, so I can finally get my cock in you."

She pulled down on his hair, the only saving grace keeping her up. Her breaths were so labored, she wasn't sure how intelligible the words came. "Keep talking like that and you'll drown in it."

"I love when you ride my face, love." She knew she heard a grin in his voice. "I can do this all day, but my cock is getting jealous."

Her hips moved instinctually as she thrashed against his face. He lapped up every little drop like her reaction to his words was exactly what he'd wanted.

She came hard, hard, hard, hard...

The way she screamed his name, she was sure her family heard it past this manor and into town at the family home.

Then his mouth finally gave her a bit of a reprieve, and she was limp and falling off of him a satisfied mess.

His lips pressed to her ankle as it fell over him and he moved again, slowly kissing up her legs as she lay there, her head rolled to the side to watch him progress up her body.

When he got to the shirt that stopped at the very top of her thighs, he growled, "I don't want you ever wearing this again."

Her brows furrowed. "It's your shirt."

"I prefer you naked." His teeth bit at the bottom of the shirt and he slowly cinched it higher.

She laughed, finally gaining the energy to lift to her elbows and watch as the shirt made its way past her breasts, leaving her bare for him. "Take that fucking thing off." He suckled on her breasts as she moved to pull the shirt off.

When she was completely naked, she pulled him up by his shirt lapels so their lips brushed together. "And why are *you* still dressed?"

He kissed her through his smile, his tongue plunging into her mouth and letting her taste herself before he pulled his shirt off.

Then he pulled away quickly so that he could pull his trousers off. And though Maya hated the loss of contact, she enjoyed the view. His dick sprung out at attention the moment it was free of his trousers. It called to her as he walked back.

She moved to the edge of the bed and her hand wrapped around the top of his cock and slowly moved down as her mouth took his tip and sucked. "I've missed my cock."

His hand fisted into her scalp and pulled. "You don't get to taste right now."

She licked around the pre-cum from the tip and sucked again.

He growled as his hips thrust into her, but he pulled her away. "I need to come inside you, Maya."

She pulled away only because she also really needed to feel him inside her. Needed to feel him dripping down her thighs. Needed it all.

He moved onto the bed and pulled her to straddle him, but he didn't lie back. He sat chest to chest as Maya placed his cock at her opening and slowly lowered herself down. Their breaths mixed as she reached the hilt.

And Maya felt the seriousness of how much she loved him settle inside her.

Their flames still licked together around them, but they'd calmed down. This was a whole other sort of pleasure, pressed together with him like this and moving oh so slowly.

She noticed the glint of her ring as she reached to trace his face and her heart constricted. "I'm your mate, Hunter. Yours, yours..." she moaned as his hips thrust up into her.

She felt his ring press into the skin of her back. "You are." Their pace had never been so slow, yet so deliciously perfect. "And I'm yours, Maya. Everything I am, everything that I have, it's all yours."

She kissed him because she needed to. More than she needed the air they breathed.

They moved closer and closer to finishing with every thrust and hip movement, but not once did they break eye contact. She clenched around him when she couldn't take it any longer, needing him to come inside her the same moment she came all over him.

And because he was hers, he listened without her needing to say a word.

4

*H*unter was grumpy when Maya insisted they shower and get dressed. She'd insisted they needed to talk to her family.

But that'd be their second stop.

"We need to talk to your family first," she said as she watched him put on his shirt and finish getting dressed.

He quirked a brow. "Excuse me?"

"I bet Warren's with your dad right now. *And* I bet your dad is eager to tell me he told me so."

Hunter's arms crossed before his chest. "Why would my father say anything to you?"

"I went to him the night you two left with Colette." He stiffened. "And again two days after that. And again earlier before coming here."

He didn't look too pleased. "Why?"

It was the first time Maya actually felt a blush come up around Hunter. "Hoping he'd have news on you."

His demeanor dropped and he walked up to her and wrapped his arms around her so they rested on her ass. "Why you would ever think I'd go to him before you is incredible."

She rolled her eyes. "He kept saying the same thing."

"Yeah? Is that what he's going to get so cocky about?" There was an amused look about his black eyes.

"And that you'd be giving me the mating ring."

He stiffened against her. "How'd he know?"

"He's your father, your partner. He's known from the beginning by just the way you'd act hearing my name. At least that's what he says."

Hunter studied her. "He doesn't lie."

"I know."

He stared down at her another moment. "I want you to answer. Why would you think I'd go to him instead of you?"

"I was scared." *That you'd actually not want me.*

She didn't have to say that last part. She knew he read it in the way she looked up at him.

"I'm yours, Maya."

She nodded. "I know. But it's that irrational caring heart of mine. I couldn't help considering the alternative."

His lips brushed hers. "I don't want that alternative to ever cross your mind again."

"Your wish," she said in a feigned serious voice as her brows furrowed together.

He laughed as he shadowed them away.

They landed in the exact spot she'd landed when she'd shadowed in earlier.

And like before, Augustine's back was to them. Though this time, he looked to be making a cup of tea rather than dark liquor.

As expected, Warren was also there, leaning against the desk on their other side. He stiffened when he saw her.

She pulled away from Hunter's hold so she could face the men, but didn't put space between their bodies. She enjoyed the feel of him at her side too much.

"I told you," Augustine called with his back still to them.

Maya rolled her eyes and looked to Hunter, mouthing her own 'I told you so.'

"I see you've met my witch, Father." Hunter sounded on edge. Like he wasn't yet sure how he felt about his father's acquaintance with her.

"My daughter?" He turned with two cups in hand and moved to hand Maya one. "Yes, of course I have, no thanks to you."

"Your daughter?" This time, Hunter's tone was more considering. Almost like he liked the way she was being referred to. As his other half, therefore Augustine's daughter.

At least, Maya thought so since that's why she liked hearing Augustine say it.

Augustine's glance dropped to their hands and his cocky gaze met hers. "Yes. My darling daughter."

Part of Maya wanted him to say 'I told you so' for the mating rings too because that cocky grin was almost worse. "Whatever, I get it. You told me so."

Augustine laughed and moved to take his seat.

Maya looked to Hunter, and from what she was reading on his features, he was as happy as he was going to be about this newfound friendship she had with his father. Which meant happy enough that there was someone else looking out for her safety, but not so much more than that.

She nodded toward the chair. "Sit."

"Why?" He narrowed his gaze at her.

"So that I can sit."

"Why do I have to sit for you to sit?"

"Because that's my chair too and if we're both going to use it, you need to go first," she said with obvious snark.

His eyes blazed. Now he looked pleased.

When he sat down, he took up the entire armchair. It looked much smaller now that Hunter sat in it.

Maya moved to him, hot cup of tea in hand, and sat on his lap, her feet tucking beneath his thigh as she snuggled in close and his arms wrapped around her.

And like when they'd been pulled out of Hell's Gate, he pulled the cup from her hands after her sip and took his own.

Warren was still staring. He looked dumbfounded, and Maya was sure it was because he'd never seen his brother like this before. She loved that.

"Shall I pick that jaw off the ground for you, Little Brother?" she teased him, and Hunter chuckled at her copy of his calling Camilla 'Little Sister.'

The blush on Warren's cheeks was light as he leaned back into the desk and his lips tipped up. "Glad you're not angry with us, Maya."

"No. But I would like to know what kept your brother away for a whole fucking week," she simply stated.

"And your wish is my son's command," Augustine said, another knowing look about him.

Maya narrowed her eyes at him. They *had* been in Augustine's front foyer when Hunter had said that exact thing to her months ago.

Hunter growled at his father like a wolf ready to attack. Maybe the analogy went further than Maya had thought.

"We had to make sure you guys were safe from The Eight—they think that's a stupid name you've given them, by the way—and then we had to make sure you weren't on Grandmama's hit list." Warren sat at the edge of the desk. "It just took a while because Grandmama was trying to convince us to work with her. She's trying to get retribution on all the families that were responsible for killing her family."

"A few months ago, I would've definitely taken the deal. I don't know how she got that type of payment. Not to mention the ability to steal all that power. Even those that don't have the Powers like demons and witches would have magic I could take. I didn't take the deal, but..." Hunter said with a small smile.

Maya narrowed her eyes on him. "But what?"

His hand rubbed her back in a soothing manner. "Calm down, love. I said a few months ago. We agreed no more trips without your permission."

Augustine and Warren both coughed to hide their laughs, and Maya sent her narrowed gaze their way.

Warren shook his head. "Not funny at all. Right call, Brother."

Maya turned back on Hunter. "So why'd it take a week?"

"We were making sure you would be safe from them. Then finding out what Grandmama wanted from us and making sure you would be safe from her retribution game. We at least learned these halfies won't work against Grandmama's word. Then I had to put my sister in her place for thinking she could threaten you."

"What made you sure you could trust their word that any of us would be safe?" Maya drank some more of the tea, then handed the cup over for Hunter to finish and place on the table beside their chair.

Hunter looked her in the eyes. "Grandmama bargained with us. Get one of the people on her list, and she'd keep you safe from her halfies."

Maya's face drained of color. "And you trust her?"

"She's been alive a long time. She knew I wouldn't, so she agreed on a dark magic that holds her responsible. If she or any of her halfies come after you, she'll begin decaying until she's a dead fucker. She even made a deal for this boss of theirs. I don't know how legitimate it is considering I don't know if she actually knows the true identity of this boss man, but I was more worried about the halfies attacking than this boss man, so it was really just a bonus. I'll figure out how to deal with him later."

"Hunter." She tried to control her breathing. "Tell me you didn't hurt anyone."

"No," he answered, and she let out a deep breath. "I just brought the elf over for Grandmama to kill herself. That's what took up the end of this week. Apparently he was somehow the most difficult one for her to get to on her own."

She stiffened in his hold. "Hunter."

Augustine whistled. "You've messed up now, haven't you, Son?"

Hunter rolled his eyes at his father. "Maya, he was going to die anyway. Might as well protect you in the process."

Maya looked to Warren. "Seriously?"

Warren's hands shot up in defense. "I told him you wouldn't like it, but to be honest…the elf would have died. We got a great deal."

Maya turned blazing eyes from one brother to the other as Warren's arms crossed before his chest as he rested on the desk. This was a side of Warren she hadn't seen before—the demon half that he'd always made sure to hide around her sister.

And as the more sinister of her family, she truly did understand their stance in the situation they were in. But she didn't like their decision.

Augustine interrupted her anger. "I see now why you waited to give her the ring, Son. She would've shadowed right over had she known your location all along. Ruined your progress."

Maya turned dark eyes on him. "Stay out of this."

His hands went up in defense, but his eyes twinkled with amusement.

Hunter raised an annoyed brow at her. "Is there anything you didn't tell my father?"

Maya's gaze darkened as she watched her mate.

Hunter blew out a breath. "Maya, I don't regret it and I'm not going to."

She finally relented because she knew he wouldn't regret it and she wouldn't change that about him. Even if she didn't like the consequence of said decision. "I know. I'm just annoyed that I understand your reasoning and honestly, I probably would've done the same thing to protect you."

"That's my darling daughter." Augustine sounded cheerful.

"Augustine!" she exclaimed.

He laughed in response.

Hunter's arms tightened around her, and his eyes were questioning again. "You didn't answer me. Anything you didn't tell my father?"

She snuggled in tighter with him and let her voice drop. "The...Bridgers one."

Warren stiffened. "It's back?"

"No," Maya answered quickly, then turned back to Hunter. "I just wanted to be with you when your father found out. Figured he's more ancient than you so he may know what happened, but I wanted you here when I mentioned it."

Hunter searched her gaze as Augustine said, "What one? What power are you speaking of?"

Maya ignored him, waiting for Hunter. "You don't need my permission to tell him, love."

"I know." She felt so safe in his arms. It was a sense of settlement her soul only felt with him. "But I wanted you to be here."

"What power?" Augustine sat up straight.

Hunter's eyes shot to his father's. "Later. Right now, we have to go deal with her family."

Maya rolled her eyes through a smile and saw just how annoyed Augustine was that he wouldn't be learning of this power now. He was probably more annoyed too that Warren knew of it.

Hunter looked pleased to be annoying his father with the little secret dancing just out of reach.

Maya stuck a finger out and guided Hunter by his jaw to look at her. She jut out her bottom lip and gave her best puppy dog eyes. "I want a kiss."

He was instantly transfixed. She could see that much as his black eyes jumped from her eyes to her lips and back again. He didn't try to argue, just leaned in dand pressed his lips to hers, his arms tightening around her.

She smiled into the kiss, satisfied.

Melted into him, content.

Maya figured Augustine was talking to Warren when he said, "You see, Son, her wish, his command."

H is brother was mated.

Incredible.

His father hadn't mentioned having spoken to Maya in the few hours he'd been home, so when they'd shadowed in, Warren had been confused. Especially about the 'told you so's.' He'd guessed they had to do with Hunter.

But the one where his father didn't even say 'I told you so,' but rather gave that annoyingly knowing look? That one had been more obvious because Warren had tracked his father's eyes.

Right down to Maya's hand.

And his own heart had stopped a moment because he'd never seen one in person. Never known anyone to wear one.

And for half a moment, Warren had convinced himself it was just a piece of jewelry.

Until his gaze shot to his brother's hand and saw the twin. The one that had been on his hand the entire week and Warren hadn't thought about enough to piece together.

His brother was mated.

Warren knew it would happen. Could see it in the way Hunter acted with Maya. But to actually have it happen was an entirely other experience.

And now to see the more possessive side of Hunter make its way out, it was everything Warren had read about but never thought he'd actually get to witness. That's how rare demon matings were.

But this newer possessive nature was part of the mating.

Hunter had always been possessive of her, but it was said that a demon grew as possessive as a wolf after their mating ring had been accepted. Even if they took the rings off after tonight and never wore them again, the bond had been accepted already.

Warren saw the truth of the matter by the way Hunter

growled at their father and held Maya closer. He'd never hidden his affections for her, but Warren truly couldn't believe how much a mating could increase it.

And Maya looked so…content. It was incredible to see it without a single smile from the witch.

She'd known they hadn't betrayed her family. Just by the way she snuggled into Hunter, Warren knew that much. But hearing she wasn't angry with them *and* she hadn't yet heard what had happened, that she'd trusted Hunter would be hers forever, solidified Warren's beliefs.

Something only a mate would do with a demon.

And a mate with a power that opened a portal to Hell's Gate —even though said power had now vanished.

It definitely was something to tell their father because as much as he pissed Warren off, Augustine Delvaux might actually know what the hell had happened. How Maya had opened it to begin with and where the power had gone.

But that power on such a formidable witch? Perfect demon's match.

Then there was that look she gave them. The one that told them she was angry to hear about the elf sacrifice and scared Warren a little.

Was he better trained and would likely be able to outmaneuver her in a fight? Yes. But there was something about *that* look that hinted at *don't fucking mess with me* that Warren trusted. He had a feeling it was a female thing.

The thought brought a smirk to his lips.

"What the hell are you so happy about?" Hunter barked.

Warren hadn't realized his smirk had been directed at his new sister and felt the wrath of the mating come off his own blood.

He widened his smirk as his eyes jumped between the two. "Just figure now I can complain to Maya if you do something that annoys me and you're going to be in trou-ble."

Maya laughed into Hunter's neck as he narrowed his eyes at Warren. "Fuck off."

"Maya," Warren whined.

Maya looked to her man, a mock serious expression on her face. "Don't talk to your brother like that."

Hunter rolled his neck. "You've got to be kidding me."

Maya laughed with Warren.

Hunter smacked the side of Maya's ass—as much as he could get with her seated on his lap—and looked to her, annoyed. "Let's go. I'm not letting you two keep this shit up."

Warren winked to Maya. "Later."

"Oh, absolutely."

Even Augustine chuckled from the side.

Yeah, this mating would make Hunter more lethal regarding Maya. But it would also make things amusing around the family.

5

Camilla watched from her position on the couch as Vera and Harry whispered to each other across from her. Their smiles were so shit eating that even the world falling apart couldn't wipe them.

And Camilla was happy for them. They deserved this. *Vera* deserved this.

Maya did too. And Camilla knew she would find that happiness for herself. Eventually.

She knew it'd take some time for Maya to get over the pain of Hunter actually betraying them, but it would happen. Camilla wasn't in denial anymore. Maya was in love with Hunter Delvaux in a way Camilla had never been in love with Warren.

So she knew the betrayal she felt must've felt tenfold to Maya.

Which probably also explained why the middle Whittle wasn't downstairs with them, hadn't been around since they'd returned from Bishop's grave that morning. If Camilla knew her sister, Maya would be in the bath upstairs, burning her body in the steam.

Hopefully the bath would help Maya at least a little bit. It hadn't helped Camilla.

She'd tried it, in the days after the brothers had left them in the middle of that room. Tried taking a bath and letting her body relax into the water, but she couldn't do it. She'd start messing with the water temperature because it was never just right. She'd keep adjusting her spot because she kept slipping and it didn't feel nice. She'd wanted a long period of seclusion, but the steam would grow too much. Overall, baths were not for her.

And even when she'd finally gotten to the perfect spot, her mind would wander over to Warren and how she could've been such a fool for him. For the second time.

And that's when she'd come to the realization that she'd never truly been in love with Warren. She'd loved him, that much was absolute. She knew she still did and she hated herself for it, but she'd never been *in love* with him. Not the fairytale romances she'd always dreamed of.

Good thing too because that made this entire ordeal so much easier to get past.

Unfortunately, Maya didn't have that luxury.

Camilla snuggled deeper into her end of the couch, feeling for her sister, just as a shadow erupted at the opening to the foyer.

A shadow.

They were meant to be done seeing those shadows in their home.

But worse than just seeing the shadowing and knowing it would be one or both of the brothers, was seeing *her* sister in between them.

Camilla gasped and jumped out of her seat, Vera and Harry right behind her. "My, what the hell are you doing with them?"

When Vera's arm swung to throw the brothers back, a shield shimmered around them. So Hunter would've been smart enough to protect them. Of course he would, he'd been smart enough to trick his way into every part of their lives.

"You need to hear their side," Maya responded calmly.

Hunter didn't look like he cared too much about their reactions, but Warren's features said he wanted to explain.

Yeah right, she'd fallen for that before.

"You can't be serious, Maya," Vera exclaimed and tried again, but got nowhere. "You cannot trust anything they say."

"Maya, he's already betrayed you once. You think he wouldn't play with you in order to do it again?" Camilla asked because this pained her more than before—for *Maya* to be so in denial.

"He never betrayed me. *They* never betrayed us," Maya stated, unperturbed.

Camilla was about to argue when Harry interrupted, "You trust them, Maya."

Camilla turned wide eyes on her warlock and noticed Vera doing the same. Vera was the first to speak. "Harry! You can't just…"

"He wouldn't hurt her, Vera." Harry's eyes moved over to her. "The same way I wouldn't hurt you." Then his gaze jumped between Hunter and Maya. "I was wondering what must've happened. Knew something must've gone wrong if Hunter had to leave to protect Maya."

Maya's eyes warmed on him. "Thank you, Harry."

"You seriously believe this, Harry?" All Camilla could think was something must be missing.

"I love Maya as much as you do, Camilla. If I truly believed her in danger, I wouldn't just be standing here. I knew he would never hurt her. I just couldn't understand what had happened," Harry responded in his cool British accent.

"Fine." Vera crossed her arms over her chest. "Then explain."

Maya rolled her eyes. "They're not going to hurt you, or me. If they wanted to, trust me, they could've. Sit and they'll explain."

Surprisingly, Camilla felt herself relent first. She wanted to trust in her sister, and she simply had no fight left in her. "Okay."

Harry and Vera moved to the kitchen to get a tray of tea ready as the others settled around the room.

Hunter and Maya moved to the end of her couch by the fire —basically their designated spot most of the time—and settled there, Maya snuggling into the crook of his arm.

Camilla narrowed her eyes on them. So she'd been wrong. Maya wasn't soaking in order to forget him. She was with him, trusting him. Camilla hated that she recognized the way Hunter held her sister now. A hug that pushed her into him and stated that he'd kill anyone or anything that tried to hurt her.

Then Camilla looked over to the other couch where Warren had taken his seat across from his brother. He had his elbows resting on his knees and watched his interlocked hands.

She felt the love she had for him. But that was it. She didn't feel an aching need to be with him and when he glanced up at her, Camilla knew he didn't feel it either. He wasn't in love with her.

If she really thought about it, he'd never been with her what Hunter had been with Maya. He'd never been in love with her.

Like she'd never been in love with him.

And realizing that now sucked.

But she still wasn't convinced they weren't playing games with her family so she was also glad for it.

Harry and Vera walked in, one carrying the tray of cups and the other carrying the kettle and a plate of cookies. They settled everything onto the table, readied everyone's drinks, then sat and waited.

"I see you two are finally together," Hunter muttered as he eyed the two across from Camilla.

Harry and Vera sat close to one another and were holding hands. It wasn't as close as demon and dark witch over to Camilla's side, but it was very indicative of a romance.

Harry's lips tipped up and Vera said in a harsh manner, "We are."

Camilla glanced around the room. Warren still wasn't sitting back, like he couldn't get comfortable. Hunter looked the complete opposite. He seemed entirely too comfortable as he played with Maya's fingers in his lap.

Camilla caught his stare and swore there was a wickedness behind those blacks that her sister loved so much. She wasn't sure if that was his way of saying *I'm going to fool her again* or his way of saying *Glad to have you back, Little Sister*. Either way irritated Camilla.

Warren was the one to open. "Grandmama looked to you guys for only a second. But when she looked at us, it was longer. *Because* she needed to speak with us."

He took a sip from his cup and that shook Camilla out of her stance as she reached for her own cup, needing something to hold as she listened.

"It wasn't like when Camilla speaks to you with her thoughts." He never looked up. "It was like hearing a phantom whisper. We needed to release Colette because that was the last puzzle of the night. If anything happened to Colette, the chains holding you were laced to kill you with Colette's electrocution. It's a crazy dark type of magic and takes forever to complete, but Colette had done it, and if we wanted you three safe, we couldn't hurt her."

"Letting Colette go essentially meant taking her to the room they were using for meetings, since Colette can't shadow on her own. We knew what taking her would mean with you lot, and so we let you think we'd done as you'd expected and betrayed you," Hunter continued.

Camilla interrupted, "My, did you think so too?" Part of Camilla wanted the answer to be in the affirmative, like she shouldn't be too hard on herself because even Maya had believed it.

And Camilla knew Maya could read that in her eyes, but she shook her head. "You guys never liked Hunter so I understood why you believed it so easily, but he's...mine. I got scared, yeah, but at the end of the day, I knew everything he did was to protect me."

A silence followed her answer. Her irrevocable honesty regarding her relationship with the Delvaux heir.

Camilla thought about this revelation as they all drank their teas, Maya and Hunter sharing a cup like they had when they'd pulled the two from Hell's Gate. Maya was convinced this story they were being told was true, but Camilla wasn't entirely sure. Was it just her dislike of the elder Delvaux that caused her to be on edge or was she the only one seeing what the others were blind to?

The way Hunter treated her sister told Camilla it was the former, that no demon could do that lest it were in truth. Not even the most cunning of demons could fake affectionate so perfectly.

Finally, Hunter spoke again. "And when we got there, we found out why Grandmama needed to come back—her reasoning—but we still don't know why *she* was needed. What the leader needs with her."

"And what was her reasoning?" Camilla asked, the slightest bit of rebuke in her tone. She was beginning to believe their story and she didn't know if that made her a fool or not.

"In the storybook, you learn that her entire family was killed," Warren answered. "What you don't learn is who the people were specifically who killed them. Turns out Grandmama knows every single family line that was involved. And it's worse than we would've thought. There're people from basically every species involved."

"And she wants revenge. Understandingly so," Hunter finished. "She can't kill those who actually committed the acts, but she can hurt their families."

"We were offered pay to bring those families in, kinda like the business trips," Warren said and Camilla hitched a breath, fearing the worse.

They *had* been gone a week.

And she had started to believe they were good. That Hunter had changed for her sister. She needed to stop allowing her soft heart to fall fool to them.

"She could easily do it herself, but it would be much faster if we do so since it's already basically our job," Hunter said. "And she's waited a long time for this retribution. Without us, it'll take some time."

"But of course we denied," Warren finished, and Camilla internally smacked herself for thinking the worst. Again.

She always thought the worst of them. Of Warren.

But this time wasn't her fault...entirely. This was the type of deal they all knew Hunter would've taken. So again, Camilla had to ask herself if he only refused to fool them into a false sense of security or if he was truly in love with Maya and refused because he knew Maya wouldn't approve?

In the silence that followed, Camilla landed on the latter.

She looked over to her sister and her demon. Maya had moved at some point so she sat between his legs, hers spread out on the couch, and he held her like he'd much prefer to take her somewhere private.

Why was that gesture the one that confirmed to Camilla it was the latter?

"Is that where you've been all day?" Camilla asked Maya, nodding to the demon she was snuggled up with.

Maya smirked. "I'm still selfish. I needed him more than I cared whether you lot believed them the enemy."

"Threatened?" Vera asked with a small smirk of her own. "That Harry and I were taking the act-ive gold medal?"

Maya's eyes twinkled. "It's cute that you think you even compare, sister."

Camilla's lips twitched up so slightly she knew it'd be imperceptible. As much as Vera and Harry had been *together* in the past week, Maya and Hunter would beat them a million times over. The fact that Vera and Camilla had caught them in the kitchen—though it wasn't full on sex—was evidence to that, the horny fuckers.

Camilla looked back to the couple in question and felt a softness grow inside her. Not for Hunter, but for what he had with her sister. If it was true, it'd be the most pure thing in their lives.

6

*a*nnoyingly, Harry had been on Maya's side when she insisted that Vera continue training with Hunter. Vera knew it was necessary. She just wasn't looking forward to it.

Hunter strolled into the empty room across from the living room like he owned the place. "At least now you won't bitch at me because you want to get in your warlock's pants."

"I could still bitch to Maya about the way you act during these sessions." Vera watched him closely, still not entirely certain about his motives.

Hunter crossed his arms and leaned into the fireplace. "Let me let you in on a little secret, Sister. She knows."

Vera rolled her eyes. "Let's just get started."

He waved a hand in her direction. "Start."

Vera narrowed her eyes, but threw out her hand.

And as expected. Poof. He was gone.

Tingling.

She turned and…he wasn't there.

Tingling. Tingling. Tingling. It almost felt like it was coming from multiple places.

She felt another one coming and threw her arm out to that location before the tingling could reach her neck.

He was leaning against the frame to the foyer when she grumbled his name.

"Yes?"

"You're going too fast."

"I see you still expect demons to wait on you." He looked so unbothered. "And that you haven't been practicing."

She grumbled and crossed her arms, the slight movement causing the shirt she was wearing—not hers—to waft up to her. Mm, distracting.

The blush started and Vera turned around. "Again."

And again the tingling shot up her arm to her neck, alerting her to a demon's presence, but it was there and gone and there again so fast.

Vera could hardly concentrate. Somehow the shirt's smell had grown stronger in the seconds that passed rather than fading away.

She knew she was going to miss when she threw out her arm.

"It's embarrassing, Sister. You definitely should've been practicing in my hiatus."

"If you don't stop, I'm going to make sure Maya stops sucking your dick," Vera bit out in her frustration. She was even surprised that those words left her mouth. But she *was* thinking about certain acts more and more recently. And definitely when a certain smell was around her.

He scoffed. "I don't think you understand how much your sister loves sucking my…"

"Okay. I'm sorry I said anything. Again."

This time he went slower. Not much slower, but slower.

She actually almost got him. And distracted with the scent of the shirt too. That was an amazing feeling.

"Good job."

It was oddly satisfying to be complimented by him. Maybe because he didn't exactly give them out, and when he did, it was known to be honest.

"Go a little slower and I could get you," Vera said smugly.

His eyes twinkled like he was accepting a challenge, then he shadowed out.

The tingling told her he would be stopping beside her, and when she threw out her arm…she almost got him. Again.

"Damn."

He was leaning against the fireplace again. "I thought slower meant you'd get me."

She rolled her eyes. "I'm a little distracted."

"With what?"

Vera blushed and looked down.

"Ah." She looked back up to him. "I thought I smelled him too. You're wearing his shirt."

"Yeah."

"Good."

What?

"Now that you're horny all the time, it'll be important to recognize the threat past those feelings," he explained.

Then she was doing well. If she was almost getting him, distracted as she was, she could definitely get him not distracted. Next time she'd remember to dress appropriately.

"Is that what you had to do? Train to get through threats with Maya on your mind?" She was always curious about their dynamic.

"Yes."

His honesty still surprised Vera, even though he had yet to lie to her. Though she couldn't be certain his entire relationship wasn't a lie. Even though Harry insisted it was real.

"After I met your sister in the forest, then again at the school, I went home and trained for three days straight to get myself to focus with her on my mind. Then when I finally had her in my bed, I spent a week trying to focus with the scents she'd left there, continued to leave there."

"And now you can control it?" A week? That didn't sound so bad.

"I spent an entire month training it with her in the room, then on memories of what we'd done, with her scent lingering on me. It was hard."

Vera quirked a brow. "It was hard or you were hard?"

Vera couldn't deny that the way Hunter spoke about Maya was convincing enough that he hadn't betrayed them a week ago. That he would've done and would continue to do everything in his power to protect her.

Maybe Harry had been right in trusting in their relationship.

Hunter smirked but didn't answer. "I put your sister through the same training. When we train her powers, I'm always there so she gets a two in one. But I've also made her practice with memories of me and my scent when I'm not there. It's important to be able to work around the distraction."

"You think you're good now?" Maybe more like a month or two.

"I'll never be good."

Her hope dwindled.

"I'll always have her on my mind, and when she's there, she'll always be a distraction. But I've mastered my power enough that I can work it harder to balance it out."

That was kinda sweet. Vera wasn't used to Hunter being sweet. Even regarding her sister.

"So I'll never be good?"

He tsked. "But you're better than the last time we trained. And you have the distraction. Trust me, Sister, you're doing better."

She narrowed her eyes at him. "Why are you being nice to me?"

His smirk grew wicked. "I'd like your sister to suck my dick tonight."

She turned around. "Gross. Okay, bonding time is over. Again."

His chuckle came from behind her before he was gone and she felt the tingling indicating to her right.

I t always amazed Camilla that her school had an astronomy tower and no one was allowed to use it. Quite frankly, it was bullshit.

So she would be using it.

Even better that no one would be around. She could lie there and look up at the beautiful skies in the solitude of her thoughts.

She'd just left the little alley she and Warren used to go to be away from the crowds of students. They'd met to talk about their relationship.

Or lack thereof.

Because really, they'd met to finally break it off.

For good. No more trying again.

Because neither one of them was in love and neither one was going to get there. They were both fully aware of that and finally willing to admit it.

Camilla needed someone who was human. At least that's what she assumed. Maybe she'd be okay with some of the other species too, but definitely not a demon. Even one as good as Warren Delvaux.

And he deserved someone who would believe in him the way her sister believed in his brother. He deserved someone who would understand some things that were more instinctual to him as a demon and not judge him for it. He deserved someone who allowed him to be himself without feeling the need to alter any part to please her.

Basically he needed a Maya to his Hunter.

And Camilla couldn't be that for him. They both knew it.

And honestly, she was more upset by her inability to accept him rather than the fact that the relationship didn't work. Because she still loved him, would probably always love him. But she couldn't *be* with him.

And she hated herself even more for falling victim to finding the worst in Warren without consideration yet again. She wasn't good for him.

So she was alone again. And part of her knew this was a good thing. Knew she needed this time in her new adult life to figure herself out before thinking about finding a fairytale true love.

The sky was a bit overcast in the winter air, but it was still beautiful as Camilla looked up at it. The light breeze that pushed through into the tower caused a bit of a flush on her caramel skin.

She didn't know what to do, where to start. She'd spent so much of her life worried about boys and going on little dates until she'd fallen in love with Liam—or so she thought—and he turned out to be a jackass. Then with Warren, and she turned out to be the jackass.

And now she was alone again. And all her thoughts revolved around wanting a man by her side the way her sisters had Hunter and Harry.

It was unhealthy.

She had to learn to be comfortable being alone. The way Vera had been before she'd found out about them, and the way Maya was before Hunter had entered her life.

Not to mention, she still had some considering to do about the elder Delvaux. Camilla believed what he'd done was to protect her sister, but something was still off. And annoyingly, Camilla knew it was her own judgmental prejudices coming into play.

But the thought of him still brought to life that evil glint in his eyes when he stood in the middle of that auditorium with the flames blazing around those kids. It still brought about the knowledge that he'd so readily snap a person's neck, and mostly because he enjoyed the feeling beneath his hands. It still brought the screams from all those witches he and Maya had burned alive.

She wanted to believe he was changed for Maya, but a larger

part of her knew he wasn't. If anything, he merely refrained from certain acts because of Maya.

But she could worry about him at another time. Right now, she needed to take her older sisters as role models and find out who she was without a man to know what she really needed in a man.

It'd be hard. To push away the desire to be held and the constant flip her heart made at the slight chance of something. Knew she'd likely get jealous watching her sisters with their men.

But she'd prevail. Her mother's strength was in her and she knew she could do it.

If Loretta Whittle could leave the love of her life and her *daughter* to protect them, then Camilla could leave the thought of love behind to protect herself. At least until she was ready.

It would just be fucking hard.

7

A Valentine's Day ball.

Camilla's literal dream come true and she didn't have anyone to share the night with. Her sisters both had a man on their arms, and though she was happy for them both, she was also incredibly jealous.

And though she knew her feelings weren't really there for Warren, the thought of seeing him there still sucked. Not to mention learning his father would be there too.

Camilla hadn't realized how much she still hated Daddy Delvaux, even though she'd never met him. It probably had to do with the same prejudice she'd given Warren when she'd found out about his demon side.

Though to be fair, Augustine Delvaux was more like his eldest, and Camilla truly hated said eldest for the longest time. Still didn't necessarily like him. Just approved of the way he treated her sister.

But now she was ready—the first, as usual—and waiting to get the night over with. Though on the positive, she felt like a princess in her blushing pink, empire waist gown.

Vera was second down in her sheath deep blue gown, and Camilla's lips tipped up at the image of how much it would please Harry to see Vera like this. She looked absolutely stunning.

"Wow," Camilla complimented her as Vera stopped beside where Camilla leaned against the couch's arm.

Vera blushed and smiled wide as she gave a little twirl. "Thank you. Though how you think anyone would beat your beauty is astounding."

Camilla winked in return, but didn't have time to say anything else as Harry beat Maya down. He was readjusting his tie—though it looked perfect to Camilla—when he stopped dead in his tracts as his gaze found Vera. Camilla actually saw his breath hitch.

Vera looked equally taken aback.

Because Harry looked *good*.

He always looked good, it came with his posh way of dressing, but there was something about seeing him in a tuxedo that added more to it.

Eventually, Camilla had to clear her throat to knock them out of their reveries. Harry's eyes instantly shot to her, and an almost imperceptible blush spread across his cheeks. "You look stunning, Camilla."

Camilla smiled, twirling her dress in her hands. "I know."

A knock at the door interrupted Harry's next remark, and Camilla was shocked to open it to find a properly dressed Hunter Delvaux standing beyond.

He looked as handsome as ever, but the real shocker was that he hadn't just shadowed into the house. "You knocked."

He smirked as he stepped into the foyer. "Don't get used to it. The ball calls for a heightened amount of decorum."

Camilla rolled her eyes and closed the door behind him.

She was about to call out to her sister when finally, footfalls fell onto the light creaks of the stairs.

She looked stunning in her cream tight-fitted dress that stopped with a slit just above the ankles and showed off her every curve.

One glance in Hunter's direction told Camilla exactly how much he appreciated the time Maya took to get ready. She'd honestly never seen the man struck stupid like that.

Then he was moving, right to the bottom of the steps to meet Maya as she descended. As she got to the final step, Hunter placed a hand to her hip and allowed his eyes to roam her figure. The way he looked back up to her sister, Camilla knew he wanted nothing more than to get her back to his manor and rip the dress right off.

And Maya's smirk told him she'd like that.

Right. Time for another clearing of the throat. Camilla really wasn't enjoying fifth wheeling. On Valentine's Day!

On the positive side, they'd be taking a limousine.

With humans also in attendance, it was advised that all creatures attend in discreet ways. Which could mean popping up somewhere humans wouldn't see—since wards would be put up against shadowing and porting within the estate—or preferably, driving in.

Hunter wanted to shadow, of course, but Maya pushed him toward the limo instead. It was actually amusing the amount of power her sister held over the demon.

And again, Camilla had to wonder whether that was Hunter fooling them or genuinely complying to her sister. And again, Camilla knew it was the latter and was annoyed with herself that she'd even questioned it. She'd spent too much time these past few months judging him rather than considering the alternative—that he wasn't a good guy and never would be, but he'd be good enough for Maya.

Gathered in the long stretched vehicle, the hour's ride was quiet.

Harry and Vera sat facing forward, having taken the seat directly beside the door to the back, and they whispered to each other through wide smiles. Their hands clasped together as they leaned in to one another, and a soft smile grew on Camilla's face because this was the happiness Vera had been looking for and she finally had it.

Hunter and Maya sat on the opposite end, being the first to get in. Hunter's legs stretched out to the side Camilla sat on in his signature lazy lounge and his arm wrapped around Maya as his free hand played with her fingers on his lap.

They were whispering to each other too. And where Harry and Vera looked to be in the honeymoon stage of just getting together, Maya and Hunter looked more seasoned.

The way Maya's red lips kissed the stubble at the end of Hunter's neck then wiped it away shot a pang through Camilla's heart. It was exactly what she'd dreamed of.

This night was going to be torture, and unlike for her new brothers, not in the good way.

***

The estate was large.

Not as large as Delvaux Manor—either one—but large.

Maya instantly wrapped her hand around Hunter's bicep and waited for the others to stop behind them. They'd be entering as a family.

The opulence of this manor was far grander than either Delvaux Manor. Gilded entirely in white marble and gold, and too flashy for Maya's tastes. But it was decorated quite romantically for the occasion.

The grand ballroom, too, which would be the room for the occasion, was larger than Maya had expected. Though understandably so, considering the Delvaux's never hosted balls, and when they—Augustine—did, it was demons only.

Whereas this ball...

It had every species in attendance. And though there were fewer humans than Maya had expected, it was packed full of every being. Oddly enough, given the occasion, it wasn't a couple's ball, and even children ran after one another around the dance floor.

As they entered the room, Maya felt the stares on her. And from all but the humans, she felt a judgement she didn't care enough to consider. Naturally everyone would be staring. She and Hunter were flaunting their relationship rather than hiding it like most would. A smirk graced her features at the attention.

Augustine and Warren watched them as they walked over.

"You look radiant, Daughter," Augustine said with an acknowledging nod to his son.

Warren shook his head as he looked her over. "Beautiful."

A low growl from her side.

She smiled and leaned into Hunter. "I know I should be annoyed, but I'm really starting to like this extra possessive side of you."

He smirked. "Yeah? Let me take you to a different room and show you how possessive that side can get."

She laughed and turned back to those around her. "Augustine, you know of my family already. Vera, Harry, and Camilla." She turned to her family. "This is Augustine Delvaux, Warren and Hunter's father."

Harry gave a single nod in acknowledgment, Vera a small smile, and expectedly so, Camilla's eyes narrowed on him. She didn't say anything, but that hateful look spoke volumes.

"Ah, Camilla." Augustine smiled. "Aren't you a delight."

Camilla's eyes fell to slits, but Maya interrupted, "No fighting tonight."

Camilla gave her the eye roll that said she was using her 'mom' voice and smiled just too sweetly. "Fine. I'm going to go...mingle."

Harry laughed as he took Vera's hand. "We'll be off too."

Maya watched them go with a smile, then Augustine's hand reached out. "May I have this dance, Daughter?"

Hunter's arms tightened around her waist. "No."

Maya giggled into him. "Yes, he can, Hunt."

Hunter clenched his jaw, blew out a frustrated breath, then released her.

Maya took Augustine's waiting hand and walked with him to the dance floor. The stares bore into her in an almost stinging manner. Augustine held her exactly how she'd always imagined a father-daughter dance.

"I think I'm really going to enjoy frustrating my son with you," he said through a smile.

"You and Warren both." Maya would enjoy it too.

Augustine watched her closely. "You two are garnering quite the bit of attention tonight."

She shrugged. "Expected."

"You know, if it weren't for that annoying side of you that wanted to keep everyone safe, you'd make a great demon."

She knew her grin was dark as she looked up at him. "Your son likes my caring side."

He quirked a brow in her direction. "Only on you, darling."

"You know, if your objective was to get me to tell you about the other power right now, it isn't going to work."

His jaw twitched, but he didn't say anything, just looked over her shoulder for a few moments, then back down at her. "Tell me, that possessive side erupt in you yet?" He was oddly amused.

"I've always been."

"But it is different with the mating, is it not? That is what I've heard." He looked too giddy.

She narrowed her eyes on him. "Why?"

His brows shot up like he was nodding behind her. "There's a demon I've heard would do *unmentionable* things to that full-blooded son of mine."

Maya stiffened and actually felt the fire in her freeze.

She turned in her spot, and there he was, her mate, speaking with a demon that looked like she was ready to do those unmentionable things before everyone in the ballroom.

There was a heat worse than flames, the kind so cold that it burned and raced blue, that clouded Maya's vision with fury.

She was moving before she even realized it. Knew she should remain calm, that Hunter would never want anyone else, but she didn't care.

Hunter glanced her way just as she was coming to a stop. "Maya, what…"

When her heat kissed that chill away, a softness erupted in her soul. That's how it felt to hear her name on his lips.

"I want to dance with my mate." She brought her left hand up to toy with his lips, perfectly aligning the ring in the demon bitch's line of sight. She saw the way the demon's eyes widened from her periphery.

Hunter smirked like understanding was dawning on him. "Your wish, love."

His eyes remained glued on her as he moved her to the dance floor, and Maya felt her insides quiver with the attention.

He took her hand in his and brought her in close as the other hand stopped at her lower back, as if showing off his own mating ring. His lips found their way to her ear. "I like this side of you too, love."

Maya's smile was wicked as she looked up at him because there was nothing she was ashamed of. He was hers and she intended the whole world to know it. "Good."

Slowly, as one song changed to another, Maya felt herself settle. Felt her body calm in his embrace.

He lowered his face so their world started and ended in that little bubble. "Sometimes I wonder what would have happened had you not walked in on me killing that priest. Had that not led to our official meeting in the forest. Would I not have found my mate?"

Her heart raced as she stared up at him.

"Then moments like these arise, and I know had I never seen you before, one glance your way at this ball and I'd have known I'd found my mate. I'd have stayed by your side all night until you gave me my dance, and you would have done it because you wanted to, even though you wouldn't admit it. Then I wouldn't have let you go. All night and every day after. I'm mesmerized by you, Witch."

Maya didn't realize her breaths were so labored until she tried to speak. "I hate you, Hunter. So. Much. I've always hated you."

His smirk held a hint of endearment. "Good."

Vera had never allowed herself to envision this life.

The one with the family and the balls and the man by her side. The one she had read about in all her romance books, but never thought possible. The one that seemed almost too good to be true.

But it was true.

And Vera had it.

She'd tried to enjoy it all. The ball with all the species in attendance, her family around the hall, the simple fact she was in a beautiful gown. But all of it was overshadowed by Harry.

His presence was all she could focus on.

His scent invaded her every thought. His touch awakened her every nerve ending. His stare. Damn, his stare stole her breath away.

So she stopped trying to enjoy it all and let herself enjoy him. Enjoy how beautiful she looked in that dress as he spun them around the ballroom, dance after dance after dance.

She didn't even care if people judged her for being in a relationship with her family warlock. It was such a freeing feeling. No wonder Maya seemed so carefree all the time. She never let others' opinions of her relationship bother her, and it felt amazing.

"We should probably stop," he said. "Make a turn of the room, show the others of our presence."

She shook her head aggressively. "No. Stay. You're all I want tonight."

A darkness filled his hazel eyes, but he gave a genuine smile. "You're all I want every night."

"Just…pretend it's only us."

"I have been." He held her closer to him, their chests pressed together. "That's why I thought you may like a break from me."

She gave him a small, lingering kiss, then whispered against his lips, "Never."

His hands moved to cradle her face, and Vera could see just how much he wanted to kiss her. Public displays weren't normally their thing, that was much more her sister's forte. But, like before, Vera was beginning to understand her sister more and more.

She tightened her hold on the lapels of his tuxedo jacket and brought him closer. "Kiss me, Harry."

He obliged her. Instantly.

This kiss did exactly as all their kisses did to her—sent her to a word so far away, they truly were the only people on it. Because when his lips pressed to hers, she forgot about everything around them. He was her beginning, middle, and end, and she was drowning in the story.

When they finally broke apart for need of air, Vera smiled up at him. She was about to tell him just how much she loved their little bubble on the dance floor when she felt a sensation to her back and a ringing in her ears.

Her eyes widened on Harry, but before she could say anything, he was moving.

He turned them around so the shrapnel Vera now saw flying through the air hit his back rather than hers.

The ringing in her ears. There must've been an explosion.

Panic filled the room as soon as the shrapnel stopped flying, and the smoke filled its spot in the middle of the room.

When Vera looked to Harry, his eyes mirrored her own question.

What the fuck?

8

Hunter had her shoved up against the wall the nanosecond the explosion hit, his back taking the brunt of the impact of what looked like wooden pieces flying through the air.

It was the hanging hearts that had been put around the ballroom for decoration. They were all made of wood and right above the dance floor.

All Maya knew was that the explosion had come from the center of the floor.

As the ringing stopped in her ears and she heard the commotion of an entire ballroom trying to figure out what had happened, Maya felt a tugging pressure on her arm.

She saw Hunter's gaze darken and was barely quick enough to realize it was Bella at her arm and stop him from doing whatever he had planned.

Bella, her ten-year-old mermaid friend and the heir to the North American mermaid line.

Maya shouldn't have been surprised to find her here too. As the coming heir, she'd need to make allies for her people.

But now she had to worry about whether or not her little friend was hurt.

The commotion around the ballroom was almost deafening as people shouted and tried to control the wreckage so that no one else was injured. Hopefully not many were hurt to begin with.

Maya bent before her friend. "Bella, are you all right? Did you get hit?"

Bella shook her head but kept tugging on Maya's hand. Maya wrapped a hand around Hunter's arm and let Bella drag her out of the ballroom and into the grand hallway. She led them to a room at the end of the corridor and closed the door behind them.

A dark lounge room.

Maya watched Bella move to the leather couch and slump into it.

She finally released Hunter's arm and moved to her friend, crouching before her and moving the strands of hair from the little girl's face. "Bella, what happened?"

Bella's eyes didn't land on her when she looked up. Instead, they landed on Hunter standing behind her. Maya didn't have to turn to know Hunter looked domineering and way too scary for the moment.

She smoothed Bella's hair again, bringing the girl's attention over. "He's not going to hurt you."

Bella didn't look scared, rather confused. "He's a demon."

Maya turned an amused look in his direction just in time to see the annoyance mar his features. She looked back to the mermaid. "He's my demon."

Bella's stare looked to be analyzing her. "I thought you were in a cross relationship. I just didn't think it would be a demon."

Hunter moved to take the other end of the couch Bella sat on, though with his larger size, he took up most of it. "What did you think, Fish?"

Maya gasped. "Hunter. Behave."

Bella shrugged, unbothered by Hunter's tone. It was definitely not what Maya had been expecting. Most ten-year-olds would've been afraid of a demon, especially considering the crap that was said about them in the other species. "I thought wolf. But demon makes sense too since they also have mating. Actually, demon makes more sense."

She knew about demon matings. How?

Maya moved from her crouched position to take the bit of space left between the two on the couch. "And why would that make more sense?"

"We're both very alike, both strong."

Maya's brows rose. It was the shock of what that comparison meant. And the plain amusement of Bella's confidence. Maya loved it. "And?"

Bella broke into a blush. "I like a demon too."

Maybe that was how she knew demons could mate. Though from what Maya understood from Hunter, most demons didn't even know they could mate.

Maya knew that comment got Hunter's attention when she felt him stiffen behind her. She turned back to him and knew from the furrow between his brows that he was trying to calculate who Bella was talking about.

Bella took Maya's hand. "A mating ring?"

Maya glanced down to it with a smile. She always smiled when she looked at it and hoped the feeling never went away. "Yes."

"I've never seen one in person."

"Not many have," Hunter remarked, sounding an equal share bored and evaluating.

Maya didn't want to rush Bella, but his tone did remind her that she'd been dragged to this room for a reason. "Bella, why are we in here? What happened? Is Brynn okay?"

She hadn't heard any news on the elder mermaid heir.

"Brynn is great. Alloy is taking amazing care of her," Bella answered. "I want your help with a friend."

Hunter grumbled behind her, and Maya kicked her foot back to get him to shut up.

"What happened with your friend?"

"She's missing, like those couples," Bella stated without emotion.

Missing? A ten-year-old? "What do you mean she's missing? That wouldn't have to do with the couples we'd found before, right? They've never touched children."

"She's older. Seventeen." Now the hints of fear showed behind Bella's eyes.

Older—though seventeen still felt young to Maya—and in a cross relationship would put her in the line of fire of the halfies. "With who?"

"A faerie. I don't know anything else about him. Like Brynn, she didn't tell me, I just found out."

Maya's lips tipped up just as Hunter said in an amused undertone, "You seem to do that a lot, Fish."

"I swear I think this man took her," Bella continued. "Last time I heard them talking about this man, but I swear they said he was human. I just...don't know how that would happen."

"That man probably just said something that made her feel uncomfortable. Human men have a way of doing that," Maya said. "But the couple missing? That could definitely be the halfies. I doubt their goal has changed."

Bella shrugged. "Just, if you find out anything, let me know."

"Of course, my little detective." Maya smoothed her hair back again. "You know, you're going to make a great leader to your species."

She smiled. "Not if they find out about *my* demon."

Maya laughed, and she swore she heard a chuckle from behind her, but by the time she turned to face him, Hunter's expression was bored. She narrowed her eyes at him, but he didn't give.

"I'm going to get back to my parents before they cause a scene about their only remaining heir going missing after an explosion," Bella remarked. The way she spoke, Maya kept forgetting she was ten. "I know it's wrong, but I'm glad the explosion gave me the chance to talk to you. I didn't know how else to get you out without my parents seeing."

Maya have a soft nod of acknowledgement. "I'll call you later, Bell," Maya called to the girl as she closed the door behind her.

Maya turned to face her demon.

"I can see why you like her so much," he said.

She smiled even though she was trying to be angry with him. "Don't call her Fish."

He smirked. "Why not? She *is* a fish."

Maya shook her head at him, though her amusement was definitely shining in her eyes. She could feel it. "You're an asshole."

His hand moved from her back to the back of her neck, and he tugged her forward until their faces were only an inch apart. "I'm your asshole."

"That's right, baby."

His lips twitched into a grin right before their lips crashed together.

H arry had been having such a marvelous time wrapped with Vera on the dance floor that for a couple of hours, he'd forgotten they were anything but human and that some of those within the species were currently being hunted. For revenge that wasn't their fault.

Harry pulled off of his tuxedo, knowing the brothers had gone home to do the same as the girls changed out of their gowns. He put on a set of trousers that were the closest he would be getting to sweats and a plain t-shirt and headed for the kitchen to get the tea ready.

Unsurprisingly, the brothers were already in the living room with their father sitting between them. Harry hadn't been expecting to see Augustine Delvaux in their house, but hoped Maya trusted him enough to allow him to remain.

Augustine looked to be in the same boat as Harry in that he'd merely pulled on a less fancy pair of trousers. Hunter and Warren, on the other hand, both wore t-shirts and sweatpants—grey sweatpants, to be exact—and lounged on either side of their father.

They sat in their comfortable silence as Harry headed to the kitchen for his usual tea and biscuits.

Maya was already in Hunter's lap and Camilla seated in the corner of the opposite couch when Harry walked out with the tray. Vera appeared as Harry readied everyone's drinks, but the silence still wasn't unbearable.

All three Delvaux men took up one couch, sons on either side and father in the middle. And only Warren looked slightly uncomfortable, but Harry figured that had more to do with the ex-girlfriend across from him than the silence in the air.

Harry mirrored their seating arrangement as he took the middle spot on their couch with eldest and youngest Whittle on either side of him.

Augustine smirked in the quiet air. "Look at us. The Delvauxs sitting across from the Whittles. Peacefully."

Harry narrowed his eyes only slightly. "Maya is a Whittle." He knew Hunter loved Maya, but still wasn't entirely sold on the family line. Demons still didn't care for the lives of others, and though Harry tried not to judge them for it, he couldn't hide that it caused a larger rift than not.

Augustine looked very amused. "She is mated. That makes her one of us now."

Harry's eyes widened as they shot to Maya's, then Hunter's, fingers. How Harry hadn't noticed until this moment was unfathomable.

Neither woman at his side would understand what that meant.

But now was not the time to discuss this.

Instead, he took his cup of tea and sat back. "You said the other night that Grandmama was looking for revenge on the family lines responsible for killing her family?"

"Yes," Warren answered.

"Do you think that's what the explosion was?" That was the only guess he'd been able to make. The only victim was a forty-three-year-old unmarried pixie woman with no children.

Hunter shrugged. He looked more interested with Maya's hair than the conversation. "What was her name?"

With that much disinterest, Harry had to wonder what Augustine was doing with them. He hardly believed the man to care more than his son did.

"Mia Ketola."

"Ketola." Warren nodded. "That was on the list we were given."

"She's getting through the easy ones first," Hunter remarked. "Begay, the elf she got before, had no family. Ketola and one other were meant to be the only single living in her hunt."

Harry froze, but Vera was the one to speak. "She already killed another?"

A single nod in the affirmative came from both brothers.

"So why now? Why in front of everyone at the ball?" Camilla asked as she sipped her tea.

Warren shrugged, but it was Augustine who answered. "Could be for a variety of reasons. She or their leader could have done so just to get a rise out of everyone. As a warning, albeit indiscreet, that she was on the hunt for the families. It's so subtle that no one would be able to pick it up, but it's still a warning. Or simply, she just found that the most opportune time. Ketola was distracted and not looking to protect herself in the middle of a ball. I suspect had the other families been there, she would've killed all of them."

"Could The Eight still be attached though?" Maya asked.

"Maybe it was a fear tactic, except they've already taken their next couple."

"Why do you think so?" Harry asked.

"I found out about a faerie and mermaid missing after the explosion. They were gone before the ball, so if it were The Eight, it would've been done beforehand."

"Do you know for sure it's The Eight?" Vera asked.

"No," Maya said, and Harry saw the twinge in her eyes that said she didn't like that the couple was missing.

"That is worst case," Harry said. "We'll assume until we have proof otherwise and start looking."

"What about how to deal with the halfies? Or Grandmama?" Camilla asked.

Harry shrugged because he knew the answer but didn't like it.

Augustine answered anyway. "Death, sweetheart." There was nothing sweet about the way he said it.

"But we don't know how many halfies there are. There could be dozens!" she argued.

"And they all have to go," Augustine concluded.

"How?" Vera asked exasperated.

Augustine's smirk appeared as he turned to his left. "Tell me, Maya. Do you have a power that could take care of it?"

Harry narrowed his gaze. Couldn't be the fire, his own son had that. The only other extraordinary power would be…

"Nice try," Maya grinned toward him. "Keep this up and you may never find out."

The patriarch rolled his eyes as he faced Harry again. "She's so annoying. You're welcome we took her off your hands."

Harry was about to argue when a growl came from Hunter's corner.

That was another thing Harry had heard about demon matings. That they were very similar to wolf ones and the possessive instincts would quadruple.

Augustine didn't look at all concerned with Hunter's reaction. "I'm sorry. You're welcome my son has taken her off your hands."

Harry wasn't finding himself liking the head of the Delvauxs. But truthfully, he had never expected to.

"She's still one of us."

9

"Why are you covered in blood?" Maya watched Hunter walk through their bedroom and head for the ensuite as he stripped his shirt.

Word had just come out that the Roosevelts, a gargoyle family from the European tribe, had been killed. That meant four adults, six teenagers, and twelve children.

Hunter didn't respond. He'd never lie, so that meant omitting the truth.

Maya stopped before the ensuite so he couldn't get through. "Hunter."

"I was on a business trip, Maya. It got messy."

"Where?" she asked. And when he didn't answer, she insisted, "Where?"

"Polish mountains." He didn't look happy about telling her, and Maya knew exactly why.

Polish mountains was the main location of the European gargoyles. Which meant he was around when the Roosevelt family was cast into a burning house.

"You did help, didn't you?"

He scoffed and looked down at himself. "I was a little busy."

"And they were burning alive! You could've disintegrated the fire, saved them!"

"I was surviving," he grit out. "I see you haven't stopped to ask how much of this blood is mine."

She paused. "Don't try to guilt me. I know none of it is yours. I'd have known if you were hurt."

She'd learned that much about the mating rings at least. Any substantial injury would be felt on both ends.

"Maya, I was in the middle of a fight. I was more worried about making it out unhurt than what was happening with the gargoyle family across the yards."

"And that stupid payout is more important than their lives!"

He grimaced. "Don't act surprised, *love*. You knew who I was when you accepted the mating."

"And you knew who I was. You knew I'd have a problem with you not helping them!"

"I helped!" His volume grew to a level Maya had never heard before. "I incinerated that house. I helped as much as they were going to get while I had thirteen gargoyles coming at me. They didn't scorch in the flames, didn't suffer. Instead, they were gone in moments. That's all the mercy I could have, Maya."

She knew she should be more worried about the fact that he had thirteen gargoyles attacking him, but he could've shadowed away and that wouldn't have been a problem anymore. He would've lost the payout, but he could've helped.

"You could've stopped the flames!"

He was an inch away when he seethed through his teeth, "By the time word got out, they were already burning. I was merciful because that is what you would have wanted. I know my mate, Maya, and don't you ever insinuate that I do not. Had this happened before you, I wouldn't even have bothered. Instead, I would've had all my concentration and energy on my project!"

She knew her mate too. Knew he was telling the truth, that

he had helped in the best way he knew how. By killing them faster.

"And what about the thirteen you were fighting? Did you kill them for some stupid payday? You told me you were only going to pick up a few books." She knew she was angry about the Roosevelts' deaths and trying to find other fights to pick, but she couldn't help it.

"They're not dead," he bit out. "Injured, but they'll be fine. I took the books and left. I don't kill innocents."

"I know," she grit out because she was still angry and she had nothing to argue about.

He finally breathed out. "They were on the list, love. As good as dead. I gave them a kindness no other demon would've."

He didn't wait for her to respond, just moved past her to the showers.

Maya stood there and breathed slowly. In and out.

Her gaze landed on the jacket he'd let fall to the floor beside his shirt. She picked up both pieces and brought them up to her nose, as if she would be able to smell whose blood it was.

A part of her swore she smelled just a little bit of Hunter's blood staining the shirt.

He was all right. She'd seen his unharmed torso, but her chest still panged with the need to make sure her mate was unhurt.

But the need to fight was also there and not going anywhere anytime soon.

***

Maya wanted to apologize. Knew it hadn't been his fault that the family was killed and he truly had done the most merciful thing. With the amount of damage that had happened before the incineration, the family wouldn't have made it out.

She didn't know why she'd been so angry with him earlier. Her emotions had been running in a way she hadn't expected.

But he was in the training yard of their manor, and Maya knew he needed some time to let off steam. In the meantime, she'd be with Vera, helping—watching—her sister try new recipes.

Maya wasn't in the most joyous of moods, but watching her sister cuss at a batch of cookies for not being strawberry enough brought a smile to her lips. It was just too ridiculous.

"Your phone, My." Vera motioned to the phone vibrating beside the stove.

"Who is it?" Her heart skipped as she stood from the stool. *Hunter?*

"Bella," Vera read the caller ID.

Bella? What could she need right now? Unless it had to do with that missing friend of hers.

Maya took the call. "What happened?"

Bella's voice was somber as she said, "They found them. I texted the location."

Maya sighed. "I'll be right there."

Vera left her baking and moved to Maya's side. "What is it?"

"They found the couple I mentioned. The faerie and mermaid."

Vera paled a little. "Harry is with Camilla, but I'm sure he'd get here quickly to take us."

She was about to call out to Harry when Maya stayed her and shook her head. "Don't hate me for this."

Maya took Vera's hand and shadowed them to the location in her texts, knowing it was close enough for her to be able to do it.

They were in the middle of a forest and Maya had a feeling the couple was left there as a show because the couple wouldn't have chosen this spot. Mermaids needed to remain near water, and they were nowhere near water.

As Vera balanced herself and came out of her shock, she turned on Maya. "That's not a dark power, Maya."

"Not now, V." She'd just gotten into an argument with Hunter and though before she had wanted something to fight about, now she didn't. She was over it.

The victims were teenagers. The girl was seventeen, the boy eighteen, nineteen at most. Babies, basically.

They lay on the forest grounds, eyes wide and staring at one another.

Bianka, Bella's mother and leader of the mermaids, walked over with her arms crossed before her chest. She was beautiful, both her daughters having taken her looks. "You think this is that halfie group?"

"My guess. Though they completed their mission last time when Grandmama was resurrected. I couldn't fathom what would be needed now," Maya answered, already looking for the ten-year-old she knew was somewhere in the area.

"Do you guys have an idea of what happened?" Vera asked, but Maya was barely paying anymore attention. Being that they were in the middle of a forest, ground level wouldn't give the kid much hiding space.

Up in the trees, north of where she stood now, Maya saw her friend.

She left Vera to speak with the others and made sure no one was paying attention to her as she began climbing the tree. Camilla had always been better at tree climbing than she was, but Maya made her way up.

Bella didn't speak as Maya situated herself on the branch and looked out at the scene before them. Maya didn't know what to say. This was Bella's friend, and she didn't know how to comfort the girl in her grief.

Eventually, Bella broke the silence. "They don't want me here, but she was my friend. I'm the one that knew she was missing."

She looked upset, but more so, she looked determined. At the very least, to not allow her friend to be forgotten.

"Do you know what happened?" Maya knew Bella wouldn't want coddling right then.

Bella just shook her head. Maya hadn't thought so.

As they looked on in silence, Maya came to the odd realization that had nothing to do with this couple. "Bella, how'd you learn to climb a tree?"

Mermaids spent almost all their time in the water, preferring it to land. Their children definitely didn't know how to climb trees. They were much better at aquatics.

A light blush settled on Bella's cheeks, and Maya felt a bit of triumph at the distraction she was able to bring to the moment.

Maya smirked. "Demons. Teaching you things that'll drive your family crazy."

The light blush turned crimson, but Bella never turned to look at her.

Bella's head fell to Maya's shoulder. "Thank you. For trying to lighten the mood."

"You're welcome, Fish."

A laugh cracked through Bella's sadness as she shoved Maya's shoulder. And that made Maya smile too.

⸻

After shadowing her sister home, Maya just wanted to get back to the manor, but Vera stopped her. "How, Maya?"

Maya looked her in the eyes. "You know how."

Vera shook her head, almost like she was trying to convince herself it wasn't true. "Was it something that happened during sex? You transfer powers to one another?"

That would be something.

"Vera, you know how," Maya huffed out.

It was obvious Vera still didn't want to believe it. "How could you, Maya? Stealing powers isn't right."

"He was dying anyway," Maya argued. "He could've died with it or he could've died without it. Either way, he'd be dead."

"Maya!"

"Look," Maya cut off her sister, "you scolding me right now isn't going to change anything. Now, I need to talk to Hunter, can you tell Camilla and Harry?"

Vera quirked a brow. "About the shadowing?"

Maya merely stared at her because they both knew the answer to that.

Vera breathed out. "I'll tell them about the couple. Go."

"Thank you," Maya said in a light voice before shadowing home.

Maya had assumed he would still be training, but heard the shower running when she landed in the hall before their bedroom. She could only imagine how much sweat he must've worked up while training, especially not knowing where she was.

She'd learned quickly that if she paid attention to the ring, she could pinpoint his location. But normally, it didn't change their ways of life. She liked that. Liked that this wasn't like having a tracker, but still held the benefits of a tracker if she needed it in the future.

Hunter stood under the water with his eyes closed and head bent as his hands scraped through his hair. His back looked tense, like he was trying to relax, but it wasn't working. Maya had a feeling he was avoiding using the rings to find out where she was, and she loved that he was trying to control the overbearing side.

After watching him stand under the water for minutes without moving, Maya began to silently undress.

With a glass wall standing before the expanse of the shower —with both ends opened for entrance—Maya walked to the end that would put her to Hunter's back. It was one of those fancy showers where the water came from the middle and could spray from all sides if they wanted. Even the side with the glass. Fancy fancy.

She moved until she was right behind him, her hands coming to rest against the middle of his back and feeling him tense for only a moment before complete relaxation finally took over his body.

It was only slightly annoying, the twinge of happiness that she'd been right and his tenseness had to do with not knowing where she was. She shouldn't be so happy to be the reason behind his distress, but she couldn't help it.

Maya's hands slipped around his form until she was hugging him from behind and resting her head on his back, the water falling over them both.

His hands clasped hers so their rings touched, and they simply stood there. It was only when Maya lightly kissed his spine that Hunter finally moved, turning in her embrace.

He cradled her face in his hands and toyed his thumb across her lips.

"I'm sorry, Hunt," she said because she'd been dying to say it and knew he deserved to hear it. "I know everything you do is for me. I know you did what you could. I don't know why I was so…" Angry? Upset? Emotional? She didn't know.

"I know, my bleeding heart."

"Thank you for being everything I need from you, Hunt. Thank you for handling me."

He watched her seriously. "Do not thank me as if I would ever hesitate to do it all for you."

"You're my perfect, Hunter."

"And you're mine, Maya." His thumb peeled her lips open as he bent over and kissed her softly.

10

Vera hated not telling Harry about Maya's new…ability.

She hadn't lied, just omitted the truth. But she still hated it.

But they also hadn't asked. How had they not asked how she and Maya had made it to the location of the dead couple? By driving, it would've been about three hours both ways, but Harry hadn't seemed concerned about that. Vera's only guess was that Harry presumed Hunter had taken them.

And technically it was Hunter's fault that they had been able to go.

Because Vera had no doubt Maya wouldn't even have considered stealing without Hunter's insistence.

Okay, maybe she would consider it, but she would never have actually done it.

So the nagging feeling that Hunter still wasn't the best of men kept coming to the forefront of Vera's mind, but at the end of the day, she knew he would do anything for her sister. And that was all that mattered.

So overall, she felt like kind of an ass for leaving it out. Especially when Harry was so good to her all the time.

But at the same time, it wasn't necessarily her secret to be giving out. No matter how much they trusted one another.

She sighed and buried herself in the ridiculous feeling of complete giddiness that came when she thought of Harry. She was twenty-seven, not seven, but damn, she felt like a child in love. Like running to her dad—because she'd never had a mom to run to, and her dad had become her best friend growing up—and telling him about the really cute boy throwing pencils at her.

But this felt like more than those giggly crushes in the best of ways. And she wanted to tell her father all about it. All about how good Harry was to her.

He'd understand.

He had to.

Even though he wasn't Mom's warlock, he had to understand that Harry wasn't around when she was growing up, so it wasn't wrong.

Vera brought the dog tags that lived on her nightstand to her chest and knew he would've understood. He would've seen how happy she was and made fun of her for how goofy she looked with such a wide smile. She brought the dog tags to her lips and kissed them as a sadness filled her.

Because Harry, with his British poshness and three-piece suits, made her heart flutter, and she wanted to share that feeling with her best friend.

Well, Harry was her best friend now.

He was now the person she wanted to share her mind with. The person she wanted to be beside to laugh and cry with. The person she simply wanted.

No, not wanted. She needed to be with him.

It was in that final thought that Vera felt herself shimmer before she was in an out-of-body experience.

Literally.

She could still feel her body lying in her own bed, but now she stood in Harry's room.

He was at the door as if he was about to leave when he jumped at her sudden appearance. "Vera?"

What the hell was happening?

"Harry, I swear I can still feel myself lying in bed." She tried not freaking out.

He traced her body with his stare before leaving the bedroom altogether. Vera followed him to her room and watched as he opened the door.

There she was, lying in bed looking like she was sleeping.

Harry turned back to face her. "What were you thinking before this happened?"

Vera knew the blush was seeping into her cheeks. She seemed to always be blushing regarding him. "You. Being with you."

His smile was more sweet than cocky, but there definitely was a bit of self-satisfaction in there. "You were thinking about wanting to be with me and it happened? Vera, you astral projected. That's incredible."

She twiddled her thumbs. "It is kinda cool."

And she was beginning to understand why Maya would want the ability to transport from location to location. After doing so herself, Vera couldn't help but want to be able to completely transport rather than just astral project.

But even the projection was pretty damn cool.

He stepped up and tried to cradle her face before his hand slipped through. "There's the non-primary power part of it. Your form isn't corporal."

"Give me a sec."

She thought about being in her body again—because she assumed that's how she would get back—and seconds later, she was opening her eyes on her bed. Harry stood at the end where she'd just been a moment ago.

He smiled and walked up to her sitting form and cradled her face. "I was going to say, I like that you wanted to be with me. I wanted to be with you too. I was coming to you when you popped into my room."

Her smile was light, but she didn't break his stare as she said, "Maybe next time you could just port me out of bed."

Because they didn't do anything in her room. It was too weird since it used to be her parents' room.

He chuckled and held her close to him as he ported them back to his room.

***

Camilla wanted to spend some time sneaking into the astronomy tower again, but instead, she'd be with Harry for the afternoon.

They'd gotten a call about a couple, and with both of her sisters missing—Vera living her human life and growing her baking business at a child's birthday party, and Maya probably with Hunter—Camilla was the only one available to tag along. They did text them though. Just in case. Locations were always sent just in case.

It was lucky that Harry was a warlock and could port them around because this one was two states over from their little town. Maybe that's why witches always found themselves in the middle of situations—they were the ones with warlocks who could take them anywhere in the world. With warlocks and demons the only ones able to travel through space, they were the obvious calls. And demons wouldn't exactly be of help.

They ported into what looked like the end of a run-down town. In the middle of nowhere, a little too far out from the rest of the town's residents to really be noticed.

Camilla's heart stopped at seeing the two shivering bodies on either side of the door of the shack they were currently sat against. They were alive.

Shaken. But alive.

A gargoyle and a nymph, both of whom looked about Camilla's age.

The lack of noise almost made Camilla forget that they weren't the only ones there. Both families stood around the shack, and they all looked too nervous to go up to the couple lest they scare them.

Eventually, an older nymph stepped up to Harry. "They won't speak to us. To anyone. Can't look at us. Can't even look at each other."

Camilla ran a soothing hand over the woman's forearm, controlling her power so she didn't invade her thoughts. "Would you mind if I walked over to them? I can read minds. If they're thinking about what happened, I'll be able to get it."

She'd done so with Vikki before, and though she hadn't enjoyed that process, it had come out useful.

The woman looked sad. Not distressed or angry or emotional. Just sad.

She moved to the others and asked the families how they felt about having a witch near their children, then gave Camilla a small nod. It was a nod that said she didn't want to know what had happened to them, but knew she had to. It was a kind of torture Camilla wouldn't even have wished on Hunter, even in the depths of her most utter hatred for him.

"Thank you." The woman's voice was soft and barely there.

Camilla tried to give a reassuring smile but didn't know how convincing it truly came out. Like when she'd gone through Vikki's thoughts, she really didn't want to be there right then. Really didn't want to go through the victims' thoughts.

She moved first to the nymph girl who sat with her knees bent into her chest. She held onto her legs like they were a teddy bear and she was afraid of the dark.

"Hi," Camilla said softly as she crouched before the girl. "My name is Camilla."

She waited.

And waited.

When the girl didn't say anything in response, Camilla added, "I'm a witch and I want to help you. I'm just going to put my hand on your arm, okay?"

Again, nothing.

Camilla sighed and readied herself as she placed her hand as lightly as she could onto the girl's arm. The fact that the girl didn't even react told Camilla that she was too far into her thoughts to realize Camilla was right beside her.

The girl's mind was a jumble. Like several scenes being played at the same time, she wasn't focusing on any one event.

Camilla waited and tried to see if she could find a stable memory.

And finally, it happened. Clouded around the montage of memories was an illusion. Camilla had learned how to recognize illusions only recently when Harry had helped her sift through the mind reading information in the Book and she was glad for it.

An illusion was a sighting that the subconscious knew wasn't real, but the mind still believed. It was a whole other type of torture—to not even have to hurt anyone else and still let your captive think it is being done.

From what Camilla could pick up, it was the gargoyle slowly being spread until limbs starting peeling away from his body.

She was going to be sick.

The memory played on a loop, and Camilla wasn't sure if that was how it had been shown to the nymph or if that's all the girl could think of. Trauma like that would haunt her.

The little bit that Camilla could pick up past the illusion was the halfie responsible for the pain the nymph was going through. She was half nymph.

And if Camilla paid attention, she swore the other half was gargoyle. But how would a non-witch or demon halfie be able to create an illusion?

She slowly pulled her hand away and watched the girl. How

would they pull her out of that trauma? How would they help her come back from it all?

Camilla shut her eyes to steady her thoughts and tried to push away the memory that was now lodged into her mind.

Then she slowly rose and turned to everyone behind her.

Maya was there. Alone. How had she gotten there? Had Hunter dropped her off?

It didn't matter. What mattered was that Camilla had to move to the gargoyle. Had to get his thoughts too. For the sake of the families. No matter how much she didn't want to.

Crouched before the boy, he looked much younger than his years. Like what had happened to him had pushed him back to childhood the way he shook in his spot.

Again, she introduced herself.

Again, she waited.

And again, she got nothing.

She placed a soft hand to his arm and entered his thoughts.

It was almost an exact mirror of the nymph's mind. A chaos of images all surrounding one illusion. And past the illusion, a half nymph, half gargoyle.

There must've been someone else in the room, a witch or a demon who was able to throw up these illusions. Had that been a question to Camilla a couple of months ago, she would've said demon, no questions asked.

But now, she didn't know.

The jumble of thoughts were all the same, and Camilla swore she noticed a white aura filter through the air around him, almost like when Lyric had tried to drain Hunter's life. Except different.

But it was there and gone in the mess that was this gargoyle's mind that Camilla couldn't properly catch it. And though the array of thoughts was the same in the gargoyle as it had been in the nymph, the illusion was different. And in Camilla's opinion, far worse.

The gargoyle got an illusion of the nymph getting taken

against her will. Of her screaming out for her gargoyle to help and protect her, and he couldn't.

She pulled out of his thoughts quickly and numbly felt the tear sliding down her cheek. She felt selfish and weak for not being able to take more than a few seconds of a memory that was now plagued in his thoughts, but she couldn't do it.

She shouldn't be crying, shouldn't be showing weakness. But that tear? She couldn't fight that tear away.

She stared at the ground as she turned and moved toward the families. Didn't raise her head as she told them everything. About the illusions and what they consisted of, and the fact that they were for sure illusions, but in the minds of the couple, everything was real.

She couldn't look any of them in the eyes as she said it. Couldn't fathom the pain she was putting the families through or how they would take care of this trauma.

It was the gentle stroke to her upper back that only Maya ever did to her that brought her out of the sorrow she felt. She looked her sister in the eyes and saw Maya's struggle at not being able to take Camilla's pain away.

As Camilla turned to look at Harry, a shadow filtered into space beyond his shoulder. Hunter.

She heard the hushed commotion from the families behind her, but didn't say anything. He'd be here for Maya and nothing more. Camilla had stopped deluding herself to think he cared.

Camilla heard the two families relax as Maya walked over to him, her hands caressing his chest as she stopped before him. A soft, chaste kiss silenced the area and sent Camilla's heart aching with greed.

She didn't know what they were whispering about, but watched as Hunter pulled out a vial from his trouser pocket and a knowing look crossed between the two of them.

A small smile broke over Maya's features as she took her lover's hand and guided him to the families.

Hunter handed the vial to the elder nymph who stood as the head, then pulled out another vial and handed that over as well.

The nymph looked down at the vials, then shot her questioning gaze to Maya.

"It's a potion to help them get over this," Hunter explained. "It won't affect their memories, but they'll be able to move on. It'll erase being haunted by the trauma, but the memory will always remain."

Camilla gasped at the thoughtfulness behind bringing the potion. A kindness Camilla hadn't thought Hunter capable of. Though she knew if it weren't for Maya, he wouldn't even have considered handing it over.

The elder nymph gave the vials back. "We do not have funds for your favors, demon."

It was well known that a demon, especially one as high up on the echelon as Hunter, never allowed anything to go by freely.

Hunter didn't move, just remained pressed to Maya's back. "No payment."

"Why?" One of the older gargoyle men who stood within the group questioned in astonishment.

"I've a witch for a mate. It's what she'd want."

As everyone's gazes jumped between Hunter and Maya, Camilla's brows furrowed. That was the second time she'd heard Maya referred to as Hunter's mate. Was that just the way demons talked about relationships or was it mates in the same sense of wolves like Felix's mating to Juliette? Camilla had the odd feeling it was the latter.

Then the 'thank you's' began.

And were quickly cut off when Hunter remarked in a bored tone, "Do not thank me. I truly couldn't care less what happened to your children."

And there was the Hunter Camilla knew.

And was growing annoyingly fond of.

Though she'd never admit that.

When they landed back at Whittle House, Hunter gave her a

small smirk. His eyes washed over her like he was picking up the pain she felt at having read the memories of the couple before he pulled out a vial from his pocket and held it in the air between them. "Little Sister."

Camilla wasn't sure if she was imagining it, but she swore there was the lightest twinge of concern in his black orbs, like he cared if she lived with the traumas in her head.

That part of her that believed he'd betrayed them was still there, but Camilla pushed it aside. She knew it was just a thing she'd have to learn to slowly let go of, because if she was sure about one thing in this world, it was that asshole Hunter Delvaux would never betray her sister.

Camilla took the vial with a single nod. "Thank you."

He winked and followed after Maya.

11

---

*V*era was reading a steamy romance novel when Harry stopped at her side to tell her everything. Camilla didn't care about any of that, she just wanted to drink the potion and wash the pain away.

It was kind of crazy, how quickly the potion worked.

Or maybe it was the placebo of knowing she'd just taken it.

She followed Hunter and Maya to the kitchen, not wanting to stand around and relive it all, and took a seat at the table to watch as her sister—and brother-in-law, if this whole mating this was legit—made dinner.

Not much noise filled the air as Camilla sat there, but she did notice the way they'd lean in to whisper to one another. And she had a feeling they were the whispers of love rather than dinner preparations.

They worked so effortlessly together.

Camilla had known as much when she'd seen them together at the Bridgers coven, but it was different like this, in the domestic environment of making dinner.

Mates.

She could see it.

She'd have to ask later if it truly was the supernatural

version of mating or if it was just what demons referred to legit relationships as, but the former was looking truer.

Maybe a mix of the supernatural version and a human version because those rings they wore were on their wedding fingers.

By the time dinner was set, Harry and Vera had walked into the kitchen and silently taken their seats. It was Maya who finally broke the silence, but kept the conversation away from their afternoon. Instead, she told them about the drawings she'd been commissioned for.

Camilla only half listened, unable to stop herself from watching Harry as he sat beside Vera. The way his body leaned into her and his hand continued to graze hers.

Another ache hit Camilla's chest and she breathed out with it.

She wouldn't be envious of her sisters. They deserved the love they had.

After dinner, Camilla insisted on doing the dishes, and when she returned to the living room, she found the couches pushed off to the sides and the coffee table moved aside to make a little dance floor. Vera was currently fiddling with the small speaker they had to play some music.

Hunter sat on one of the couches at the other end of the room as Maya came to a stop beside Camilla. "Do you want to talk about it?"

Maya was always the one who didn't want to talk about things. Camilla always wanted to talk about them.

But Camilla was finding her sister's way better at the moment. "No."

"You'll be fine," Maya consoled in the best way she could.

Camilla's lips quirked up a little as her eyes moved to Hunter. "Thanks to your mate."

A small chuckle left Maya. "I think I'm going to write down the date and time and keep this as a memory. No other way to prove you thanking him."

Camilla laughed. Then she sobered right up. "My?"

"Hm." Maya's gaze was on the demon as he annoyedly watched Vera fiddle with the speaker.

"I'm sorry." It wasn't what she'd meant to say, but it slipped out and now Camilla knew she had to finish the apology. "For everything I put you through with him. For making an already more difficult relationship even more so and not supporting you."

She shrugged, but never met Camilla's gaze. "I know."

"Maya." Camilla grabbed for her sister's arm and turned her so she met Maya's dark browns. "I'm serious. I am sorry. I see now…I *accept* now that he would never betray you. I know it hurt you every time I said he was only around to take advantage of you, and I feel like a jackass."

Maya's lips twitched up. "He's a jackass too. I seem to attract them."

Camilla gave a breathy laugh. "He's here for you. I knew it before too, but I had it pushed so far down that I wouldn't allow myself to believe it. But I need to say it, for you to know I see it —you're all he cares about."

Maya analyzed her for a few long seconds, then finally muttered a small, "Thank you."

They turned back in time to see Hunter wrestle the speaker out of Vera's hand so he could put on the song she was having trouble doing so herself. And though Camilla accepted Hunter as part of Maya's life, it was still annoying that any fondness came when she looked at him.

"What does demon mating mean?" She finally asked what she'd meant to before. "What are you to him?" Camilla guessed Harry knew the answer, which meant Vera would know too. Camilla would be the only one out, and she wanted to hear it from her sister, the one person in her life whom she'd known her entire life.

"Werewolf matings, have you heard about those?" Maya asked.

"Territorial. Loving. Affectionate for only the one person. Well, more affectionate towards one person," Camilla answered. "And that the two mated were born for one another. There never would've been another option. It's not like humans picking husbands and wives; they known instinctually."

Maya's eyes shined as she watched her mate. "Basically. Except demons don't realize what that instinct is because they're not used to those feelings. And they're *only* affectionate towards that one person, no *mores* about it."

"So he told you you're his mate and you kinda have to deal?" Camilla had a feeling Hunter wouldn't have done that to Maya. Had she been asked a week ago, the answer would've definitely been the opposite.

But now?

Now she let herself accept Hunter's feelings for her sister.

"No." A twinge in Maya's tone told Camilla she was tired of the remarks against Hunter, and Camilla was about to apologize for the way it'd come out—because she truly was done hating on him—but Maya continued, "The demon's mating ring is made specifically for the couple using both of their blood. It takes ten days. Which meant Hunter got our blood, made the rings, then presented them to me. They basically connect us without magic or technology. Old world magic, he calls it. If I never accepted it, we would technically still be mates, but we wouldn't have been mated. Does that make sense?"

Camilla numbly nodded as she watched her sister. "And if either one of you takes it off?"

"Doesn't change what's already been done. We could never wear the rings again, but we've officially been mated." Maya looked to her. "But there would be no reason for us to stop wearing the rings."

Camilla didn't say anything in response because she knew anything that came from her at the moment wouldn't sound right. Even though she truly meant no harm in her questions.

Camilla turned back to the others.

Finally, they played "Hero" by Mariah Carey, and Vera turned to find Harry's arm already outstretched.

A small smile graced Camilla's lips as her eldest sister and the family warlock met in the middle of the makeshift dance floor.

Then she caught sight of Hunter behind them, eyeing Maya and motioning to the dance floor as if asking for his own dance.

They, too, met in the middle, and Hunter pulled her in close and held her tight.

Camilla remained on the outskirts and watched the two couples. She enjoyed their happiness. The way both men held their partners and leaned into them. The way they smiled down at her sisters. The ache of jealousy in Camilla's chest was still there, but it was getting beat out by the contentment of finding her sisters happy.

Camilla watched Hunter's lips move against Maya's ear then remain there, not speaking to her, but just breathing her in. His gaze met Camilla's, and he gave her a wink.

And Camilla hated to admit it, but she smiled back. Her heart shattered in annoyed gratitude for him, and he knew it. He was maddening, but he was her brother now. Her sister's mating made that much clear.

How had they become the most stable relationship she'd ever bore witness to? It was absurd, but that was love. It didn't play by the rules made up in heads; it worked its own magic.

The ache settled back into her heart. Except this time, it wasn't for her own wishes for a partner. This time, it was for the couple dancing before her.

Hunter and Maya. Demon and witch. Mixed.

A very dangerous position to be in at the moment. Even with how powerful he was. They both were.

Camilla had to make sure nothing happened to them. To either one of them. Because she wouldn't be able to comprehend life without her sister, and said sister wouldn't be able to comprehend life without Hunter.

So they had to both be okay.

L ike the Valentine's Day ball, Harry could spend the entire night dancing with Vera and not have another care in the world.

And like the Valentine's Day ball, their dance would be interrupted. By a knock at the door this time.

Harry opened it to find Lila and Tamire Bridgers. And a swaddled baby in Lila's arms.

Harry allowed them in and followed them to the living room, where Vera was turning down the music and Hunter and Maya were moving off to sit at the ottoman before the fireplace.

The new couple looked shocked to see Hunter in the room, cuddled by Maya's side, but they didn't comment on it. Instead, Tamire held Lila a little closer to his side as Lila huddled her child closer to her chest.

There was a genuine smile on Camilla's features when she saw the bundle. "You had the baby."

"Yes." Lila lovingly looked down. "This is Aurelia. She came about two weeks after your visit."

"It's a beautiful name." Vera smiled.

"Thank you," both parents whispered as they sat at the couch Hunter had previously been on.

"Come to show us the child?" Harry knew that wasn't the case, but didn't know how else to open.

The edge behind their smiles came back in full force as the new parents met his gaze and Tamire said, "There was an attack at our cottage."

"Why you? You're not a mixed couple. Could your ancestors have anything to do with Grandmama's family?" Camilla muttered before anyone else had the chance.

"No," Hunter answered. "No witches or demons were involved in those killings."

Again, both of them looked genuinely surprised at how domestic and unthreatening Hunter was. Harry had forgotten this wasn't his usual way of being since it'd become so normal to see him in this manner.

"Then…" Camilla started.

"We don't know," Lila answered. "We just know with Aurelia's safety as our first priority now, we couldn't risk it. We figured the safest place would be here, but if it's an inconvenience…"

"Absolutely not," Harry interrupted.

Tamire eyed Hunter, but didn't say anything more when he realized Hunter wouldn't be attacking or threatening or causing any harm. "Only until we figure out what happened."

"As long as you need," Maya insisted. "You can take my room."

"No! We don't want to put you out of your room," Lila insisted as Tamire's arm tightened around his wife's waist. "The couches will be fine. Tamire will grab Aurelia's bassinet, her bags, and a little infant rocker. That's all we'll really need."

Harry smiled and saw his entire family do the same. "Oh, you won't be putting her out."

Maya's grin was just shy of wicked. "I live with Hunter. You won't be putting me out."

"Live?" Camilla asked. "Planning on telling us you'd moved?"

Maya shrugged. "Not until this whole mess was over."

Now both Lila and Tamire eyed the two with such profound curiosity, Harry was surprised they stopped themselves from asking. He had a feeling the questions would come his way later though.

Camilla rolled her eyes, but it was the sort siblings did to indicate amused annoyance. With her acceptance of their relationship, at least slightly, all the tension that had come with finding out about Maya and Hunter was gone. Finally.

Vera brought the conversation back to its hinges. "Do you have any ideas what the attack could've been about? By whom?"

They both shook their heads as Tamire said, "That's what we're worried about. We've stayed so low key, we don't know why we'd be bothered."

"Well, you don't have to worry about that tonight," Camilla said. "I'll show you to Maya's room and you can enjoy the night as a little family. I can bring you guys some tea if you want?"

"That'd be amazing." Lila smiled warmly. "Thank you."

Camilla turned to Maya right before leaving. "Goodnight, horn-bag."

Hunter's smirk was immediate as his hands cupped Maya's shoulders from the back as they rose to their feet. "Goodnight, Little Sister."

Maya shook her head, but the smile she wore spoke volumes—a smile that said she was happy they were finally getting along. She turned to where Harry and Vera stood. "Goodnight, you two. Don't be too loud now. There's a baby in the house."

Harry laughed as the two shadowed out of the room and his gaze landed on Vera. "I did mention that the rooms are charmed, right?" He took a step forward as Vera stumble back.

"Maybe."

Another step and a quirked brow. "Maybe? Hm, seems you don't believe me." Closer. "Shall we test it?"

Her back hit the wall. "Harry."

"I'll make you scream so loud your voice will crack." He reached her and caged her in as his body hovered right over hers. "Then we can ask our guests if they heard a peep."

She was shaking her head, but the way her pupils dilated and her breathing hitched, Harry knew she was convinced.

"Shall I have you here, love?" He pressed his body into hers and felt her arch against him.

She was beet red when she shook her head. "Your room."

He chucked as his hands rounded her waist and cupped her ass. "Let's go, love."

Her fingers clung to the bottoms of his hair and pulled

lightly as he ported them right onto his bed. He fell over her, loving that his body caged hers in. That she was his prey.

He ground his hips into hers, the moan that escaped her lips just shy of loud. He thrust into her again, his hardening cock pressing into her through their layers. She bit her lip to muffle some of the sound.

She was actively trying to keep quiet.

He tsked into her ear as his hands traveled beneath her shirt and pushed the cups of her bra aside so he could take her breasts in hand. They filled out his hands so perfectly. "I think you need to trust me, love."

"I do," she whispered.

"Then why be silent?" He nibbled down her ear to the side of her neck. "The charms will hold in however violently you scream for me."

Her skin heated beneath him and he knew it was part arousal, part embarrassment. Her hands fumbled beneath his shirt and pulled up wantonly.

He pressed a long kiss behind her ear, loving the sound of her whimpers in his ear, then sat up to his knees so he could take the shirt off. He slowly unbuttoned the vest and peeled it off before loosening the tie and finally, he unbuttoned and pulled the shirt off.

It was slow, but he knew how much she enjoyed watching him.

As he pulled away from her completely to remove his trousers and shoes—they were quite nice and he'd like to keep them so—she busied herself with pulling her own clothes off.

A positive of carefully taking off his clothes so as not to ruin them was that he got to step back and stare at Vera's naked body anticipating him.

He crawled up her body and paused between her thighs for a kiss before she clamped her knees together and locked him in his spot. She pushed back and completely closed her legs. "No."

He smirked up at her. "No?"

"I just want you inside me," she argued.

"Liar." She just knew how loud she was when his tongue and fingers worked her.

"Harry," she begged for him, her deeper skin reddening even more. It was impossibly intoxicating when she burned for him, even if part of the reason was out of embarrassment.

He kissed her knees and saw the way her thighs pressed tighter together as his face inched up. He laughed as he moved north and suckled one nipple while palming the other. "Relax, love. I'll just allow my cock to have all the fun tonight."

Her breathing was already heavy as her head lolled back and she enjoyed herself. He slipped a hand between her thighs to spread her legs apart again. She complied and allowed his fingers to slip over her cunt and inside her. Lords, how he wanted a taste.

But it wasn't about his wants.

He switched to the other breast and gave it the same attention its sister had received as his fingers moved in and out of her slowly. Her hips bucked beneath him, riding his fingers.

"Harry, please," she moaned into his ear, and he could tell it was getting a bit uncontrolled.

He gave her nipple one last pull and enjoyed the way her back arched for him, then moved up her neck and took his time there. His fingers never once breaking rhythm inside her.

Her hands touched him too, and he didn't shy away from letting her know how much he enjoyed every time those fingers scraped his back, grabbed his ass, pulled his hair.

He loved the sound of her gasping to tell him to be quiet as he moaned out her name. And at the same time, telling him to say it again. And again. And…

"You're not playing fair, love," he teased as he pulled away just enough to look down at her. "If you get to hear me call out your name, I think the act should be reciprocated."

"I am," she panted as his fingers continued to pump in and out of her wet cunt.

He tutted. "Louder, love." He bit her neck and relished in the sound that came out of her. "It's only fair."

Her breathing grew ragged, and Harry could tell she was getting close so he pulled away from her and brought his slicked fingers to his lips. At least this way he'd get a little bit of a taste.

Her disappointed moan was the loudest one yet.

He chuckled because she was shy, but when she didn't get her release, she forgot all about being bashful. Her skin didn't even redden the same way, just the heat of desire glowing on her every inch.

He guided his cock to her wet lips after he got every morsel of her taste off his fingers and slid it from opening to clit, but never entered her. "Say my name, Vera."

"Harry," she whispered.

"I can't hear you." He really exaggerated his accent. He knew how much she enjoyed the sound of it.

"Harry," she called louder as her hands fisted into the sheets at her sides.

"I'm sorry, love. The charms are too strong. You're going to have to be louder than that." And fast. He wanted nothing more than to enter her, but instead he kept a steady rhythm sliding his cock up and down her cunt.

"Please," her voice dropped, "please, Harry, please."

He didn't even dignify that with a response.

Because he knew exactly what his disregard would do to her.

Her fists whitened as they dug into the sheets, and she arched her back as she cried his name so loud he almost came just hearing it.

"Finally," he growled and pushed into her, not caring to be gentle about it.

They gasped together as he filled her completely.

He brought her knees up to her chest as her hands reached for him in relief and he moved inside her, deeper and harder with each thrust. Her nails dug into his sides with each stroke he made over her clit.

And it was like filling her made her forget all about her reservations. Her breath hit his jaw as she said his name over and over and over again, each time just a little bit louder. Just a little bit more breathless, until he couldn't understand her any longer.

He could hardly pay attention anyway because his entire being started and ended with one word—Vera.

He was coming before he realized it'd happened, and that's when the real scream came out of her as she clenched around his cock and finished with him. Her nails dug into his back, and he felt his healing powers working the wounds closed already, but loved that she'd needed to dig into him like that.

When he found himself back from his high, he breathed in her being, then finally mustered the strength to pull out of her and slump just to the right of her body so he didn't crush her with his weight.

His lips quirked into a grin as he recalled how loud she'd been. "We can ask our guests in the morning if they heard that."

The shy reddening of her cheeks came back as she hid under his bicep. "Stop it."

12

---

*H*unter did not particularly enjoy the mornings when Maya left while he was still asleep. Especially after they'd had such a long night together and she'd wiped him out completely.

And she knew that much.

Which was exactly why she did it. He knew that was the reason. She thought it was funny to tick him off.

Hunter grumbled as he rolled out of bed when he realized she wasn't beside him after turning toward her for another round. And after searching the property and finding her nowhere to be found, he'd thrown curses into the air as he'd readied himself for the Whittle home.

He'd reprimand her in the most delicious way. He didn't care if her entire family was around for it.

He shadowed to the kitchen, figuring it the most neutral territory in the house. He truly tried never to check the ring for precise locations unless it were required. He didn't want to control her every movement, and knowing where she was every second felt very similar to that.

At the silence that rang throughout the house, he grew suspicious. She hadn't messaged him with any new developments.

Now he would use the ring.

To find she was in the house. Her office, to be precise.

He should've guessed. It wasn't always that she played music as she drew. Sometimes she preferred the silence that echoed around her. She said it was like listening to the air around her—Earth's own form of music.

He moved silently through the house to the back where the glass door to the office sat just wide enough for him to pass through.

But he stopped beforehand.

Because she was sitting behind her desk drawing.

With a baby in one arm. It looked to be sleeping as it rested against Maya's breast.

Hunter's heart raced and broke all at the same time. He'd never experienced something like this before. He'd thought Maya's accepting the ring was the most exhilarating feeling, but this one was coming right up there.

Because this was his future.

Maya would be the mother of his children, and he would wake up every day to find her like this.

He could not peel his stare away from the picture quickly filling around her.

Maya sitting in *her* office in Delvaux Manor, rocking *their* child to sleep as she finished another commission. She could never work another day in her life if she wished, but Hunter would never take her love of graphic design and drawing away.

But that little one rocking against her breast? His brown hair and her brilliant eyes.

He pictured a little girl, just like her mother.

Hunter finally swallowed the fantasy away and forced himself to move.

He was quiet as he slithered into the office. Maya's darting gaze met his with a small smile before it dropped back to her work. That smile said 'hello' and 'you better shut up, the baby is sleeping' all at once. Very motherly of her.

He walked around the table until he was standing behind her chair and leaned down to whisper in her ear, "I'm going to get you pregnant, love."

Because his heart was beating too fast at the thought and he wouldn't—couldn't—wait for their future.

Maya was in the kitchen with Aurelia in her lap when they returned from the unfortunate call they'd received. Maya had given Lila and Tamire the opportunity to go with the others while she watched Aurelia. Vera still wasn't sure if that was because she genuinely wanted to watch the baby or if it was because she hadn't wanted to join them.

Vera couldn't fault her sister if it was the latter.

And if nothing else, Lila and Tamire trusted her—their entire family—fully so even though they hadn't wanted to leave their daughter, they'd done so. At the very least, to find out what was after them. If it had anything to do with those the Whittles were hunting.

"What happened?" Maya pushed her sketchbook aside and watched them all take their seats around the kitchen. Hunter took the sketchbook and leaned back in his signature lounge beside Maya as he sifted through the pages.

"That same gargoyle and nymph couple." Harry sighed. "Killed this time."

"How?" Maya asked as she placed a sleeping Aurelia in her infant rocker.

Harry leaned his elbows over the table and looked distractedly handsome in his three-piece suit. "The families were angry. When we got there, they were ready to rip our throats out, as if we had anything to do with it. Nae, the elder nymph, was the one who had called originally. They wanted to know the same thing since their kids were dead and they had no idea what had happened."

"Basically, we're pretty damn lucky we have Lila on our side right now. I can only read thoughts the person is actively thinking about, so I would've been no help," Camilla said.

Hunter's gaze moved from the sketchbook to Lila, but moved back down as if he still wasn't interested. Maya, though, insisted on learning more.

Lila shrugged. "I'm lucky with a non-primary power that works really well. I can go through memories from the most recent memory backwards. It works on the dead too, but if they've been dead too long, I can only get more recent stuff. Lucky for us, I needed more recent stuff *and* they weren't dead long at all."

Tamire took his wife's hand and looked to be eyeing Hunter with a bit too much suspicion. Vera felt for Hunter; no matter what he did, everyone was always wary of his intentions. Though, to be fair, last time they'd seen each other, Hunter had threatened to kill their unborn child. So maybe the looks were a bit justified here.

And though the demon didn't care, Vera knew Maya hated it.

"I went back to when I figured would be most important—the last time you guys saw them. Saw Hunter giving the potion to aid them." Lila also gave Hunter a wondering gaze. "Then saw them take the potions. Both had pretty similar memories even though their families had taken them home separately. But I have to say, they were thankful for that potion—it was exactly what their minds and bodies needed to finally be able to rest." She watched Hunter with some consideration even though the demon continued to flip through Maya's sketchbook like he couldn't be bothered with the story.

"They woke up with the illusions feeling like nightmares," Vera continued the story Lila had recited as she'd been going through their memories. "All they wanted was to see each other again, so they met in the woods."

"I sped through the next part." Lila's lips tipped up. "Didn't exactly need to see what they did then."

Maya gave a soft, knowing chuckle, and even Hunter's lips tipped up into a grin.

Lila's smile dropped. "Then…the halfies. Gargoyle-nymph to be exact. Almost like they were getting revenge on couples that were similar to their parents. They said they were going to kill them because they couldn't listen to the simple rule of staying within their own race. That they'd already gotten whatever magic their bodies held for T…I don't know. The halfie stopped herself before saying the name."

"That has to be what I saw!" Camilla exclaimed. Since she'd been more focused on the families when they'd been on the site, she hadn't heard this part. "It looked almost like when Lyric was draining Hunter's life. They were draining magic!"

Hunter looked up, more intrigued now, but didn't say anything.

Vera, on the other hand, sat up a little straighter. What could they possibly need to drain magic for? This had to be Grandmama's doing. The halfies seemed too focused on their revenge to want anything more.

"But the halfies couldn't do it," Lila continued. "It looked like the death shot came from an older woman."

"Which had to be Grandmama," Harry interrupted.

Lila shrugged. "I saw this intense shine hit them when they fell to the ground. When they realized they weren't making it, they just stared at one another, like they wanted the last thing they saw to be each other."

"That's where it would've come from," Vera whispered under her breath, but she realized too late it was loud enough for everyone to hear. A blush filled her cheeks as she looked up to everyone. "I can astral project." She ignored the gasps and continued talking, Harry's hand on her thigh a lovely distraction. "I didn't realize I'd done it, but I was hovering over you guys at one point. Saw this shimmer on their faces. I bet it came from that shine. I don't think it's anything to worry about. I'd just been so confused."

"Was there anything specific with the shimmer?" Hunter spoke up for the first time, intrigue filling his black eyes.

Vera shrugged. "A pentagram with a dagger through it, I think. It was split between both of their faces so it was harder to tell."

Camilla gasped as Hunter's eyes shined. "The Book showed me a page the other day with a pentagram with a dagger through it."

Hunter's lips tipped up in giddy excitement. "Dark magic."

"As in, that's what they're using now or that's what was used to make Grandmama?" Tamire asked.

"I don't know what they're doing, but I can guarantee it's with dark magic. I'd wondered if they'd try it. I figured it'd been used to make Grandmama because regular magic wouldn't have kept her alive all this time." He leaned back in his chair and brought Maya closer to him like this was relaxing to him. "Now things are really getting interesting."

13

ace down, ass up. Is that the way you like to fuck?

Of course Maya would find a way to distract him while he was on a trip. She rolled her eyes every time he chastised her for these messages and always found a way to argue that they were simple questions.

Yeah, simple questions that had his dick hard in the most inopportune times.

"Distracted on the job?" Warren smirked his way. "Didn't you tell me once never to be distracted on the job?"

Hunter growled at him. "Find a mate and I'll allow you the inconvenience."

Warren's smirk dropped and a line of worry filled his hazel eyes. Hunter knew what his brother was thinking, could guess it merely from Warren's human side. He was worried he would never find a mate. Most demons didn't.

"I see both my sons are distracted today." Augustine stepped forward.

This was a more unusual trip. Hunter wasn't used to trips with all three of them. They'd done so before, but it was far more common for him to only be with one. Actually, it was far more common for him to be with neither one of them. But since his father had learned of Maya, he'd wanted to rejoin Hunter's trips, and now Warren wanted a piece of the money to begin his own line. So they'd quickly turned to family business trips.

Maya thought it was cute, that they did these jobs together. Hunter couldn't care less for the sentimentality of it. He enjoyed these trips with his father and brother over other demons, sure. But he preferred them most when he could just finish them himself.

Luckily, this one would be short and quick.

There's just something about the way your fingers move inside me that hits different. Mine don't feel half as good.

Hunter strained his neck as another growl escaped him. Maya was really testing his control.

That's not a question, he texted back, though he knew it was stupid to engage.

"How is my darling daughter?" Augustine asked as they walked into the sewers that would lead them to their prize.

A pain in my ass, Hunter thought, then chided himself for thinking of Maya and ass in the same sentence. She had such a delectable ass.

"None of your concern," Hunter bit out. Especially right at that moment, entirely none of his father's concern how Maya was.

Augustine chuckled, but said nothing more. Even he knew when not to test his son's limits. Especially now that Hunter was mated.

Their trip was quite a simple one: to apprehend a serial killer who had gone a little far and killed a demon.

Now the demon's family wanted vengeance.

It was realistically not a difficult job, but that was the thing with demons—they loved paying others to do the work for them. And Hunter loved taking their money.

So they were tracking a human serial killer.

A twelve-year-old human serial killer.

And they said demons were bad.

"So, why is it you're here, War? Finally giving into the demon side?" Hunter needed a distraction.

His brother shrugged. "Giving up these jobs got me nowhere. I still lost Camilla for what I am, *and* I have to stay under Dad's wing because I can't afford to do otherwise. I've come to find your way was probably the best decision—not fighting against the fact that you're a demon and making a life for yourself. It sure as hell got you Maya."

Augustine clapped his youngest's shoulder. "Ah, don't be upset, Son. She was never your mate to begin with."

"I know," Warren said with no conviction in his voice.

They rounded the corner to find the kid with a stake in one hand and a knife in the other. His crazed eyes told Hunter that he truly thought he'd win.

"Remember," Augustine said, "money comes for a live, healthy boy. No one wants to play with an already injured one. Not as much fun."

Hunter rolled his eyes, like he needed the reminder. Though he knew it was more for Warren's sake than his.

Warren shadowed behind the boy and punched into each of the kid's elbows so the weapons dropped. Putting him in a chokehold afterward was no work.

Augustine shook his head. "Son, you can have more fun than that."

"I don't want to hurt a child," Warren grit out.

Hunter rolled his eyes. "A serial killer child. Even your humanity should understand that."

The kid punched his elbow into Warren's distracted gut. Then he was running.

Hunter smirked and shadowed before the kid, sent a back hand across his face, and watched him fall to the ground. Still uninjured—basically—and still very much alive.

"That's how it's done." Augustine strolled up. "Though you could've had more fun than that too."

Hunter's phone pinged and he pulled it out of his trousers. She'd ignored his message and sent another definitely not a question.

Don't worry, I finished. Just imagined slobbering all over your cock. But I'm so wet now that you'd slip right in.

"I'm going to kill her," Hunter spit through clenched teeth as he shoved his phone back into his pocket.

"Ah." Augustine chuckled. "So the Missus is why you're not having more fun today."

Hunter glowered at him. "Fuck off."

They still had to take the kid for their payment. A few more hours before he could see his mate. And even then, they had a conversation with his father that needed to take place before he could take her home and punish her for distracting him.

Sometimes Maya wished she were more of a reader like her older sister. But drawing was the art form that brought her most pleasure.

So she sat in her chair in Augustine's office as she waited for the boys to return before the fire that blazed beside her. It was adorable to Maya that they were out as a family on this little trip. Hunter rolled his eyes every time Maya said so with her wide grin.

Plus, it gave her a bit of peace of mind to know that Augustine and Warren would be around to look after Hunter if it were needed.

Though Hunter would be offended if he heard that.

She sat in the office and drew for the better part of an hour as she waited and got a beautiful—and graphic—portrait of her mate done before their shadows appeared. She pushed her sketchbook to the small table beside her chair as Hunter walked immediately toward her and his brother and father moved for the bar cart.

His finger played with her waiting lips, peeling the bottom one open before leaning down and kissing her roughly. It was a short kiss, but fuck, did it tell her how much he missed her when they weren't together. "Next time you try sending me those messages, I'll keep you up all night peaking, but never reaching orgasm. Understood?"

"You wouldn't dare." Her tongue toyed with his finger.

His nostrils flared. "Try it next time, love. And see if I'd dare."

When she didn't answer, his hands moved to her hips and hauled her up to wrap her legs around his waist. The squeal that escaped Maya's lips caused a wicked grin to form on his features as he kissed her neck and turned them so he was sitting in the chair.

Their chair.

She straddled him as he leaned back like he ruled the world, his hands caressing her ass like he possessed it.

Well, he did possess it.

"If you two planned on creating my grandchild right now, I'd prefer you shadowed to *your* manor." Augustine's voice behind her reminded Maya they weren't alone.

Hunter smirked, his stare never leaving hers as the memory of his demand that they get pregnant came fresh into her mind. "We *should* be working on creating that grandchild."

His hips thrusts into her as Maya shook her head. "Would you stop it! We're at your father's!"

He smirked, uncaring. "I can take care of that rather quickly, love."

She tried to pull away, but he held her tight as she mouthed, "Stop. It."

His grip on her ass was territorial as he pushed her closer to him. "I'll do as I wish with what is mine, Witch."

Her breathing hitched, and she hated how wet her panties grew with that one comment. Hated how quickly she was ready to relent to him. "Maybe we should go home," she whispered against his lips.

He chucked and tsked. "We have to talk to my father, remember?"

He knew the affect he had on her, could smell it, and sometimes he liked to make her wait for it. She really loathed him those times.

She eyed him through slits. "I hate you."

His answering smirk and deep inhalation told her just how much he was enjoying her scent. "Good."

After controlling her breathing, she finally turned in his lap to face her new 'father.' It was still weird, that though Augustine was Hunter's father, their dynamic didn't work the same as just about everyone else's might. The uncaring nature wasn't just about the welfare of others, but it also meant that it wasn't disturbing or embarrassing or gross or any other feeling when Augustine saw Hunter and Maya interact. To him, it was merely the sight of two mates.

Warren sat at an armchair beside his father, and his stare told her how amusing he found the entire situation. At least with Warren, it was the reactions Maya was used to and expected. And as *Hunter's* brother, rather than her own, Warren's was more teasing than disturbed.

As Maya watched the two sat across from her, she realized how much Warren looked like his father. Hunter really only shared the black eyes with Augustine. Warren shared just about everything else.

Including that wicked smirk they both stared at her with.

She tilted her head at them. "You two find something amusing?"

The shakes of their heads came quickly as both insisted, "Absolutely not."

Yeah, pretty damn similar. Too bad Warren didn't love that side of himself. Maya hoped he'd grow to. She loved all of Hunter, and at least fifty percent of that lived in Warren too.

She hoped now that he wasn't trying to hide his demoness from her sister, he could grow more confident in who he was.

Maya leaned back into Hunter and let his arms circle around her middle and hold her close as her head rested against his neck. She breathed in his scent to prepare for the conversation.

Without moving, her gaze found Augustine. "The power..."

Augustine stiffened. Maybe he was expecting them to string him along and never actually get to it.

"It came only once, when we were at the Bridgers coven, then...disappeared. Hunt and I tried to see if we could bring it back, but nothing."

"Vera was dying. They had a hold on her that was knocking her air out, so we assumed it was based on anger. Maya's anger for almost killing her sister, so I took her down to your dungeons and tried on some of those we have down there, but nothing," Hunter explained.

"It could've been the combination of Vera getting hurt and Melusine trying to kill you. There were icicles thrown at you, at all of us," Warren said. "It could've been a protective instinct. But Camilla told me you tried that too."

Maya shook her head. "We did. With one of the pieces of shit in your dungeons. After Hunt told me what he'd done, he was allowed to attack. Nothing. I wanted to try again, but *my mate* wouldn't allow it."

Hunter looked almost annoyed with her. "I'm not risking you almost getting hurt again for it."

Augustine's eyes narrowed on all of them. "So what is the power?"

"It's a dark power," Warren said.

"Obviously, this is my daughter we're speaking of." Augustine was serious, but still, there was pride in his eyes as he watched her.

"It's never been seen in a witch before," Hunter added.

That got his father's true attention more than anything else had.

"And from what I understand," Maya finished, "it's as old as Hell's Gate itself."

They waited and took in Augustine's scrutiny. Warren had guessed his father would be able to figure it out with hints.

It took only another minute before Augustine's eyes widened, and he looked her over as if seeing a completely new person. "Impossible."

"Apparently not so." Hunter's hold around her waist tightened as he pulled her into his chest until they were basically one.

Augustine didn't pay attention as he placed his drink on the arm of his chair, and it went falling as he leaned forward. "*You* can open a portal to Hell's Gate?"

Maya shrugged. "Not anymore."

He shook his head. "Once you have it, it's there. We just have to figure out how it was triggered."

"This will not be something you advertise for the family's gain, Father," Hunter growled.

Augustine's eyes were still on her as he said, "No, no. Not until she's in full control."

Maya swore Hunter's growl vibrated through the room as she soothed a hand up his arm. "He won't do it without us, Hunt. He's an ass, but he respects us—you—enough for that."

Maya turned back to Augustine.

"I knew you'd be the greatest asset to this family the second I realized *Hunter* was mated, *Maya*." Hunter almost leapt out of his seat at the use of her name, but Maya forced her weight down and continued stroking him. Augustine's black eyes shined like Hunter's reaction was his intent with using her name. "Now, Daughter, we must find out what makes *you* tick."

14

_M_aya sat at a stool in the kitchen holding a cup of black coffee and was staring straight ahead when Camilla walked in holding baby Aurelia in her arms. Camilla was only half surprised to see her sister, given Maya technically no longer lived with them.

Camilla was even less surprised to see her sister so focused when she noticed Hunter preparing breakfast at the stove.

"Morning," Camilla opened just as Harry and Vera strolled into the kitchen.

Maya nodded toward her, and Hunter turned to acknowledge her when his gaze landed on the baby in her arms. They widened, and he quickly turned.

Camilla turned curious eyes to her sister as Maya laughed.

"When I watched Aurelia and you guys went out to the nymphs and gargoyles, Hunter showed up and Aurelia kept crying to be in his arms," Maya explained.

Camilla's bottom lip jut out. "That's so sweet."

Hunter didn't turn back around. "It's annoying. The only child I want clinging to me is the one I make with your sister."

Camilla rolled her eyes as she sat beside her sister. "That would be sweet too if you hadn't added the first bit."

"Where're Lila and Tamire?" Harry asked as he readied himself a cup of tea.

Camilla shrugged. "They asked me to watch this little bundle. Said they were headed to their cottage to see if they could figure anything out without having to worry so much about Aurelia. So, I'm guessing still there."

"I wish they'd mentioned something." Harry fell into his stool. "I would've gone with them too."

"That's probably why they didn't. They wanted to leave the family warlock with the family," Maya said.

Harry rolled his eyes. "You lot have Hunter now too."

"But we can't call to Hunter by simply saying his name into thin air," Vera argued as she pushed her stool as close to Harry as it would go.

"Yeah, yeah, yeah." Harry leaned in to give Vera a chaste kiss.

Camilla smiled at them before she looked down to find the baby's wide eyes on Hunter's back. Camilla smirked as she looked up to her new brother. "I think she's realized you're here, Big Brother."

Camilla swore she *heard* Hunter's teeth grind. "Tell her to fuck off."

Maya gasped. "Hunter."

"Sorry, love." He most definitely wasn't sorry, but what else was expected from him?

He finished plating the food and placed it in the middle of the island. It didn't happen often, but sometimes they'd eat standing—or sitting on the three stools—around the island rather than the table.

Hunter made an omelette. Camilla loved Hunter's omelette's. She'd never tell him that though.

He'd barely gotten two forkfuls onto his plate when Aurelia made her desires known. She reached out to him with the most adorable puppy dog eyes Camilla had ever seen. She even saw the way Maya turned to Hunter with 'isn't that the cutest thing you've ever seen' eyes.

Only to receive a quirked brow and annoyed eye roll.

Aurelia kept reaching out.

And the bastard was really ignoring her.

He was about three mouthfuls into his breakfast when Aurelia gave up silently asking to be held. Her wails rang through the kitchen as she practically fought Camilla's hold, as if at three months she could leap for Hunter's arms.

"Hunter, come on," Vera begged from the other side of the island. "Think of it as practice for yours and Maya's baby."

"I don't need practice for our child."

"Hunter," Harry called as he sadly looked on to the child.

The demon truly was unbothered. "No."

Maya took Aurelia into her arms after another minute of Hunter's ignorance and handed the baby to her mate. "Pretend she's ours."

"I'm not pretending that annoying thing is ours." He took another forkful.

"Hunter," Maya admonished.

He finally huffed out and took Aurelia into his arms. "I'm not pretending she's ours."

The silence that echoed as he took her was deafening.

"Wow," Harry said. "She really does love you."

Hunter didn't look amused as he adjusted the little girl in his arms. And now Maya was the one mesmerized by the demon.

In the quietude of clinging utensils as they all ate their breakfast, Camilla couldn't help the way her gaze kept shooting up to her sister and the demon.

And the child in his arms.

They looked like a family. Like a true family. Father, mother, baby.

With their food consumed, Camilla watched Maya ready a bottle for Aurelia and hand it to Hunter. The way he did it, Camilla assumed Maya had made him feed the baby the day before too because it did not look like his first time.

And Maya was hypnotized again.

Camilla couldn't hear them as they whispered to one another, but the smiles and low laughs coming from both parties told her it was something good.

Or dirty.

Probably dirty.

But it made Camilla content. That after all those months of hating on them, she was finally happy for what they shared.

"It smells amazing in here," Tamire's voice came as they turned the corner and came to a halt at the sight before them.

Because the man that had threatened to take the life of their unborn child was now holding and feeding her. Camilla held her breath and had a feeling everyone else in the room was doing the same because honestly, this situation could go one of two very different ways.

Lila and Tamire watched Hunter, then their gazes slipped to Maya beside him and their very satisfied daughter in his arms. And slowly, Camilla saw their acceptance of the situation and forgiveness to the past.

Witches were like that. They forgave easily. Sometimes even too easily.

But in this instance, they had Maya's assurance even without speaking that nothing would happen to their daughter.

They moved toward the island and took the last bits of omelette left on the large plate in the middle. Maya heated it up for them so it tasted straight off the pan rather than microwaved. Camilla loved that part of Maya's power.

Camilla broke the semi-awkwardness that had seeped into the room. "How was the cottage?"

Lila took Maya's forgotten stool and smiled to her husband as he set a plate before her. "We were there for two hours to see if we could find any evidence of The Eight. We don't think it's them, but just in case, you know. Nothing."

Tamire stood beside his wife so they could share from her plate. "But we were attacked again, so at least there's evidence that they are definitely after us. And even more reason to be glad with leaving Auri here."

Brows shot up.

"Same person?" Harry asked.

Tamire shrugged. "That much, we can't tell. We didn't see them the first time, and we barely got a look this time. We have Aurelia to think about now, so we had to make sure to make it out fine, so the fight didn't exactly last as long as it could've."

No one responded. How could they? They had no idea what it was like to have a child to return to.

Hunter placed the bottle on the island and pushed the baby out just as Tamire and Lila finished their plate. "It's done."

Maya smacked him. "Hunter, stop it." She pushed Aurelia back toward him and placed a bib on his shoulder. "She needs to be burped."

He looked down to his mate as he placed Aurelia to his shoulder and started smacking her back, and there was a lightness to his black orbs that had never been there before. Or that Camilla had never noticed. Never *allowed* herself to notice.

"I'm only doing this so you'll see how nice it'll be when ours comes," Hunter teased her.

"You're trying?" Tamire asked.

"No," Maya insisted.

"Every. Single. Day." Hunter ignored her with that smirk that said he was mostly teasing.

And at the same moment, Aurelia burped so loud a grown man would be jealous, and everyone laughed because how could they not?

Hunter looked to Maya again. "Now can I give it back?"

Maya blew out a frustrated breath and motioned for him to do so. "But stop calling her an it."

Tamire took his daughter as Lila said, "It's weird. It felt less trained than before. It's the only reason we think it wasn't the same person. Or at least, if it is, they're devolving."

Camilla was only half paying attention, most of her focus on the baby, whose gaze never left Hunter as her chubby little hands reached out for him.

Again, he was completely unbothered.

But Maya melted as she stood pressed to his front.

Before Lila could say any more, a man ported into their kitchen. Just like the first time Harry had ported in months ago.

Just poof and there.

But this man was younger, probably closer to Maya's age. And obviously a warlock by his way of entrance.

Camilla jumped in her spot at the suddenness of the entrance as Tamire handed Aurelia to his wife and stood before them and Hunter pushed Maya behind him and glowered. Camilla had to admit, that stare was kinda scary.

Harry froze too, but he didn't put Vera behind him. Didn't try to protect any of them.That simple choice told Camilla this warlock, whoever he was, wasn't someone to be afraid of.

"What are you doing here?" Harry's tone was demanding as he ground his jaw. It wasn't often that Harry became serious like this.

But if *Harry* was angry, then this man wasn't someone they could entirely trust. Camilla was astounded by how much she could pick up by Harry's small acts.

The man smirked something Hunter would be proud of. "Brother. Good to see you too."

Camilla turned on Harry the same moment Vera and Maya did. "Brother?"

Harry inhaled a large breath. "Not real brother. We're both old warlocks so he calls me that. Mostly to annoy me."

"That's great," Hunter growled. "Now what the hell is he doing porting into the house?"

"Don't worry, Demon. I wouldn't imagine touching your mate." The warlock's amusement was still there. And he was unafraid of the demon before him.

Camilla wondered how quickly that would change if Hunter attacked.

"How does he have access?" Camilla asked, flabbergasted.

The smirk turned on her, and his gaze trailed her skin slowly before landing on her lips. "That's a pretty little mouth you have, darling."

Harry moved faster than Camilla had ever seen before, slamming the new warlock into the fridge. She heard the remnants of the fridge move and crash, but couldn't focus on that.

Because Harry was angry.

"Do *not* speak to her like that," he ground out.

"Sorry, chief."

Camilla scoffed because he was like the warlock version of Hunter. Amused and having fun in this situation. Asshole.

Harry's hold on his shirt didn't loosen. "What are you doing here, Kai?"

His own hazel eyes, lighter than Harry's by leagues, shined. "Calling in your favor. I want to help in our mystery search."

Vera spoke before Harry had the chance, "What favor?"

Kai's gaze moved past Harry's shoulder and landed on Vera. "Ah, you must be the beautiful Vera." Harry slammed him against the fridge again, but Kai seemed indifferent to it. "I was the one that found out about your history, Sister."

Camilla's breath caught.

She'd been told about Vera's past a couple of days after Grandmama had come back to life. Harry and Vera had sat her and Maya down and told them about Vera's sickness and their mother's inability to see her for a quarter of a century.

All Harry had mentioned was that he owed some favors for the information.

Kai's gaze moved back to Harry. "Now, Brother, let's be cordial."

Harry ground his teeth but finally released his companion and moved back to stand beside Vera. Like being near her would calm him in the same way touching calmed Maya and Hunter.

Camilla narrowed her eyes on the man. Her dislike of him

wasn't immediate like it had been with Hunter, but after this little show, it was just as strong as her dislike of Hunter had been. "What do you want?"

He fixed his shirt in the most dramatic of ways, then faced her with a wicked smirk. "First, I'd like to introduce myself. Kai. At *your* service, darling…Camilla, I'd wager."

He bowed in front of her, and Camilla wanted to smack him across the property for his theatrics. "I don't like you."

He looked to her through his lashes in his still bowed position. "There's a shocker. Does Miss High and Mighty like anyone?"

Now her jaw clenched. She guessed that was a dig at her failed relationship with Warren, though how he knew about that was at question.

Hunter's chuckle came from behind her. "I like him."

She turned a dirty look on her new brother. "Shocking." Asshole for asshole.

Not even a moment after the word left her mouth, Aurelia's cries hit the skies. In the disturbance of the new warlock, Camilla had forgotten about the baby's desire for her sister's mate.

Her arms reached as far as they'd go and she practically jumped from her mother's grasp as the tears fell down her face.

Lila tried to hush her, but none of it worked. She wanted only one person.

Lila looked to Maya, like she knew Hunter wouldn't care, and Maya smiled warmly before she took Aurelia into her arms, then handed her to Hunter again. Hunter didn't say anything, just rolled his eyes and took the child.

He held her lazily so Aurelia's back hit his chest, but she didn't seem bothered. Just being in the demon's arms was contenting for the baby as she played with Hunter's thumb balancing her chest back.

He wrapped his other arm around Maya's waist and brought her into the other half of his chest as he grumbled, "Happy?"

Maya kissed his jaw. "Very."

Camilla smiled at the scene before Mr Full of Himself interrupted the moment. "Isn't that sweet."

Camilla turned on him again. "Go away."

He ignored her and met Harry's gaze. "So what are we working on?" When no one spoke, Kai grinned a little too cunningly. "A favor's a favor, Brother. I *insist* on helping."

Harry gave a choppy nod, and Vera broke the tension by telling the new warlock—Kai, he had a name and Camilla had to not be petty enough to use it—everything.

Vera didn't know how to feel about their new companion.

He was cocky, and she could definitely see how that would annoy just about anyone, especially her little sister, but something told Vera he was a genuinely nice guy. Almost like he was putting up a facade. Or that the years he'd been alive had taught him to hide the nice guy.

Or maybe it was the years of being alone as a warlock that had hardened him to assery.

But he'd definitely be helpful.

After she finished telling him everything, he'd been the one to insist they reach out to the gargoyles since they had a good standing relationship with Uzark, the gargoyles' leader. If they could start somewhere—especially considering one of theirs was a recent victim—then they could possibly learn of any more gargoyles in relationships and slowly expand to keep all species safe, though Vera couldn't see the same tactics working on all species.

Kai's plan was the reason Vera knew he was a nice guy hardened by time. Because at the end of the day, he could act like a demon, but he would always be one of them—part of the witch species.

Camilla hadn't seemed too happy by his good idea, and

really, she had a reason to be annoyed with the young warlock. He *was* being the biggest ass to her. Not to mention, he did remind Vera of demons, and Camilla was still warming herself to the species.

Harry had whispered to Vera it was because of Camilla's past with Warren. Kai's best friend when he'd first taken the immortal life was a halfie just like her little sister's ex. Demon and human.

The man had passed long ago, but Kai still missed him every day.

Vera would not argue with Kai's insistence that they do this. It was something they'd all wanted—to know who was in these relationships in order to better protect them. But they'd never been deluded enough to think the couples would give themselves up.

But Kai sounded so sure the gargoyles would.

Camilla stayed home with the excuse she had homework to get herself out of spending any extra time with the new warlock.

Maya stayed with Hunter since they weren't exactly sure the presence of the demon who had allowed his lackeys to destroy the gargoyles' property would be accepted. Or whether his mate would be accepted.

Kai had insisted they both stay, and Vera had wondered how Kai knew so much about their family. Or about what Hunter had done. The warlock was like an encyclopedia of recent events.

And Lila and Tamire stayed behind with their daughter, so that left their little group of three to port to the middle of the woods.

Uzark was waiting for them by the front when they arrived.

He looked nervous as they approached. "I don't know how the lot will feel about giving up that information. We are still not the most accepting of species. Nothing like the wolves."

The wolves.

The most accepting of mixed relationships.

Though theirs came instinctively because their matings could happen with any species. And their matings were more important than any other matter.

It was one of the instances that other species allowed—mating with a wolf. Because they knew it couldn't be helped.

But not always. Sometimes even the mating wasn't enough to look past the prejudices they held.

Kai spoke first. "No, but you have made it easier on your lot. They trust you, and though they may fear what their peers will think, they won't hide it from you if you ask. If you *need* to know."

Uzark narrowed his gaze on him. "What makes you think that?"

Kai gave that little smirk Vera was coming to recognize in their short acquaintance as his signature. "I hear things."

Uzark's gaze moved to Harry's then hers, like he needed their reassurance. Then he simply turned and walked into the manor. They followed as he said, "Everyone is in the great ballroom now. They're expecting you, but haven't been told of the reason."

Vera grabbed for Harry's hand as they walked. She was nervous for those in relationships within the room and needed his calming nature.

The space looked more like a darkened, expansive room than a ballroom. All the residents were lined up on every available bit of wall, most huddled together, given there were too many of them to stand single-file.

They stopped in the middle of the room with their backs to one another, and Vera noticed Uzark's sigh of nervousness before he spoke. "Like I said before, I'm going to make this quick. No consequences will be held out. I want everyone's full honesty. And I need you all to know this is for your safety. With the group of halfies going around, it's more important to me that you remain safe and alive than the prejudices of the species."

Vera's heart hammered in her chest.

"I need you all to be honest with me and with your peers," Uzark continued, his voice all authority and love mixed together. "Step up if you know of a mixed couple within our people."

Know of a mixed couple.

Which meant they were not necessarily incriminating themselves if they stepped up. That would take some of the fear out of the moment.

Slowly.

So slowly Vera almost thought they wouldn't do it, one gargoyle after another stepped up around them. In the end, there were twenty-seven women and men who knew of someone that was in a relationship outside of their species.

Maybe Kai had been right and Uzark's people truly trusted him because that was far more than Vera had expected to step up.

"Thank you." Uzark was obviously shocked that they'd stepped up *and* at the amount of them there were. But he hid it well. "Now take another step if you yourself are in one of these relationships."

One minute.

Two.

Three. Four. They weren't going to do it.

Uzark turned doubtful eyes on Kai, and when he got the reassuring nod, turned back to his tribe. "All those who stepped forward, remain. All others, get about your duties."

Vera hated the fear she knew was running through every single one of these individuals. Hated that they believed they would be outcast and treated differently for whom they chose to love. And hated that in many other species, they definitely could be outcast.

Harry's thumb softly caressed her hand as they stood there.

They weren't necessarily needed in order to make these confessions happen, but Kai had mentioned he believed the tribe may feel a bit safer if witches were standing about too. Like they'd be witness to any confessions and would be able to hold others accountable if something were to happen to them.

She'd have to ask Harry how Kai knew all this.

When the room emptied, Uzark motioned for everyone to line up on one wall.

"I repeat," he said calmly, "no consequences. I only wish to know for your own protection. You will be free to continue your relationships, but I *need* to know. Step up if you yourself are in one."

One minute.

Two.

One woman stepped up, her chest rising and falling so slowly it was obvious she was trying to control her nerves.

After another minute, two more women stepped up.

Then the men obliged.

In total, out of the twenty-seven, thirteen were in relationships outside of their species.

Uzark nodded through his shock. "Thank you." He looked to the others still standing about. "Minus those who have stepped up, are there any other relationships you know of?"

One female stepped forward. She looked nervous, like she didn't want to be the one to out her friend, but felt it better to keep them safe than sorry.

Uzark gave her a small nod. "You may all step back. Please wait here, I'll walk our guests out, then come back to speak to you."

Vera's hand was full-on sweating by the time they walked out, but Harry didn't complain or pull his hand away. Everything had gone well, but she couldn't help the fear she'd felt for them. With them.

Uzark stopped at the gates of the property and turned mainly to Kai. "Thank you."

Kai's eyes were warm and strong all at once. "Your only job now is to make sure they feel secure enough to stay with the species. Better yet, if they bring their significant others here so they're not caught sneaking around. I have a feeling, and I'm sure you can agree, that's how these couples are getting caught."

"Thank you." Uzark gave a final smile and headed back inside.

Kai met their gazes. "That's one species that should be safe now. The easiest one too. The others wouldn't be this accepting."

"You think it'll help?" Vera asked hopefully.

He shrugged. "I hope so. It's really all we can do to protect them. Help them tell others, even if it's only a leader. But if we keep them safe from the halfies, then it's one less problem we have to worry about, and we can put the rest of our focus on this Grandmama character and whoever their puppet master is."

They'd already warned against Grandmama's list of victims.

And they had no idea how to go after this puppet master.

But it was one problem down, slight as it may be.

15

$\mathcal{M}$aya had thrown a pot at his head in the manor's kitchen.

A whole fucking pot.

And all because he'd said he wasn't in the mood for a four-cheese mac 'n cheese with grilled cheese on the side. How that had warranted a pot to the head, Hunter didn't understand.

So he'd tried to kiss her goodbye—which she quickly shut down—and shadowed to the Whittle residence.

He couldn't have her getting angry with him for not upholding his trainings with her sister too. He could only imagine what she'd throw at him then.

Plus, he needed her to calm down before that afternoon when they went to visit Zathrian and Acacia, the only real friends he'd had before meeting Maya, and another demon-witch mated pair.

"Where's your cocky, I-own-this-world stride today?" Vera asked as he walked into the empty room they used to train.

He grimaced her way. "I'm not in the mood, Vera."

Her smile was cocky and amused. "You're in trouble with my sister, aren't you?"

132

"No." He crossed his arms before his chest as he stopped in front of her in the middle of the room.

That smile wasn't going anywhere. "Liar."

"Forget about your demon sensing for a moment. Try throwing me back," he said.

She narrowed her eyes, but her smile was still there. "I've done it before."

"Great." He was in no mood to play. "When you run into unsuspecting victims, you can easily get them. But after the first throw, they'll be ready. Not to mention if they're not unsuspecting. Throw me."

She shot her hand out, and it took zero percent of his energy to get out of the way. He only moved a foot to the right.

Now the smile she'd worn was gone.

She tried again.

This time, he moved back to his original position.

He could see the frustration building in her as she failed again and again. All he'd do was shadow a foot or two in either direction and always just out of reach.

And since shadowing was so second nature to him, he didn't really have to give it much of his attention. Instead, his attention could go to his mate, who was still at home. He could feel her through the ring, and if he truly focused on it, he could feel her emotions running wild.

Annoyance and anger and guilt and...he smirked, horniness. His witch was always horny.

"This isn't funny," Vera growled as she threw out her arm again, obviously believing Hunter was teasing her with the smirk.

Hunter brought his thoughts back to the moment. "You're not thinking about your actions. You're just throwing your arm out. Think of it like a sport. Like baseball. When they throw the ball, they don't throw it straight to the spot the bat is at that moment. They throw it at an angle to the spot they believe the bat will hit."

Vera closed her eyes and breathed in, then opened them again. Her eyes were so similar to the only pair that intrigued Hunter that he almost got distracted from the training.

But his focus did retract back to his witch as he shadowed out of the way again, but felt the edge of Vera's power brush him. Good, she was learning quickly.

Maya's emotions were jumbled through the ring. Hunter figured that had to do with the fact that they weren't so strong that the emotion would transfer to him, but he still wanted to fix it. She felt guilty—he assumed for throwing the pot at him—but more than that, annoyed. And something told him, it was annoyance at herself rather than at him.

Why?

Was it because of her emotions that began running wild right around the time he'd left with Grandmama?

He had a feeling that was the case and didn't know what to do to help her with it. Was it his fault she was going through this?

He shadowed to the left, narrowly missing Vera's power, and ran straight into another blast. Clever girl had thrown two so she'd catch him in either direction.

He hit the wall and immediately came out of his thoughts. Hunter smirked to Vera as he stood up. "Good job."

Her smile was wide "Thank you." Then she looked him over. "You're distracted, aren't you?"

"Yes." He wouldn't lie, no purpose in it. "But that's not why you were able to get me. You did well. Don't try to make excuses past it."

She took a sip of water, then placed it back on the fireplace's mantel. "Why is she mad at you?"

He looked heavenward. "Because I didn't have a major craving for cheese for lunch."

She paused. "That doesn't sound like Maya."

His quirked brow spoke for him—*You're telling me.*

She gave a superior scoff. "Maybe that shadowing ability is

affecting her more than you thought it would. Demon powers shouldn't be in a witch."

He laughed at her jab, but continued the training. In which he got thrown around a couple more times. And as they reached the end of their session, their conversation came back to Hunter and he froze.

Vera was right. Demon powers weren't meant to be in witches.

He didn't allow himself to think about it as he controlled his breathing and tried to clear his mind. "Let's finish this, Sister. I cannot have Maya getting angry with me for not completing our sessions."

Vera smirked. "Yes, sir."

Camilla's gaze wandered around her literature class. It was her favorite class and had quite the attractive professor to top it off.

But it was also the one class she shared with Warren.

She'd tried to convince her mind she wasn't looking for him, but knew she couldn't lie to herself. Even though they were broken up and she knew she wasn't in love with him, she still felt love for him. Still wanted to know he was doing well.

Especially because she had been the jackass in their relationship. He'd been nothing but the best he could be.

He didn't show up to class. Which was very weird because Warren hated missing his classes.

Camilla tried to forget about him—at least for the time being—and focus on the lecture at hand. Professor Jenkins was talking about ancient magical worlds and how literature had depicted them.

These stories would've intrigued Camilla to no end a year ago.

Now, they were running havoc on her life. Because that's

what *Grandmama Told Me* was—an ancient magical world within literature.

Professor Jenkins, for his part, looked excited to talk about this section of the course, and seemed to appreciate Camilla's input whenever she was able to fully focus on the material at hand. The gleam in his eyes as he spoke of the control that magic could give to a person within the stories spoke volumes about his passion for the subject at hand. Camilla was glad to have such a dedicated professor.

It was on her way out of class, after she'd waited for the large part of the class to shove out of the room, when Professor Jenkins called her to the side. "You seemed very interested in the topic, Ms. Whittle."

She gave him a warm smile. "I've always been a fan of literature."

"And this subject in particular? Is it especially interesting to you?" He sounded so genuinely curious about what she thought. And his gaze focused on her like her opinion was the only thing in the world that mattered.

Magical worlds? Now that she was part of one, yeah, it was especially interesting.

Her smile expanded. "I think it's fascinating. The worlds that are created in literature. They must come from some reality."

There was a glimmer in his eyes. "I agree, Ms. Whittle."

The way he said her name had her blushing. She couldn't help that the man was closer to her parents' age than hers. He was fucking attractive, and she had every right—like every other girl in that class—to blush when he gave her attention.

She was going to respond when Professor Porter called for Jenkins' attention. He almost looked perturbed to go to him, but politely nodded, then looked down to Camilla. "Maybe we can discuss literature to a greater extent some other time? Maybe outside of my teaching periods."

Camilla swore she was as red as a tomato. "I'd like that."

He nodded with an almost mischievous glint before walking past her.

There was a lightness in Camilla's step as she left the lecture hall. She hadn't taken the time to truly talk to her professors that semester and hadn't realized how much she appreciated the one-on-one time, even if it wasn't a very long discussion.

Especially with professors as attractive as Timothy Eli Jenkins.

Swoon-worthy.

Camilla walked along the path that crisscrossed for students to get to every single building around the lawn when she saw Warren from a distance. So he was at school and just not in class. Was he skipping because of her?

Couldn't be. He'd be the first one to insist that there was nothing between them.

And he was headed for the Theology building. He didn't have any classes in the Theology building.

But his family did have a little demon lair down there.

Camilla rushed across the quad and followed him into the building to find the door that led down to the basements closing.

She tried to be silent as she walked down the steps.

And she was being silent. So much so she barely heard herself breathe.

But still, it was too loud. Because before she could react, her back hit the wall by the landing and a hand wrapped around her throat.

Camilla clutched at the arm, her breath leaving her faster than she'd imagined possible. She reached out with her thoughts. *Warren, it's me. It's me, Darren. Please.*

Those simple words in his mind startled him out of his death grip around her neck. "Camilla?"

She coughed as she nodded.

"Camilla, what the hell are you doing sneaking up on me like that?" He sounded irritated, no doubt because he could have seriously injured her.

Camilla heard the accusation in her responce. "Why weren't you in class? What are you doing walking down here anyway? I thought you stayed away from this little lair."

Warren huffed out a frustrated breath and caught her stare straight on. "I've fought what Hunter does for a long time." The way he looked at her, Camilla knew he was going to be more honest with her in that moment than he ever had been before. "Too long. For years, I judged him for working trips that afforded him the life he has now. But I'm a demon too. And as much as I try to fight it, I'm more similar to my brother than I've tried to convince myself I'm not. He has his own place, never relies on our father, on anyone. I want that life."

He wasn't done speaking, but Camilla couldn't stop herself from interrupting. "And these *trips* are your only option?" There was judgement in her tone. Too much judgement.

She wanted to retract, but Warren already smiled at her with no humor. "I was the same way. Always judging these trips. But they're not so bad. Some of them maybe, but I don't have to take those. But at the end of the day, my demon side is stronger than my human one, and I'm tired of being ashamed of it or trying to push it down and hide it, Camilla. This is who I am, half demon and half human. And the human side really threw caring for others into the package, but otherwise, I'm a demon, Camilla." He looked her over. "And these trips aren't all only about personal gain. This last one, we stopped a twelve-year-old *human* serial killer."

Guilt ate Camilla up.

Not slowly. No. All at once.

"I'm sorry, Warren." She sighed. "Not just for this, but for making you feel like you had to hide who you were our entire relationship."

"Don't be," he said. "It wasn't all you. I was still trying to convince myself I was more human than demon. Our relationship wasn't in the cards, but I don't regret it, Cam."

He gave her a final once over, then simply turned and continued down the stairs to his destination.

Camilla fell against the wall behind her and sighed out again. She had to go to the astronomy tower, allow her thoughts to figure themselves out. Because she was working on not hating on demons because of their species, and obviously, she still had a ways to go.

There were different levels of feeling bad.

One, when something sucked or you were sorry, but eh, you could brush it off.

Two, when you were angry for something justifiable and said something you might not mean.

Three, when you knew you were angry for a dumb reason and you were ready to apologize for it.

And four, when you knew you were angry about something stupid, and it made you emotional for being angry about something so stupid, and that made you angrier, and the cycle continued.

Four was the worst.

And Maya hated herself for how angry she'd gotten with Hunter earlier.

But technically, she was justified. He'd really had the audacity to say he didn't want mac 'n cheese and grilled cheese. He said it was too much cheese for one meal. *How could there be too much cheese?*

And that's when the rational side of her brain yelled at her that it was, indeed, not a justifiable reason. Then the tears would prick her eyes at the memory of throwing the pot at his head, and yeah, all around terrible time.

She was pacing a random hallway when she jumped at the sound of his voice behind her. "Are you all right, love?"

She turned and was running before her mind caught up with her decision to do so.

He caught her in his arms as her lips crashed against his and kissed him for all she was worth.

"Never talk about cheese like that again." Okay, so she couldn't drop it, and honestly, she didn't know why.

His chuckle rumbled between their chests. "Never." He kissed her again as he slowly put her down. "Ready to go?"

Her eyes widened in excitement as her smile expanded. "I'm shadowing us this time?"

"All you, love." He spread his arms to give her space to hold him and work her magic.

She'd been so excited when he'd said he wanted her to try shadowing him such a long distance. They hadn't tried anything past the property or the shorter distances like when she'd shadowed Vera to meet with Bella and the found couple.

But now she would be trying just outside of Quebec, Canada to visit their only other demon-and-witch-couple friends.

If anything happened and she couldn't do it, he'd be ready to take control. Maya really hoped he wouldn't need to take control.

But she had nothing to worry about because his trainings around the property had done her justice and he didn't, in fact, need to help her.

Awesome.

It was absolutely freezing when they landed, but they'd figured no point in bulking up when they'd be inside in moments. The seconds spent outside were quelled by the fire raging in both of them.

Hunter's hands landed on her hips as they made their way

into the little shop Zathrian sold his beautiful pieces out of. And heard some very not so pleasant sounds coming from the back.

Zathrian came out with a tired smile as the crow sitting on the ledge by the register cawed. "You're here, good. Lock the door behind you and come in back."

He quickly turned back around and left them in the middle of the shop. Maya looked to Hunter and found an equally confused stare. But he complied and locked the door behind them, then his hands on her hips guided her to the back.

It was a small space, but was beautifully furnished with sofas and armchairs and side tables. Rugs and pillows and beautiful curtains accented the room.

As she and Hunter took their seats on a sofa, Maya realized just how comfortable they were too. "This place is heavenly."

Then the sounds redoubled from the bathroom and Maya was brought back to the situation at hand.

Hunter sat stiff beside her as Acacia's heaving breaths reached their ears. "What is going on back there, Zath?"

Zathrian walked out with the same tired smile. "My mate is pregnant, friend."

Hunter stiffened even more beside her, then the smirk grew across his features and he moved to congratulate his friend with a hand-shake and bear hug.

Hunter pulled away slightly to look his friend in the eyes. "Aren't you a bit old to be procreating?"

Zathrian smacked him across the back of the head. "I'm not even forty, asshole. And my beauty is far younger."

"Oh, I have nothing to say about Acacia." Hunter wore such a large grin. "But you, old man?"

Zathrian smacked him again before they gave another bear hug through their laughter.

It was still odd to Maya, to see Hunter hugging anyone else. To see him happy to be around anyone else.

She kicked up to give the demon a hug too. "Congrats, Zath."

She looked to the open door that lead to the bathroom. "Though that sounds like torture."

Zathrian nodded. "Demon pregnancies aren't kind to the carrier, especially if the carrier isn't demon herself. They're different on everyone, so we didn't know what to expect, but apparently hers is very close to humans' with all the vomiting. It was only every other day or so before, but my love hasn't stopped throwing up all week. I'm only hoping it stops soon. With demon pregnancies, the symptom can only last a few weeks or the entire pregnancy. But they're always harsh on the carrier."

Maya turned an accusatory look on Hunter. "And that's what you want me to go through?"

He smirked. "Love, pay attention. He said they're different on everyone. Colette's mother didn't even have symptoms. Though to be fair, she was too far off normal witch territory to be affected."

"Or we could wait until we don't have The Eight and Grandmama and whoever else is behind all this to worry about before I'm running off throwing up all the time," she insisted.

"Or you could throw up on them." He was far too amused.

She shook her head and had to bite down on her lower lip to try to stop the grin. It didn't work. He was just so sexy when he looked down at her like that.

Zathrian's smile grew just as Acacia weakly walked out to stand beside him. "You want a baby?"

Maya was surprised by how much of the bump she could already see. It meant Acacia had been pregnant the entire time Maya had known her because that bump indicated she was at least a few months along.

It was probably one of those times when one day you looked the same, and the next, the bump just jutted out.

Zathrian moved her to the sofa, and Hunter shoved Maya towards the opposite one. She smacked him for the move, but he only grinned in return.

"I want a family with my mate," Hunter said, and though it was the first time he'd called attention to their mating in front of his friends, they didn't seem surprised.

"That's sweet." Acacia smiled at them.

Maya kissed Hunter's shoulder. "It is. He knows when to be sweet, apparently. And somehow it's never around my family."

Hunter gave her a cheeky grin. "Funny how that works, isn't it?"

"Why are you such an asshole?"

"It's so much more fun than not being one." He leaned down to press his lips to hers, and she hated how quickly she forgave him anything when he kissed her.

"I hate you."

He kissed her again, and she was melted into his side by the time he pulled away. "Good."

Zathrian cleared his throat. "You've got an old man in front of you."

Maya laughed against Hunter's lips and turned to face the couple as Hunter said, "My apologies, my elderly friend."

Acacia laughed, but threw a pillow at Hunter. "Do not call my mate old."

Hunter lounged back into the couch as Zathrian pulled his mate into his side, and Maya loved how comfortable the acquaintance was.

"How's the bird?" Maya asked them. "Looking over my parents still?"

Zath smiled warmly at her. "Always."

"And how are they?"

"As much of a pain as they always have been," Zath said with a grin, and Acacia elbowed him in the gut.

Maya laughed. "Good. And birdie?"

Maya genuinely was curious about the bird that was like a familiar to Zathrian. It was like watching those shows where the black cat named Salem helped the witch, except this was a crow.

And it was named Adramalech.

And it was helping a demon.

"Birdie is upset with what's happening with Acacia, so he likes to fight me about leaving the shop. He wants to stay around her for protection." It was obvious how attached Zathrian was to his bird. Even when he spoke annoyedly about the bird, there was a joyful shine about his eyes.

Maya wondered what that bond would be like, but familiar-like animals only came to you. You could not summon them like the movies.

And most were not lucky enough to have them.

Like, almost as rare as Maya's portal.

"That's a good birdie," Maya called out and got a caw in response.

Zathrian smirked, but it was more reprimanding than teasing. "Don't compliment him or he won't leave Acacia's side until she gives birth. Then he won't leave the babe's side."

"A very good birdie," Hunter called out and got two caws in return.

Zathrian threw another pillow at him, and they all laughed as Hunter deflected it by pulling a boomerang shield that sent the pillow flying back to the older demon.

"That's one I haven't seen before." Maya knew her eyes were wide as she smiled at her mate, but it was so interesting seeing all his hidden powers.

He smiled down at her. "One of the first I took at thirteen. It's not strong in me, but I think that's partly because I was young when I stole it and it was grouped with a bunch of others I took. But maybe not. Maybe it's just weak in me."

"How come you don't use it more often?" she asked. "That didn't seem weak."

"It was a pillow. Really, anything with actual weight, it doesn't work."

"Yes, yes, yes. Our demon that steals too many powers for his own good," Zathrian teased.

"Oh, shut up." Hunter's black eyes shined with mirth.

"Maya, you may become a widow very soon if your mate continues speaking to mine like that," Acacia challenged Hunter, and her eyes shined like she knew she'd won.

Maya laughed, and Hunter's elbow lightly dug into her gut. "You're going to allow her to threaten your mate like that?"

Maya met his stare, their faces so close they shared breath. "If my mate stopped being an asshole, there would be no threats."

He leaned in. "When we get home, I'll have to teach you how one is meant to treat their mate."

Maya's blood boiled as their lips skimmed. "Please."

Zathrian cleared his throat again. "Keep it in your pants, Delvaux."

Hunter's lips tipped up. "Which Delvaux?"

"Both of you," Acacia answered.

17

Their presence had been cordially requested by Devon and Bianka, leaders of the North American mermaids. The shocking part wasn't the request, but the warm inviting way in which they did it.

It'd be their original family of four, plus Mr. Warlock Hotshot.

The mermaid's above-water quarters were beneath a cave by the edge of the ocean, the sand from outside still trickling into the depths of the space. It was their way of remaining by the water while still accommodating the needs of every other species.

And to shock Camilla even more, their presence hadn't been the only ones requested.

Harry stopped and brought their group to a standstill in the middle of the cave. "We did not realize we would have more company."

Devon nodded. "We have invited the faeries," he nodded to their right, "because our dead was with one of their dead. The gargoyles," to their left, "because my daughter ran away with one of them. And you, because you seem to be the neutral zone in this mess."

"And the purpose of this meeting?" Harry jumped straight to the point.

"To find out what you are doing about the mixed relationships. Word has reached us that you have aided the gargoyles in protecting their citizens," Bianka answered.

"Their presence was more support than anything else," Uzark answered. "I asked my people to step forward with their relationships and they did. I made it clear no repercussions would be made and that they would be safe to remain within the species. I just couldn't have them sneaking about to meet with their lovers anymore if I wanted to keep them out of harm's way. If anything, I'm merely surprised they gave it up. I see what fear these creatures in cross relationships have."

Finlan, the faerie leader and superiority complex extraordinaire, sneered. "So you accepted the cross breeding."

"I have also opened the manor for the other species my gargoyles are with. By way of suggestion," he glanced their way, but Camilla knew it was all for Kai, "if both parties are under our property, they have no reason to sneak off and therefore will remain unharmed."

Finlan's features grew more grim. "Despicable."

"If you do not intend on accepting the relationships, at least enough to protect your people, then why call us?" Camilla tried to keep the annoyance out of her tone.

"Two of mine are missing. That's including my daughter. She may not be dead, but she's not with us and that makes her vulnerable. Just because we do not approve of her choices does not mean we do not still care for her. We need to find a way around this," Devon answered.

"By accepting the couples," Maya dumbed down. It was a statement, not a question.

"No." Devon didn't hesitate. "Accepting such ludicrousness from the small percentage will cause havoc in the majority."

"Well, then what do you want from us?" Vera's frustration was growing.

"Sometimes I wonder how low on the totem pole your lot would be if you weren't gifted with the Powers. At least demons show themselves deserving of such magic," Finlan said, then slowed his speech as if speaking to a child. "We need your assistance on an alternative."

"But you just heard Uzark tell you that he has accepted them and intends to keep their relationships safe. That has nothing to do with us," Camilla argued.

She felt Kai's gaze on her, and when she turned to him, he was silently taking it all in. Why wasn't he speaking up now? This was basically his fault.

"And what guarantee do you have that they will speak up?" Devon grit his teeth.

That's when a little girl who looked like the spitting image of the leaders of the mermaids spoke up, "They won't."

Camilla really didn't want to argue with a kid. "The gargoyles did."

"That is because the gargoyles trust their leader and do not fear him the way ours do," the girl said. "Mermaids and faeries are not dumb enough to drop their defenses because of pretty words. They won't put themselves into positions like that knowing there could, and most likely would, be consequences. Even if the consequences waited until after the halfies were taken care of."

"That is enough, Bella." Bianka's eyes narrowed on her daughter.

Bella only rolled her eyes and took a seat at the end of the room. Camilla hadn't even noticed she'd been there to begin.

"She is right though," Kai finally spoke up. "There is no way either of your species would speak out, even with us there. We would have to figure out how to find out who was in the relationship and not tell you. It is the only way it would work."

Devon sneered now. "And how would that help us in keeping our people safe? We would continue to remain in the dark."

Kai shrugged, unperturbed. "If we know of their statuses, we can aid them in meeting with their lovers so they're not caught. Set up for them to meet somewhere specific with other couples around so no one is caught in the fire line of the halfies."

Finlan crossed his arms. "And who would do something so ridiculous?"

"Juliette," Maya said so quickly Camilla doubted she'd thought it through. "The Juliette that helped your faeries a few weeks ago. She's mated to a wolf, so she's also crossed. They would help."

"It would be an anonymous collection. Unlike the gargoyles, we'll have your people come in individually so they don't have the fear of being judged by their peers," Kai continued.

"And what makes you think they would tell you?" Bianka asked.

Kai shrugged like he didn't care either way. "We cannot force them to do so, just hope that they care for their significant other enough to take the offer."

Camilla looked heavenward as Finlan asked another stupid —and unhelpful—question and Kai answered like he was used to the lunacy of answering dumb questions.

Maya hated how much everyone ignored Bella just because she was ten-years-old. She was brilliant. Especially if you looked past her age. She was well spoken and intelligent and sneaky. One of Maya's favorite people.

And she would make a great leader for her people.

That was, if she wasn't thrown out the way her sister had been for *her* mixed relationship. With a demon, no less.

Maya saw Devon and Bianka sooner calling Brynn back with her gargoyle than allowing for Bella to remain heir with a demon by her side.

It was sad, but Maya didn't see a plausible way either sister would keep their hold on the leadership of their species if their parents didn't start accepting cross breeding.

She took a seat beside her little friend and reached out to take Bella's hand. She skimmed her thumb across the top of it as the girl rested her head on Maya's shoulder.

Maya had often wondered who this demon was her little friend had fallen for. What he looked like, how much older he was than her, how they'd met. Bella had kept him her well-hidden secret because of the stigma she had to endure daily from her family on mixed relationships, and especially the stigma against demons, but Maya hoped Bella would trust her enough to hold the secret.

She whispered down to her so no one else would hear, "You know, my demon has a name. Does yours?"

Bella's gaze didn't waver from the leaders a few feet away as they continued to debate Kai's inputs, but a blush lightly colored her features. With a sheepish smile that she tried to hide, Bella whispered so low Maya almost didn't catch it, "Vincent."

***

The meetings with the Whittles had been made mandatory by both sets of leaders. The rumble outside the charmed doors reminded Vera of the unknown anticipation of being in school and waiting to go into the auditorium for a 'talk.'

Except the difference here was everyone would be coming in alone, and the charmed doors wouldn't allow for anyone to hear beyond these walls. That included the leaders.

And even though neither North American population was the largest—mermaids being the largest in Australia and faeries in South America, mainly Argentina—they had hundreds of individuals to get through.

Vera found rather quickly that mentioning Maya's relationship status warmed some up to the idea of letting their own relationship be known. And to others, hearing about Maya's relationship just sent wider sneers toward her family.

As each person left the room, a vow was made—forced—onto each person that they would not tell the others in line what was being asked of them. They couldn't have people preparing reactions and answers.

Or worse, running off.

Kai and Harry stood with their arms crossed on either end of their group, leaning against the walls at their backs and watching each person as he or she came in. Vera sat oldest to youngest with her sisters, and across the table left an open chair for each new person who walked in.

Overall, throughout the thousands plus people they spoke to in a few short days, they found fourteen mermaids in relationships and sixteen faeries. Kai mentioned that there were definitely more. That even their presence wouldn't open everyone up to revealing themselves.

But at least they had some numbers to go off of.

Vera was shocked at finding how few the numbers were before remembering that cross relationships were more rare than her first few months in the supernatural world led her to believe. It was a major reason why the prejudices still remained —most people genuinely didn't get out of their species.

And if they did, the only 'understandable' reason was normally mating a wolf. That was something that could not be controlled on either end.

Which also showed Vera how little the species knew of demons because demon matings were quite literally the same and couldn't be stopped, but no one considered them. Though to be fair, their matings hardly ever happened, whereas wolves mated all the time.

And from what Vera understood, even most demons didn't know of their own matings. It would be hard pressed for any other species to know of them.

With the relationships revealed, the Whittles told the individuals about the meeting house Maya had Juliette and Felix set up. A place where Juliette and Felix, and Celine and Kellan, and Cora and Rory, at the very least would be around. A place to keep them safe while they met with their partner.

And to those who snickered at them or refused to give it up, Vera made sure to mention that they could always come back and talk to them. Ask for help. That even though they didn't feel it now, if ever they found anyone in another species, they wouldn't have to sneak around and possibly be killed for it.

Overall, the days were long, but productive.

And, to Camilla's annoyance, Kai was coming out helpful. He didn't do much, but Vera had to admit, his confidence every time they did something made Vera feel better. And it made the leaders trust them even more. Harry had mentioned it was partly because Kai had actually trained to be a warlock, unlike Harry and Bishop.

They'd been more forced into their predicaments.

Kai had wanted this life.

Harry had been nervous to have him around. He'd told Vera it was because Kai could be a lot to handle since he loved to pry into other's business and snake his way into situations, but Vera had to disagree. Kai was good.

Though it did teach Vera how the warlock was able to know so much about everything. Sometimes his cockiness would outshine him, but Vera was glad to have him around.

Plus, he was very easy on the eyes. A fact Harry wasn't pleased about.

If she didn't already have Harry, Vera would definitely be checking Kai out every time he came around.

Honestly, a large part of her was shocked Camilla wasn't doing just that.

But she honestly hadn't been.

Though Camilla was still getting over her own failed love, so it was more than understandable that she wasn't looking to move on quite yet.

18

*H*is mate may literally kill him for this.

Hunter opened his eyes slowly to find it difficult to lift his lids for long moments after he awoke.

He tried to move and felt the ache writhe through his body as he realized his arms were chained above his head with power-restraining cuffs and his toes barely scraped the floor.

He was alone in a dark room.

It wasn't a dungeon, that much was obvious to him, but it looked to be an attempt at one. This room was much nicer than a dungeon.

It was completely empty but for the chains that littered the grounds at the edges of the room and him hanging in the middle of it. A single flickering light above his head made most of the room too dark to truly make out, but his years of experience told him he was alone.

He shut his eyes hard to erase the fog clouding his thoughts, then opened them again. Whatever he'd been hit with, he wouldn't be surprised if he had a minor concussion.

He'd been taken.

And a simple tracking with his ring—which thankfully had been left on his hand, as most didn't know about the demon's mating rings—told him Maya was nowhere near him. She was far off, safe in her family home.

Good, he had a purpose for getting caught.

The room itself didn't tell him much other than the fact that it was a nice area. They hadn't even been able to turn their 'dungeon' dingy enough to compare to a demon's true dungeon.

The chains littering the grounds around him were just that, chains. Nothing special and frightening about them. All they truly said was that multiple people could be held down there at the same time. And though the sight may frighten others, Hunter found it amusing.

Before he could assess anything else, a halfie walked in.

And surprisingly, *not* his sister.

But she was a demon and witch halfie. Like representing half of him and half of his mate. He'd figured this would be the case when Camilla had mentioned that two gargoyle and nymph halfies had taken that last couple even though they'd needed a witch or demon halfie to throw up the illusion.

"Hello, demon," it said. "Nice of you to wake up. You're lover's been waiting for you in the other room."

Hunter didn't let an ounce of emotion show on his features, but the boredom that was his signature. He could even hang there like it was a lazy lounge. He'd done it before.

"Your sister tells me you're quite in love with the witch." Her smile was sinister, and it almost made Hunter laugh that the halfie truly believed he'd be the victim here.

"I'm sure my sister would tell you lots of things." He let the boredom drawl through each word.

It smiled at him like it was winning. "Yes. Like learning that you come to her rescue in seconds. I hear your abilities have strengthened in order to keep her safe. That's quite the dedication."

Hunter didn't know if that was necessarily true, but then he remembered all the training he put himself through in order to fight while distracted by her. He guessed that did make him stronger, more dedicated. All in order to protect his mate.

This halfie didn't need to know any of that.

Hunter looked around the room, trying to see if he could make out any other giving tales. This halfie was boring him.

"I'm curious what you would do now to keep her safe?"

It almost looked like the entire place was made of steel, the flickering light above him showed him enough of the door that led out of this room to indicate that even the hallway was made of steel. If he went off of the last place they'd been with The Eight, he'd guess another warehouse. These creatures had a thing for warehouses.

The halfie before him slashed a dagger across his chest, the blood immediately trickling down his torso. "Pay attention to me."

He moved his gaze slowly, so much so he knew it would infuriate her, to finally meet her gaze. "What do you want, mutt?"

She growled as her teeth ground together. "I'm going to kill your girlfriend."

He smirked down at her. "I don't have a girlfriend."

I have a mate.

She slashed another aggressive swing of her dagger, leaving yet another mark on his chest. He chuckled at her and loved the sight of her anger boiling up inside her.

He hadn't been in a position like this in so long, Hunter had forgotten how fun they could be. Especially when the person 'holding him captive' was so easy to rile up.

He studied her as she glowered at him, a few choice words spit toward him.

She wasn't a strong halfie, which was surprising since this master of theirs had somehow found so many strong ones. Hunter still wanted to know how this boss had convinced the more powerful of the halfies to join him. To be his bitch.

His sister included.

And that Lyric chick.

But one's like this dagger-wielding one would be easy. Simple revenge on those in relationships like the parents that had abandoned them would be convincing enough.

"You're going to have to try harder than that, mutt." He knew his grin held too much mirth and his eyes were a little on the dangerous side of psychotic.

She raised her arm to slash him again when another halfie walked in, and the original paused.

Still not his sister. Just like Colette to avoid him.

But again, this was a demon and witch mix.

"Your witch is crying for you. Would you like to hear her?" the new one asked.

Without waiting for a response, she held up her phone and pressed play on a voice recording. Of Maya crying and screaming out to him.

He held his breath to control his fury. Even knowing it was fake, his mating instincts told him to rip the world apart to protect her.

He leaned down as much as the chains would allow and made sure each word landed with some spit. "Kiss. My. Ass."

She grit her teeth, but did not waver. Instead, she moved to the side and threw up an image of Maya chained to the ground. An illusion.

So this was the illusionist in the group.

And in walked a male in the picture.

Hunter ground his teeth, knowing exactly what illusion they would be showing. Unlucky for them, his father had trained him and Warren on illusions. They knew exactly how to block out the falsehood they were presented and allow their eyes to see a new picture.

So instead of the...non-consensual act they tried to show him, Hunter saw the demon's lounge in the Theology building right after Maya had gotten her shadowing ability. That had been a great night.

He even heard the way she moaned for him rather than the cries this halfie was trying to present to him.

The smirk he wore as he relived that night obviously pissed the two halfies off because the illusion dropped sooner than he'd thought it would and another blade was coming across his chest. "React, you heartless shit."

He winked down at her and never stopped grinning. She raged at the simple act and dropped the knife. She threw her arms out and used him as her own personal punching bag.

He only laughed.

And looked back out to the rest of the room. There was nothing giving enough. But he knew there was more to this. Knew they wouldn't have taken him lest it were important. Or at least, lest his sister was around.

But she wasn't.

So Hunter had to wonder where the fuck Grandmama or this puppet master of theirs was. What was the point of allowing the halfies to have their fun? Hunter was getting rather annoyed with the lack of information from these halfies.

He laughed at the halfie as it beat tiny fists into his abs.

And when her friend's rage grew too and he had two halfies beating on his chest, he laughed and laughed and laughed.

From what I heard from Loki, the trip finished a couple of hours ago.

Warren's text told Maya exactly as she'd expected. Hunter should be back from his business trip by then. So where was he?

"Maya." Harry's hand landed on her back as she sat frozen on the kitchen stool. "Are you all right?"

Maya felt through her ring and picked up on his location. She'd done it before, but figured it would have to do with his trip, so she hadn't paid much attention to it.

But he wasn't meant to be on a trip any longer.

And if she really paid attention through the ring, she could feel the pain slashing through him.

Her breath caught. "Hunter's in trouble. I can feel it."

Vera dropped the spatula she was mixing her batter with. "I was afraid this would happen."

Maya knew her entire family had been afraid something would happen to them since they were in a cross relationship. She had the same fears. And they were coming true.

Maybe.

Maya didn't know exactly what was happening.

Camilla's hand stroked down her back. "Let's go get him."

Maya swallowed back her fear and turned to tell Harry where to go exactly as Camilla ran up for some invisibility serums. She couldn't shadow this many people at once yet. Plus, she needed them focused and not caught up on her new ability when they got there.

When Camilla returned, they each took a bit of the serum before holding onto Harry and porting out of their kitchen and to the warehouse Maya explained he was at. It was still insane to Maya how she knew the exact location through just the ring.

When they landed, all hands moved to her so that she could lead the way. Because Hunter was there, she could feel him getting closer.

Somehow they'd been able to port into the building. It rushed warning alarms to Maya's brain, but she ignored them. All she needed was to find her mate. To find out why there was so much pain lacing through the ring.

The pain was getting worse quickly.

She moved them down a dark corridor of steel, the only lights flickering from the rings of fire strung up on the walls every few feet.

Her heart stopped when a pain worse than anything she'd ever felt rushed through the ring and into every nerve ending of her body. If it was strong enough for her to feel it this intensely, then she couldn't imagine what he was going through.

She threw out that part of her brain that told her to remain slow enough for her family to keep hold of her and sprinted down the corridor. Honestly, with the amount of noise her feet made, they'd be able to follow her. And their invisibility serums would be for not. But oh fucking well.

Another rush through the ring almost tripped her in her steps as Maya skirted around a corner and found the open door. Either there was no one else around in the warehouse or they truly didn't care that Maya and her family were there.

She didn't know why the latter would be an option.

And as she stopped in the middle of the room that Hunter hung in, she realized what the pain shooting through her was. Lyric was back.

And the bitch was using her power on Maya's mate.

Maya didn't wait for her family, just felt the fire lick up her arms as she shadowed to the other end of the room. A single shot of flames to Lyric's hands stopped her immediately.

Her periphery told her Hunter's body instantly eased as he hung with his arms above him. His head drooped down, but his eyes remained on Lyric. Maya had a feeling he could've gotten himself out of the chains, that Augustine would've taught him some maneuver or another, but that he'd realized she was around and wanted to keep Lyric's attention on him rather than her.

And if her feeling was right, she was going to kick his ass for it.

Lyric's widening eyes told Maya she'd realized Maya was there.

But Maya didn't care. Just let her darkness fade into the room and envelope them all in it as she shadowed behind Lyric. Her arms set an ambiance to the room as they roared with flames.

Before Lyric could turn around to face her, Maya placed both hands to either side of the halfie's face but didn't let the flames devour. "You chose the wrong mate, bitch."

She didn't allow the halfie time to respond. Instead, she consumed her arms in flames so Lyric screamed in Maya's arms.

Screamed and screamed and screamed, each one causing the smile on Maya's face to expand. Lyric would burn for what she'd done to Hunter in the past and in this moment. She'd be the example the halfies would look upon when thinking about messing with *Maya's* mate.

Maya recognized the invisibility serum evaporating as the halfie went limp in her arms, more carcass than body.

The burnt stench in the air created a happiness in Maya's heart she hadn't realized she'd wanted.

As she brought the darkness back, she saw the two other halfies lying on the ground. Harry had probably taken care of them quickly. Shame.

Another glance down at Lyric settled Maya's thoughts a final time. Knowing she was gone and couldn't touch Hunter again was all Maya wanted.

On afterthought, she realized she or Hunter could've stolen Lyric's power. It would've been one hell of a steal.

Too bad.

Another breath before she lifted her gaze to the eyes of the room. She guessed Vera had used her levitation to break Hunter's chains and lower him to the ground, because when her gaze finally landed on him, he was watching her in awe as he slowly breathed in and out, his chest bleeding out.

She held his stare for a second before she ran to his side and fell to her knees beside him. She slowly took his head in her lap and ran a thumb over his cheek. "Tell me you're okay, baby."

He grinned up at her with a mischievous glint. Of course he wasn't okay, but he would never admit to it. "Just take me home, clean me up, and give me a nice, long fuck."

The laugh choked out of her as she shook her head. "You damn near came to losing your soul and your mind is in the gutter right now?"

That crooked grin matched the awe-filled desire in his gaze. "My mind will remain in the gutter until I get you pregnant."

Maya quirked a disbelieving brow. "Really?"

"No." His hand shook as it reached up to take her face. "It'll remain there even after then. Probably more so actually. You're going to be so fucking sexy knocked up, love."

She tried to restrain her laugh, but there really was no use. She dipped her head to meet his lips. "I fucking hate you."

His lips pressed onto hers. "Good."

Colette paced back and forth across the warehouse grounds.

The agitation in her was so great that she had to walk the longer distance of the warehouse to calm herself. Especially being that she was in front of Grandmama and the Boss. She didn't really care for the Boss, didn't even know the fucker's name, but she didn't want to disappoint Grandmama.

But she was angry.

So. Fucking. Angry.

The news that her narcissistic older brother had been caught had elated her to heights she hadn't deemed possible. All she'd wanted was to speed over as quickly as possible and play with him.

But she'd been with the Boss. And he hadn't allowed her to go. He'd known how badly she wanted this, more than anything else she could ever desire, and he didn't allow her to have it.

She hated Hunter.

Warren she could deal with. He was annoying, but it was Hunter who drove her mad. It was Hunter who was the best of them, and it was Hunter who was favored and always above her.

Fuck, even those witches had chosen him over Warren, and Warren was so obviously the best candidate for a witch.

Hunter, Hunter, fucking Hunter.

But the Boss had insisted she stay put, and it was important that he get anything and everything he asked for. Grandmama insisted his needs and plans be put above any of their own.

Though Grandmama's goals seemed to be equal to the Boss's.

But that was justified.

Grandmama deserved to get her revenge. She'd waited a millennia for it.

So Colette went along with the Boss's plan because she hated disappointing Grandmama. Refused to do so.

"Child," Grandmama's soft voice broke her thoughts, "you will have your chance when the time is right."

When the time was right. When would that be?

They'd actually gotten him because of his weakness for the fucking dark witch. How were they supposed to duplicate such beautiful results in the future?

But nonetheless, Colette controlled her breathing with a small technique Grandmama had insisted they learn and turned to the woman. "I know, Grandmama. I just cannot believe they were allowed to get away."

"We needed the two, not the entire lot. I do not have time for the trouble the entire lot would have caused, little one," Boss spoke sweetly to her. It was a tone she hated more than any spiteful one.

And it still killed her. They could've stopped the Whittles, overpowered them. But instead, Boss had insisted they get away.

And whatever Boss wants, Boss gets.

"Their time will come," Boss said from his seat beside Grandmama at the end of the room.

Colette scoffed into the air as she continued her pacing. "Mixed couples are one thing. Those two are beginning to get on my fucking nerves."

Harry landed them in the middle of the upstairs hallway. Camilla figured that was so Maya could get Hunter into the shower easier.

Camilla stood in the hall and watched as Maya got Hunter to sit on the toilet as she readied the shower. The door was left wide open, and it gave Camilla the time to look her new brother over.

He was shirtless, blood smeared over his chest, and Camilla could see the cuts from one end of his torso to the other. He'd suffered before Lyric had gotten her hands on him. She couldn't imagine how much it was killing Maya to see him like that.

Maya's smile was warm and loving as she stepped between his legs. He leaned his head into her stomach and gave her thighs a hug. The asshole was slowly chipping away at Camilla's heart.

"Let's go, baby." Maya pulled on his arms, but got nowhere. Camilla couldn't blame her. The man was double her size.

Hunter grumbled through his smile as his lips pressed into Maya's stomach. "You hear that, baby? Mommy is speaking to you."

Camilla shot her hand to her mouth immediately to cover

the laugh as she turned to see Vera doing the same. Harry's century of life helped hide his own amusement, but Camilla could see it in his hazel eyes.

Maya didn't hide her laugh. "Hunter."

He grumbled into her stomach and gave it a small kiss before getting to his feet. Maya's hands were on the buttons to his trousers before she turned to the rest of them in the hall. "You guys planning on taking in a show?"

Vera smirked. "Well, if he's as impressive as you say he is, I..."

Harry grabbed her arm and pulled her away, and Camilla couldn't stop the laugh this time. Maya closed the door, but Camilla didn't move. Just stood outside the bathroom and leaned into the wall.

She wondered if the charm had been taken off of this bathroom—and if so, why—because she could perfectly hear through the door to the laughs and inaudible whispers within.

Who would've thought that a few months ago when Hunter Delvaux had come into their lives that this was how it would end up? Not only would he end up sleeping with her sister, but mated as well? It was unbelievable.

Especially to Camilla's past self.

Not a few weeks ago, she still hated him. Didn't trust him in the least and knew—was so convinced that she *knew*—he was trying to use and betray Maya. Trying to hurt her.

Boy, how wrong she'd been.

Camilla was so lost in her thoughts, she didn't hear her sister coming out of the bathroom until Maya stood before her with the door closed behind her.

Maya looked her up and down with furrowed brows. "Cam?"

What *was* she doing out there? "Is he okay?"

Maya's eyes narrowed. "Do you care?"

"Surprisingly." Camilla hugged herself. "And I know how much you care."

Maya didn't say anything, just analyzed her.

After another minute, Camilla filled the air. "I kept expecting the worst from him."

"I know." Maya's voice was small. She was always so confident, but Camilla could imagine how tired she was about fighting her on this matter.

"And he keeps proving me wrong," Camilla finished.

There was a pride in her older sister's eyes that filled Camilla with joy. She'd never realized how much the comments that he didn't want her, but was only using her, could also affect Maya.

"I know he loves you," Camilla said.

Maya opened her mouth to say something, but nothing got past.

"His desperation to get past that shield so Lyric wouldn't touch you a few weeks ago, I think that's when I really saw it. I knew before, of course, but I turned a blind eye. I didn't want to believe it. But that? I think that solidified it for me. That man is so in love with you it almost makes me sick."

Maya gave a breathy laugh as she met Camilla's stare. "I know he is."

Camilla shocked herself with her next words. "I think I could come to love him too, as a brother."

Maya gave her a crooked grin. "You have no choice. He's mine, and he's always gonna be around."

Camilla's smile was genuine. "I know."

Maya had been ridiculously thorough as she took care of him in the shower.

After her hands had finished, she made sure her mouth kissed—sucked—away any other hurt. Hunter genuinely couldn't think of a better mate.

And now it was time she get angry with him. Because before they could go back to their manor and have that nice long fuck he'd wanted, they would be speaking with the family. Everyone wanted to know what happened, and Maya really wasn't going to like the answer Hunter had.

He took his usual spot on the couch by the fireplace, Maya situating herself by his side as the others slowly trickled in. He gave her a disgruntled look. "What are you doing?"

Her chocolate browns were a beautiful mix of worried and confused.

"That isn't your seat." He eyed his lap, then looked back to her.

She rolled her eyes. "Hunter, you were just being tortured. Your body needs to recover, and I don't think my extra weight will..."

His hands were on her hips, moving her, as he interrupted, "You don't need to think. I know your extra weight will help me."

When she was snuggled onto his lap and he could wrap his arms around her waist, he truly felt himself settle. He hadn't been trying to be an ass; having her on his lap honestly did help.

Like the first meeting after Grandmama's reemergence, his father took the seat to his side and his brother took the end of their couch. The Whittles found their spots on the opposite couch, and Kai pulled a chair beside the fireplace to sit backwards in.

Lila and Tamire had taken their daughter to visit their old friends, the witches that were part of Felix and Juliette's pack, so it would be just them. Good, he really didn't want that incessant child crying for him as he tried to hold his mate.

Harry readied everyone's tea, then sat back and took his witch's hand.

"You have the shimmer." Vera was the first to speak. Unsurprisingly. The girl couldn't sit in silence for long.

Maya's head snapped to him, and she tilted away just enough to look at his face at an angle. "You do."

Her brows furrowed in worry, and Hunter had to run his

hands down her arms to calm her. "It won't hurt me, love. My guess, it'll go away in a week or two."

Her hands traced his face as she looked him over. "How do you know?"

"I know what it is." He gave his usual cocky grin.

She gasped. He knew the others had too, but she was all he could focus on.

His hands settled at her back as he tried to ease her worry. "Love, I'm fine, and I'll be fine. It's just the remnants of the power that knocked me out, how they were able to keep me unconscious to transport and chain me up."

Yeah, that didn't exactly help her frantic little heart. He could feel it thundering under his palms.

"Do you know what power it was?" Warren asked.

Hunter didn't take his eyes off his mate. Couldn't. "Grandmama's. It makes sense. She was made with faerie dust, but mixed with a greater power. The shimmer is just the remnants of the faerie dust. It'll go away soon. The only reason you saw it on the dead couples was because it had only been a day or two since they'd been hit. Or because they were dead. Maybe it doesn't go away on the dead, I don't know. But faerie dust always goes away on the living, love."

"How do you know it was Grandmama that hit you?" Kai asked.

"How were you hit in the first place?" Harry added.

Maya finally breathed out, like she was just now processing what he's said, and leaned into him. She kissed his neck and hugged him a little too tight before loosening her hold and resorting back to their original little snuggle.

Augustine was the one to answer just as Warren scoffed. It was no surprise that they'd been able to guess his answer. "You purposefully allowed them to catch you."

Maya's head snapped up as all eyes shot to him. "That's ridiculous."

Augustine's knowing smirk told her otherwise. And when

she saw Warren lounging back at his end of the couch, small smirk across his features, she turned wide eyes back on Hunter.

"Tell me that's not true, Hunt," she almost begged.

"I could never lie to you, love." He brushed her hair back.

"Are you insane?" Camilla's cry came out at the same moment her eldest sister yelled, "You could've been killed!"

Maya was breathing hard, clearly trying to control her emotions. Emotions that had been acting out lately, so Hunter had no hope that she'd succeed. "Why?" Her voice was feeble.

"When something is happening and we need to learn more, we always send someone in to get that information. I've done it a hundred times before." He tried to keep his tone reasonable even knowing it wouldn't help.

"We do it for all of our bigger mysteries, Daughter," Augustine cut in, thankfully being helpful rather than goading her on. "We train well. I've trained my boys hard enough that they could ignore illusions and even get themselves out of chains. He would've been in no real danger."

He'd been told the story alongside Warren and Kai when Hunter had been in the shower.

Maya ignored Augustine completely. "You could've died. Lyric was on you."

Hunter didn't allow the smirk to grace his features. It most definitely wouldn't help him at the moment. "Lyric was on me because I knew you were there. I wasn't going to get out of the chains and allow her to turn on you."

Maya watched him for a minute. She let her eyes take in his dark ones, his lips, the stubble along his jaw, every unhurt inch of his face.

Then she flew out of his lap and paced before the couch his family sat on as her hands rung into her hair. "You've got to be kidding me," she whispered to herself, then turned on him with quite the roar. "You went on a death mission just so you could find out some information? Are you fucking insane?"

Not that the information was very useful, Hunter thought to himself. He hated when the information wasn't all that helpful.

Hunter could feel her heart racing through his ring. The ring only transferred feelings if they were strong enough, so if he could feel it, it meant she was more upset than he'd thought.

And she wasn't done. "You could've been killed! And I don't care about whatever goddamned training you think you've been through. They could've done it while you were unconscious. Had Colette been there, it definitely could've turned out differently." Flames sparked over her arms, and Hunter noticed everyone visibly push away from her. "They could've harmed you beyond repair, killed you, Hunter. They could've killed you and taken you away from me! Do you not get that? Did you not fucking think about how this would affect your fucking *mate*?"

Hunter swallowed as he watched her light up. She was so fucking beautiful. He slowly rose from his seat to face her. "I knew I'd be fine, love."

She turned away from him and screamed her frustration. Yup, the emotions were undoubtedly out of control. With the scream, her entire body lit aflame as the room shuddered into darkness, the only light coming from her.

And from that light, Hunter saw everyone in the room move closer to the fireplace so they'd be behind him and far away from her wrath. Hunter had to hide the smirk at seeing that even his father had moved.

"Love?" He slowly moved to her.

She turned on him. "I need you to think for two fucking seconds. What if I'd done that? What if I'd almost gotten killed because *it'll help us gain FUCKING INFORMATION?*"

The anger that hadn't been within him a moment ago grew. She would never be in such a ludicrous situation. He wouldn't allow it. "You could kiss my ass if you think you're putting yourself in harm's way."

"You putting yourself in harm's way *is* putting me in harm's way!" She pushed him as she yelled. "Did you think at all past your demon upbringing to the fact that we're mated?" Another push. "That as your mate, I couldn't live without you?" One more. "Did you think at all that I'd ever be okay with your possible death without me?" He hit the fireplace mantel with the final push and noticed the others squirm away from his periphery. "I'll kill you myself before you ever try that shit again."

She stormed out and took the darkness and flames with her.

The room took a few minutes to relax after her departure. As Hunter peeled off the fireplace, Camilla pushed him back into it, a rage blazing in her eyes too. "Are you fucking insane?"

He blew out a breath as he quirked a brow. "You too, Little Sister?"

"Yes, me too, you fucking asshole," she yelled. "How could you be so reckless when you know Maya's here waiting for you? When you know it would kill her if something happened to you? How could you risk it?" She pushed him again, and the mantelpiece bit into his back. "You either stay away from her or you fucking behave."

Hunter swallowed back the pain he knew his mate was feeling in the moment. The fight left him as he looked down to his little sister. He couldn't imagine ever being as sincere as in that moment. "I couldn't stay away from her if I wished. I am hopelessly hers."

Camilla came in close so her short stature was only inches from his face. "Then behave."

Maya Whittle—correction, Delvaux—was quite the sight to behold in that living room. Augustine had believed her an asset before, but after that show, he was quite certain she was the greatest gift his son could've brought to their family.

And now she was out in her snowy yard, letting the whiteness blanket her flames.

Augustine didn't dare interrupt her. She needed this time to cool off.

But he did watch her from the kitchen door.

Augustine Delvaux was never one to admit fear, but the look in darling Maya's eyes had pushed him away too. Because that was a dangerous look. The flames rang around in her eyes said only one thing: Hell's Gate.

Augustine himself had never been down below. Most people topside hadn't, but from what Hunter had told him, and everything he already knew, it wasn't fun. And as he'd recently learned, his new daughter had the power to open a portal to the one place that brought fear to demons as powerful as himself.

Now, watching the flames die down beneath the flakes, Augustine knew the power didn't have to do with anger or pain at all. If that were the case, then she would've sent Melusine under for hurting her sister or any of their prisoners for the stories she'd heard of them.

No, this power was solely based on one thing.

Her mate.

How far that connection went was what Augustine had yet to figure out, but a sureness in him told him that had Maya lost any more control in that living room, the ground would've quaked beneath them and possibly all of them would've been dropped to the prison.

And as the memory of what he'd heard of the first and only time she'd opened a portal came back to him, he knew he was right.

Because the portal didn't open for the pain of anyone but her mate. Even back then when she hadn't known him to be her mate, she'd protected him as best she could. Because icicles had been flying through the air around her, and all she'd seen was one pierce straight through Hunt's chest.

That would've destroyed a mate.

That would've sent her into oblivion.

And she definitely would've opened true hell on earth for retribution.

Augustine had a feeling only the subconscious awareness that Hunter had been fine had stopped Maya's portal beneath only those few Bridgers witches.

Hunter passed him through the door and walked up to his mate in the snow-covered yard. His hands slowly circled around her waist, and Maya leaned back into him.

The fire had faded out of her, and she was back to herself. The pain of possibly losing him obviously having pushed the anger away.

Hunter turned her in his arms and cradled her face. Augustine couldn't hear what was being whispered between the two of them, but he had no doubt apologies and declarations were part of the ordeal.

When a single tear slid down Maya's cheek and Hunter caught it with his thumb, Augustine couldn't believe the small grin on his own features.

"It's even touching you?" Warren's presence beside him shocked Augustine. "They really must be something, huh?"

"Quite," Augustine whispered as he watched Hunter lean down and kiss his mate, soft and reassuring.

He may not have the powers of Hell's Gate, but their feelings were one and the same. Augustine could see how affected his son was by this witch.

But Maya wasn't just a witch. She was a great value.

His new daughter was more than just a key to Hell's Gate. She controlled the prison. The greatest asset possible.

20

News was out that another one on Grandmama's list was gone.

They'd done their best to inform all those Warren and Hunter had mentioned were on the list, but Grandmama still found a way around it. If it weren't so horrendous, Vera would be impressed with her dedication.

Vera sat solemnly in the living room as she tried to distract herself with a spicy romance novel that didn't seem to be working. The book was amazing—the spice definitely something she'd be trying with Harry later—but she couldn't concentrate.

And especially not with Camilla and Kai strolling around the house every two seconds.

Camilla grumbled as she threw herself on the couch and took a pillow to cuddle with. Kai didn't seem to care that she threw her scariest death glares his way as he sat as close to her as he could muster and his arm flew over her shoulder.

He leaned into her. "How about instead of pretending that you hate me, we go upstairs and have some fun?" His smirk only grew as Camilla grimaced his way. "Okay, you can continue hating me. But we could still fuck while you did that."

"Harry," Camilla called out, "please take your garbage out."

Kai only laughed as he leaned a few inches closer as Camilla tried to push herself into the couch.

Vera shook her head at the two. They really should just fuck at this point. She wondered if Hunter were here if he'd be able to pick up whether or not Camilla was affected by the warlock's advances.

Harry threw Kai a death glare of his own as he came out of the kitchen. "Get away from her." He fisted Kai's shirt and threw him to the other end of the couch. "Dinner's ready."

Camilla jumped from her seat as fast as her little body could muster. Kai strolled up in an almost Hunter-like way and looked pleased with himself as he followed her to the kitchen.

It was surprising to Vera how much he really was just trying to piss Camilla off. Maybe her little sister's treatment of Warren bothered the warlock more than Vera had initially believed.

Vera laughed to herself as she followed them to the back of the house, where the wafts of meats and cheeses enveloped Vera in happiness. She might be the best baker, but Harry was the best chef, hands down.

Harry and Kai froze, and before she could ask what happened, Harry turned and shoved her behind him while Kai was stepped in front of Camilla. Vera caught her sister's eye and they both turned.

And gasped.

Harry and Kai blocked them, but past their shoulders, standing in the middle of the living room, were Bishop and Loretta Whittle.

Her parents. Alive.

Her dad. Alive.

Vera's eyes prickled with unshed tears, but she didn't move. There was a reason the boys felt the need to stand before them. The same one beating Vera's frantic heart—these couldn't possibly be *the* Bishop and Loretta Whittle.

But if they weren't, how had they gotten access to the house?

"What kind of sick game is this?" Harry seethed.

Loretta's lips tipped up at the edges as her eyes twinkled. She turned to her husband. "I told you that's what he'd say."

Bishop, Vera's best friend, rolled his eyes. "That's because you know him better."

"Yet you still bet me." The smirk Loretta gave him was so Maya-esqe, Vera's heart hammered harder.

A low growl passed through both Harry and Kai.

Vera had never seen Harry react this way. He'd always been protective of them, but not in such an animalistic way. Was it because it was her parents—his old friends—in question that it was affecting him more than usual?

Either way, it was fucking attractive. No wonder Maya didn't mind when Hunter went all crazy mate on her ass.

"It's us, Harry," Loretta softly said to him.

"Prove it." His fists were clenched at his sides, and though Vera understood the magnitude of this moment, she couldn't help the way her body reacted to the sight. It was really fucking attractive.

She wondered if Kai was finally affecting Camilla, because the warlocks' stances mirrored one another, and she couldn't fathom her sister not getting at least a little turned on by it.

Bishop Whittle, with his dark skin, tall height, bald head, and shining brown eyes, looked to her past Harry's shoulder. "Hey, baby girl."

Vera swallowed back the tears begging to fall as the whisper escaped her. "Hey, Pops."

He smiled to her as Loretta spoke to Harry. "After you were banished from my life to remain with the European coven, I called you back when Althea tried to kill Maya. You picked up the fireplace poker and stabbed her through the chest with it."

Harry froze like the realization that this was the real friend he'd thought was dead was too much to process. Because that's what that confession meant. Other than Harry and Loretta, no one else had known about that event.

Then Maya had seen it happen in Hell's Gate.

Most knew Althea had died because of the Whittles, and after Maya's birth only a month later, most had guessed it had something to do with that. It's how Lila had known Maya was the dark witch responsible for her mother's death and how Melusine had known about Maya's abilities. After Melusine had heard her friend mumbling to herself about the dark witched Whittle, that friend had turned out dead because of the Whittles.

But no one knew exactly what had happened.

Harry stood numbly in front of her. Vera leaned into his back, unable to move forward. To reach for her father. Her real father who *wasn't* dead.

But Camilla wasn't in the same boat. Harry's acceptance was all she needed.

She tried to push past Kai to get to her mother, but the warlock wouldn't let her through. She beat against his back, but his stance was as protective as any Hunter would set before Maya, Harry before her if this were any other situation.

"How?" Harry breathed out.

Vera was glad he could still speak because nothing was coming out of her.

"It's a long story," her father said. "One you will definitely be hearing. But not until I hug my little girl."

Like hearing the words *my little girl* broke her, Vera pushed past the warlocks and into her father's arms.

It was like getting transported to being five years old and running to her father every day after school. Like being a teenager after her first heartbreak and crying into his shoulder. Like settling into his embrace every year when they celebrated her mother's birthday even without Loretta's presence.

Her father was alive.

And she was ugly crying into his shoulder.

When she finally fell from his embrace, her thumbs reaching to wipe her tears away, he leaned in and kissed her forehead. "I've missed you, my girl."

"I've missed you too, Pops."

When Vera turned back to the room, Camilla was beside her in their mother's embrace and the boys had moved forward.

Vera watched Camilla move to her father as she moved before her mother. The woman Vera had been raised to love all her life but had never known. "Hi," she said weakly.

Loretta's hand brushed back some of her hair. "My first born. I've missed you more than you can imagine."

She pulled Vera into a hug, and even in this hold, Vera felt the same sense of rightness. Of belonging. She finally had a mother.

When Vera released her mother from the hold and turned back around, Kai was lounging on the couch, obviously far less affected by the news than the rest of them. Rather, he looked contemplative, definitely taking all of this in and storing it in the back of his thoughts.

Harry stepped before them and gave Loretta a hug that said he'd missed her too. She was like a sister to him and he'd thought her dead, so Vera could only imagine how much this was affecting him as well.

When Harry finally pulled away and gave Bishop a hug too, he looked awestruck. Then he pulled away from his old friends and gave Vera's hand a squeeze of reassurance before he moved to the couch opposite them and fell into it. "How?"

Vera moved back to her father's embrace and tucked into his side as they sat down. Loretta took the spot beside her husband, and Camilla her other side.

Vera reached for her phone when it vibrated and saw a message to the group chat. *Maya, you should probably get home. Like right now.*

"I never died," Bishop opened. And before Vera could throw her anger at him, he finished, "I had to make it seem so. We had to let this event play out. This was Loretta's last chance."

Vera caught Harry's eyes, then glanced to Kai. Neither man seemed to catch on. "What?"

"There's a reason our coven is hunted. A reason I left." Loretta played with Camilla's hand in her lap. "Dark magic runs in our veins, and the bit that touched me made it so I could live."

Camilla shook her head. "What?"

Bishop took Loretta's hand into his so he could hold all of them. "Think of it as a cat's nine lives."

"It's exactly a cat's nine lives," Loretta said. "And I'm on my last one."

Vera gasped. "How?"

"The way I was able to be here now." She looked down at all of their hands jumbled together in her lap. "Every time I come back, my life moves back to a certain moment in time. The moment things turned south and led to my death, and I relive it. And every time, it turns out different. But obviously, every time, it doesn't come out positively."

"A little over two years ago, it happened again," Bishop continued. "She came back a final time. And told me everything. That's when I decided we couldn't risk it. I wouldn't risk losing her. This would be it, no more coming back. I would lose my Lore."

"The thing about my coming back is that I remember every other life, but no one else does. Bishop couldn't remember losing me every one of those times."

"I could imagine the pain," Bishop breathed out and looked to her in such a loving way. Vera hadn't realized how much she'd missed those looks her father had only ever had when speaking of her mother.

And now she was witness to those looks, and they were so much better in person.

"So, I decided I wouldn't come back to you." Loretta spoke mostly to Camilla as she said that bit. "Not for long, anyway. I'd come back enough to make it look like I'd passed naturally, then go to Bishop."

"She spent her time in Canada, in a little cottage hut we used to go to…" He smirked and wiggled his eyebrows. Both Vera and Loretta shouldered him on either end, but they both wore large grins.

"We had to let events play out. And a year and a half ago, Bishop faked his own death to come to me."

Bishop's hold tightened on Vera's hand, but he couldn't look at her. "I had to be with her. If this was the last time, I had to go with her. I know it's selfish, but..."

"I get it," Vera said softly. She wasn't angry with her father. She couldn't imagine losing Harry either, and they had just gotten together. She couldn't fathom all those decades of love. She squeezed her father's hand in reassurance and caught his thankful look.

Then her phone vibrated again. *Maya! You could suck his dick later! Get home!* Camilla sent into the group chat, and Vera had to angle her phone away so her father didn't read the message.

Maya, this is important. Vera tried to private message her.

"So we stayed away and let things play out. Every day, we wanted to come back to you. Every day, I thought it was different and I could come back. Then finally, a year later, you finally found the Book." Vera met her mother's stare. She was so beautiful. Camilla had taken her likeness. "And we were glad we never gave in. Because that was the moment I'd been waiting for. It just happened a year later than I'd expected it. Each time I came back *was* different, so it wasn't too surprising that the timing would be different too. Especially when we'd changed things juristically by faking our deaths. But that also gave me hope, that this time would be right."

"You three got together, and Harry came to you, and all was going well. But we still needed Maya and Hunter to meet," Bishop continued.

Vera's breath hitched, but it was Camilla who asked, "They still met? In every other life you had?"

Loretta smiled sweetly to her. "They're mates. They met in every one before and would continue to meet in every one after. There's no changing that."

"Why was it important for them to meet then?" Kai spoke for the first time as his gaze assessed them.

Bishop and Loretta looked to one another but neither answered. Instead, Loretta said, "Why don't we wait for the entire family?"

Vera met Camilla's eyes, caught Harry's and Kai's, then moved back to her sister. They were all thinking the same thing —who knew when those two would be done fucking the shit out of each other? And with Maya's recent temper, no one particularly wanted to get on her bad side.

Loretta watched each of them closely, her glittering hazel eyes meeting her husband's before asking the room, "Where is our other daughter?" The knowing look in her eyes told them she already knew the answer.

***

Maya watched the top of Hunter's head as he lay resting on her stomach. He whispered so low to her belly, she couldn't hear it.

But she had an idea of what he was saying.

He was talking to their 'child.' She shook her head and hated how much the sight of him talking to her stomach actually made her want it to be real.

She played with his mussed hair as her other hand grazed small circles on his bicep. "You're going to jinx it, Hunter. Stop."

He looked up at her with a wicked grin and mumbled into her stomach, "You hear that, Mini Maya? Mommy doesn't want me to jinx it."

Maya giggled. "Hunter, stop it."

His smile was wide as he met her stare. "You're going to look absolutely radiant with a belly."

Maya's eyes bugged out but she couldn't help the shit-eating grin across her face. "Hunter. No!"

He picked himself up on both arms and caged her in on the

bed as his face met hers. "Hunter. Yes," he whispered against her lips.

Her knees locked around his hips as her hands reached for his jaw, and her fingers traced his features. She stared up at him only a few inches from her face and felt the fireworks going off in her chest. He was her everything, her forever, her mate.

And she wanted to memorize every tiny bit of him, ingrain him as the only thing in her memory, and take it with her till death.

"What are you thinking about?" His breath mixed in with her deep inhalations.

"You." Her finger traced his jaw to his lips. "I'm always thinking about you."

"Always?" The question was a mix of cockiness and sincerity.

Her thumb brushed his lower lip and she was mesmerized by it, then her gaze flickered up to meet his, and she melted in her favorite sight of blackness. "Since the moment I saw you in that church. I hated myself for it back then, but I wanted you immediately. I actually had to train myself with thoughts of you before we met in the forest because I knew how I would react." She shook her head lightly. "I knew I was excited to see you rather than afraid."

He smirked. "That was the mating bond coming alive in you."

She smiled slowly. "And when did it come alive in you?"

She knew it'd be later. Even with the mating bond, his demon indifference didn't allow it to instantly click. She'd learned that much from a small conversation she'd had with Augustine about demon matings.

His nose brushed hers a few times as he leaned into her before pulling away so he could look her in the eyes. "The first time I heard your name."

She gasped. She'd definitely been expecting later than that.

"It was…eerie. Like hearing your name clicked something inside me."

Her thumbs both brushed his bottom lip, playing with it to stop herself from leaning up and kissing him.

"I'd wanted you before then. You were beautiful and I was intrigued with your power, especially on a newbie witch. I thought about you that night when I came. It was the first time I'd actually thought of anyone because of how much I wanted them. I'd gone my entire life getting it done because I was horny, not because I *needed* that person."

"Good," she growled.

He chuckled and softly kissed her thumbs. "You don't understand how excited I was to see you walking into that forest alone, even without the piece to the key. I wanted *you*. Then you said your name, and all I wanted was to be yours. I had to say it, taste the way it sounded on my tongue. I had to be yours."

She gave him a crooked grin. "You don't understand how much it affected me when you said my name."

He smirked down at her and took in an exaggerated breath. His hips thrust against hers, and his cock throbbed as it moved up her wet folds. "I remember."

She whimpered as his cock rubbed against her lips, brushing her clit in the most enticing way, but didn't fill her. She met him thrust for thrust as Hunter made his slow dance up and down her folds.

But never entered her.

"When did you know you wanted to give me the ring?" she asked through a slightly labored breath.

"That second time Colette attacked you." His hands moved to cradle her face as he continued his slow rock against her cunt. "I realized then how lucky I was that you hadn't been taken. That every time something happened, you could call me. I couldn't take that risk again, especially knowing Colette knows how I feel about you. I needed a way to get to you without magic." He kissed her jaw. "And..."

She rocked her hips up until his cock finally met her entrance.

He slowed his hips even more, the most torturous game he could play with her, as he entered her. "And I needed to be mated to you. We technically already were, whether it's accepted or not, you were already my mate. But…" He breathed slowly as he made slow inch after slow inch into her. "It's been different since we officially mated."

When he was all the way inside her, she clenched down around him, loving the sensation of being filled. "Yeah, I've kinda become obsessed with you."

He smirked as he pulled out, groaning as she continued clenching around him. "Don't kid yourself, love. You were always obsessed with me."

He could joke all he liked, but it *was* different. There was a need, that wasn't merely sexual, that was constantly there. She needed him in order to survive, the same way he needed her. They'd become one with the mating.

She smiled up at him as he pushed back inside her. *I love you, Hunter Delvaux.*

He leaned down to kiss her as he pulled out again, never breaking his speed as he deepened each thrust. His tongue played the game too, thrusting into her mouth and exploring the warm cave.

She moved her hips to his rhythm, meeting him every time.

He licked to her ear. "Say my name, Witch. Tell the world who you belong to."

She moaned his name in a breathy sigh. It was involuntary, like her mouth wanted to please him before her brain could catch up.

He chuckled his way back to her lips. "Good girl."

Her moans grew a bit louder as her hands moved from his face to wrap around his form. They found their way to his bare ass and took pleasure in gripping a cheek.

He growled against her lips. "Louder, love. Let me hear you."

She was already so wet and hearing him speak to her like

that wasn't helping. But again, she obeyed because she liked pleasing him.

She moaned louder, made sure the world heard her rasp his name.

It was exactly what he wanted because with each time she yelled his name, his thrusts became just a bit more frantic, and her name flew from his lips in throaty groans. It was those sounds that sent her over before she realized it.

"That's right, love." His final thrusts were uncontrolled. "Drench me in your cum."

She screamed louder, her orgasm never-ending as she thrashed beneath him. She swore she'd had two.

Then finally, he was filling her.

Lords, did she love when he filled her. The hot liquid shooting into her always sent her over again. It was an addicting feeling.

When he pulled out and his cum dripped down her thighs and onto the sheets beneath them, she had to bite her bottom lip and dig her nails into his back to keep from jumping him again.

He would need his rest before she could do that.

21

*A*nnoyingly, Maya's phone vibrations alerting her to plenty of missed calls and messages meant they had to go to her family home rather than find a new room in the manor to fuck after their shower.

Though, if Hunter were honest, he wasn't sure there *was* a room in the manor they hadn't fucked in yet.

He took her face in his hands and kissed her. He teased a light moan out as he shadowed them to the kitchen of Whittle House. He didn't stop kissing her when they landed, but took in every last sigh and whimper until they needed to pull away for air.

Their lips still touched as Hunter baited her, "We could still go back home."

"Mm." She skimmed her lips against his. "Tempting."

Then a light bout of laughter came from the living room and Maya finally pulled away. What the fuck could be so important if they were laughing?

She pulled him by two fingers to follow her as they made their way to the front, the scent of Harry's meat and cheese dish strong in the air. She paused abruptly at the opening to the living room, his constant awareness of her body the only thing that stopped him from bumping into her.

When he looked up, he found the reason for her sudden rigidness. Sitting on the couch across from them were Bishop and Loretta Whittle.

They were back.

Finally.

Silence rang through the room as everyone realized they were there. Hunter wasn't sure how Maya would react in the moment, but held her by the hips to steady her in case she needed it. He doubted she would, but then again, her emotions were playing with her at the moment.

Her heart raced a million miles a minute against his chest, but Hunter knew that was out of excitement at seeing her parents—her mother—rather than fear. Or the unbelievability of the situation.

She made a steady breath out, then the edges of her lips quirked up as everyone rose to stand before them.

"You've finally decided to show yourself." There was a smile on Maya's lips.

Loretta's warm smile dropped, a worry Hunter couldn't understand clouding her eyes. Bishop's hand immediately moved to his wife, like he was ready to port them out. *What the fuck?*

"What do you mean *finally?*" Loretta whispered to her daughter.

"I found out about you a couple of weeks ago," Maya said, and Hunter didn't have to look down to know there was a glimmer in her eyes.

Bishop's hand tightened around his wife's as they both stepped away from the others in the room. Almost like they were preparing for an attack.

Hunter stiffened behind his mate, but tried to keep himself steady for her. *What the hell was wrong with the two of them?*

"What do you mean, you knew?" Camilla screeched. "You found out they were alive and didn't say anything?"

Maya shrugged. "I was sworn to secrecy."

Neither Bishop nor Loretta looked happy. "How?"

"If you wish to keep it a secret, you probably shouldn't use Zathrian's bird to keep tabs on the girls. I *am* one of his only friends," Hunter answered his new father. He didn't like the sound of that. One father was plenty enough for him.

Camilla met Hunter's gaze with a new bit of shock. "You have a friend?" It wasn't said sarcastically. She sounded genuinely curious.

Hunter looked heavenward. "Why is that so shocking to you lot?"

"Because you're an asshat," Maya answered him.

He pinched her sides and loved the sound of her little giggles at the feeling.

Maya looked to her sisters. "Apparently the cottage they liked to stay at is owned by Hunter's friend. I met him and his mate last month. He told me. And made me swear some mate-suffering promise to keep it to myself. I think we all know I won't allow my mate to suffer."

Bishop's jaw clenched. "We specifically asked them not to tell."

"He trusts Hunter," Maya simply rebutted.

"And as my mate, Maya too," Hunter added because he really didn't like the way the two were acting. They were her parents, and from what he understood about these feeling creatures, they should be happy to see their daughter.

Vera turned to her father. "Why's that such a big problem? She's your daughter. So what if she knew a couple weeks sooner than the rest of us?"

"The reason we came back now is because we felt the rumble last night from when Maya found out about Hunter's stunt," Loretta said softly. "She controlled it, didn't allow it to wreak havoc."

Now everyone but Maya was scoffing.

Rather, she elbowed him in the gut. Semi-softly. He kissed her crown with a grin. "You were fucking sexy while you were trying to kill me, love," he whispered for only her to hear.

Loretta gave a small laugh in response to everyone's scoffs. "She did control it. Didn't allow anything worse to happen. That would've never happened before."

"But now, we can't know if it was fabricated to get us out," Bishop finished. "If they knew we were alive…"

If he weren't Maya's father, Hunter would already have him pressed to the wall, beating the truth out of him rather than listening to these little insinuations towards his mate. "Meaning?" Though he tried to keep his voice calm, a growl escaped him.

Maya seemed to realize something was happening then. She stood taller as if creating armor around herself to protect against whatever they said. But Hunter didn't miss how she fell a little deeper into his chest, as if sheltering herself into him.

"What happened?" she finally asked them. "Why leave?"

Loretta brushed a calming hand down her husband's arm, then turned warm eyes on them. "Why don't we all sit back down?"

Loretta took her seat on the couch again, probably realizing their cold welcome wouldn't make Maya want to embrace, her husband falling close beside her with a daughter on either side. Harry pulled the ottoman to sit beside Vera so Hunter could take his now empty spot on the other end of the couch Kai resided on. By the fire, exactly how they liked it.

He took the edge, his hands never leaving Maya's hips as he placed her in his lap. Her forever seat.

She snuggled into him like she could still feel the apprehension coming from her own father, and Hunter wanted to knock the man around for it. He wrapped Maya as close as he could, then watched her parents for their explanation.

Loretta looked at him with a softness in her gaze, almost like she was thanking him for caring for her daughter so well.

Then she began the story she'd already told the rest of her family. Of leaving after her final death and choosing to stay away so the same fate didn't become of her. It was a tale of multiple lives that was rooted in dark magic, and knowing that the current Whittles didn't delve in those matters, Hunter had to wonder what past Whittles were like, the Wittlieffs. Were they far darker than their successors?

Loretta told them of the need to wait until he and Maya met again.

Again.

Hunter's heart swelled as his hold on Maya hardened. He pulled her closer. Needed her as close as possible.

Again.

Meaning they met in every life Loretta had lived and would continue to meet in every one after. He'd always known it to be true, but it was an entirely other experience to have that knowledge verified.

"And that is where she ended her story with us and refused to continue until you two got here," Kai brought them up to speed as he tapped his fingers against his jaw, impatiently waiting for the rest of the story. He *was* a nosy bastard.

"We had to wait because that was the point where things truly began to change in each version I lived. Sometimes it happened pretty much right away, and other times it didn't happen for months. That's why we've been waiting it out," Loretta explained.

"But why? What does their meeting have to do with you?" Vera asked.

"It's not necessarily their meeting. It's more how Maya reacts with Hunter. How her dark magic mixed with her mating and her feelings for him. That determined what course the rest of the life I lived moved in," Loretta clarified.

"Okay?" Camilla said softly, but not demanding.

Loretta breathed a large inhalation, then nervously looked toward Maya, her glance jumping to her other daughters but eventually landing back on his mate. "The last three times I died, I didn't go back and have a new course. Instead, I woke up and died again maybe ten minutes later."

Hunter narrowed her eyes on the woman. He couldn't guess where this was going, but had a feeling from her constant stares that his mate wasn't going to like it. And if his mate didn't like it, he loathed it.

Loretta looked down to the hand that clasped her husband's on her lap. Bishop's thumb ran soothing circles on her knuckles. "In every one of those three lives, I was chained to the ground of a dark cellar when a cloaked figure came in with its weapon."

A nagging recollection hovered over Hunter's mind, but was pushed aside when Maya stiffened on his lap. Her hand clenched his arm and her nails bit into him through his shirt.

"Maya." He turned her face to look at him, and the rest of the room froze. "Maya, love, look at me. What happened?"

She swallowed and whispered, "Cloaked." Her glazed over eyes stared at him, but didn't meet his gaze. "Hammer," her voice was barely audible as it mixed with her deep breaths.

But those simple words from his mate brought the nagging recollection back to his mind. Of the dream she'd released onto him.

"Knife," she breathed.

Hunter couldn't believe this to be true. But it had been a dream in Hell's Gate. The one location where any past events were used against a person. Even events the person was not aware of. Like her almost exorcism before her birth.

"Axe," she whispered in a final exhalation.

Or a life she wasn't aware she'd lived.

Two gasps from the other couch were all the answer they needed. Maya's dream had been Loretta's past lives.

Maya jumped from his lap and ran for the half bath in the hallway. Hunter was behind her before the others could react.

He dropped to his knees beside her as she barely opened the toilet seat fast enough.

He held her hair back and soothed her back and left light kisses on her spine. He didn't know what to do to help her. His potion had helped her release the trauma the memories brought her, but learning they weren't just dreams, but reality, would be a new sort of evil. His only hope was that she'd be able to compartmentalize it as a nightmare since she didn't remember that life.

Maya vomited.

Over and over and over again.

Any morsel in her stomach long gone. When the dry heaving started, Hunter was ready to rip his heart out and lay it down for her just to make it all stop. He needed to do something, but there was nothing he could do.

"Focus on me, love," he whispered into the back of her neck. "My voice, my breathing. Focus that annoying little heart on me, love."

Like the words clouded the spiral she was in the middle of, she pulled back and rested her forehead onto her forearm as she took slow breaths in and out to match his.

Then she pulled away completely and flushed the toilet. She closed the lid as she stood at the sink to wash out her mouth. Hunter didn't break the way his hand soothed her back. He knew his touch was helping keep her calm.

She grimaced as she spit the water out and reached for the mouth wash. Everyone hated throwing up, but Maya *hated* throwing up.

She gurgled the mouth wash, then spit it out, washing her mouth out a final time before shutting off the faucet and turning to him.

She must've seen the concern in his black orbs because she gave him a weak, reassuring smile. "I'm okay, baby. Let's go."

Hunter's hand caught her at the stomach to bring her back before him. One hand reached to cradle her face as the other reached around her stomach and held her at the small of her back. "Maya," he reprimanded.

She needed to process what had happened, not just throw herself back out there.

Her eyes fought him for all of two seconds before she sighed and closed her eyes. Her head leaned into his chest as she wrapped her arms around him. Her hands found their way under his shirt and pressed into his low back.

He kissed her crown.

She needed to touch him to calm down just like he needed to touch her. This whole mating thing had pushed his need and possessiveness for the witch to unfound proportions.

Long minutes passed before she looked up, and her lips quirked up the slightest bit. "Thank you."

His lips twisted into a crooked grin. "Don't get used to it, my bleeding heart."

Now she wore a large smile. And leaned in for a kiss.

It was soft and reassuring and he made sure to throw in his possessiveness for her into it. His tongue was beginning to explore when she pulled away, and he grumbled, "I wasn't done, love."

She allowed him one more small kiss before pulling away. "I seriously am fine."

He eyed her body with a wicked grin. "Oh, I know."

She giggled. "Hunt, stop it." And turned. "Let's go."

He rolled his eyes and bit down on his bottom lip to fight the large grin as he smacked her ass. "Fucking tease."

She smiled back at him but sobered up by the time they were turning back into the living room. He knew where this was leading and wanted to shield Maya from it, but of course he couldn't do that.

He eyed the quiet room as they made their way back, silently threatening anyone if they tried anything toward his witch.

He retook his spot on the couch and didn't get the chance to reach for Maya before she nestled onto his lap. His hand snaked into her shirt and rested against her bare stomach, thumb rubbing soothing circles around her navel.

Hunter could tell they wanted to ask if Maya was okay, but she wouldn't like that type of attention. His gaze told them they better not try it.

Instead, Loretta eyed them with…he didn't know. Endearment? Fondness? Love? "You know, even without the demon's mating, I have no doubt you two would've found each other."

Maya played with his free hand. "Because of my dark powers?"

"No." She gave a warm smile. "You had a gravitation to fire and darkness even without your magic. But the way you are? Colder and morally grey compared to your sisters. You'd be able to accept a demon easier than most witches. I knew you'd fall in love with a demon when you were a child."

Hunter froze beneath Maya. It was a phrase demons didn't use, and he couldn't fathom understanding. *Falling in love.*

Maya's fingers skimmed up his forearm like she was telling him to relax. He flexed his hand over her stomach and leaned in to inhale her scent. Aromatic. A mix of woodsy and lavender.

When it seemed that enough time had passed, Kai tentatively asked, "Cloaked figures?"

Hunter growled at him, but Maya soothed his hand and whispered, "It's okay, baby."

Hunter ground his teeth, but allowed for the conversation.

Loretta's gaze dropped. "Yes. The sixth time, the cloaked… person came in and killed me. Then again the seventh. And the eighth. The difference was in the tool used."

Harry's gaze shot to Maya. "A hammer, a knife, and an axe?"

Loretta nodded wordlessly.

Everyone looked to Maya as she cocooned deeper into him, but somehow still made herself look confident and lethal. She was a mix of everything that fascinated Hunter.

It was Vera who finally asked, "How'd you know, My?"

Maya swallowed deeply, but his mate was strong, sometimes

annoyingly so. "It was…the second memory I had in Hell's Gate. I thought the first one was a memory and the second a dream, but I guess not."

Bishop and Loretta both froze and leaned forward like they wanted to wrap their little girl up. Hunter snuggled her closer. There was no need for anyone but him to hold her.

"What exactly did you see?" Bishop asked.

"I stood in the corner and watched…Vera uncloak with the hammer." Gasps all around. "Then again when Camilla uncloaked with the knife." Another round. "Then…I was in the body as I…"

As she beheaded her mother, the blood spraying over her skin and a cold laugh bellowing out of her. She'd told him all about it one night as the tears had tumbled down her cheeks. The potion may have wiped away the trauma, but when Maya thought about the dream in enough detail to recite it, it brought all the fear back to her.

"You remember," Loretta said breathlessly.

"It's true?" Camilla and Vera exclaimed, Kai and Harry leaning forward in their chairs to hear the answer too.

"Hunter gave me a potion to help with the emotions surrounding it, but I remember seeing it. Almost like a movie." She faced him and kissed his jaw. "Finding out it was real was just…too much."

"Understandably so." Kai briefly broke his gaze from the older couple to nod toward her.

"Mom. Mom, that can't be true." Camilla's eyes were lining with water.

Loretta clasped her daughter's hand. "It's not your fault. Any of you. But it's why we waited. That time around, Maya's mating with Hunter got them into trouble, and to get out of it, they did a lot of messed up things. But at the end of the day, they're mates. If you asked them now, they'd still do all the messed up things to remain together."

"She's not wrong," Hunter threw in.

"And because they got into the messes, you two got in to protect your sister. It got out of hand, and you three were lost. Not *my* daughters anymore."

"It's why we had to make sure Maya wouldn't go off the deep end with the Hell's Gate portal power," Bishop said, and Kai's head snapped to Maya. "Especially considering we don't know how it works yet either. The other lives only told Loretta she could wield the portal, nothing more."

"Between us alone, warlock," Hunter bit out before Kai had the chance to open his mouth.

Kai threw up his hands in the defensive and looked back to the older couple, but there was curiosity lining his eyes that Hunter couldn't argue he'd feel too if the roles were reversed.

"When we realized how well you controlled it," Loretta continued. "And how well Hunter took care to make sure you remained the same caring witch you always were, we knew it was time to come home."

"My bleeding heart," Hunter whispered into Maya's ear and felt her shiver against him. His cock twitched, but he pushed that thought down.

"So…what now?" Vera asked.

"And what is the meaning of the different lives?" Kai asked the more important question.

Bishop threw his arm around his daughter and brought her in close. "Now, we help you guys with whatever you're dealing with. Then live out our lives together."

"And when I die this time, it'll be with Bishop to the afterlife," Loretta said with a *look* to her husband.

He returned the look and leaned in to kiss her.

Vera threw her father's arm off her shoulder with a wide grin. "Ew, parents. Gross."

They all laughed as Bishop pulled away from his wife and turned to Kai. "Lore's lives…we believe was because of me. My dark bloodline is the reason Maya has that power, and we think is the reason Lore had to suffer."

"What about your background?" Vera asked.

Bishop patted his daughter's hand. "Why don't we speak of it another time? I'd like to sleep knowing my family is finally all together tonight."

"Of course," Vera whispered to her father with a loving shine in her eyes.

"They can have my room," Maya offered. "I live at Delvaux Manor anyway."

Hunter held her tighter. He loved when she told her family she lived at Delvaux Manor. Like she was owning being mistress of the household. Owning being his.

Vera shook her head. "Lila and Tamire are in your room. They can have mine. It used to be theirs anyway."

Bishop turned loving eyes on his daughter. "Sweetheart, we're not putting you out of your room."

"I think putting her out will be my brother's job," Kai said, knowing Vera would burn up with the remark. They all knew Vera would burn up. Then he turned to Camilla with a suggestive wiggle of the brows. "And I can put you out."

Hunter choked on his laugh and tried to hide it in Maya's hair when she elbowed him. "I really like this guy," he whispered to her.

Loretta and Bishop both looked to Harry who was also flushing. "Oh?"

Harry ignored them, his gaze jumping between his youngest charge and his warlock friend. "Why continue flirting with Camilla knowing it bothers her?"

Kai's knowing eyes skimmed Camilla's body. "It doesn't bother her."

"Kai," Harry insisted, and Bishop sat up a little taller at the insinuation that his youngest daughter may be feeling uncomfortable.

Kai looked to Harry with a wicked grin. "You're my brother, so your lover has to be my sister. Can't flirt with my sister." He nodded toward Hunter. "I'm not flirting with the mated one. I'd like to keep my life." Hunter's grin grew wider than the Grinch's. "So that leaves the elusive *Camilla*."

Camilla grit her teeth at him. "Kiss. My. Ass."

Loretta gasped and was on the verge of reprimanding her daughter when Kai leaned over his knees. "Open it, darling."

The man seemed to have no shame in front of her parents.

Camilla growled and threw a pillow at him, but Hunter's heightened scent detection picked up the slight hints that the phrase had worked on his little sister.

But just slight. He had a feeling Camilla truly wasn't looking for companionship at the moment.

ila and Tamire's introductions to dead and deader went...well.

They were obviously shocked, but that was normal. Vera herself was crazy stunned too. Even after the night's rest, she still couldn't help the jump her heart made when she saw her father. Alive and standing before her.

He was making chocolate and strawberry pancakes—her favorite breakfast from childhood—as Harry gave him and Loretta a breakdown of everything that had happened since they had received their powers. A crying Aurelia in her mother's arms the only other participant in the conversation.

Bishop looked to Lila with a knowing smile. "Girls, right?"

Loretta smacked his arm as he laughed.

"Listen to the sound on that little one," he defended himself. "Our girls were just as rowdy."

Loretta scoffed. "They were not."

"It's all Hunter's fault." Lila tried hushing her daughter.

"What did my daughter's mate do?" Loretta asked with a hint of tease in her eyes.

"He carried her one time, and she's become obsessed. Sometimes she'll cry until he takes her. It's disheartening as a parent to see your child want someone else so desperately." She looked equal parts upset and annoyed.

"Especially when said someone else doesn't care for her in the least," Tamire grumbled beside his wife and daughter.

"But he's not around," Loretta argued. "How is *this* his fault?"

"It's not," Lila answered. "But it would stop right away if he took her."

Like speaking of the devil conjured him up, Hunter and Maya shadowed into the corner of the kitchen just as Aurelia's cries hit a crescendo.

Lila breathed a sigh of relief and immediately walked over and deposited her daughter into the demon's arms. Hunter only grimaced, but took her into his arms without complaint. The silence that followed was deafening.

Bishop scoffed through a smile. "You weren't kidding."

Lila shook her head as she looked at the two, mumbling beneath her breath, "What are we going to do when we finally leave here and he's not always around?"

Hunter took a seat at the head of the table, Aurelia falling to his lap and Maya settling her hands onto his shoulders. "You know I don't like her, right? What kind of a mother continually gives her child to someone who is just as likely to hurt it?"

Lila rolled her eyes but didn't look at him as she cut oranges for their breakfast sides. "You won't hurt her."

Vera had to stifle her laugh. They all knew he wouldn't hurt her.

He quirked a brow anyway. "Aren't we so sure?"

"You may not care for Aurelia, but you care for Maya. You wouldn't want to upset her," Tamire answered for his wife.

Hunter strained his neck with annoyance as Maya laughed and leaned down to kiss the side of his throat. "They gotcha, baby."

Vera smiled at them. With Aurelia in his lap and Maya leaning into him like that, they truly looked like their own family. Vera had never been able to picture them as a family before, but now? She saw the way Hunter would dote on his mate and child, even if he didn't show it on Aurelia. He'd be their everything, their protector.

Not long after, Bishop and Lila were bringing breakfast to the table and everyone was beginning to dig in. Hunter even got Aurelia to rest in her bassinet off to the side without complaint. The kid was literally in love with him.

Harry sat beside Vera, his leg lightly rubbing against hers and causing flutters to explode within each one of her cells. The same thing that would happen before they'd gotten together. She'd thought it would stop when she finally had him, but nope.

Every single one of Harry's touches sent all the cells in her body fighting to be in that spot. Maybe she could take him back upstairs after breakfast.

Or better yet, he could port them somewhere else. It was so weird knowing her parents were in the house as she was getting it on. Silencing charms or no silencing charms.

By the end of breakfast, Vera watched Hunter take her sister's face in hand and give her a soft kiss, telling the family— but really just her—that he had to go.

"Before you go, Hunter," Tamire interrupted the conversations. "We need some information."

Hunter quirked a brow.

"We got a call earlier from a demon family, saying they have some information on the one attacking us. We're going to meet with them in a bit. Anything about the family would be appreciated," Tamire said.

Hunter's lazy lounge was back as he crossed his arms before his chest and waited.

"The Heisenbergs," Lila said.

"The Heisenbergs?" Kai asked at the same moment Bishop asked, "Why would they trouble themselves with your problems?"

"You know them?" Vera asked.

Bishop nodded. "An important demon family. Nowhere near his highness over there, but important enough."

Hunter wore a smug look at her father's wording. But he remained silent.

Vera couldn't see it, but somehow, she knew her sister's hand was running up and down the demon's thigh as she said, "Baby, what do we have to know?"

Hunter relented without hesitation for Maya. "Dagen is their head. His power is incineration, which is why they became part of the powerful families. Heat related powers are always higher up and more rare. It's part of the reason my family continues on top; everyone always has heat related magic. And with Maya as my mate, and having as rare powers as I do, rarer even, it'll catapult us."

"So getting burned alive is something to worry about?" Lila said unenthusiastically.

"No," Hunter said calmly. "With Maya there, he won't be able to get you. She can stop it. It's basically a specified version of our power." He watched them for a moment, then continued, "His wife, Zella, also shouldn't be a problem. Zoolingualism. Surprisingly a light power, so it still shocks me that he ended up marrying her, even if her power has come in plenty handy for them."

"Are they mated?" Camilla asked.

Hunter tsked. "Most demons don't mate."

Vera had been shocked to learn that unlike wolves, who are the only other species to have matings, demons usually didn't mate. So when wolves 'married,' it was always to a mate. When demons 'married,' it almost never was to a mate. Hell, other than the top families, most demons didn't even know about matings.

But that still brought to question why a top demon family would marry a light-powered demon.

"So unless they have animals around," Hunter continued, "there isn't too much to worry about. If you do see animals, warlocks hold on and prepare to port out."

"What about stolen powers?" Camilla asked, surprisingly non-judgmentally.

"Or non-primary powers?" Vera asked.

"They have multiple powers like any of the rest of us, but they're weaker powers. They quite literally rely on their primaries to keep power. And they don't have stolen powers. Dagen is bent on being a *proper* high born, so he wants everyone to know that all their powers are theirs because they're superior." Hunter rolled his eyes. "The idiot could be so much more powerful if he just allowed himself to steal powers."

"Some people have morals," Camilla argued back.

Hunter smirked to her with a wink. "They'll lie and cheat everyone out of their funds and lives. They don't have morals. At least my family never lies. Everyone is clear on our 'morals.'" Arguing was their thing. "The kids are the ones to look out for. The oldest, Jayce, is about Camilla's age. His power is petrification, so you need to watch out for that. But again, Maya will be there."

Vera threw a half-eaten strawberry at him. "How many times are you going to insinuate Maya is better than the rest of us?"

"She is."

Her parents laughed from beside her, and she couldn't help but add in her own chuckle. They were probably delighted by the way Hunter praised the grounds Maya walked on.

"As I was saying, Maya will be there, so Jayce's petrification shouldn't be a problem. It works on a freezing basis, so Maya should be able to melt it away. The second son is like Warren, melting. Just watch out that he doesn't touch you. Unlike War, he needs touch to get his power to work. Not sure if it's just because he's unpracticed or because War is more superior."

"Yeah, yeah, we all know you think Warren's more superior." Harry smirked at the demon.

Hunter smirked back, but it was Maya who said, "Of course he is. He's a Delvaux."

Hunter was smug as he continued, "The third is techno-pathetic. I don't see how that can do anything, just the psychic ability to control technology. But in case there's anything that seems robotic, be on your guard." His hand moved to Maya's back, and Vera didn't know why, but that small move made her heart ache in a beautiful way. Like it was showing his affection for her without realizing it. "The last son is said to only have astral projection. Apparently his father's greatest disappointment, and still, he won't let the kid steal. Dagen says if the kid doesn't grow into some powers, he doesn't deserve them. He's young though, has time."

"Anything we have to worry about regarding the family itself? The way they deal?" Tamire asked.

Hunter shook his head without consideration. "They're liars and cheats, but that's it. They're greedy as any other demon, but because they're so interested in forcing their way into deals, they make mistakes often. I'll trust you lot smart enough not to fall for anything. Especially when they're such awful negotiators to begin."

"High compliments." Bishop gave him a crooked grin and got a wink in return.

Maya would be porting in with Tamire and Lila as Harry took her sisters. Loretta and Bishop would stay behind to watch the baby since the world didn't yet know they were alive.

Hunter pulled Maya close. His arms wrapped around her shoulders and brushed her back. "I don't think they know about us. I've gotten some *congratulations* from the families higher up like mine about our mating, but not all. They don't pay attention to witch business, like the morons they are." Maya giggled. "But they definitely pay attention to my family. I'd assume they know we're sleeping together if nothing else. If that's all, they shouldn't try anything because they won't know I care for you.

But in any case, be careful. Especially if they know about the mating already or see the ring and put it together. I don't care about keeping the shadowing a secret—if anything happens, you get out of there."

She quirked a cocky brow at him. "They're going to mess with *your* mate?"

"I don't know what they'll try, but I'll rip their entire line apart for even thinking about it," he growled.

Maya gave him a long kiss, then mumbled against his lips. "Good."

He brushed her hair from her face, then cradled her jaw firmly. "It's killing me not to go with you, love."

"I know," she whispered against his lips. "But we have to get used to not doing everything together. You know how much it bugs me when you go on those trips?"

He smirked down at her. "Always with the good points, Witch."

She kissed him again because she had to. And he shadowed out of her grasp as her mouth was opening for more.

She gasped at the air and shook her head to herself. "Asshole."

She turned for Tamire, who stood with the rest of the group handing Aurelia off to her parents with a final kiss.

Heisenberg Manor was large. Nowhere near either Delvaux's, but fucking enormous.

Maya dropped Tamire's hand when they got there, and when his eyes widened at her, she simply gave him a wink.

The lackeys out to guide them to Dagen felt more like royal guards from a fantastical story than demons. Maya had to stifle her laugh at the ridiculousness of it, and as she caught Tamire's amused stare beside her, the realization was clear that Hunter hadn't been kidding about a *proper* high born family.

They were lead into what could only be described as a throne room before the guards closed the large doors behind them. Wow. This demon really wanted to think highly of himself.

Dagen smiled from his place on the throne, his eyes shining in delight that he'd be able to cheat them out of something more than what they were there for. "Tamire." He raised his hands in welcome. "You've brought quite the entourage."

"I have five, you have five. It is only fair," Tamire responded coolly.

His wife stood off to the edge of the room, hands clasped before her hips like a proper lady. She looked subdued and tranquil, like she was too weak and meager to go against her husband.

Maya scoffed beneath her breath. She wondered how much of it was an act and how much of it was years of being broken down by said husband.

"Last I recall, you only had a wife." The demon played with the arm of his throne.

"Call the others close friends." Tamire's tone never faltered. "Now, what do you have for me?"

"Past pleasantries, are we, Warlock?"

"I do not have time, nor care, for your games, Demon." Again, no falter. Impressive.

Though really, he was like two hundred years old. He shouldn't be faltering.

Three of Dagen's sons stood on the other side of the dais, straight backed and trying to be frightening. They were young though—nineteen, seventeen, and sixteen—and looked like their father had been telling them their whole lives they were better and they truly believed it.

"I know the woman that's been attacking you. She came to me for aid in taking you down." He looked cocky.

"And you are informing me?" Tamire quirked a brow.

"She doesn't have much to offer that I care for. You do." His smile grew disturbingly wide. "But by all means, if you refuse, I will simply take what she gives me."

Tamire's eyes narrowed on the man. "What do you want?"

Where was the final son? The twelve-year-old weakling.

"I hear you have gotten your hands on some unicorn blood," Dagen teased out.

Tamire's brows knitted together. "You're a demon. I got it from your kind."

"It is a form of status to carry unicorn blood within your arsenal," Dagen explained. "Only *the* most powerful families have any. It is the only thing holding my family back."

Maya really had to hold back her scoff that time. *Yeah, the only thing.*

Tamire didn't answer, his eyes taking Dagen in like he was thinking about it.

After a moment, Maya felt a presence in her mind. *He needs to speak with you.*

Camilla had figured out how to allow multiple people into the conversation, but hadn't yet gotten to a point where it could be private. She may never get to that point.

Then Tamire's voice was in her head, *Can you get me a vial from Hunter?* He sounded apprehensive, like he didn't like that he had to ask the favor. But of course the answer would be yes, She wouldn't allow anyone to hurt his family. If for nothing else, little Aurelia had great taste in her mate. She had to protect the little witch.

No problem. Maya didn't let her gaze waver to him as she answered.

Thank you, he responded before her mind was clear of them.

Tamire breathed out like he'd finally considered all alternatives and was coming to a decision. "Deal."

Dagen's smile was getting creepier by the second. "Her name is Sarah Bridgers." No surprise finding out it was a Bridgers witch. It made sense she'd want retribution for her lost coven. "She blames you two for giving away information that lost them the battle to the Whittles. Which I'm presuming are these close friends of yours." After a pause, he added, "For two vials, we can take care of her for you."

"No need," Tamire said smoothly. "You'll receive your vial tomorrow."

Dagen's eyes hardened as they turned to leave. It was obvious he had wanted more than a small bargain of this sort.

Turning to the wide doors, Maya finally saw the youngest son blocking it. When she turned back around, he was also standing beside his mother. Astral projection. Right.

"Yes, Vincent is the weakest of my lot, but useful enough," Dagen spoke to their frozen stances in the middle of the throne room.

Vincent.

He was about the right age for Bella. Which also meant he wouldn't truly be helping his father. Especially if he knew of Maya's friendship with Bella. She'd have to confirm with Bella this was *her* Vincent.

"I have changed my mind, Tamire." Dagen moved in his throne like he was trying to look bored, but the greed in his eyes was too bright to pass off. "If you can so easily agree to one, why not ten?"

"The same reason you seem to find it so difficult to get any. I can only get you one." Tamire's composure was breaking. Just a little.

Maya then felt the petrification attempt to hold her and not get past because of her heat. But if it was being tried on her, it'd most definitely be used on the others too. She sent her heat into everyone's bodies and felt the effects of their petrified stances. Maya simply undid the magic holding their bodies still.

Dagen's eyes bugged out when he saw none of them were stuck, and when the wide eyes of his son met his, he turned narrowed ones onto Tamire. He was no longer holding that disturbing smile.

Then his gaze flickered to Lila. But Maya's power was already in everyone's body, ready to help them when necessary.

So she felt when his incineration attempted to make its way into Lila's body and pushed it back without a problem. Hunter's trainings were coming in very useful at the moment.

Dagen drew in a breath, his hard gaze flickering through them all. "They say the Delvaux heir is fucking a witch. The man goes around without touching anyone his entire life, then finds himself in a witch? Even one with such rare dark powers, it is despicable. But I think I am beginning to remember that she is of the Whittle line. And if I'm not mistaken, she is here with you now."

Maya loved that she was the first person who Hunter had taken publicly. He'd done it to save himself any false pregnancy allegations, making sure never to allow a chance of procreation in the past with spells.

But he hadn't done that with her. Not once.

A growl vibrated through her chest, but she shoved it down before it could bring any attention to her. She really didn't like thinking of Hunter with anyone in the past.

Finally, Dagen's eyes settled on her. When his gaze roamed her body, Maya saw the equal shock and horror fill his eyes as he shot from his seat to stand at the dais. "Impossible."

Ah, so he'd seen the ring.

"Keep it up, Dagen," Tamire said coolly, "and you won't get the one vial."

Now that he'd seen the ring and knew that Maya was technically a Delvaux herself, he'd know that if he tried anything against her, he'd be calling war against a ruling family. And as much as he liked to think highly of his little group, they were nothing against the Delvauxs.

There was a fury so deep in the patriarch's eyes as Maya winked at him. Mostly because she knew it would anger him more.

23

Maya called Bella later that afternoon.

An enthusiastic "yes" from the other end told her they'd be having a visit immediately. It saddened Maya more than she cared to admit that Bella hated it at home. Mostly because there was nothing she could do about it.

They were seated at Brynn and Alloy's private beach as the couple made them some sandwiches and drinks. The way they were always smiling and hugging one another made Maya happy that they'd chosen to leave.

"So why are we here?" Bella asked as they watched the waves.

"What?" Maya looked down at her.

Bella gave her knowing grin. "You definitely have something you want to talk to me about."

Maya rolled her eyes. "You're too observant." After their light chuckles, Maya sighed. "Tell me, is Vincent, Vincent Heisenberg?"

Bella froze beside Maya, and her head shot over, a gaping expression that was hidden too late on her face. Maya smirked down at her.

"I met the family earlier. Not the best." That was the kindest way she could put it.

Bella scowled and turned back to the waters. "His parents are the worst. They treat him like garbage because they think his primary power is astral projection."

Maya watched Bella's profile for a moment. "And what is it actually?"

There was a hesitant pause as Bella looked to her before settling back on the water. "Biokinesis," she said softly.

Maya's eyes widened and her breathing stopped.

Biokinesis, the complete control of a person's biology, their insides. Another *very* high-level dark power. Smart kid to keep it from his parents.

Maya's love for the kid beside her grew as she realized Bella trusted her enough to keep this to herself.

"He can make people internally bleed without any effort," Bella explained softly but didn't look to her. "You can tell Hunter."

"I wasn't going to." She honestly wouldn't have, even knowing Hunter would never abuse the knowledge. Even before she was in his life, he wouldn't want Dagen to know because that would put the Heisenbergs at the top with the Delvauxs, and he wouldn't like that.

"I know." Again, the trust made Maya's heart expand. "But that would be like me not telling Vincent something. I'm the only person he's told, and he said it would be okay for you two to know in case..."

A small smile rose on Maya's lips. "In case he ever needed help from a demon, he needs one he can trust?"

Bella shrugged, but looked to her with confidence. "You think Hunter would mind?"

Maya threw her arm around her little friend. "Having a biokinesis as an ally? No, I don't think Hunter would mind."

Bella laughed. "That's not what I meant."

Maya smiled back. "I know. But seriously, he won't mind. If Vincent needs anything, we're here."

"Thank you," Bella whispered as her sister and brother-in-law walked out with their picnic.

Maya brought Bella's crown to her lips for a kiss. "Don't get used to it, Fish."

Bella laughed and pushed her away as the food was placed before them.

Maya had to compliment them on their food. After this whole mess, she'd come to Brynn for some lessons. Maya was good in the kitchen, but there were some recipes here she definitely wanted to steal for Hunter.

Maya looked between the couple as they ate. "You know, technically you two could go back. Uzark has been accepting his mixed couples."

"Thanks to your lot." Alloy wore an almost thankful look.

Brynn snuggled into Alloy's side. "But my parents won't like it. We don't want to cause a problem for the gargoyles because they have the mermaids heir in their 'lair.'"

"Fair point." Maya looked out to the ocean.

"Plus, why would they give *this* up?" Bella exclaimed as she looked on to the water crashing against the shore.

"Another fair point." Maya threw her arm around the girl and brought her in close.

***

Vera was in the shower, getting the remnants of being at Lila and Tamire's cottage off her skin before having to meet with Hunter for another lesson.

She'd gone with them while her parents had watched Aurelia, and they'd waited for hours, inspecting the cottage along the way, before the witch had showed up.

Sarah Bridgers.

The information Dagen had given had afforded them the

ability to use a spell to track Sarah down and allow her the falsehood that she'd catch Lila and Tamire unawares.

They'd known she would try to attack immediately when she arrived.

And she'd done just that.

But Vera had been able to stop her. To push her against the wall and stop her. Though, that witch had been trained, and it was almost like trying to get a handle on a demon. She'd never admit it, but Vera knew she had Hunter's training to thank for her ability to stop Sarah.

They'd questioned her lightly before killing her, and as Vera took her shower, she thought back to what the witch had said.

It had been mostly useless threats, even though *she* was the one about to die, but one stuck out to Vera—*Melusine will have her retribution. She will end you for what you've done to this coven.*

Vera hadn't understood it then, and she still didn't understand it now. Melusine was dead. Hunter had taken care of her.

She shook her head of the thoughts because Sarah hadn't been willing to give any more information and they'd finished her. Finally, Lila and Tamire might have their peace with their daughter.

Vera was tired and not entirely in the mood for this lesson, but that would be a lesson in and of itself—in the future, she wouldn't be able to choose when she was attacked. How tired she was or how much not in the mood wouldn't matter.

So she showed up.

Especially now that she had an audience.

Not a large one. Just Maya. But still, Vera had never had anyone watch them before.

Maya'd taken a spot on the ground, placing a pillow to her back and leaning on the wall as she watched them prepare in the middle of the room. "V, seriously, if this is going to make you uncomfortable, I don't have to watch."

Vera gave only a small eye roll. "You can stay."

"Good." She beamed. "Because I want to watch you kick my man's ass."

That faith in her was definitely helpful too.

Hunter leaned over his mate and gave her a chaste, loving kiss. "Thanks for the vote of confidence, love."

Maya's smile only grew, unconcerned. "You're welcome. After all, you are the one training her."

And his trainings and advices had been helpful, even outside of these sessions. Vera had started wearing one of Harry's shirts to acquaint herself with distraction. Her attention was still stolen at the scent of him, but she'd gotten better at putting a handle on it. And every time Hunter was around, she'd get better and better at pretending the tingle that spiked up her hand to the back of her neck wasn't pleasant. Like a Pavlovian dog, she trained herself to fidget to attention anytime she felt the tingle now.

She hated to admit it, because the demon certainly didn't need an ego boost, but his methods worked. And he was good to her after pushing aside the asshole part of his personality. Especially considering it actually wasn't his fault that being an asshole was in his blood.

Hunter turned on her, and wordlessly, the training began.

The first ten minutes were like their earlier trainings. Meaning, she wasn't getting him. But unlike those earlier ones, she was getting close. So close that soon, she had him flying through the room.

And he hadn't even been any more distracted by Maya as she silently sat at the edge of the room. Vera knew there was a bit of distraction with her presence around, but he'd been deflecting her throws perfectly for their first half of the training, so this was all her.

He picked himself up from where he'd hit the banister to the stairs and gave her a crooked grin. "Good job, Little Sister."

Vera narrowed her eyes at him. "Camilla is Little Sister."

He chuckled. "And what am I meant to call you? You're also younger than me."

Vera rolled her eyes. "I'm just saying, she might get jealous that you're using it on me now too."

He laughed. "I'd like to see that." He strolled around her in the room. "Go again."

And they did.

It was like a darts game where most of the of the attempts didn't meet their target, but every so often, she'd send him flying through the air, and each time, it got just a bit easier to recognize when to strike.

Maya laughed. "Getting your ass handed to you there, babe?"

"Oh, yeah." There was no shame or hurt of pride. "You're going to need to kiss my wounds better later."

Before Maya could respond, Vera interrupted, "No. No. No flirting. No dirty jokes. No anything. None of that please." The way he continued looking at his mate bypassed everything Vera had just forbade. "And no undressing each other with your eyes."

He gave Maya a final once over before turning to her. "We're going to try something else. You're beginning to get a good handle on detecting me and throwing me around. But in a real situation, I most likely won't be immobilized by one throw. And I absolutely would never take my time getting back up. I need you to be ready for another strike immediately, because when I fall on my ass, I could shadow straight from there and end up standing behind you. I don't *have* to get up if I'm just going to be shadowing again."

Vera breathed out in concentration. "Got it."

She didn't get him at all the first few attempts. But then the tingling shot up her hand, and she was throwing her arm out before it reached her neck, and he hit the wall and was gone in a matter of half a second, landing to her side. And again, she shot her arm out, just barely getting him flying through the air. This time, he shadowed midair. And landed behind her. He hit the banister as she threw him back while she turned, and before his body could hit the ground, he was gone.

Behind her again.

And she was exhausted. They were going much faster than she'd expected.

She bent over her knees to catch her breath as a "Good job" came from behind her.

She breathed out again and moved for her water, needing the liquid more than she'd ever needed it working out. She was actually sweating a little bit too.

Hunter stretched his limbs as he walked around the room, allowing her to rest. His gaze landed back on his mate like he couldn't pull away for too long. "I'm definitely going to need those kisses later."

She bit her lip. "Trust me, I'm ready to give them. Everywhere just to be sure."

"My dick especially hu…"

"Hey!" Vera struck. "No! No. Bad. Stop it!"

Hunter cracked a grin as Maya laughed. Hard.

24

Hunter was alone in the Whittle kitchen when parents one and two walked in. He poured his black coffee and leaned against the counter, finding no desire to fill the air with conversation as they bid him good morning and began preparing breakfast.

Maya's mother talked a lot. Maybe that's where Vera got her incessant need to fill the air with conversation. It was irritating.

There was a glimmer in Loretta's eyes every time she looked at him. It was in Bishop's as well, and it oddly made Hunter feel uncomfortable. It was such an odd feeling to have Maya's family look at him with joy rather than annoyance or anger or hatred.

The hatred had washed off the faces of his new family. Anger too, a bit, but annoyance was always there.

Hunter's gaze settled on Bishop. "Tell me, why don't you oppose of my relationship with your daughter?"

Bishop chuckled. "You're her mate. I'd be hard pressed to keep you two apart."

Hunter rolled his eyes. "You couldn't keep us apart. That's not what I'm asking. But you don't seem bothered by our relationship."

Bishop shrugged. "You make her happy. As a parent, that's all we could really ask for."

"It's something even your cold heart will learn in the future," Loretta added.

Hunter analyzed her before his gaze flickered between the two of them. They weren't kidding. Weren't putting up a face for Maya's sake, they truly meant this. Hunter didn't know how to feel about these witches being honestly excited about being grandparents to *his* offspring. So he didn't think any longer about it.

Their eyes shimmered again, and Hunter was glad to have finished his cup of coffee so he could turn his back to them and pour another. Hatred or annoyance he was accustomed to and could brush off without a worry. But this acceptance? It was odd.

He turned back and watched them with narrowed eyes when Camilla strolled in. "Hunter, are you bothering my parents?"

Hunter rolled his eyes as she took a seat at the table, Lila and Tamire close on her tail. Then the rest of their little group trickled in just in time for breakfast of a veggie omelette and muffins to be placed in the center of the island for grabbing.

As plates filled, Tamire opened, "What happened this morning?"

Hunter had forgotten that Maya had texted him that Harry had gotten a call from Juliette asking them to check out a problem with her banshee friends she couldn't get to. Two more had been found dead—a banshee and a dwarf—and a survivor was found with them.

Mostly because he didn't care for these people so he didn't cloud his thoughts with the information.

"There were three missing banshees. Two were found this morning," Harry answered solemnly. "Iris was found dead next to the dwarf, but Ayla insists they weren't lovers. But she said she doesn't know where Lyra ran off to."

"Poor girl blames herself for her friends' death and Lyra's disappearance," Vera added.

"But what happened?" Maya asked around her bite into a sliced orange.

Hunter really didn't care what happened. All he wanted was his mate. Simply watching her eat was enough for him, and he didn't know whether he liked this foolishness the mating was taking him down.

But he couldn't help it. He wanted to watch her do any and all mundane things.

"I think," Harry answered somewhere in the background of Hunter's focus on Maya, "that Hunter's little stunt getting himself captured actually got us some useful information."

Hunter snapped his head to the warlock, then back to Maya with a little smug smile.

"Wipe that grin, Delvaux." She wasn't amused. "You're still in trouble for that."

He could also watch her reprimand him for the rest of his life. It was sort of erotic.

"Information like what exactly happened when they're captured, but also the people doing the torturing. It's always someone who is half of both of the people in the relationship," Harry continued.

"We already guessed as much," Camilla said.

Harry shrugged. "I think if what Ayla is saying is true, maybe they couldn't find a banshee-dwarf couple for the specific halfie that needed the release, so they resorted to friends."

"If they're beginning to resort to friends, this is going to get more dangerous very quickly," Lila said.

Harry looked out to the others. "That's what I'm afraid of."

"Then we need to focus on Lyra," Bishop said. "As a banshee, she could've gone to protect a group the same way I hear this Juliette went after that group of faeries. That's both best case, because it means she's most likely safe, and worst case, because it means a larger group may be in danger."

"A mermaid friend of mine gave me a list of some couples she knows of. Some of the men she didn't know the partners to, and they were the ones that didn't volunteer the information when we asked, probably because they're guards, so they're extra cautious. But that's a starting point," Maya said behind another orange. She'd single-handedly eaten two whole oranges and was moving onto her third.

Vera shook her head as she nibbled on a muffin. "It's so messed up. Colin and Iris weren't even part of what the halfies hate. They were just friends."

"And they knew mixed couples, which they looked like, are being hunted. They should've taken more care to make their outings private. Or so public they couldn't be confused as romantic," Kai argued.

"It's not fair." Vera sighed.

Hunter shrugged. "They took the gamble." He finished his coffee and placed it on the counter behind him. "For instance, I would rather be around Camilla than you, but then I must reap the consequences of being around the little brat."

Camilla gasped at the insult as Vera asked indignantly, "Why her?"

He smirked, knowing Vera's cheeks were about to explode with color. "Because Camilla's hormones remain stagnant most of the time. Yours throw a party every time Harrison there is around or his name is mentioned. Or worst off, I can tell when you're thinking of him even with no mentions of his name. And this was even before you two finally gave in and fucked too, Little Sister. It's revolting."

Camilla froze. "I'm Little Sister."

Vera was red. Not pink, red. And her family was laughing on the side lines. But instead of arguing what he'd just said, she simply commented, "I told you she'd be jealous of you calling me that."

Hunter laughed.

And when Harry tried to console Vera with a shoulder rub,

Hunter looked to him. "You're not any better, Warlock. It's a nightmare to be around."

That comment sobered Harry up and turned his lighter cheeks pink.

Though Hunter had a control on the power and could normally ignore scents, sometimes they'd be too strong. It wasn't as often as he was making it sound, but he liked being dramatic once in a while. And Maya knew it as she laughed and shook her head at him.

And though she was obviously enjoying the scene before her, Camilla turned on Hunter. "They're a nightmare to be around? It's a blessing none of us have that power. I cannot imagine being around you and Maya with that!"

He let his gaze drink his mate in as he said, "Touche, Little Sister." And when he saw the desire in Maya's eyes and smelled how much she wanted him, Hunter turned back to said little sister. "But next time you argue me, we can find out what happens with yours when a certain someone," he let his eyes flicker lightning fast to Kai and back, "is around."

She sobered up quickly.

But Kai caught the flicker.

His smirk was as wide as any Hunter could muster as he strolled up beside Camilla and threw his arm around her. "The offer still stands, darling. Allow me to put you out."

She elbowed him in the gut, but that didn't wipe the pleased grin from the warlock's face. Camilla looked to Hunter like she wanted to kill him, and Hunter had to wonder just how often she actually got aroused by the warlock. He'd only scented it a couple of times, and each time had been very light, but the way she reacted now felt like it had happened more than *a couple times*.

Or maybe she was just embarrassed enough for those couple of times.

Her parents were adamant they join when Maya mentioned they were headed for Zath and Acacia's. So, this time when Hunter landed her before the cottage shop that Zathrian sold his crafts from, they weren't alone.

Her parents shivered beside them, and Maya was reminded that the heat within their bodies kept her and Hunter warm. She sent some of her own so that her parents didn't freeze in the few moments they spent outdoors.

Small snowflakes were falling outside and lining them all in flurries. Maya watched them fall on Hunter's pristine hair with a smile, unable to imagine him getting any more attractive.

"It's absolutely beautiful, isn't it?" her mother asked. "I always wanted to bring you girls, but it didn't feel right without Vera and your father."

"It wouldn't have been right." Maya hated how much guilt her parents lived in, because at the end of the day, everything they'd done was to protect their daughters, and Maya would never fault them for that.

It was the same thing she would do for hers and Hunter's children. They didn't even have any yet and she already loved them beyond compare.

But not more than Hunter.

She couldn't imagine loving anything more than Hunter. Which Maya also found as a positive because it meant her kids would see what love looked like always.

"Let's get inside before we become real life snowmen for Zathrian." Her father jogged for the door to the shop and held it open for them.

Caw. Caw.

Adramalech was sitting guard at the front desk, as always, and cawed an extra bout this time, which Maya guessed was because of her parents. He flew to Bishop's shoulder and sat there waiting to be pet.

Bishop laughed and obliged the bird. "Yeah, yeah. I'll pet ya, even though I know you told my daughter on me."

"Don't be ridiculous, Pops." Maya pushed him. "He didn't tell me."

"Oh, shut up." Her father pushed her back, and Hunter growled as his hands landed on her hips.

Maya held the hands on her waist and pulled them closer. "Calm down, baby."

Adramalech cawed twice more before Zathrian showed up from the back and paused abruptly. "What is this I'm seeing?"

"An annoyed warlock and witch who asked you to keep their secret that you blatantly ignored." Bishop narrowed his gaze on the demon.

"I'm sorry, friend." He sounded far more amused than sorry. "But how could I say no to that beautiful face?"

Maya beamed at her parents as Hunter pulled her in closer to his chest. "He couldn't."

Zathrian laughed and nodded to the back. "Come, come. Let's sit."

Adramalech flew back to his perch at the front desk and the rest of them followed Zathrian back.

"How's Acacia doing? Still throwing up?" Maya asked with a grimace.

"Better now." Zathrian looked back to her with a beaming smile. "Still throwing up sometimes, but mostly better now. We got lucky. The demoness of it all is being kind to her."

"Why is she throwing up?" Loretta's concerned voice sent Maya back to childhood for a moment.

"She's pregnant." Zathrian jumped a little with his step in his excitement.

"Truly?" Bishop asked. "That's incredible, Zathrian. No wonder you couldn't keep your yap shut. You're overwhelmed with your demon pregnancies that act like they want to kill the witch carrying."

Zathrian laughed. "Be careful there, Bish. Your daughter is going to carry a demon."

"I imagine Hunter will be just as annoying," Bishop retaliated, and Maya laughed.

Her father was truly annoyed that the secret had been let out, and honestly, she could imagine Hunter being the same level of annoyed. As men who want to protect their women, all their concern would be on making sure nothing harmed their woman. And telling a secret when specifically asked not to could possibly harm that woman.

So Maya understood.

But she still found it amusing.

Acacia jumped from her seat when she saw Maya, then paused at the sight of her parents before smiling wide. Then she was moving for Maya for a hug. "Good to see the lot of you!"

Maya hugged her back, then instinctively fell to the little belly jutting out. "Hi, baby. Thanks for treating your mommy a little nicer."

Hunter reached around her to kiss Acacia's temple, and his hand fell over Maya's on her stomach. "The babe's excited." His hand moved for Maya's stomach. "To have a friend."

Maya pulled on his hand so they moved and muttered under her breath, "Hunt, I swear to the lords, I hate you so much sometimes."

He fell to the couch and pulled her so she fell half on top of him. "Good, love."

Then her parents were on Acacia, hugging and congratulating and touching the belly.

"I'm so happy for you, Acacia." Loretta's eyes shined.

"And not for me?" Zathrian joked as his hands landed around his mate's waist from behind.

"No, you old man." Bishop chuckled.

Acacia smacked at Bishop's hand. "Don't call my mate old."

"Yes, ma'am." Bishop pulled at Loretta so they fell on the long couch opposite Maya and Hunter's tiny loveseat.

Maya still wasn't used to it, seeing her mother so lovey-dovey with a man. She wondered if the same weirdness was how her family viewed her and Hunter, since before this demon, Maya was never touchy and lovey with anyone.

But she was happy for them nonetheless. Happy they got to be together again fully.

Zathrian pulled Acacia so they took the end of the couch her parents had taken, then turned on them. "Do we owe any pleasures to this visit?"

"Just visiting friends who can't keep their yaps shut," Loretta teased.

Maya shrugged. "And just visiting the only other friends Hunt has."

"Only other?" Zathrian asked as if he were offended. "What other friends does Hunt have?"

"And I'm the asshole," he barked into her ear.

"We're friends with a wolf-banshee pair who're very similar to us. I think you'd like them too."

Zathrian chuckled. "So any couple, as long as they're mated."

"Basically." Maya giggled as Hunter grumbled into her ear again.

"And we're here to see if you have any leads on his master puppet leading this entire mess *my mate* has found herself in the middle of," Hunter concluded. "Heard anything?"

With all the custom orders that Zath picks up, he's kind of like Kai in that he learns a whole lot of shit.

He shook his head. "Sorry. I've been taking on less with the pregnancy. Now that the vomiting isn't as bad, I may continue back up, but haven't heard anything yet."

Hunter shrugged. "It's what we figured."

"Don't you have a power in that arsenal you call a body you could employ?" Zath joked. "Or are they just uselessly sitting there?"

"Acacia, dear," Hunter's voice held a teasing undertone. "That babe may end up a bastard before it's even born."

Maya elbowed him in the gut. "Behave."

Hunter's grin was wide as he pulled her closer to his side. "I'm sorry, love."

"No." She uselessly fought him. "You're not."

"No." He bit her neck. "I'm not."

Her parents laughed alongside her friends as her mother said, "Behave before your mate makes your babe a bastard before it's even created, Hunt."

"Impossible," Bishop laughed.

"Very possible." Maya elbowed her mate again and shrugged. "I got his sperm before, I could do it again."

Hunter laughed into her ear as he forced her jaw around to face him. "I'm sorry, love. Don't go procreating without me."

He kissed her before she could respond.

25

In order to keep the suspicion off of the men they wanted to speak with, they called Bianka, the mermaid's leader, and asked for a private meeting with each of their guard units. Vera made sure to make it sound like it was to find out information about whether or not they'd seen anything suspicious, like couples frolicking off, so Bianka wouldn't be too dubious.

Harry ported them to the edge of the mermaids meeting cave, then left to allow them to follow through with this avenue.

They were lead to a meeting room with a table in the center and three chairs on either side. The mermen guards were always in groups of threes, and they were there specifically to talk to two of those groups. Though getting through them all was necessary so they didn't give those two groups away. Plus, they could always actually learn more.

Left alone in the room, Maya was quick to throw up a silencing charm to make sure no eavesdropping took place. They intended on keeping secrets the same way they had before.

The first group would be one they didn't need. In case Devon or Bianka intended on prying on the questions they were asking. They would keep everything surrounding mixed couples and their safety. Around the safety of the species. Nothing more.

Walt Hembrow, Jack Skylet, and Grove Williams.

Bianka and Devon's best guards.

Their most loyal. Almost telling that they would have the same mentality as their leaders.

Vera and her sisters sat in birth rank with Maya in the middle as the three guards took their spots across the table.

"This shouldn't take up too much of your time," Maya started sweetly. "But we have some questions regarding what you know about mixed couples within the mermaids. Anything you know can keep your species safe."

She was a lot more diplomatic than Vera would've expected. Maybe Hunter had taught her that too.

The middle one, Walt, whom Vera had to guess was the ring-leader, spoke. "I can tell you we don't know a damn thing about them. If we did, they'd be in the dungeons, not running about embarrassing the whole of our species."

Jack to his right added, "It's ridiculous we're even putting this much manpower in helping them. If they want to plague themselves with another species, they don't deserve our assistance. There're plenty of beautiful men and women within our own species. Going out for another is asking for a death sentence."

Or maybe there was no ringleader and they were just a perfectly matched set.

"And you, Grove?" Maya kept her voice level.

He shrugged, almost uncaring. "I do not think their lives are forfeit, but it is a distraction. At least they should know to stay away from one another at the moment. We still have our normal guard work to do rather than making sure someone who broke species rules and tainted themselves with another is unharmed."

He was less harsh about his beliefs, but they were still exactly those of his friends. Vera figured that's how these groups were paired. Or maybe their similar ideologies were because they spent basically all their time together.

It was a good thing Maya could keep her composure because Vera could feel the annoyance steaming off of Camilla and herself. Instead, Maya gave the men a small smile. "Thank you for your time. I see that you do not know anything that could assist us."

They got up to leave without another word before Grove turned back and his eyes caught Maya's. "It is not prejudice. I do not believe all should stay apart. Witches and demons, for instance, though different species are part of the Powers."

"We are completely other," Walt added, and the resentfulness that was in his tone earlier was gone. They truly believed this.

"And humans come in handy for those like the banshees who only have females in the magical line," Jack added.

"But for most of the species," Walt finished, "interbreeding is unneeded and harmful."

As they left, Vera hated that they actually made an argument for their stance. Not anything to change her mind about, but it made sense.

The next group, one of the ones they actually needed, walked in.

Theon Forsyth, Dexter Bell, and Beckett Allaway.

They took their seats across the table, and again, Vera allowed Maya to do the speaking. "We have some questions regarding mixed couples. Ones where the answers will not be shared with your leaders or anyone of your people. Your friends before you will be telling them it is a routine questioning about knowledge of mixed couples for our aid. This room is charmed, so feel free to speak freely, as you hadn't the last time we were here."

They each sat stiffly and stared blankly at them.

"Look, we won't be telling anyone. We just need to know what species each of your partners are," Maya continued. "Because rest assured, I know each of you is in a relationship."

Dexter did an impressive job at furrowing his brows into confused irritation. "Is this some trick? We are not in mixed relationships."

Vera didn't know how they were going to convince them to talk, but Lyra's life could depend on it.

Then Maya crossed her arms before her chest and leaned back in her chair. "Brynn told me."

The guards stiffened to a point of breaking, their eyes giving away immediately that they had been caught and were, indeed, in these relationships.

"And do not go off blaming her. She did it for your safety," Maya argued for her friend. "She trusts us, and we need you to do the same so we can continue to protect couples like yours."

Beckett signed as if giving up. "Pixie."

Dexter followed quickly after. "Gargoyle."

Then Theon finally said, "Werewolf."

"No banshees?" Camilla spoke for the first time.

They each shook their head.

Vera looked to each of them in turn, then asked, "Know of anyone who is with a banshee?" It was a long shot, but worth it.

Theon slowly nodded. "My girlfriend's brother is with a banshee. Mated. I don't remember her name though. Elle, I think. Or something with an L."

Vera held her breath. "Lyra?"

His eyes shined. "Yeah, that's it." Then worry edged his tone, because as the brother's mate, this was technically his girlfriend's family they were speaking of. "Is she okay?"

"We don't know," Camilla answered softly.

"What's your girlfriend's name?" Maya asked at the same time.

Theon watched her momentarily before choosing to trust them. "Knova Alcott."

"Thank you," Maya said. "We'll check on them."

Theon looked hesitant, like he wanted to go check himself,

but knew he wouldn't be able to get out of his duties right after this meeting.

Finally, as the three guards rose to leave, Vera asked something that was wiggling in the back of her mind, "Are you her mate?"

Theon turned back to face her, his friends waiting at either side. "No. But sometimes it takes time for the bond to stick."

Vera nodded softly, but she swore that wasn't the case. Matings normally happened instantly, though giving in to them could possibly take longer. Maybe that's what he meant.

When the room was empty of anyone but them, Camilla turned. "We can't leave now. They'll know something happened with that specific group. We have to play this out with the others."

Maya shook her head. "You two play this out. I'll go check in with Knova and her brother."

Vera's heart froze.

She was going to shadow.

Camilla was going to find out about her shadowing ability.

Before Camilla could argue, Maya looked to her. "Don't hate me." Then simply shadowed out of her seat.

Camilla's widening gaze stared at the blank space for a whole minute before turning on Vera. "What. The. Fuck."

They were all very aware that shadowing was a demon specific power and exactly how Maya would have come across it.

And Camilla looked *very* angry with the knowledge.

Maybe her good streak with Hunter would be breaking after this.

Maya landed on wolf territory. Like her fire power, she couldn't imagine giving up shadowing. She'd come to love it so much. Even if most of the time she still allowed

Hunter to shadow them places, she still loved that he'd given her this power.

Hayes, the North American wolf leader, stood with his back to her as he watched a lot of his pack's children train their fighting abilities. He was tall, with blonde-brownish mussed hair and a muscular frame. Before Hunter, Maya may have even gone for him. But she couldn't even consider it now. He was too much a friend and nothing more.

"Still with the demon?" he called out to her and made Maya push out of her stance.

"Still with the demon." She moved up to stand beside him with a wide grin.

"Consensually?" he teased.

Maya smacked his shoulder as she laughed. "Shut up, asshole."

After a beat of silence watching the kids, he asked, "Does your mate know you're here?"

"What?" Her smile slipped. *Did he just call Hunter her mate?*

He was wearing a smirk as he watched the kids. "Your mate," he repeated, "does he know you're here?"

Maya didn't know what to do with that question. "I mean, he can track where I am if he wanted to, if that's what you're asking."

Hayes scoffed through his smile as he shook his head. "No." He turned to her. "Does he know you're here? Alone." His gaze bore into hers. "With me."

"Technically no." Maya didn't understand where he was going with this.

He didn't break his gaze as the edge of his lips twitched up. "I don't think he'd like it."

Maya's brows furrowed. "Why? He has nothing to worry about."

"No." Hayes took her in. "Because you're his mate, so you couldn't fathom it. And because I'd never consider touching another man's mate."

Maya's heart stopped. He couldn't be saying what she thought he was saying.

She was normally one to hold her expressions in, but she knew a bit of shock bled into her eyes as she stared up at him.

He laughed at her obviously panicked state. "Don't worry. I didn't need a ring to tell me you're his mate. I knew from the *consensual* markings." He wiggled his brows at her. "And the mating scent was on you two the day I met you."

Three things slipped through Maya's mind at that moment.

One, that Hayes knew of the demon mating rings, which was extra shocking because even most demons didn't really know of them.

Two, even though they weren't wolves, being together physically had transferred scents. So much so that a wolf could pick up the mating within their bodies. Before the official mating with the rings. It was an exhilarating new fact that she couldn't wait to tell Hunter.

And three, Hayes was coming on to her. Sort of.

And he was right. Hunter would not approve.

The memory of the demon flirting with him at the Valentine's Day ball flashed before her eyes, and the fury she'd felt then bubbled back up. If being around Hayes brought Hunter even close to that type of rage, then she probably should stay away from coming to him alone.

Because she'd experienced that wrath herself and knew he wouldn't be overreacting. His mating bond would be doing all the talking, and she understood how possessive the mating bond could be.

Then Hayes's words came back to her, *I knew from the* consensual *markings,* and she cracked a grin. She smacked him again. "You're right. He probably wouldn't want me here alone."

He looked to her with a quirked brow. "I may not yet be mated, but I can tell you definitively that he would not want you here. No probablys about it."

Maya smiled to him because he was a genuinely good guy

and she couldn't wait until he found his own mate. He deserved it. "So tell me where the Alcott family is and I'll go."

He watched her inquisitively, but didn't ask for further explanation. Instead, he trusted her with his tribe and told her the location. He really was a good guy.

She walked back and turned to watch the kids one more time. Hayes was so good with them, and Maya could already see them growing to be some powerful protectors.

She landed in the patch of land Hayes had told her about. Really, just a clearing in the tribe's bit of the forest.

And there, she saw a lone wolf. Then took a gander at which sibling this would be. "Knova?"

The wolf transformed before her, a woman a couple of inches taller than herself stopping before Maya, defensive stance at the ready. So she'd been right.

"You smell of a witch, but you move like a demon?"

Maya chose not to answer that. Telling her she'd stolen the shadowing ability probably wouldn't earn her pointers at the moment. "I'm looking for your brother."

Knova growled lightly. "So am I."

Maya's brows furrowed in concern. Not knowing where both parties in the relationship were was a bad sign. But she remained calm before the wolf, not wanting to cause any more worry without proof that her brother truly was taken by The Eight.

Maya looked around to make sure they were alone before meeting Knova's gaze head on. She knew wolves weren't secretive about their mates, but she wasn't sure if Lyra had been. "Is he with Lyra?"

Knova inhaled sharply and stared at Maya with wide eyes.

"Theon told me."

Now she was back to growling.

Maya raised both hands to show no offense as she tried to bite back her smile. She would react the same if Hunter was brought up. "I just want to make sure your brother is all right."

Knova watched her for long, quiet minutes. Then finally backed down, her shoulders slumping slightly inward. "We always went to them together. I don't know what happened. He's never gone off alone."

Maya grit her teeth. "I was afraid you'd say that."

After that, it was a little too easy to convince Knova to go home with her.

She was desperate to find her brother, and merely hearing the Whittles were ready to help had her shadowing along with Maya.

And as Knova told them anything she knew of her brother and his mate—which wasn't much—Maya tried to ignore Camilla's hateful glares in Hunter's direction.

Knight and Lyra didn't have a spot they considered theirs.

Didn't have a location they met in that Knova hadn't already checked multiple times.

It all came down to mean they would need to divide and conquer areas that didn't seem plausible, but could be where the couple was hiding. Basically, they were working blind.

arren would be working with Knova.

There was no real reason behind it other than the fact that he didn't want to be with Camilla, and both Harry and Hunter would want to be with their women. Camilla's refusal to be with Kai meant Bishop would be taking her. Since the couple had a baby, Tamire and Lila stayed behind with Loretta to watch over the house.

Warren shadowed them to a cul-de-sac he'd heard multiple demons speak of. When they repeatedly got no results from the alcoves Knova knew of, Warren had chosen this spot.

Specifically for the privacy of it.

The cul-de-sac looked like normal homes of the happy American family, but instead were known as areas couples—or groups—who wished to be alone for private matters could spend their time. From what Warren had understood, it was usually a demon with another species.

Cumminghome Lane.

Appropriate.

After knocking on the third door and not finding them, Knova finally broke their silence. "So tell me about you and Camilla."

Warren looked to her with knitted brows.

She chuckled. "You two have tension. And not the good kind, like your brother and his mate. What happened?"

Warren didn't answer as they walked up to the fourth house and knocked, a demon woman immediately opening it. Behind her, Warren could see a human and another demon. She looked them both over, then smiled wicked and wide. "Would you like to join? I've never had a wolf before. Want to show me a good time?"

Knova smiled at the demon, but her gaze didn't fully reach. "Sorry, wrong house."

"Shame," the demon woman responded. "If you don't find the right one, please, come back."

Warren tried to stifle the light chuckle that escaped him as Knova kept her eyes down as they walked back to the sidewalk and over to the next house. Then, finally, he answered her, "She couldn't handle it."

Knova didn't understand correctly. "Oh, I'm sure she would've handled me a little too well."

Warren smirked down at her. "Without a doubt." When Kova finally looked back up at him, he explained, "Camilla. She couldn't handle it. When we got together, she didn't know she was a witch and I was half demon. When she found out, and after she was done being angry with me for not telling her, we tried. I could see it bothered her, but I tried. Tried to be more human and push my demon side down so we could get past it, but in the end, she couldn't get past it. She kept expecting the worst from me, and honestly, I was tired of pretending I was more human than I am."

Knova sighed and looked to the house they'd paused before. "Not as understanding as her sister?"

Warren watched her. She was beautiful and Theon was a lucky man, but the part of him that had known from the beginning that Camilla wasn't his mate knew Knova wasn't either.

That same part knew Theon wasn't her mate either. He could already imagine the pain when they finally ended it.

When she turned to him, Warren looked to the skies. "Maya's not understanding. That would mean she sees the problem and makes sense of it. She doesn't do that. She just accepts him. She never took any aspect of Hunter and tried to *understand* him. She just saw it as who he was and fell harder for him for it."

Knova looked to him softly, like she could see the pain and envy in his eyes. But she didn't voice it.

Maybe she understood it. Her brother was mated and she wasn't. They were in the same predicament.

His pocket vibrated and ended their moment. A text from Camilla into the group chat he'd been made a part of. *Another pixie found dead. Guessing it's Grandmama's work since she was alone.*

Knova looked down at his phone, then knocked his shoulder. "C'mon. Let's finish these houses so we can get outta here."

Warren smiled thankfully at her and walked up to the fifth house.

***

Hunter allowed Maya to shadow them so she could get her practice in. Plus, he loved seeing that wide smile when she did it.

They were in a patch of land Felix had told him about one time when they were discussing some of the illustrious places they'd had sex with their mates. The illustrious part of this one was seen only in the fall when the weather turned this patch of land 'magical.'

He expected, given it was just turning spring, to land in a lush spot of greens and slowly blooming flowers. Instead, Hunter picked up the scent of blood immediately and narrowed his gaze.

He slowly led Maya out of the patch and after a few minutes, found his way into another one. This field was nowhere near as nice as the last as he stared out at the six bodies.

A pixie, a faerie, and a banshee. Two dead. But there was their missing banshee, alive and possibly fine.

Three wolves, two dead and one obviously weakened but in a defensive position anyway. A simple breath through his scenting powers told Hunter the wolf was mated to the banshee he was protecting.

And though they were not there to harm them, Hunter immediately pushed Maya behind him. One mated male against another. And Hunter's powers, both natural and stolen, gave him a widely unfair advantage.

Flames instinctually licked up his arms as the wolf growled at them. Hunter had a family to protect and even the slightest threat wouldn't go unpunished.

Maya's hand on his forearm soothed him down, but he didn't take his eyes off the threat across the clearing.

"Knight?" Maya's beautiful voice calmed him just the slightest bit more. "Lyra?"

The wolf growled, but instead of pushing forward, he pulled his mate farther away from them. Smart man. He would know that any strike would lead him burned and his mate unprotected. He wouldn't risk it the same way Hunter would never risk leaving Maya in harm's way. And wolf boy's scenting was stronger than Hunter's power. He'd know there was a mating bond between the two of them even without knowing that demons could mate.

Hunter tried to fight her, but Maya persisted as she pushed past him and stood between the two of them. And though her back pressed to his front, every instinct in him was screaming to push her back. To get her out of the way. To shield her.

"We're not going to hurt you." She ignored Hunter's low growl behind her that indicated he didn't like her new positioning and kept her eyes on the couple before them. "We're a mated mixed pair too. We just want to take you back to your sister, Knight."

It was Lyra's hand on his arm that finally broke the wolf, the same way Maya's touch had relaxed Hunter.

Knight backed down—barely—but it seemed to be enough for Maya as she turned to the carnage around them. "What happened here?"

And though Hunter knew they wouldn't attack, that Knight wouldn't try anything, especially hurt as he was, he kept a cold stare on the man.

Then Knight finally backed all the way down, like hearing the question broke him a little. His mate helped him to the tree where he leaned back, his breaths coming in harsher now.

"It's a long story," Lyra said, though she turned her back on them as she placed her full attention on the wolf. "Knight was hurt helping them."

Maya stepped up, but stopped when Hunter's hand forced her. She made a blatant turn so he could see her roll her eyes, then turned back to the couple. "I have four warlocks at home who could heal him. And a wolf-banshee couple who could take you to a little safehouse for mixed couples. If you'd like."

Knight groaned. "We don't need your help."

Lyra ignored him and turned warm eyes on them, the look so similar to the pain Maya had worn when she'd cared for him after he'd been 'taken' by The Eight. "Thank you."

Hunter rolled his eyes and dropped his lips to the back of Maya's head. "Or I could take *you* home, my witch. And maybe you could take care of me."

Maya elbowed him in the ribs as she pulled him by the hand to the couple by the tree. "I'll send someone after to care for these four."

Lyra gave another thankful smile as Hunter shadowed them away.

Hunter shadowed them into her office so that she could text her family they were coming. Maya thought it would be easier on their new couple to meet everyone at once rather than having Knight jump into a growl every time someone showed up.

Then she texted Juliette. If these couples wanted to go to this house that Felix and Juliette had running, Maya wanted them there and ready.

Maya could see the tension rolling off the both of them. Off Knight, it was the need to keep his mate safe. But from Lyra, it was fear. Fear that Knight was harmed and there was nothing she could really do about it but wait until the warlocks got to him.

As she watched them, Maya wondered what their plan would've been had she and Hunter not shown up. They don't have the ability to transport like demons and warlocks, and Knight's speed would be impeded by his injury, not to mention having to carry Lyra on his back. Because there was not an ounce inside Maya that believed he would leave her behind.

When the thumbs up text came in telling her they were all in the living room, Maya led the couple, Lyra attempting to support her mate's weight, to the front of the house. When they paused before a dozen people, the tension mixing through the air around Knight was palpable. Then his gaze met his sister's, and a part of him relaxed. He was obviously nervous about this situation, but Knova's presence and Lyra's constant tugging to get him to a couch finally broke him into movement.

He fell into it, a sigh he tried to hide falling from his lips. Lyra took one side and Knova rushed to the other. Maya hadn't realized that Theon was there too, following behind his girlfriend.

Hunter's arms wrapped around her waist as she said, "You don't know any of them, so it really is a names game. Harry, Bishop, Tamire, or Kai?"

He looked to her with a quirked brow.

Maya smirked. "Guess he doesn't care."

Harry was the first to move, crouching before the wolf and letting the warmth of his hands hover over the man's chest. He would be able to detect all the wounds in that position and heal them. It just normally went faster if he was hovering directly over the wound. Lyra had her arms wrapped loosely around Knight's shoulders as she pulled him to rest across the couch, his head landing in her lap.

As Maya watched Harry heal Knight in the quiet of the room, Hunter pulled her back so he was leaning against the wall and she fell into him.

He drooped his face into her hair, lips pressing lightly into her neck, and his eyes closed as he breathed her in. Maya imagined he had some relaxing of the heart to do himself. She may not have been hurt, but the mere threat, light as it was, was probably pushing him to take her back to their manor and never let her out.

She kissed his temple and turned back to those around her.

Lyra was watching her with what seemed like envy. Though not in a malicious way. More like she wanted their openness. And if she told the banshees, she'd have it. With the possibility of full acceptance since this was the outcome of a wolf's mating bond—something that could not be helped.

When Harry finally turned away, Loretta stepped up with a cup of tea, which Maya assumed had some healing and drowsiness remedies within it. It would be required since there was no way Knight would voluntarily fall unconscious and allow his body to rest with Lyra in a house of strangers. He wasn't altogether wrong to be on edge, but his body needed the rest.

Knova stood at the end of the couch as her brother fell asleep, the rolls of tension falling off of her, no doubt in relief that he hadn't been taken by The Eight.

And as the room settled, Maya turned in Hunter's arms to

face him, his head picking up to look her in the eyes. "Love," he whispered.

"You okay?" she whispered back, her hands resting on his chest and feeling his heartbeats come in evenly.

His hands pulled her closer around the waist, creating their own little bubble away from the rest of the room. "You're safe and in my arms. That's all I care about."

His breath mixed with hers as their foreheads touched, and Maya smiled against his lips. "It's all I care about too."

He scoffed jokingly. "Liar."

She gave an airy laugh against those inviting lips. "Okay, so I also care about my family, and the friends we've made, and making sure all these creatures are safe from those maniacs." He bit her lip through a smile. "But most of all, I care about this. Us."

Their lips pressed together for long moments. "Good."

It wasn't too long after that, maybe an hour, before the door-bell rang. Knight was up from his rest, a short one that Lyra didn't look too happy about, and froze at the disturbance. But Maya paid it no mind as she opened the door and allowed her friends into the house.

As they turned into the living room and Maya moved back into Hunter's arms, she saw Lyra's eyes bulge out. Maya wasn't entirely sure if it was recognition or surprise.

Lyra's body moved on instinct to protect her weakened lover, and Maya found it adorable. Because that's exactly what she would've done. Hunter bit the side of her neck, likely thinking the same thing.

Maya made introductions. "This is Felix and Juliette, the couple I told you guys about."

Lyra looked them over a moment before her eyes landed on Juliette's amused one. "That's your wolf?"

Juliette finally gave in to her laugh as Felix's hands tightened around her waist. "Yes." Her hands settled on Felix's like she were trying to calm him.

Maya shook her head as Hunter bit her again. Mates, how overbearing.

"And that's yours," Juliette finished.

Lyra gave an unsteady nod as she sat beside Knight, her body still lightly covering his, and his annoyance seeping visibly higher and higher. Lyra then turned to Knova. "And that's his sister and her merman."

Juliette looked them over silently. There was no question they'd be accepted to the house. "Maya said you might be interested in coming to the safehouse? We have a dozen couples there right now, including ourselves, and a few friends. Everyone does their own things, but Felix has also been training everyone to fight. You're welcome to join, then maybe your wolf can also help in the trainings."

Juliette had mentioned the trainings to Maya before. Felix would do as much as he could, then go to Hayes for help because wolves were never cast out. So Hayes was always an ally to them. And Hayes was a good guy. A great guy.

Lyra watched them for a long minute. The decision was ultimately hers, since Knight didn't exactly have anything to hide and the sneaking around was for her sake. Then her gaze moved and settled on Maya and Hunter still huddled by the wall.

Maya was about to ask if she had any concerns when Lyra looked back to Juliette and answered, "Maybe. But I want to tell my family first. Knight doesn't need to hide us, and I don't want to anymore."

Juliette gave a warm, knowing nod. She'd understand that better than any of the rest of them in that room. She was also a banshee who had been afraid to tell her family. And for all the right reasons. She'd been cast out without a second's thought.

Knight turned Lyra around to face him, his hands cradling her face as she hovered over him. "You sure about this, baby?" When she nodded, he breathed into her. "I love you, Ly."

She kissed him. "I love you more, baby."

He scoffed as he pulled her in for another chaste kiss before she moved away with a light blush. It was obvious he wanted so much more. She likely did too. But they had an audience.

Lyra fell into Knight's side as Juliette looked to Knova and Theon. "And you two?"

Theon was more quiet, and he blushed when the attention of the entire room fell on him as he answered, "I agree. I want to tell my species. To not have to fear getting caught by the mermaids."

Juliette looked happy with the decisions, like it was what she was hoping for. And Maya could understand that. There was nothing like facing the fear and telling the world you were in love.

"I hope it goes well for you. I really do. But if it doesn't, the safehouse is always open to you. We could always send Cora or Rory, our resident witches, to get you," Juliette closed their conversation.

27

*L*yra had insisted on going to her family as soon as Knight was up for it.

And Knight had insisted immediately that he was up for it.

The short argument between the two was eventually won by Knight and Maya was calling the banshees to tell them Lyra had been found.

Then it was time for Hunter to shadow them to a patch of woods in front of an expansive house to meet the family. Maya truly couldn't imagine a life without shadowing or porting. Having to move the distances all on foot or by vehicle would take incredibly longer. She couldn't fathom it any longer.

The second they landed, Lyra's family rushed to her, pulling her into tight embraces. The sight gave Maya the dangerous hope that they would approve of their daughter's relationship.

Especially since it was to a wolf.

After long moments of their reunion and Knight attempting quite thoroughly to settle his jittery need to be holding Lyra again, Lyra pulled away from her family and moved back to them. They watched her inquisitively, but didn't disrupt.

"I have something to tell you guys," she said as she stepped beside Knight. "Something important."

The way her family watched her felt like a huge puzzle they were trying to solve, but they were ignoring the most obvious parts. Because the way Lyra and Knight stood together, their hands grazing, was already giving them away by itself.

But it wasn't until Lyra took his hand that things began to click together. "This is Knight." She looked up to him as she said the next part. "My mate."

Knight's returning grin was gut-wrenching and hopeful.

But things wouldn't be so positive. Maya almost berated herself in having the same hope. In trusting that they would at least accept, even if they don't want to, because she's with a wolf. It was a first step for mixed couples.

But no. Because a simple glance in Lyra's family's direction showed just how upset they were with the revelation. After a moment's silence, the air filled with multiple voices. "We will have no association with a mixed couple," and "No child of ours will be with a wolf," and "An animal," and "Lyra, do not taint yourself so," and many more that Maya couldn't make out.

Lyra looked heartbroken as she clutched onto Knight's hand.

Maya was the one to step up, Lyra obviously too overwhelmed at the moment to do so. "You were so worried. She's here, and she's safe because of him."

They quieted down as an older woman Maya knew as Lyra's aunt sneered in her direction. "Of course you would stick up." She glanced behind Maya, then looked back to her. "Your relationship is even worse. A demon. A Delvaux demon, no less. *You're* disgusting."

Uh oh.

Hunter shadowed behind one of Lyra's cousins, the aunt's baby, and placed a hand to either side of her head like he were ready to snap. The screams quieted down quickly as Hunter's eyes narrowed on the aunt. "Oh, please, continue. Continue that speech, and you can say goodbye to two girls tonight."

There was raw hatred mixed with fear in the aunt's eyes as she looked between her child and Hunter's unforgiving stare.

Hunter lips made that cruel smirk that sent Maya's thighs pressing together. Completely inappropriate, but when were her bits in the right state of mind?

"Apologize." Hunter smiled.

When no one moved, Lyra's aunt especially, Hunter's hands dropped. Like giving them the hope that the girl was safe, then pulling it right out from under them as a single hand grabbed for the girl's neck before she could run off. His shoulder burst into flames that were slowly moving down.

Shaking, the banshee in his arms cried out, but Hunter was unperturbed. "Apologize."

The aunt turned to Maya and spit, "I'm sorry."

Tsk tsk. Hunter would not be happy with that.

The flames came closer to the girl's neck. He leaned into her ear and stage whispered, "That didn't sound very sincere. I don't think mommy dearest favors you very much, does she?" His gaze grew colder as he met the aunt's eyes again, but no matter. They were Maya's favorite black orbs. "You better hurry, fire can be an ugly way to go."

The girl in his clutches tried kicking out, the tears snotting up her face, but it was no use. Hunter's strength could over-power her without trying.

The aunt screamed, and when she tried to move toward her daughter, Hunter's flames moved faster. She paused so quickly, it was almost like watching her get petrified.

Then she turned to Maya and dropped to her knees and apologized in so many different variations, Maya was sure she'd made some new ones up in her desperation to get her daughter out of harm's way.

"Good job." Hunter dropped the girl and lazily walked to Maya as mother and daughter reunited. Hunter stopped beside her and turned to them. "You can say all you'd like about me, but another word about her and I'll rip your daughter's heart out and hand it to you. Understood?"

The aunt gave a shaky nod as she pulled her daughter closer.

Maya turned to Knight and Lyra before she could see the family's responses. "What do you want to do?"

Lyra turned heartbroken eyes on her. "We'll join Juliette and Felix."

Maya gave her a small, encouraging smile and reached a hand out. Hunter wrapped his arm around her waist and shadowed them out, the banshees silent behind them in the fears that Hunter could still retaliate.

Vera didn't release Harry's hand as they landed in the cave the mermaids used for meetings with the aboveground species. She'd called Devon and Bianka and insisted they had something important to discuss.

And now that they were there with Knova and Theon, she and Harry would be taking the backseats and waiting to see how things played out.

When the two leaders walked into the meeting room, their gazes landed instantly on Theon and narrowed.

"What are you doing out here, Theon?" Devon asked suspiciously.

Theon took a deep breath, the anxiety rolling off of him in waves as he faced the only people who had ever taken care of him. Most of the men put out as guards were orphans with no one else in their lives but their guard brothers and their leaders.

Then Theon took Knova's hand. "They brought us here so I could tell you about Knova. My..." he struggled to finish the sentence, "...girlfriend."

The blank stares that followed caused a blush to deepen on the man's cheeks. He likely wasn't used to so much attention as a guard.

Then the stares turned to scrutiny as they assessed Knova then moved back to Theon. "Truly, Theon?" Devon asked. "You too? How could you?"

How could you? Like he was killing off magical creatures and not just a man in love.

"I didn't choose this, sir." He barely met their stares. "It happened."

"Well then, choose now." Bianka's stance didn't waver as she stared at the man before them.

Vera's breath hitched, and she looked to Knova to find the pain and fear in her eyes. One look in the girl's eyes earlier had shown Vera the same thing she'd felt before finding this family —loneliness and fear. She was a firecracker of a wolf, no doubt, but she would be too nervous to stand up now.

"I love my species," he argued. "My loyalty to keeping them safe remains."

"So it shouldn't be a difficult decision," Devon responded.

There was a desperation in his eyes as Theon looked between Knova and his leaders before he squared his shoulders and...

And released Knova's hand.

He stepped up to his leaders. "My people will always come first."

Devon and Bianka smiled warmly at him, but all Vera could pay attention to was the heart-wrenching pain that filled every inch of Knova's features.

Theon turned to her, but didn't move forward. He looked pained as he met her gaze. "I'm sorry, Knova. But I'm not your mate. This will be a good thing for you too."

Devon's arm opened for the guard as he said, "Do not worry about the indiscretion. Everyone has their missteps. We will not make it known. In fact, your loyalty was tested to the highest degree, Son."

There was pain in Theon's eyes as he moved away from Knova, but Vera also saw the pride he felt from Devon's praise.

Then the three were gone.

And Knova was still standing frozen in the middle of the cave.

Vera moved slowly over to her, a hand landing on her shoulder. "I'm so sorry, Knova."

But the wolf didn't move. The tears filled her eyes, but not a single one dropped.

Then eventually, she turned and said so softly, Vera almost didn't hear it, "Can we just go?"

Vera didn't have to turn to Harry. He walked right up to them and ported them back to the house, leaving Knova in the back family room to cuddle up alone as they moved to the front of the house to let the family in on what had happened. Her mother and father would care for the girl.

They were in Harry's room—their room now—and Vera fell onto the edge of the bed, shoulders slumped as her mind raced back to Theon releasing Knova's hand.

"Vera," Harry spoke softly as he sat beside her, his hand taking hers and rubbing soft circles.

"I know they're not mates." She stared off into nothing. "But for him to just walk away as if she didn't mean anything to him, as if he weren't breaking her heart."

"I cannot pretend I know the pain she is going through," Harry worded carefully, "but it's a good thing it happened. Not only because they're not mates, so eventually she would've found someone else anyway, but because if he found it so easy to walk away from her now, he would've done it later too. Better to go through the pain now than waste her time on him and still go through it later."

"You're right." She finally turned to look him in the eyes, and the hazel honesty staring back moved her. "But all I can think of is what if you did that to me? I can't..." She couldn't finish the sentence, the thought.

He took her face softly in his hands. "Don't think that,

because it won't happen. I will choose you, Vera. Above all else, above your family even. I won't ever leave you like that."

"Promise?" Vera asked quietly, the memory of her lonely upbringing with only her father washing over her.

The even worse memory of that time after he'd 'passed' and before she'd found her sisters. It'd been so lonely.

"I lay an oath to you, Vera. I will be by your side, choose you first. For eternity." His gaze didn't break from hers, like he needed her to see how sincere he was being.

Then he kissed her softly and thoroughly. Passionately.

And they were falling on their sides, the kiss not breaking for even a second. "I love you, Harry," she whispered into his mouth and felt him freeze against her.

Then froze herself.

Fuck. She hadn't just said that.

Her eyes widened and she began to pull back, but couldn't get far as he held her still. He swallowed and watched her like he was memorizing this moment. "Good. That's good." His lips tipped up as his eyes shined, and Vera felt her heart running at a gallop. "Because I'm so far in love with you, Vera Whittle, I cannot imagine a life at my immortal age any longer."

She gasped, and now her eyes were widening for an entirely different purpose. "You've started aging again?"

He stroked her cheek with his thumb as he nodded. "I started the night I kissed you out in the yard. Before I kissed you. I knew that even if you rejected me, it was my time. I didn't want to keep going on without you in this world, didn't want to remain young while you aged without me."

Vera couldn't believe what she was hearing.

Sure, she'd thought about it—more than she cared to admit —but she thought she'd have to bring it up to him. That he might be hesitant about letting go of the body he'd had for a hundred years.

But no.

He'd done it all on his own.

For her.

She kissed him again, with all the passion and desire she could muster. He pulled her in close as he groaned into the kiss.

Fuck, she loved this man.

253

28

Knight, Lyra, and Knova would be picked up as soon as Cora or Rory could muster. Until then, they were staying at Whittle House. But Maya couldn't worry about that because she had a mate to deal with.

"What the fuck did I just hear from your father?" She wrapped the blanket around her shoulders as she stood before him.

He looked down at her with narrowed slits. "I don't think I enjoy your little relationship with my father."

"I don't give a fuck what you enjoy." She was well past annoyed, and for the first time in their relationship, she was thinking about sending him to sleep on the couch. "We agreed that you wouldn't be so reckless anymore."

"What is my father doing coming to you with anything?" He circled back.

"I asked him how the trip went," she bit out. "I thought I'd hear the same old 'fine' or 'annoying' or 'bit of work, but we got through it.' But no! You know what he told me? That you guys had quite the time dealing with the *halfies*!"

He clenched his jaw. "I'm going to kill him."

Her brows rose indignantly. "You plan on never telling me, asshole?"

"Watch your tone, Maya." He sat at the chair by the fire. "I told you the trip went fine. I never lied to you."

"You're right." Lords, she wanted to kill him herself. "You didn't lie, just forgot to mention that you tried getting yourself caught again so that you and your father could finish off the halfies on your own."

"Don't you think you should be happier about hearing that?" His voice grew as he flew out of his seat. "Shouldn't it sound romantic to you that I keep risking my life to make sure you're out of this mess sooner? So that you don't have this stress hovering over you?"

"Romantic? Ro-fucking-mantic?" she yelled back. Really yelled. "You think it's romantic that you went off on the same little mission that we fought about before? All I'm thankful for is that the halfies grew some fucking brains and didn't fall for it. It wasn't fucking romantic. It was a death wish. Even if you two could get out of it, they could've gotten you and killed you immediately, no games. Don't you think that would've caused me some *stress*?"

"I don't care whether you like it or not, Maya," he spit out. "I'm going to continue playing with them until I kill them off. Because I'm not going to sit around and allow a threat to constantly hover over you. I *will* protect my family."

"And you don't care how that makes me feel?" She should feel the urge to cry, but she didn't. She just wanted to smack some sense into him. "Maybe I should play the same game, see which one of us prevails. Maybe I can lure the halfies out and kill them off so you can stop."

His entire body froze and his lip sneered up. "I will chain you to this bed before you even consider doing something like that."

"Tell your mating bond to kiss my fucking ass, Hunter." Her voice was slowly rising again. "If this is what it means, that you're going to throw yourself onto Death's doorstep and think you can control my actions, I don't want it."

The black of his eyes grew darker than she'd ever seen them as he stalked right up to her, but she didn't care because she felt the flames rising in her. "I don't give a fuck what you want right now. You're mine, and I will protect you. Hate me all you want for it, but do not attempt baiting me. I will cast you to this manor and not allow you out in order to protect you." He moved to the wall with such speed, Maya could barely see it through the fury in her. Then he hit the wall, and his words came back to her.

I will cast you to this manor and not allow you out in order to protect you.

He would never do such a thing, but the threat alone sent Maya's rage to such new heights, she swore she felt the ground rumbling beneath her. And it was only on hindsight that she realized the panicked look that overtook the angry blacks in Hunter's eyes when he snapped his head to her was a warning. Not to stop the argument, but that something else was happening.

Because seconds after she felt the ground rumble, she felt the same sensation of pulling that had happened when Warren had sent them to Hell's Gate.

Except this time, she was the one doing the sending. And she didn't even know how.

Hunter tried moving to her, like he wanted to get to her before they could fall through, but didn't make it before they were falling into the portal.

And though they weren't touching, they landed in the same cage.

Except unlike last time when Maya had fallen on top of Hunter, she took the brunt of her fall entirely. She'd been right all those months ago—Hunter's fall had definitely been worse.

Hunter somehow only took a couple of seconds to catch his breath before he was crawling frantically to her. "Love? Love, are you all right?" His hands traveled her body, his thumb rubbed her stomach as his worried black orbs stared down at her.

Maya breathed in again, then pushed up, allowing the blanket to fall off her shoulders as she pushed him away. "Fine."

He growled as he strained his neck, fingers turning white. "We just got pulled into Hell's Gate and you want to continue this ludicrous argument? Really, Maya?"

She ignored him. "Why does it feel different than last time?" She didn't know how to explain it, but the same fear that trickled into her the last time they were down there didn't muster. And it wasn't because of familiarity. She just didn't know what it was.

He was obviously still annoyed with her, but he answered, "You have control now. I doubt this'll be like last time at all. I doubt we'll even have anything happen to us, unless you want to see me in pain again, of course. But you should be fine." The 'hopefully' wasn't said, but Maya heard it.

She turned dark eyes on him. "I hate you, Hunter, but..."

"Good." His dark gaze met hers, unnerved.

She clenched her teeth and breathed the frustration through her nose as she said, "But I'm not putting you through any pain. If what you're *guessing* is true, we'll be fine. Hopefully, I can just figure out how to get us out of here."

"Or we could stay." He leaned into the pillar. "At least this way I'll know you're safe from The Eight. Or my sister."

"Why can't you understand that you can't put yourself in dangerous situations anymore? That you have me to worry about now too?" she fought him.

"Why can't you understand I'm doing this for you? Because I need to keep you safe?" he growled.

She finally felt the tears prick at her waterline as her energy gave out, and she just stared at him from the middle of the cage. "Because the same desire you have to keep me safe, I have. I want to lock you up until all harm has subsided too, Hunter.

The thought that anything could threaten you kills me, and yet, I trust that we're in all this together and that we'll figure it out *together*. I understand it's harder for you, that you're not used to *feelings*, so you want to control everything, but that's not how caring works, Hunt. You going over my head and putting yourself in harm's way...it kills me, Hunter. I genuinely don't think you can understand the fear that spikes through me knowing what could have been."

K nova kept mostly silent, speaking with her brother to make sure he didn't worry too much about her, but keeping to herself otherwise.

Camilla didn't blame her. She still had some recovering to do.

While they'd been away the night before dealing with the banshees and mermaids, her parents had gone to the clearing with Tamire and Kai and dealt with the other species and their dead, promising an explanation from Knight once they had one. Camilla had been glad to not be included in the plans, using the time to head to the astronomy tower at school and stare up at the skies.

Seeing Warren had been much easier, and she was beginning to feel a sense of peace at being alone, something that had never happened to her. She'd always worried too much about boys, always wanted someone too much that she'd never focused on her mind and what it needed. Lying under the skies, she'd felt content.

And that morning, they would be getting the explanation from Knight and Lyra before they moved on to the safehouse.

"Jhon and Lhake had come to me with news saying they'd met someone that could take them away with their partners. It's why I was so cautious when Maya said the same thing in the clearing," Knight opened as they sat around the table in the kitchen. "Though mentioning Knova was different, that she'd known personal information like that."

"Plus, he was hurt, so I didn't really care," Lyra interrupted. "I just needed him healed."

Knight rolled his eyes, though he smiled down at her. "I told them that it wasn't the best time to be trusting strangers, especially if they smelled like halfies. But they were adamant they had to protect their mates. I told them not to do it, but they were going to whether I joined or not, so I followed to make sure they were safe."

"I felt death coming near Knight," Lyra started her side. "That's why I left Ayla and Iris. I couldn't tell who it would be, but just the slightest inclination that it could be Knight getting hurt had me running to him."

"Which we're still fighting about," Knight threw in under his breath.

Camilla smiled at the way Lyra threw her mate a death glare. "I found him hiding from the others right before those halfies attacked."

Knight was staring off into space as he picked up, "It was just as I'd expected. They didn't even need to capture anyone. Jhon and Lhake were so blinded, they walked right into the trap. They immobilized Jhon and Lhake first, so they weren't hurt, like they wanted to play with them rather than quick deaths. So I attacked to keep the boys and their mates safe." He looked down to his hands, and Camilla felt a crack prickle into her heart for the pain he was re-experiencing. "When they realized there was another one of us, and I was too quick since I didn't have a mate to worry about—or so I thought—they panicked."

"Then I came out screaming because, well, because that was my mate in the middle of a fight with Powers," Lyra said.

"And my concentration broke because now I had the fear of Lyra's safety to worry about. That's why they got the two couples. They were quick deaths, but then they were on us."

Lyra wrapped a hand around his arm. "It was my fault they're dead."

"No," he growled. "It's their fault. I told them not to go." Knight sighed. "When they realized I wasn't going down, even hurt I would fight until I tore them apart, they threw out some portal and got out of there."

Bishop shook his head. "So now they're luring couples out? We need to find them, kill every single one. That's the only way to end this."

Camilla stared at her father for long moments, then looked out about the room that held everyone but her sister and the Delvauxs.

Well, just the Delvauxs if Maya being a Delvaux now was true.

Her father was right, they needed to rip these halfies apart. And coming from Camilla, that meant something because she was always worried about protecting everyone.

But she couldn't be blind anymore. These halfies had caused so much harm, they needed to be taken care of.

29

Camilla was the type of weird who would wake up Monday mornings happy that it was a Monday morning. And every time people would call her crazy for it, she'd smile and go on her merry day. Maya had always been like that too, though their mother hadn't. They always assumed it'd come from their father.

Waking up that morning to find Bishop already in the kitchen with a bright big smile, Camilla knew it was the case.

Her literature class with Professor Jenkins had all of three people in it so far. She was half an hour early, so Camilla just moved to her spot and got settled in. She was so thankful to still be in school. It was the one thing still grounding her to her life before everything happened.

Warren walked in about ten minutes later and surprisingly walked right up to her, pointing to the seat to her left. "Is this seat taken?"

Camilla sat up straight. He hadn't initiated contact between the two of them since they'd broken up for good.

He gave her a small close-lipped smile. "I wanted to talk to you about the reading for this class. Did you get through it?" She nodded, her eyes narrowing at the turn of conversation, but she didn't have time to question him as he continued, "Good. Because reading them got me to thinking about The Eight and their boss. They're both about a power claim, and we already figured that had something to do with it, but what if the reason this boss is so okay with allowing the halfies to kill the couples is because before they do it, he gets the magic out of them? Because even the lowest of creatures have magic in them."

"So it's not about breaking up mixed couples. He just allows the halfies to have their fun so he can get what he wants?" Camilla thought it through. "That would make sense. I think I saw an aura taken from their bodies when I was going through the memories of that one couple. But Hunter didn't mention anything like that."

He shrugged. "I remembered a demon storybook I'd read as a child. When so much power is taken in order to have complete dominance, a.k.a. rule the world, have everyone bow down kind of crap, you need to be strong enough to hold it all down. I think that's what's holding this boss guy back. He's allowing the halfies, and maybe even Grandmama, to do their killings because until he can find a vessel strong enough to hold it all, he can just collect all the magic."

"But where would he be holding it until then?" Camilla asked.

Warren shrugged nonchalantly. "It wouldn't be difficult to hold powers in small vessels, like little bottles like the ones used for potions and serums. It's putting them all together that would require something strong enough."

Just then Professor Jenkins walked into class and began setting up at the front of the hall.

"What would count as something strong enough?" Camilla turned her whisper back to the halfie beside her.

"I don't know. I figured a strong witch or demon. Since we have the Powers, we're already more capable of holding magic than any of the other species. But even the strongest of us, I don't know what exactly would classify it as enough."

The professor called to everyone's attention as class was a couple of minutes from beginning, and Warren moved to rise for his seat by one of his roommates a couple of rows up.

She stopped him before he could get away. "Why come to me?"

He shrugged. "I don't hate you, Cam. I want to be civil, friendly. Plus, I thought of it last night, and my father is away with business and I can't find Hunter anywhere, though I know he's not on business, so I'm assuming he and Maya are preoccupied."

Camilla held in her laugh and caught the knowing glint in Warren's eyes, then gave him a warm smile. "Thank you. I'd like to be friends."

He smiled back, then looked past her shoulder and winked. "Have fun."

Camilla's brows furrowed and she turned just as Warren left for his new seat. Walking right up to her was Kai.

Fuck, sometimes she wished she knew his full name so she could use it against him. There was something about a reprimand that came with a full name that hit differently.

"What the hell are you doing here?" she seethed as he took the empty seat to her right.

"I'm long overdue for a literature course." His smirk told her he knew just how annoyed she was, but he'd turned his eyes forward before she could say more.

Then Professor Jenkins was speaking.

And surprisingly, Kai left her alone the entire class, and for the first time in months, she could focus like before she found out about the supernatural world.

Kai didn't even disturb her when class finished and she was on her way out. It was one of the best classes she'd had in a *long* time.

"Ms. Whittle," Professor Jenkins called to her before she could make it too far past his podium up front.

She turned for him, the same handsome glint in his eyes as the last time they'd spoken just the two of them. "Professor?"

"I was wondering if you would like to grab a cup of coffee? My teaching hours are complete for the day."

Camilla was about to respond—with a very excited yes—when Kai's arm landed on her shoulders. "You getting us one-on-one time with the professor, babe? I would say that's cheating the rest of the class, but they could always meet the professor after hours too, so it's really not."

Camilla wanted to smack him, but stopped herself from doing so in front of her professor. Kai had already placed his claim on her, and as much as she wanted to smack him for it, she didn't see it very worth it.

Especially since she knew he was doing it on purpose. That he saw the blush that graced her cheeks when Jenkins gave her attention and he wanted to ruin it.

And the other part of her knew he was doing it for her protection, no matter how much he didn't like her. He had joined their hunt for the protection of magical creatures *and* her family. So he would lay a claim to protect her if he thought something dangerous, and to be fair, if Jenkins weren't so attractive, it wouldn't be an appropriate situation. He'd basically asked her out.

But the blush was still every present as Camilla looked from Kai to Jenkins and back again. "No, *babe.*" She hoped he heard her annoyance in the way she emphasized the endearment. "The professor and I are just very interested in magical literature outside of this class. It's just nice to have someone to talk to about such interests."

He pinched her nose, and the sparkle in his hazel eyes told Camilla how much he knew this was bothering her. "Why don't we go home, and you can tell me all about it while I have some dessert?" He wiggled his eyebrows.

She gasped as Jenkins coughed uncomfortably.

She grit her teeth as her elbow bit into his gut, and she gave him her best death glare. She wore the most apologetic look she could muster and turned to her professor. "I'm sorry, Professor. Maybe next time."

"Yes, yes." He looked between her and Kai as he shouldered his bag. "I'll see you next class, Ms. Whittle."

Her close-lipped smile was barely contained until he left the lecture hall, and finally, they were alone. Her elbow flew into Kai's gut even harder, and she pushed his arm off her shoulder instantly. "What the hell is wrong with you?"

"He's too old for you."

"He's my professor. We were going to talk about lit."

He was completely unconvinced. "Please."

"Look," she said frustrated, "it doesn't matter what we were going to talk about, what the hell was that?"

"Just sticking by your side," his smirk didn't hide the annoyance in his own eyes as he mocked, "*Ms. Whittle.*"

"You could stay by my side and not insinuate, *to my professor,* that you're going to go down on me when we get home."

He smirked down at her with a wicked shimmer in his eyes. "You're right. Next time, I'll make sure he knows I'd enjoy my dessert anywhere, not just at home."

She gasped, but he was already walking away. She grumbled and followed after him, her next reprimand on the tip of her tongue.

H unter finally stopped.
    Truly stopped.
And listened.

And Maya didn't know which part of what she'd said clicked for him, but he looked at her like he was finally understanding.

He walked up to her and took her face in his hands. "I'm sorry, love." His thumb brushed the tear that got away, and his eyes drank her in for long minutes. "I make you this bond today the way I made you the mating one weeks ago. A bond, meaning the two of us joined together, that we are in every decision together up until the very basis of your safety, because, love, I don't care how much you hate me for it, if your safety is on the line, past simple threats, but really put on the line, I will not hesitate to kill myself to save you."

Her heart stopped. He was never shy about his feelings for her, but his declarations still took her breath away every time.

Her hand reached for the one stroking her cheek. "And I make you the same bond, Hunter. Until the basis of *your* safety."

He didn't like that—the flare of his eyes said that much—but she didn't care. Because as much as she did hate him for what he did, every fiber in her needed to protect him. She had no doubts that if he were in real danger, the same way he'd been before, she'd kneel before the enemy to keep him safe.

His thumb brushed her lip, then his mouth took over, kissing her with a feverish softness. Almost like he wanted to be rough, but forced himself to slow down.

When he pulled away, he stared down at her with a small quirk to his lips, then let his hands skim down her form until they reached her hands.

He stepped away. "You plan on figuring out how to get us out of here?"

She rolled her eyes. "If only I knew how I got us in here."

An amused breath left him as he dropped her hands and turned to the blanket she'd thrown to the ground. He opened it wide and set the large cloth on the dirt ground of the cage. He kicked off his boots and stepped onto it, taking a seat and looking up to her. "It's a good thing you had this on you, love. I don't feel like getting dirty right now."

She laughed through closed lips as her head shook and she moved forward. "I truly do hate you sometimes."

His hand reached for his heart as she kicked her shoes off. "How can I make it all the time?"

She sat facing him so that the sides of their thighs touched. "Keep annoying me."

He smirked as an arm fell over the leg he had bent and his other hand fell between her legs to hold himself up. "I can do that."

"Oh, yes, it's second nature, isn't it?"

"I think it's part of the mating." His eyes twinkled. "To keep things interesting."

"You know what I think?"

"Hm?" His eyes shined as they studied her face.

"I think we should play twenty questions." They had talked and told each other a lot, but there was still so much they hadn't gotten to.

Plus, she really didn't want to think about how to get them out of there at the moment.

His brow quirked in amusement. "You always want to play twenty questions."

"And you always comply." She smiled sweetly.

His gaze dropped to her lips and dilated. "Because I always know where it'll end."

She smirked, her finger lightly grazing his chin and pushing his gaze back up. "Then we play. And I'll be nice and allow you to go first."

Surprisingly, he didn't have to think about it. "Are you opposed to taking the Delvaux name?"

She hadn't been expecting such a serious question to begin. But it was something they hadn't spoken of. She'd never opposed it when he or his father indicated her as part of the family, and to be honest, she'd never really put much thought into it.

But it was like hearing the question, and the dash of uncertainty in his voice, that solidified her answer. She shook her head softly. "I figured I was already a Delvaux."

He shrugged. "You've never said it."

"I don't know." She wanted to touch him, but doing so early

in the game wouldn't allow them very many questions before their desires took over. "I guess I just didn't know how it worked. We're not married, technically, like the humans and witches—most creatures, really—so I didn't know how the naming would go. It's simpler with marriage. The second you say your 'I do's,' it's understood that the name transfer has taken place."

The small twist of his lips was genuine. "It could work the same way with us. You accepted my ring."

She shrugged again. "I don't oppose it, no. I actually love the sound of it. Maya Delvaux. I think it fits better than Whittle."

"I do too." He leaned in so his lips brushed hers. "But if you'd like, we could have a small wedding too. Then we'd be married and mated."

She smiled and pushed back so his lips didn't press into hers. His black gaze glinted like he knew what she was doing. He'd win out. They both knew it. They hardly ever actually got through twenty questions.

"My turn."

"Indeed, love."

She watched him for a moment when a question, more random in nature, came to the front of her mind. "What did you think when you saw me walking through town with 'the piece' in my hands? Did you think me dumb enough to actually hold it so openly?"

His eyes drifted off as he remembered the time, and a smile brightened his features and made Maya's heart swoon. "No, I didn't think you dumb. I thought you a new witch who didn't fully understand the dynamics of the magical world. I thought you greedy in the way I am, that you were attempting to hold the power for yourself. I thought you intriguing, and honestly, I wanted to know everything about you, including where you were going with that piece."

Maya didn't really know why that had mattered to her, but

the prideful part of her wanted to know he didn't see her as a little dimwit. "Good. Your turn."

His gaze dropped down to her lips before meeting her gaze again. "We both know we would've ended up together no matter what, the mating bond solidifies that. But do you think if Warren hadn't sent us down here, you would've come to me after the Bridgers coven?"

Maya actually had to think about that one. "I think so. I think as long as you still showed up at Lila's and helped us out, I would've come to you."

He bit his lip. "You know I went to their cottage in the hopes your bleeding heart would hear of it and come to me."

Her grin grew. "Good. Because I didn't really know how to lure you out to me."

The hand he had rested over his knee reached up and pushed her hair back. He rested his elbow on his knee and allowed his hand to remain skimming the edge of her face. "Your question."

She watched him for a long time. "If I'd actually had the piece in my hands, and my family hadn't been around to bludgeon you," her lips quirked up into a cocky grin, "what would you have done? What was your plan in following me into the woods?"

He considered the question a moment. "Initially, I was intrigued, of course, but I still only planned on taking the piece and shadowing out." His fingers grazed her cheek. "Then I heard your name, tasted it on my tongue, and I knew there was no way I was leaving without you." Her lips. "I thought you were a new witch, so it would still work in my favor to get the piece away from you, just in case that bleeding heart of yours woke up, but…" His thumb parted her lips, and his brows furrowed as he studied her. "But I intended on taking your hand then. Shadowing us back to my manor—*my* manor—and taking you in a hundred positions. All I knew was I needed you."

Her breath hitched.

His manor.

The manor he had never allowed anyone to before her. He had been ready to take her there even though all he'd known about her was her name, her power, and that she was a new witch.

His eyes were far too wicked. "You like the sound of that."

Her desire spiked. She bit down on her bottom lip and nodded, far past the ability to speak.

"You know what I thought about last time we were here?" His thumb grazed her cheek as his face hovered closer to hers.

She looked up to him curiously, because if he had Lust down his neck the same way she had, she could only imagine what he'd thought of. "That's not a real question," she answered breathlessly.

"Sure is." His crooked grin was far too wicked for this game. "Answer it."

She shrugged. "How annoyed you were with your brother for sending us down?"

He tsked. And thankfully didn't continue playing with her. "I thought of shoving you against those pillars and burying myself between those legs."

She knew by the way he smirked down at her that her eyes grew black with desire. Her breathing ragged as she asked, "Your tongue or your cock?"

"My tongue *and* my cock."

She bit her lip in anticipation. "Well, we do have *some* time."

30

Maya was still not around. And not answering her calls. Hunter either.

And Augustine Delvaux was at their house.

He didn't seem pleased to not have heard from either one of them yet, but Vera doubted that was what he was there about.

"Word has just gone out." He took his usual spot in the middle of the couch, Warren filling the seat beside him, and an odd emptiness to the other side. "Dagen Heisenberg is sending a mass threat to the whereabouts of his youngest son."

Vera looked to the others around the room, and when not a single one of them could come up with something to say, her mother finally said, "And you have come to us, because?"

"I was hoping my son and daughter would be here," he grit his teeth in annoyance. "I believe it was by The Eight."

Vera's brows shot up. "Why would you think that?"

"I'd heard a private conversation between the two, and Maya seemed far too concerned about the boy and another girl, though I didn't catch the species. It makes me believe he may be their youngest victims yet."

"You were eavesdropping." Camilla quirked a brow.

He smirked. "In my house, it is not eavesdropping. If they didn't want me listening in, they should've gone to their estate."

Their estate.

It still shocked Vera that the entire Delvaux family so naturally referred to Maya as part of the family. So naturally spoke of all of Hunter's belongings as Maya's. They never slipped up or said that it was all Hunter's, and never once did they call the manor *theirs* with any condensation. Rather, they spoke as a matter of fact.

"In any case, though he is the weakest of the lot, Dagen doesn't like being played. Naturally." He looked more bored than concerned, and though it was Warren who shared his father's looks—like, really shared his father's looks—it was entirely Hunter's personality that the patriarch carried. "He cares more about the reputation of his family if his son could so easily be taken. He's threatening to war with the demons, and though most of us would like that so we could just wipe them out, they're an easy scapegoat any time there are cases the rest of us don't want to deal with. Dagen believes himself better when it falls to his lap, like we couldn't handle it."

"So you want us to deal with him?" Vera asked.

His smirk grew condescending. "Of course not. I will deal with him. I need you lot to find the child. I figured you would like to, considering he is with The Eight."

"You assume," Camilla argued.

His smirk didn't falter. "I don't have to assume, darling. I access. It is how I knew before ever meeting your sister that she was mated to my son. And it is how I knew you definitely weren't."

Camilla sat straight, her eyes darkening on the father, but Bishop interrupted before Camilla's temper got the best of her. "Thank you. For coming to us. I know you did it for your own gain, but still."

"I did not only do it for my own gain." Augustine looked to

him. "Maya's heart still remains witch, and she would care for the child. I am doing this for my daughter."

"Because she's such a great advantage to your family?" Vera asked.

"Indeed." He wasn't shy about his state of affairs. And maybe that's what made them—at least Vera herself—so able to work with him even though she didn't agree with him.

"We'll look into it," Loretta finalized.

Augustine didn't stick around much after that. He merely stuck around like he was waiting for something—which Vera would assume was her sister—then left without so much as a goodbye. Warren gave an apologetic shrug and shadowed out after him leaving the family alone for the first time in a while. And if they knew where Maya was—or where her manor was— or if the middle Whittle would answer her phone, they could be a whole family.

Vera realized in that moment that they had yet to have a moment of just the five of them—Bishop, Loretta, and their three daughters.

And like they were telepathically connected, she and her father rose for the kitchen at the same time. He threw his arm over her shoulder and hugged her close to his side as they moved for some tea as her sister and mother followed.

Vera loved her mother, always had since Bishop had made sure of it, but it was nowhere near the love she had for her father. After Harry, he was her best friend and she had no doubt he always would be.

"Why don't I make us some teas and warm some of those muffins you made earlier and I'll meet you girls in the dining room?" Bishop squeezed her closer while he spoke in that tone that told Vera that would be what was happening.

She smiled to herself as she turned to the formal room that was hardly ever used in the house and sat with her mother and sister. It'd been a while since she'd heard him boss her around like that and she'd missed it. She'd always be his little girl and the time apart while he'd faked his death had only magnified her want to remain so.

"I know Maya's not here and you'll have to repeat it all to her later," Camilla opened to her mother, "but can we know now? About everything?"

Loretta gave her a knowing grin. "Everything, darling? That's quite a bit."

Camilla rolled her eyes in that loving way of hers. "We can start with why we never really knew about dad? Vera knew about you."

Loretta's grin dropped and she looked up to find her husband coming back with the tray of teas and muffins. He sat beside her and took her hand softly. Vera loved seeing them together.

"Vera..." her father opened. "Vera accepted that she did not have a mother. Accepted that for some reason, she couldn't see Lore even though Lore loved her. She did not have someone beside her to scheme with."

"You girls on the other hand," Loretta took over. "You girls had one another to scheme with. And I know at some point one of you would have gone to the other and demanded to know more. I know you would've worked together to track him down and we couldn't risk it."

Camilla looked like she wanted to settle with those words but couldn't. "But you never mentioned it. Even when we were young."

Loretta reached for Camilla's hand and clasped it fondly. "I tried, my love. But your sister, her fire. She loved hearing about your father, but sometimes she would grow angry about him loving us and not being there. The older she got, the more I saw it. And the older the both of you got, the more I knew you would lean on one another. I couldn't risk anything. Couldn't risk even accidentally seeing Vera, so I had to make you believe there was no man to speak of. It was the hardest thing I had to do with you two."

Camilla nodded like she understood and sympathized with their mother. Vera knew she did. She could not imagine having a child with Harry and having to act like Harry meant nothing, that he was nothing more to them.

In the quiet that followed, Bishop stared at her and Vera could tell immediately that he knew her brain was ticking away.

"What is it, my girl?" he asked.

She shook her head softly, a furrow entering between her brows, as she said, "When you were telling us about Mom's different lives, why do you think that had to do with you? Maya's makes sense, she's your daughter, your blood. But why Mom?"

They both looked solemn, but Loretta answered, "We left the European coven for a reason, my girls. It wasn't an easy one. Everyone was against it, because they knew something would happen."

"We don't necessarily know how," Bishop answered. "But we were told even then not to be together, warned against it."

"My mother, especially, did not want us together," Loretta continued. "Not because of his warlock status or any cultural background, but because she could sense trouble. That was her primary. More like you, Camilla, non-active. She told me I would be cursed to spend my life with Bish."

"She didn't hate me," Bishop corrected before Vera could jump to that conclusion. "The coven was quite fond of me, actually. She was only protecting her daughter. Adela, she...she hated me when we left the coven, but only because of what it could and would mean for her daughter."

"We did it to protect them," Loretta argued. "I was okay with being cursed. I was okay with whatever came of me as long as I got to be with your father. My family, my coven, they hadn't signed up for that."

Vera gave a weak smile. "He *is* the best."

Loretta reached to softly clasp her hand. "Absolute."

"But if you two were together at the coven too, then what's the difference?" Camilla asked.

"Uniting," her father said. "Marriage. It is so common that people forget how powerful it truly is. Especially to us supernatural. Think of your sister's mating except we weren't fated as strongly as they were."

Vera smiled to herself. *Fated as strongly.* Because her father had always known he was fated for her mother.

"The night before we married," her mother continued. "It was a small ceremony for us and a couple of witnesses. But that night, I had a dream, a warning. That's how we knew it would be nine lives and this is my last."

Bishop prepared the teas and handed them off to everyone to drink, placing a muffin to make sure they all ate as well like he always had.

"It was vague though. I wasn't entirely sure what it meant. We thought when everything happened with my Vera that it was the curse keeping us apart. It was not until death three that I really started to piece it together and realized that this curse wasn't meant to keep us apart, but to test fate."

Bishop answered both hers and Camilla's confused stares. "Fate. Our continued relationship through being separated, but especially the fate of our family. Because Lore continued dying based on how Hunter and Maya reacted to being together. That fate. We believe my bloodline, though dark, was attempting to alter itself."

She stared up with a warm smile. "And it has happened. My going to Bishop that last time, us running off. It has altered fate so beautifully. We think the curse was there in disguise, helping us right whatever wrong came with Maya's love for Hunter while I was around."

"We realized then that as much as we want to be there to guide you girls," Bishop said. "It is about guiding yourself. When we left, we were nervous beyond compare that without us, things would go worse that before because Maya wouldn't have her mother to run to."

"But that's the difference," Loretta said solemnly. "My leaving forced her to become the mother in some ways. It forced her to be more apprehensive. In all the lives before, she came to me and I helped her through whatever and she always had me to lean on. As much as it pained me, I needed her to make her own decisions and mistakes. I am so proud of how far she's come."

"If only she were around to hear it." Camilla gave a knowing smirk.

Loretta smiled. "I believe she knows, but I will definitely be telling her. But she did. She became stronger. You all did. You all fought for your family before boys and turned the clocks on the fate of your blood. Maya didn't fall into the darkness that surrounds her, but forced Hunter out into the light."

"He is to her what the night is to the stars. Allows her to shine her brightest," her father said fondly. "All because she needed to fight for you girls instead of simply allowing herself to fall. Because though you may see it as Maya going to the enemy a few weeks after meeting to sleep with him; though you may see them sleeping together and going to one another constantly even when you still hated him; though you may see his uncaring side, their relationship is pure now."

Loretta looked proud as she smiled toward Camilla's quirked brow. Vera could already hear her little sister questioning *how* Maya had waited.

"I understand that it doesn't entirely seem that she fought it to you," their mother said. "But she did. Because she had to be wary and that protected her. In the past lives, I was there so she didn't feel the responsibly to protect her family. In the past lives, by the second meeting they were obsessed with one another. They were clouded in their desires and their mating. It gave them less of the fight and control we know Maya holds over Hunt."

Camilla gave an airy laugh. "He does love her."

Vera was shocked to hear the words, especially from the little Whittle, but felt how true they were.

"And he has always and will always, in every life," Loretta said, always with a soft look about her when speaking of the demon. "But this life afforded them the opportunity of real love over obsessed love. They fight for each other, but they continue to be their own people."

"They are pure," Bishop concluded.

Vera gave a warm smile thinking of her middle sister and her demon. They were a mess of dark magic and impropriety, of passion and strength, of selflessness and family. They were to Vera in some ways how she always pictured her parents when she was a little girl. "They are."

31

Because Hunter's fantasy had specifically started with her against the pillars, he didn't move as she got up and walked to the edge of the cage. His mouth watered as her back kissed the pillars and she faced him.

The same fantasy of being between those legs sprang to Hunter's mind, but it was so much worse this time. Because now he'd been between those legs an infinite amount of times, so he knew exactly what was waiting for him. And it was so much better than any bit his imagination could have rendered.

He rose slowly, taking his time in moving to her and watching her eyes dilate to match his black orbs as her anticipation grew.

He stopped three feet away. "Take your shirt off."

"Why don't you do it for me?"

"I want to watch you undress for me."

She swallowed, but he saw how much she enjoyed what he was saying. She didn't rush the movement so it was entirely seductive and not even a little bit stumbled.

He drank her in. Her glorious breasts spilling out of the black lace of her bra. "Unhook the bra, love."

Her eyes never left his as the bra slipped to the ground.

"Good job." He licked his lips because bare from the waist up, all he could think about was how much he wanted to taste each browned peak. "Now cup the girls for me, love. Play with your nipples."

There was not a single ounce of brown left in her eyes anymore. She was so filled with desire he didn't need a scenting power to smell it.

But again, she complied and took each breast in hand. Her fingers tweaked over her nipples and her back arched into her hands, but she never broke his gaze. His mouth was so jealous of those hands.

Hunter peeled off his shirt and saw the way she froze in anticipation. He dropped the shirt. "Did I tell you to stop?"

Her breathing grew more ragged, but her fingers continued to tease his favorite girls.

His hands reached for his trousers and he saw the immediate drop her gaze made to his hips. She licked her lips in excitement.

And he enjoyed pleasing her.

Hunter jumped between watching the way her hands kneaded her breasts and taking in the way her eyes glazed over with desire as they waited for his trousers to fall.

And then they fell, and his cock was free and hard as a rock.

She licked her lips and moaned his name, her hips thrusting with an obvious need for friction.

He smirked as he watched her battle with herself, on the one hand wanting to reach out for him, and on the other knowing she had to stay rooted until he told her to move. "That's my girl," he teased as he grabbed for the base of his cock.

She whimpered as she watched the pre-cum drip over his tip and fall onto his hand as he stroked. Her thighs pressed together so tightly, Hunter knew she was hoping to get some friction from her jeans pressing into her clit.

"Should I take pity on you, love?"

"Please," she cried out, her fingers working overtime on her luscious breasts to make up for the lack of friction farther south.

He stroked twice more, his cock so ready to fill her. "Take it all off, love."

She sighed and moved quickly, naked in the matter of moments. Her fingers were already working their way to fill the need her body was so desperate for.

"Did I say you could touch yourself?"

She froze just below her navel and looked to him desperately. "Please."

He tsked and pumped his cock again. "Arms around the pillars. Legs spread. I don't want you rubbing yourself either."

She whimpered, but listened like the good girl she was.

She moaned as she watched his hand work himself, a bit of drool falling down her chin. She *did* love the taste of him. Maybe he should be kinder to her. She *was* the one controlling whether he was tormented down there or not.

He dropped his cock and stepped up to her, watching the way her back arched so their skin would touch. It didn't happen, but he could see how much she was straining for it.

He let a single finger slide down her form, straight down the valley of her breasts and past her navel to where she desired him most. He let his finger just brush the tops of her folds before removing it entirely.

She cried out in frustration. "Hunter, I swear to the lords I'll have Hell's Gate torture the fuck out of you if you don't stop playing."

He smirked. *There was his girl.* "Is that a threat, Mrs. Delvaux?"

She gasped and her arms gripped tighter to the pillars.

"You like the sound of that?" His finger brushed a nipple. "Mrs. Delvaux?" His finger moved slowly until he was playing with her bottom lip.

Her tongue reached for his finger, in an obvious need to

taste any part of him. "Love. So fucking much." Her hips thrust forward. "Too fucking much."

He removed his finger from her lips and slowly dragged the wet digit back the same route it'd been on before as he leaned in to her ear. "Good." He dropped to his knees, looking up at her with hooded eyes at the same moment his finger reached her pussy. "Because you're my property."

She nodded vigorously as she thrust her hips into him over and over.

He gripped her hips, knowing the pressure would leave bruises, but not caring. He couldn't wait to see his fingers marked into her skin.

He kissed the bottom of her navel. Each hip bone. The tops of either thigh. Her thighs were spread as wide as she could manage while still standing, and he continued to purposefully divert from the one spot she needed his mouth.

He kissed her stomach. The valley between her breasts. Her stomach again. Down one thigh to her knee. Then up the other leg from knee to hip bone. All while she strained against his hands, but he was much stronger than she and had no problem holding her still.

She growled. "Hunter, I swear I'll make them mindfuck you with something worse than the Blood Eagle."

The breaking of each of his ribs. It hadn't actually happened, but Hell's Gate had made his mind believe it had. Torture.

He dipped his face between her thighs, but didn't touch her. Just let her scent fill his senses. "There's my mate, as persuasive as ever. But I believe I enjoy torturing you too much to care what becomes of me."

"Hunter," she begged.

He chuckled, dark and seductive. "I love it when you beg, love."

He swore he saw her nails break into the pillars as her head fell back. "Then I'm begging. I'm fucking begging, put your fucking tongue on me."

His chuckle grew as he breathed her in. "That's a good girl."

She moaned so loud when his tongue finally touched her sensitive—and insanely wet—center that if they weren't currently stuck down below, he was sure the entire town would've heard her. A release of ecstasy so intense, she came into his mouth after one flick of his tongue.

His grin grew devilish. "Ejaculating prematurely, are we?"

She completely ignored him, one hand slipping into his hair and pulling at the roots as she looked down at him, whimpering. "Tongue fuck me, baby."

"Your wish," he licked from opening to clit and suckled, "is my command, my mate."

Her head fell back into the nothingness between pillars and she moaned every curse he'd ever come across between calling out his name.

His tongue slipped into her opening and tasted every ounce of her, overdosing on her mouthful, relishing in her cries. "Fuck, love, let's never leave. I can survive eternally with only your taste."

His fingers finally slipped from her waist, reaching for her thighs and lifting her to sit on his shoulders. He wanted her to suffocate him between her thighs. Loved losing his breath as she pressed her thighs closer together.

Her fingernails scraped into his scalp as she tried to hold herself up with the other against the pillar. "Please, please, *please* don't stop."

Never.

He'd never stop.

He'd never give up this delicacy.

She was coming again. Screaming so hoarse, he couldn't make out her words any longer, but he couldn't be bothered with trying to. All he cared about was licking up every last drop.

Every.

Fucking.

Drop.

He was standing over her by the time she came back from her high, his fingers pulling her lips apart as his tongue invaded her mouth. "Taste yourself, love. Taste how fucking good you are." Their tongues fought as his hands took her breasts, thumbs running across her nipples.

"It's your turn to come, baby." She bit his lip. "Preferably inside me."

He tsked. "It's still your turn."

He lifted one of her legs to wrap around his waist, opening her up to him as she held onto the pillars behind her. He didn't wait, filling her to the hilt and groaning as her cunt clenched around his cock.

They both stared at the spot they were connected and watched as he pulled out, completely covered in her juices, then slipped back in. He left the space between their bodies so he could continue watching his cock invade her most delicious area as she pressed into the pillars, leaning so far back he had to support her lower back so she didn't fall.

But in this position, he also got a beautiful view of her lips parted in ecstasy, her eyes rolling back, and her breasts bouncing with each time he pounded into her. Each timed perfectly to get a cry out of her as he rolled over her clit with every stroke. "You're so fucking beautiful, love. Alluring. I can't get enough."

She mumbled something incoherent as he stabilized her with one arm and moved the other hand to her cunt. His thumb rolled over her clit as he pounded into her, and in less than a minute, she was covering his cock in her orgasm.

He felt the need to come sliding down his spine, but pushed it aside. It wasn't his turn yet.

He pulled out before he gave in to the bliss of her pussy clenching him as she came and turned her around. He bent her over, her arms still gripping the pillars for support, and stroked his juice-covered cock down her ass.

He noticed the way her ass clenched to the possible intrusion, the way her back arched, and her head fell back to spill those locks down her back as she moaned out.

"Don't worry, love." He palmed her ass in either hand. "I won't be taking this today. We'll leave that discovery for another day."

"As long as you come in me, I don't care what you do to me," she begged.

His fingers slipped down to her pussy as the other fisted her hair, pulling her head back as his fingers slipped into her wet folds, and she breathed in the feeling of penetration yet again.

"You're dripping, love. And I haven't even come in you yet."

His cock lined up with her crack as his fingers picked up pace and his thumb rubbed her sensitive nub. He leaned in and bit the side of her neck. He needed everyone to see she was his.

"I love when you mark me, baby," she moaned, pushing her ass into his cock like she wanted it.

One day.

One day he'd claim that hole too, and she'd be entirely and utterly his.

He bit her shoulder, then moved to the back of her neck. He'd leave so many bites on her, he'd have the entire magical world questioning whether vampires were real.

Her voice cracked as she screamed his name the next time she came. She was so broken, she couldn't even hold herself up on her own any longer.

Hunter chuckled as he guided his cock into her cunt, then took a strong hold of her waist so she wouldn't fall as he pumped into her. He took her savagely, intoxicated with the sight of her ass bouncing off his hips with each thrust.

"Fuck, baby, fuck, fuck, fuck, Hunter, Hunt, Hu…" Unintelligible words followed her screams.

He throbbed with the need to come. Felt it at the very base of his cock.

But it wasn't his turn.

"That's right, Witch, cry for me." He grit his teeth. "Beg me, Witch."

She was so sensitive, she was coming before the next words could leave her.

Her shoulders slumped into the pillars when she recovered.

But.

He.

Was.

Not.

Done.

With.

Her.

He licked up her spine and felt her writhe beneath his tongue. When he reached her ear, he bit down. "One more?"

She whimpered, but couldn't answer. He knew how much she wanted him to finish inside her, and he was prone to giving her whatever her heart desired. Always.

He fisted her hair and pulled her back into his chest, turning them around so she could see the blanket still lying in the middle of the cage. "Face down, Witch."

She could hardly stand, but eventually she stabilized her legs enough to walk over and fall onto the blanket. No more seduction without a stumble. She was an utter mess.

She crawled just enough to put herself in the middle, then rested her chest to the ground as her ass lifted up into the air for him. She looked to him with the darkest hunger he'd ever seen before.

"It's time to give you what you want, my mate." But when he kneeled behind her and took a quick bite of one cheek, he couldn't help the need to taste her again. "Almost." He smirked as he spread her cheeks to give him a glorious view of her dripping wet pussy.

"I hate you, Hunter," she mumbled. "So. Fucking. Much."

His smirk grew. "Good." He took her clit with his tongue, sucking it and listening to her cries grow.

Her hips moved of their own accord, and he allowed it, his hands only business keeping her spread for him. She rode his tongue, her arms reaching out before her and digging into the dirt.

Sensitive.

She was so sensitive.

And so fucking mouthwatering.

After coming so many times, she'd been more than wet for him. She was dripping down her legs and covering the entirety of his face in her juices.

She was coming again, and he was getting a mouthful. He made sure to lap up every last bit, from her orgasm that exploded into his mouth, to the bits trickling down her thighs. All of it. It was all his.

"You taste so fucking good. And you're all mine, Witch."

"Yours, yours, yours, yo…" Each word barely understandable through her cries.

She was losing her voice, so as much as he was enjoying this little torment he was giving her, it was time to finish.

He pulled up to his knees and positioned himself at her opening, her ass floating in the air waiting for his attentions. He spanked her hard enough to leave a print—because he intended on marking her, even if he'd be the only one seeing it—and pushed into her.

And because he'd just tasted and fucked her multiple times, he was on the brink of exploding. His balls so ready to fill her, his vision clouded.

This was so much better than he could've ever imagined it four months prior.

And because he'd tortured her this entire time, his mate took her turn in playing with him.

She reached a hand beneath her arched body and cupped his balls, playing with them with the tips of her nails, so no matter how much he wanted to, there was no way he would be able to hold out any longer.

"Maya, Maya, Ma..." He screamed as he erupted into her so hard his vision blacked out, and instead of stars, he saw white flames. He'd luckily been holding onto her hips as he pounded into her so he didn't fall over, but he was damn near ready to. Every last ounce of being within him left his body and entered hers. He roared so loud, he swore the cage rattled a bit.

And before he'd even pulled out, he was dripping down her thighs. That had to be even more than the first time he came in her.

He had just enough strength left in him to pull out and flip her onto her back. He fell between her jelly legs, his chest taking in the warmth her cunt still radiated, not caring that it covered his chest in their mixed juices. Their sweat stuck together as he rested his head on her stomach.

"You win." Her head drooped to the side. He looked up to her with a furrow between the brows. "There's no way I'm not pregnant after that. I *felt* that hit my ovaries."

He laughed into her belly. "Oh no, I think we should keep trying." He kissed her navel. "And trying." He kissed the bottom of her breast bone. "And trying." The valley between her breasts. "And trying." The dip between her collarbones. "And even when your belly is so large it physically keeps me from being on top, we can keep trying from behind." His lips brushed hers.

The ground rumbled as they kissed, but he was so lost in her, he didn't care. It was incredible that he still wanted more after that. Yes, his cock definitely needed a moment to ready for it, but he *wanted* more. Needed more. Needed to be inside her again.

When he pulled away, they were lying on their plush bed, out of Hell's Gate.

His eyes shined down at her.

32

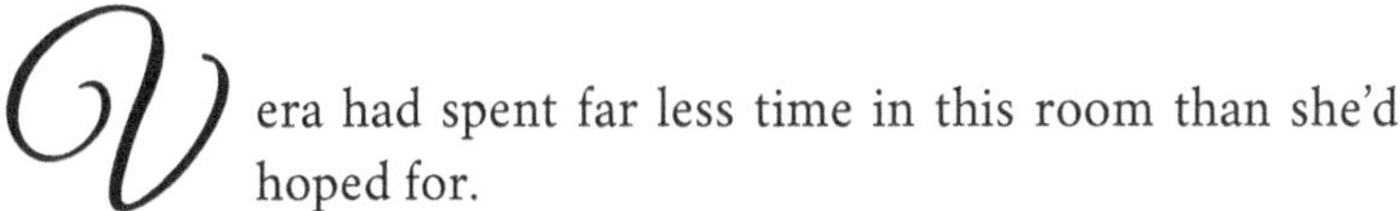

era had spent far less time in this room than she'd hoped for.

In the past months, she'd never gone more than a couple of days without playing the piano and recently, it'd been far longer than that.

With the amount of people in their house and the stress of everything happening really beginning to get to her, she hadn't prioritized taking care of herself. And that meant she hadn't played—something that never failed to soothe her soul.

And it was her space with Harry.

She knew if she went, he'd follow, and she loved their time together in the piano room. It was different than their times in the room, the bed. It was intimate in a non-sexual way.

Most of the time.

She was playing the melody she'd written specifically for Harry before they'd gotten together when his hands settled on her shoulders and his body pressed into her back. He kissed her lightly on the crown and whispered, "My beautiful love."

She tilted her head to kiss his hand. "My handsome love."

His chuckles hit her hair as he straddled the bench beside her. "You're playing my song."

289

His hand on her thigh was a bit distracting as she nodded, but her fingers knew the keys so well, she didn't falter. "I think I should change it."

His brows furrowed in the most inviting way, she wanted to kiss the spot between his brows.

"Why?"

She shrugged. "I wrote this when I wanted you and couldn't have you. I can have you whenever I want now."

His lips twitched up in a proud smirk. "But that's my song."

"I'll write another. One that's not me crying out for what I can't have."

"I don't want another, sweetheart." His hand moved to play with her bottom lip. "This song was written for me. It tells me how you've always felt for me. I love it exactly as it is." He kissed her tentatively. "Although, if you want to write me another, you're very welcome. I'd welcome a million songs all for me."

A giggle left Vera without her permission. "Then it's settled. I'm writing another."

"Okay." He kissed her again. "As long as you always remember to play this one. It will always be my favorite."

She rubbed her nose against his in an eskimo kiss. "How about I give you some lessons? Then you can make a song for me."

He laughed against her lips. "You can teach me all you'd like, sweetheart, but a hundred years wasn't enough for me to get it, so don't hold your breath on receiving that song."

Vera laughed as she pulled away and motioned for him to turn to the keys. "Just put your hands over mine. I'll play something easy."

His hands settled over hers and ate them whole, and Vera had to tap into her training with Hunter to ignore her feelings so she could concentrate on the song. Harry always had a way of making her falter on the keys.

She moved over the keys slowly so his fingers had time to

follow, but even then, Harry's fingers spasmed over the wrong keys.

"Harry," she teased. "I'm playing for you. How are you still messing up?"

He smirked in her direction. "I told you a hundred years couldn't teach me."

Vera kissed his shoulder and continued to play. "We have our lifetime. I don't care how long it takes. You'll learn."

His fingers continued to follow over the ones she had playing, but he turned to stare into her eyes. "I love you, Vera. And when you say things like that, I'm reminded of how very lucky I was to survive that attack on my family a hundred years ago. How lucky I was to befriend your parents and be the one they trusted to come to you. How lucky I've been that you chose me."

She leaned her forehead against his as her fingers danced across the keys. "I'll always choose you, Harry. Don't you know, us Americans love a British accent?"

His hands fell over hers as dead weight and the room rang with the finals keys before it was filled with silence. And all the while Harry stared into her eyes.

Vera hoped he could see how earnest she was as she said, "You say you're lucky, Harry, but you cannot imagine how lucky I feel. Not only for having this family and getting my father back, but because all of it means I got to you. If feeling that loneliness my entire life meant I'd get you, I'd do it over and over and over again."

He cupped her cheeks. "Kiss me, sweetheart."

A shy smile graced her lips as she leaned into him. His lips were her favorite taste in the world and she truly felt herself fall deeper in love with him in that moment sitting at the piano bench.

"My warlock," she whispered against his lips when he pulled away enough to stare into her eyes.

Maya walked down to the kitchen at Whittle House and met questioning gazes. It was Camilla who broke the silence. "Where have you been?"

Maya smiled, thinking back to her time with Hunter. Somehow, they'd only been gone a day and a half in Earth time. "With Hunter."

Camilla grimaced. "I don't want to know."

Kai grinned wickedly as he leaned over the counter. "I do."

Loretta looked amused too, but she didn't further the conversation. Instead, she looked to Maya. "While you were gone, Augustine came around. Have you spoken to him yet?"

Maya froze, but tried not to let it show on her features. *Had he figured out the Hell's Gate portal already?*

She just shook her head. "Haven't seen him."

"Apparently another kidnapping by The Eight." Vera sighed.

Maya's brows furrowed. "Why would Augustine care?"

He wouldn't.

"He wouldn't," her father repeated her thoughts. "But he knew you would. This one specifically, apparently."

Maya's brows furrowed. Juliette and Felix? But they were hidden at their safehouse, and the rest of her family would care for them too. Alloy and Brynn? But how would Augustine know about them? "Who?"

"The youngest Heisenberg," Harry said as he evaluated her.

She froze.

The youngest Heisenberg. *Vincent.*

If Vincent was taken by The Eight, then the counterpart would have to be...

Maya turned instantly, reaching for the phone in her back pocket as she paced to the living room, phone already ringing. And falling straight to voice mail.

Another attempt proved futile. Then she called Brynn.

When Brynn picked up, sounding cheery and unsuspecting, Maya forced her voice to gather. "Hey! Have you seen Bella?"

"No." She sounded almost teasing. "Why?"

Maya ignored the question and asked another, "Have you heard from her at all today?"

Brynn's tone fell, worry beginning to etch in. "No. Why, Maya?" The fear was filling quickly. "Has something happened?"

"No!" Maya dispelled quickly.

She would find Bella before Brynn even knew something had taken place. No one needed to know about her and Vincent.

Well, no more people.

"We just had a fight and she's not picking up."

Brynn laughed. "Oh, she's like that. Give it a few hours. Maybe another day. She'll call and act like nothing's happened. She usually stays away from technology after a fight to annoy the other person even more."

Maya couldn't get herself to smile, though the picture of Bella doing just that was an easy one. She just thanked Brynn and let her phone fall from her hands as she realized what *had* happened.

Because there was only one explanation.

Bella had been taken by The Eight. That, or she'd realized Vincent had been taken and she'd gone after him. Because this was Bella.

Bella, who would destroy herself if something happened to Vincent.

Bella, who would fall prey to her parents if she didn't have Vincent to counter off of.

Bella, who would ruin anyone who tried to hurt Vincent.

Because it's all exactly what Maya would do for Hunter, and Maya knew instinctively that those two were mated. It was just incredible that they'd found each other so early.

Maya couldn't breathe. She could feel her lungs contracting to fill with air, but barely processed anything entering.

"Maya." Someone called to her. "Maya, honey, calm down. " Her mother was by her shoulder, trying to comfort.

It wasn't working.

Bella couldn't be taken. They couldn't be doing to her what had been done to the others. *She was a child.*

Maya turned back to her family as Camilla's reasoning came together. "Wait. Bella? As in Devon and Bianka's heir *Bella*?"

Maya shook her head as her breathing accelerated. "You can't tell. You can't tell." Bella couldn't have her relationship broken so early. "You can't..."

She couldn't breathe.

Then she was seeing spots.

The only image one of Bella and Vincent hanging by their arms the way Hunter had been when she'd found him. Their bodies rolling with shocks of electricity, or worse, with the illusions thrown at them. Because neither one was trained to look past illusions. Even Maya wasn't trained for that yet—though it was a problem Hunter intended on rectifying soon. His family guard Loki was an illusionist.

All she could hear as the world moved around her was their screams for it all to stop. Their cries to get away. To get to one another.

Her lungs were calling for air.

Her heart was pumping, but she felt none of it.

***

His father was waiting for an answer.

Hunter quirked a brow at the man, but didn't answer.

Warren looked amused at his end of the office as Augustine asked once more, "Why couldn't any of us contact you or Maya?"

"I was too deep inside her to worry about what the lot of you wanted." It wasn't a lie.

"Hunter, be serious."

Hunter knew his father wasn't concerned per-say, but he wondered about the man's interest.

Hunter took a swing of bourbon to burn down the tingling

of the scar he'd acquired while training with Loki before his father had interrupted for this meeting. It'd heal quickly, but still, it was bothersome. "You interrupted my training to ask what my mate and I do with our private time? Weren't you the one that raised us never to interrupt trainings?"

Augustine looked like he was going to open a new lecture when a shock of dread ran through Hunter. It most certainly wasn't his feeling. Which only meant Maya needed him.

His brother and father seemed to notice his change in behavior—the stiffening of his form and the way his hand reached to touch his ring—immediately as Warren asked, "Maya?"

Hunter gave a single nod and didn't wait to see what they would say as he shadowed to Whittle House.

Maya was sitting on the edge of the coffee table. And she was hyperventilating.

He moved to kneel before her instantly. "What happened?" he grit out, barely able to control his rage. *What had they done to her?*

"We told her Vincent Heisenberg is missing," Vera said from behind him.

Fuck. "And Bella?" he muttered.

"Not answering," Kai said, though he sounded like he didn't entirely know who Bella was.

Hunter took Maya's face in his hands as he leaned in so their brows touched. "I need you to come back to me, baby," he whispered. "Maya, love, come back to me. Listen to my voice and breathe for me, baby." When their breaths mixed and Hunter realized hers was calming, ever slowly, he continued speaking to her, knowing the sound of his voice was helping more than anything else. "We're going to get them, okay? I'll find them if I have to burn this world down. Just come back to me. *Breathe* for me."

Hunter eased as her breaths mixed perfectly with his own, her glazed over chocolate browns meeting his. Bella in trouble, added with her heightened emotions at the moment, Hunter was glad to have bought her down so quickly.

"We'll find them, love."

Hunter had realized very early on that Maya saw the little fish as a sister and a daughter wrapped into one. So he could only imagine how frantic her little heart felt at not knowing what had happened to her.

And from what he'd learned of Vincent, Hunter didn't want to lose him. That type of power was some of the best to ally with.

Maya's eyes closed as she leaned into his embrace before she pulled away and faced her family again. Hunter dropped his hands to her thighs and rubbed them up and down slowly, knowing she needed his touch still.

"I told the lot of you the boy was involved with another species," his father's voice came from behind him.

Hunter turned to see Warren and Augustine both standing within the group. So they'd followed along.

Unsurprising.

Warren cared for Maya, his human heart probably wanting to make sure his new sister was all right.

And Augustine?

Augustine would want to make sure his new asset was okay, if nothing more. But Hunter figured a part of him cared for Maya the way he cared for his sons.

Loretta's hand reached for her daughter's shoulder from her spot sitting beside Maya, softly caressing her in a comforting gesture. "Do you have something of Bella's? Something we can track her with. I am assuming her parents don't yet realize she's gone, so the sooner we can get her back unharmed, the better."

"Especially if they do not know of this little relationship of hers," Kai added.

Maya nodded wordlessly, then was out of the room.

Shadowed.

Right in front of everyone.

Well, that little secret was out now.

Bewildered eyes met his as he stood and turned to the rest of the family. He only smirked, feeling a sense of pride that Maya was his, as he said, "She's quite something, isn't she?"

His father and brother were the only other ones who looked amused. The Whittle sisters didn't seem shocked, but not amused either.

Maya landed beside him with a photo of her in a framed shell. Hunter remembered Maya showing it to him, telling him how the little fish had spent a week carving the shell to fit the picture perfectly.

33

arren didn't know why he'd chosen this group to join.

He moved to the side of the building with Loretta, Camilla, and Kai. As one of the last to choose a group, he'd honestly had his pick of any.

Kai had been immediate to move for Camilla's side, and Loretta had taken her other side after seeing the slight irritation there.

Warren found it amusing that the warlock bothered her so much. Maybe it was just the thing she needed, someone to get under her skin. Not someone who changed himself to be approved by her like he had.

Though he still loved her as a person and knew part of the reason he joined this group was to make sure she wasn't hurt, he knew the other part was because he liked Kai. The man was amusing, to say the least.

And maybe *he* would be the one that needed protection if he continued infuriating the little Whittle.

They would be taking the basements, Hunter's group focusing on the ground floor and Vera's group on the upper level. This warehouse was different than any of the ones they'd been to before. It felt bigger, and Warren hoped that meant all the halfies would be here and they could finish this off.

They walked the hall in alert silence, taking in the basement level. It was clean.

Far too clean, even for Warren's upbringing.

Which made him believe his sister lived here. She'd always been a clean freak. Warren had assumed she liked the control keeping an area pristine gave her when she had so little control over the people in her life.

A shock of wind hit him before he could take another step forward and he dropped to the ground to get out of the way. Warren turned to find his 'team' dropped to the ground right beside him.

Before another shock could lower down to them, Loretta had her arm cast out, freezing the others in the room to their spots. "Get up. Move."

She moved behind a tall chair by the wall. Not hidden, but enough out of the way that the halfies would have to step out to see her. Warren watched Kai throw Camilla between him and her mother before moving himself. He was there to protect them, which meant being the last to move and first in the direct line of fire.

The time freeze must've run out because Loretta was barely paying attention, too much of her focus on her daughter, when three halfies stepped out right before them. She barely turned around in time to freeze them again, then they waited. If there were more halfies, they needed to come out first.

Five more stepped out just as the others were coming to again. And again, Loretta had them frozen as they remained 'hidden.'

Kai smirked. "Guess we found their lair."

Warren had a feeling this was done on purpose. "Meaning the Boss is done with them. He wants us to finish them off."

"What makes you think that?" Camilla asked as Loretta froze

them again, her breath accelerating with the exertion of so much of her power.

"A hunch. He probably has everything he needs from them and now wants us to finish them off so they're no longer his bother. It's why it was so easy to find Bella, why they would take a demon from a well-established family. It's why we got in so easily."

"Or maybe we got in so easily because they want to end us all on their grounds," Camilla argued.

Warren shrugged, but didn't take his eyes off the eight halfies. "Maybe."

When they unfroze this time, Warren didn't wait. He was behind one, dagger already out and piercing through her neck before she had so much as a second to blink.

When he looked over, Kai was doing the same thing and they had three killed in the matter of seconds.

Then the others caught on. And so did Loretta, freezing them all to the spot. But not before one got the chance to throw a dagger at her.

Warren didn't think, just shadowed into the dagger's way and felt the sting as the cool metal pierced through his chest.

The last thing he heard was Camilla's scream as he fell to his knees, the blood beginning to foam in his mouth.

***

Hunter, Maya, and Bishop took the front entrance, walking into an empty hallway that lead directly to two wide doors that opened up to yet another hallway, this one with door after door of rooms.

It was excessively clean.

Her mother had raised them to be clean, but not this much. It almost made her uncomfortable.

Then a halfie walked out of one of the doors, and though she looked shocked to see them, she didn't attack. Instead, her eyes moved over them and stopped on Hunter, lingering around his waist as they trailed down his form.

She threw him a seductive grin. "Boss didn't tell me he was sending me a treat today."

Maya rolled her eyes as she sent a throwing star at the girl, watching the blood splatter out of her throat instantly. She'd recently learned of throwing stars, and with the two months training Hunter had given her, she was pretty amazing. A natural.

Bishop smirked down at her. "Looks like you've got some competition."

Maya looked to Hunter with an amused grin. "Is that so?"

His lips quirked cockily. "It's adorable if you think it's only her."

Her smile dropped to a scowl, and a growl left the back of her throat just as another halfie came toward them from the end of the hall.

Hunter didn't break eye contract with her as he shadowed behind the girl and snapped her neck—his favorite method— and was back before Maya, only an inch away this time. The amusement was still alive in his eyes as he leaned in close. "Don't worry, love. You're the only reason my dick gets hard anymore."

"Good," she barked and turned right as her father ported to the end of the hall, whipping both arms out and daggering two more halfies before they could suspect anything.

So, positive, their presence wasn't known yet.

Negative, they didn't know how many halfies would come at them once it became known. But Hunter didn't look worried, and neither did her father. Rather, they looked ready. Hunter even giddy with excited adrenaline as the three prowled down the hall again, turning in the direction the last two halfies had come from.

A quick look through the tiny windows in each room

showed small spaces for sleeping. More comfortable cell than bedroom.

Around the corner, they came into a room that looked almost like a lounge. The 'almost' part coming in with the too clean of the warehouse. The room didn't look like a place anyone could lounge in.

And inside, there were five halfies. No doubt more walking through this way to 'lounge' or head to their cells.

Hunter didn't hesitate. But he also didn't leave her side.

His flames shot out, and two whole tables were on fire, incinerating the three people seated immediately. So fast, they didn't have time for screams.

"None of them are prepared for a fight," Maya concluded as she watched her throwing star fly into the chest of one of the halfies—a guy this time, a rarity—on a couch at the opposite side of the room.

Bishop tsked beside her as his dagger flew into the chest of the final halfie in the room. "They wouldn't be. This is home, and I have a feeling they've been comfortably safe here for so long, they see no reason to be on edge."

Hunter took a large inhalation.

Bishop narrowed his eyes on the man. "The smell of charred bodies turn you on, Demon?"

Hunter smirked at the man, and Maya knew something inappropriate was going to come out before she could stop it. "The only body that turns mine on is your daughter's, especially when she's clawing at my back and screaming my name."

"Hunter!" she admonished.

He quirked a nod. "Almost like that."

She punched him in the arm. "Stop. It."

He bit his lip when he looked down at her and there was desire there. He liked when she was not-real mad at him. Really liked it. Usually tried to invoke it.

Her skin began to flush as her *father* watched the way her mate acted with her.

When Hunter decided he was done playing with her, he looked back to Bishop. "Children have a different scent than adults. I can smell them. At that end."

His head thrust to the left of the room as the doors burst open on either side. From the left, three halfies. From the right, at least ten. Probably more. So they'd been alerted of their visitors.

Hunter had a neck snapped and another in flames in the time it took Maya to burn the third alive. Hers wasn't as quick, so a bit of a cry was heard. Though through the noise in the room at that moment, she doubted it would be the thing to stick out.

Bishop had two in headlocks as a pixie-wolf halfie leaped on him. He waited just long enough for the halfie to fall before pushing the two in his arms at her and stepping aside. The three crashed together, and before the halfie could realize what she'd done, her wolf claws had taken out her peers.

"You two go." Her father turned to the oncoming halfies, looking almost as excited as Hunter. "I'll take care of the rest."

Maya hesitated for a moment. She'd just met her father, but she didn't want anything happening to him. And especially not when she could've stayed and helped.

But after he killed two more halfies in the blink of an eye, Maya turned and ran with Hunter at her side.

L ila, Tamire, Harry, and Vera took the right side of the building. They'd dropped Aurelia off with Cora and Rory in hopes to help the Whittles end at least the halfie part of this magical problem.

They took the steps leading to the top floor. The men sandwiched them in from the front and back so if any attacks came their way, they'd be ported or blocked instantly. Harry had learned from their trip to the Bridgers coven and now refused to drop Vera's hand.

Though the only reason he had before was because of his increasing feelings for her that were distracting him. Now he had an out for those feelings—every time they talked or shagged, he'd get a release of the pent up emotions he hadn't been able to months prior.

That tight grip on her hand was highly favored as Vera tripped over a step and heard the echo like a sharp ringing in her ear. It was too quiet for any disturbance not to sound like a lightning strike.

She breathed a silent sorry to the others, but they didn't look angry with her.

The top floor looked more like a wide open dance hall with flickering lights all up the middle. Vera had a feeling the halfies, if there were any up here, and something told her there would be, would be hiding out on the edges.

They were themselves still hidden by the darkness at the edge of the stairs.

As Vera moved to take a step forward, figuring drawing them out would be most ideal, Harry tugged on her arm to push her behind him. She wanted to ask what he was doing when a scene came to life before them. It was the four of them. Or rather, a great rendition of the four of them, in the light where the halfies would definitely be able to see them.

They looked astonishingly realistic.

She turned to Lila beside her with wide eyes. She'd always assumed that reading memories was Lila's primary power, but with the intricateness of these illusions, Vera had a feeling this was her true primary.

Tamire gave her a knowing wink over his wife's shoulder, then turned to watch the show.

As the image figures made it halfway through the flickering lights, six halfies emerged from all around, circling around the images. They looked ready to play.

When one finally moved to attack—a half gargoyle and... Vera couldn't tell—the mirage evaporated and opened again behind them as if they'd just ported out of the way.

Tamire nudged her over Lila's shoulder and handed a piece of paper. *Cast a shield wall around them.* When had he taken this out to write? She'd been so mesmerized she hadn't even noticed.

Tamire or Harry could've cast this shield, and it probably would've come out stronger, but Vera knew they needed to remain alert to port out if necessary. She cast the spell, whispering softly into the air, and watched as the six trapped into invisible walls with the mirage of the four before them.

The illusion of Lila was the one to speak, and again, it was incredibly realistic. "I think it's time we had a chat."

Camilla wanted to turn on the halfie that had thrown the dagger at her mother. The dagger that had lodged into Warren's chest.

But all she could do was fall beside him, the tears streaming down her face as she screamed, "No! Warren. War, no, look at me. War..."

She was forcibly pulled from his body, and she was ready to turn on Kai, yell at him that Warren wasn't gone, couldn't be. But Kai didn't give her the chance. Just handed her off to her mother and bent before Warren, his hands turning bright, something Camilla had only seen happen when really bad injuries needed healing.

She almost screamed again when Kai pulled the dagger from Warren's chest and more blood gushed out.

Blood.

Kai was covered in it. Camilla barely forced her eyes around the room, where all the halfies lay dead. Kai had done that. In the time Camilla had taken to fall to the ground, he'd killed the other halfies and pushed her out of the way to save Warren.

She didn't like him. But for this, she would be forever grateful.

Especially considering it only took moments before Warren's chest was rising and falling again. His eyes fluttered open only a few seconds later.

And Kai looked so relieved.

It was weird since he didn't really know Warren, but his relief almost felt as palpable as her own.

Camilla helped Kai get Warren up as Loretta cleared her throat, her hand flying back up.

Camilla turned to see six more halfies.

Then her father was beside her mother. A bit of blood marred his arms and clothes, but overall, he looked ready to finish the halfies. Good, they needed someone else while Warren recovered.

"I'm good," Warren said, trying to pull away and join the fight.

Kai was the one to push back. "Rest. For a few more minutes. Your body needs at least that much."

Warren narrowed his eyes at the warlock, but it looked more like amusement than resentment. "You'll finish them off by then."

Kai shrugged as the halfies came back. "Sucks for you." Then he and Bishop were porting behind them, daggers at the ready as Loretta played with their ability to move.

34

The halfies tried to make a run from the mirages, tried to break through the shield. But Vera maintained her concentration, and eventually, they had no choice but to turn to the images before them.

They looked a lot less excited about the confrontation now.

The Tamire illusion spoke. "Hello, friends. I believe now we may speak."

Vera bit the inside of her cheek as she glanced to the real Tamire. The fake version didn't talk like the real.

He flickered his gaze to hers and gave a grin and a shrug.

They didn't answer, but one stepped up with newfound bravado. "Why would we tell you anything, *Warlock?*" She spit the last part like it was acid on her tongue.

And it was like that little comment spurred her friends on as each stood straighter, spitting foul words at the mirages standing before them. For a group that used illusions on their victims, Vera was surprised they were so bad at telling them apart.

Or maybe they were more used to the illusions of a specific scene and not these ones that interacted. Vera didn't even know these existed.

Harry's thumb brushed the top of her hand and she turned to see him whispering under his breath. A silencing charm.

She narrowed her eyes, but there was a tug on her other side before Harry could finish.

Tamire.

He was handling her a vial and another note. *Spill a drop over each one. Just a drop.*

Vera glanced at it, then met his gaze again.

Her power took the vial and moved it through the air until it was beside Lila's creation. Then she moved farther until it was within the circle. The halfies scowled as they looked up to it, but none of them stopped their harassment.

Vera ignored them and allowed her magic to uncork the vial and tip it just slightly so that a single drop escaped and fell to the 'leader' of this pack.

It took less than half a second before a blood-curdling scream came out of the halfie's lips. Her friends froze suddenly, and Vera stiffened beside her friends. So that's what the silencing charm was for.

Harry squeezed her hand to bring her back, and she moved her magic again, allowing a single drop to fall onto another member of the group. This scream was just as horrific. Maybe it was a good thing she was in this group and not Camilla.

That second scream was enough to silence the others and have them running straight into the shield that surrounded them. They clawed into the air, which Harry was now helping her keep up, and Vera felt a surge of retribution spike through her that they'd finally be feeling a bit of the pain they'd caused those innocent couples.

None of their attempts for escape would deter Vera. She allowed another drop over a third, fourth, fifth halfie.

The sixth had a bit of piss falling down the side of her pants as she pushed against the air to get out of there. When the single drop fell over her, her cries were as sharp as the others'.

Tamire's phantom spoke again, "Any more willing now?"

One of them scowled in the mirages' direction, spit flying as she yelled a "Fuck you."

Probably not the smartest of ideas. But hey, they were loyal.

"You sure about that?" Harry's mirage spoke, and Lila even got the British accent in there.

The original Mrs. Bravado glared at them. "We're going to kill you."

Vera watched for another few seconds before turning to Tamire and seeing the single nod that told her to allow one more drop on each member.

One. On Mrs. Fuck You.

Two. On Mrs. Death Warrant.

Three. On Mrs. Disgusted Scowl.

Four. On Mrs. Tough Guy.

Loyalty was strong for a master who gave you the retribution you've been craving all your life. But it only went so far when pain was involved and you held no love for the one you were loyal to. Because these halfies definitely didn't love one another, and they certainly didn't love their boss. Grand-mama, Vera was less sure about.

But five and six seemed to have taken the hoarse cries of their companions as sign enough to give in and tell them what they wanted to know.

It was six who screamed with her arms reaching beside her face—as much as possible in her fetal position. "What do you want?"

As they waited for Lila to make one of the phantoms speak, Harry whispered in Vera's ear, "The first drop is painful. The second is worse. A third may kill them."

Shock ran through Vera at finally getting a bit of explanation.

Just one more and they'd be dead?

Though from the sounds of it, they probably wished they were dead already.

It was Lila's phantom that did the speaking, "Your sole purpose?"

"Revenge on the species that abandoned us," she cried. "I needed a pixie and mermaid couple to get back at my parents. That's all it was for us." The tears stained her cheeks as she shivered away in fear from the bottle that still hovered above her.

Vera's heart shriveled up with empathy, but she knew she had to be more like Maya and fight it away. These halfies didn't deserve any empathy.

"And Grandmama's plan?" Lila's mirage asked.

"Revenge too." The other pushed her frail body away from under the vial. "She wants to rid the families that killed hers."

All things they knew. Or had guessed. It was nice having them verified, but now the most important part. Boss.

"Cowards," Mrs. Death Warrant hissed. "You two are traitors. Fucking cowards."

Vera gave it to her for sticking her ground, but a light squeeze of her hand told her to go ahead with exactly as she'd been thinking.

Drop three.

Her screams echoed for long moments, and just as Harry had said, her body wasn't able to take it. Her heart likely gave out before her will did. But finally, the silence rang in Vera's ears.

"And your boss?" Vera jumped at hearing her own voice from a few yards away. It was incredible how well Lila worked her illusions.

They all shivered away from Death Warrant's body, the tears falling faster and faster.

The vial shook above them, and before Lila could make the illusions speak again, Mrs. Tough Guy broke, "He wants power."

"We figured that much," Vera's voice came from up ahead. "How's that happening?"

"He has Bason take the power of anyone we're about to kill

and put it away in a vial for him to use later." Number Five again, Vera hadn't given her a name.

"Later use meaning?" Vera's voice rang out.

When no one answered, she shook the vial above them like a lottery of which one the drop would fall onto.

Mrs. Fuck You screamed as she pushed her body against the shield. "He can't take all that power. It's like stealing powers from demons or witches. Your body needs to be able to hold everything you take." Vera had never thought about that point. Never considered that some people may steal powers that their bodies couldn't handle. "He needs a vessel that could hold it all for him. Someone he could control so the power is all still his."

"How?"

"We don't know," Number Six screamed like she was tired of the interrogation.

Mrs. Disgusted Scowl finally joined. "You guys are pathetic. They're going to kill us anyway. Why give them what they fucking want?"

Vera's lips twitched up, and that bit of sympathy she'd felt was beginning to wash away. The vial tipped, and a single drop hit Disgusted Scowl.

For her part, she tried to keep the screams contained.

They didn't work, but she did try.

Tamire's phantom spoke when there was a bit of silence again. "Anything else we should know about this boss of yours? For instance, his name?"

"T-T-T…" Number Five began convulsing. Vera had a feeling it was shock of everything happening because she hadn't dropped another bit on her.

"TJ," Mrs. Fuck You cried and pushed farther back as her companion foamed at the mouth. "That's how we know him."

"I-I-I don't know. He's secretive," Number Six cried.

"What's he waiting for?" Harry's phantom asked.

Mrs. Tough Guy was the one to answer, and like her name, she decided to tough it out rather than wallow away like the other two. "What does it matter what we say? You're going to kill us."

Vera gave her props for going back to sticking her ground. Because she was right, they were all dying one way or another.

The third drop hit her before she could say much else. Her convulsions had the other two crying into their legs in their fetal positions.

"*What* is he waiting for?" Harry's phantom asked again.

Mrs. Fuck You answered, "Someone powerful enough to hold it all. Someone who can steal magic, a ton of it, and hold all of it."

"We don't know who," Number Six cried.

Vera looked to Tamire beside her and saw the nod back, informing her to bring the vial back. Because all of them would be dying, but not all of them had to die in the same horrific ways.

She had the vial in her hands, cork already screwed back on, when Lila dropped the illusion and the boys muttered something under their breaths. Then both warlocks ported and daggered both halfies silently.

Bella was breathing slowly when Maya and Hunter turned the corner into the room she and Vincent were held in. Maya could see the light barrier of the shield holding them apart in their own little boxes. And Vincent's attempts to get out of his and reach Bella.

He had power draining cuffs on. They'd been smart enough to hinder his abilities even though he was known for being the weak one.

But when Maya's gaze landed on Bella, her heart stopped. Bella's breaths were coming out too slowly, her lips chapped. Less like she'd been tortured and more like she needed something.

Like water.

She was a mermaid. Without water, she wouldn't be able to survive. And the assholes here knew that.

Maya was running to her side before she could think it through, but Hunter's arms around her waist stopped her at the door of the room. She tried fighting, but he calmly leaned close and whispered into her ear, "I'll hydrate her. Just calm down. I'm not letting you run into a trap."

Maya's heart raced as her breathing equalized. He was right. They couldn't be reckless if they wanted to get the kids out.

And he had a handy stolen power.

He kept one hand around her waist as the other lifted and sprayed out to Bella's form, drenching her. She gasped like a human coming out of the water for air. Then her mouth opened to take in the water her pores were already fighting for.

And thankfully, Hunter didn't pull away immediately. He allowed the water to flow out of him and cover her. Vincent also seemed to relax against his shield a bit as Bella looked lively once more.

Hunter only pulled away when a voice from the darkened shadows at the back of the room spoke. "How nice of you."

Maya froze.

Somehow, even though she'd never heard it herself, she knew the voice as Grandmama's.

Grandmama looked less corporeal coming out into the light now than she had when she'd been brought to life, but there was a bit of a sheen on the outskirts of her form that gave away something wasn't entirely right.

Hunter moved, pushing Maya behind him and keeping his hand on her stomach to push her back again when she tried to move beside him. She still saw Grandmama past Hunter's arm though, and the woman looked like she could've been a cute old grandmother. Except there was also something in her eyes that wasn't entirely inviting. That was the part that Maya suspected meant she would only be the cute grandmother to her family—the only ones allowed to go up the mountain to visit her.

"It is for this girl," Grandmama spoke in her soft yet authoritative tone, "that I suspect you did not agree to my offer the first time."

"It is," Hunter said with no attempt to conceal their relationship.

"Hm." Her old hand delicately touched her neck. "Does it not inflame you that you must lower yourself to helping those you do not care for just because she wants you to?"

Maya had no idea where she was going with this. Because she was obviously trying to knock Hunter's masculinity down enough to do something stupid that would get Maya angry with him. Except as a demon who didn't care for others, and in turn didn't care what others thought of him. It wouldn't work on Hunter.

"No." Simple. No more information about how strong their relationship was. Though an effortless glance in their direction would tell any stranger just how strongly Hunter cared for her.

Grandmama smiled at them, but there was something sinister in the way she did it. Her glance dropped to Vincent, then Bella—Vincent's form stiffening alongside Maya's—before coming back to them. "You know, it is my fault that my family was killed."

Quite the change of subject.

"Oh?" Maya answered because it was obvious Hunter wasn't going to.

A sadness glazed into her eyes, and it almost overtook the dominance. "Yes," she said solemnly. "Had I been around to protect them, not been made of stolen faerie dust as I am, they wouldn't have been killed. It was a protection against the magical creatures to kill my family."

"How so?" Maya asked to get her to continue talking so she wasn't focused on the kids. But also out of curiosity.

"The way I was created, it was outlawed long before I came

along. But no one knew of my existence, so life went on. But I got cocky up in that mountain, and a certain *someone* saw me and made sure the whole of the magical world knew I was alive and had offspring. The plan was to kill me too, you see." There was more vengeance in her features than sorrow. She'd had a thousand years to grieve. Though the pain was likely still there, she was over that stage. Now she just wanted payback.

Though, Maya had to say, she was getting revenge on the wrong people. The family lineage of those responsible had nothing to do with what their ancestors did.

"I only have one more family left," Grandmama's eyes twinkled. "Except I will not go after everyone in this family. Only the one who holds the power that truly caused my pain."

"You didn't mention a family where you were only after a single member," Hunter responded without asking who exactly she was speaking of.

"No." Her eyes shined brightly as she stared between the two of them. "I didn't. But I am close. I almost have my retribution."

Her eyes shined on Maya for what felt like an eternity, but was likely only a second.

Then she was gone. As if they'd finished their conversation. Vanished like an apparition.

"What the hell was that?" Maya whispered into Hunter's arm.

"I have no idea," he said through a clenched jaw, his gaze still analyzing the spot Grandmama had been standing.

Maya knew the room was safe when she stepped out from around Hunter and he didn't stop her. If he believed there to still be a threat, he wouldn't allow her an inch. He'd allow the kids to die in front of her, but wouldn't allow Maya any closer to danger.

A quick spell broke the shields holding them apart, and the second they were down, Vincent ran to Bella's side. She was looking livelier than when Maya had arrived, but she definitely didn't look like her normal self.

"She needs to swim!" Vincent demanded.

Maya rested a reassuring hand to his shoulder. "We have a pool at the manor. She'll be safe there."

The manor no one else knew the location to but her. It was her manor now too, so she could invite them without asking permission, but when she looked up to meet Hunter's gaze, he didn't look annoyed. He honestly didn't look like he minded at all that she'd offered to take them to the one spot he'd done an amazing job at keeping hidden.

She pulled out her phone and texted her family that they had the kids and were leaving. When she put it away again, Hunter was looking back to the spot Grandmama had been standing. It was probably killing him not knowing what she'd been talking about.

He came up and wrapped his arms around Maya's waist again, Maya keeping her hold on Vincent, who had a tight grip on Bella. Then they were all shadowed out.

They landed in the pool room, Bella pushing out of Vincent's arms and coming to stand. She hugged him tight, like she was scared something would've happened to *him*. Like he had been the one on the verge of dying.

But Vincent pulled away quickly. And pushed. Pushed Bella back, back, back, against her protests. His protective instinct needed to get her in the pool.

Though his efforts were pure, Bella wasn't bound to let go anytime soon, and so when Vincent finally got his way and pushed her into the water, he was falling with her.

Seconds passed before they both breeched the water laughing, Bella looking more and more alive as she floated in her mermaid form. A form Maya had yet to have seen, but realized just how beautiful she was in it. Almost more siren-esque than mermaid in her allure.

Then there was a splash. Then another. And another. And they had begun a little war, not without drowning attempts and water wrestling. But their smiles and laughs were intoxicating.

Maya turned in Hunter's arms, clasping her fingers together at the small of his back. His bored gaze watching the kids—if she didn't already know better, she wouldn't have been able to believe that he didn't find the scene before them endearing—dropped down to meet hers and turned bright as their foreheads touched.

"You know," Maya kissed his chin, "a few little ones running around the manor is sounding better and better."

The sparks in his eyes burst like a show of fireworks as his ever present smirk grew to reach his eyes. "You wanna go right now?" He wiggled his brows.

She pulled away as much as his arms would allow and pointed a finger at him. "Behave. We have children in the house."

He always enjoyed when she was not-real angry with him. "Is Mama Maya getting angry?"

"Hunter!" she shrieked with an incredibly wide grin as her body hummed with happiness.

His hands skimmed down her back and took handfuls of her ass. "Mama Maya *is* angry. We should fix that."

Thank the lords the kids were distracted in the pool.

Maya couldn't help the laugh that bubbled out of her as she muttered, "I hate you."

He pulled away from her and took her by the arm as he led them out of the pool room and into a hallway. He only turned into one other hallway to give them the semblance of privacy and pushed her into the wall. His lips brushed hers as his hands made their way over her body. "Good."

Maya's text that she'd found the kids was a heaven-sent, because after listening to all those screams, Vera just wanted to go home and let the shower wash the day's events away. Harry joining in the middle to remind her just how lovely her life was now was also a plus.

Though she still wasn't a hundred percent on the whole having-sex-with-your-parents-downstairs part. Maya was lucky in that aspect. She had a whole private manor to do as she pleased.

Augustine was sitting in the middle of the couch when they came down from their shower, most of the rest of the house coming from different parts of the house to meet in the living room.

Vera didn't know when, but somehow, at some point, the living room had become the meeting room rather than the kitchen. Maybe because their group had become too big to manage in the kitchen anymore.

Everyone took their spots, a round of hot chocolate being passed to each person as brownies and cookies were placed in the middle of the table.

Hunter and Maya shadowed into the foyer, and on their way

to their spot beside his father, Hunter grabbed for one of the gooey chocolate chip cookies.

Maya held their shared cup in her hands as she took her spot in his lap.

With the whole family together, they could finally discuss what happened. Starting with a question from Augustine that Vera had forgotten about in all the chaos.

He turned on his son. "Now that you're no longer busy running after your mate's feelings"—Hunter's eyes made it clear he had to tread lightly when speaking of Maya—"where were you two these last couple of nights?"

That was right. They'd been gone two nights. Odd of them to take a vacation at the moment.

Hunter ignored his father, enjoying his cookie as he seemingly allowed Maya to decide whether or not they would answer that question.

Maya's face flushed, but she complied. "Hell's Gate."

Vera almost spit out her sip of hot cocoa as the others around the room choked and Augustine's eyes bulged. "Excuse me?"

Maya swallowed, but looked him in the eyes, almost like she was telling him something extra. "We were fighting. About what you told me the other day." Vera could only wonder what that would've been. "And…I don't know. I was so angry, then the ground was rumbling and we were in Hell's Gate again."

Augustine looked equal parts horrified and fascinated. Actually, more fascinated. Vera was definitely more horrified, the consensus of the room seeming to match up with her.

"How'd you get out?" Camilla exclaimed right before Vera could.

Maya shrugged. "We were just…lying on the ground one moment and in our bed the next."

Hunter drank some hot cocoa, gave it back to Maya, then pulled her in close so his nose settled into her neck. That man's love language was definitely physical touch. "It was the best fucking time of my life."

Maya's eyes glowed in that way they always did when there was mention of hers and Hunter's sex life.

"Gross, My," Vera muttered, only to earn a wicked grin in return and a couple of chuckles from around the room that solidified everyone understood exactly what had been happening in Hell's Gate between the two.

"No dreams this time?" Harry asked the actual important question.

Maya shook her head. "None."

"How?" Loretta looked contemplative.

"Hunter thinks it has something to do with my control of the portal. He thinks it gives me enough control so that we weren't hurt down below."

"Interesting," Bishop and Kai said at the same time. Warren looked equally as interested.

And Augustine? He looked to be far off, like he was piecing a puzzle together.

"You were fine then? Nothing happened?" Loretta asked with concern.

Maya's lips tipped up, and Vera swore she saw Hunter's wide grin even though his face was hidden in Maya's neck. "Like Hunt said. It was the best time."

Camilla scoffed with a shake of her head, but it was more disbelieving than disgruntled. "Which means we don't need to focus on that right now. Or ever, you know." Maya stuck out her tongue to her sister, but Camilla ignored it. "How about the kids you guys got? How are Bella and Vincent?"

"I think they'll be all right. Bella's a lot stronger than people give her credit for."

"Then let's focus on the one thing that's still sticking out. Why?" Lila said, though the way she glanced Maya's way said she was still concerned for the children. Maybe becoming a mother did that to you.

Aurelia was asleep in her bassinet at the edge of the room, but Lila's gaze kept flickering over like she was afraid something would happen to her daughter. Having children sounded like too much worry.

Maya shrugged again. "I have no idea. Grandmama told us she has one more person she's going after. That the entire family is around, but she only wants one person from the group, that she holds that one person the most responsible. But I honestly don't think it was Bella or Vincent. We can't figure out why *they* were taken. Even if it was for the halfies, there are definitely other demon-mermaid couples they could've found that weren't kids."

"The halfies told us," Lila said, "that the Boss, T.J., was waiting for someone. Apparently he needs someone that's strong enough to hold all the power he's been collecting over each killing."

Camilla's head snapped to Warren as he sat up straighter and whispered under his breath, "I knew it."

"What?" Tamire asked.

"That he's not strong enough to hold all that power. There aren't even many demons who could steal that much power. I highly doubted someone hiding behind the magic that birthed Grandmama would have that kind of strength. He's trying to get someone strong enough to carry all the magic for him. I'm guessing he has all the magic separated now?"

"Yes," Harry answered. "Each in its own vial."

"That's what I thought," Warren muttered.

Kai spoke over him, "So basically this T.J. guy allowed the halfies to have their revenge in order to get the magic out of those killed. Which means he's done with that because he let us kill them all earlier." He sat backwards on his chair as usual and leaned over a little more. "I would assume he's doing the same with Grandmama, taking the magic from those she kills, but it's more of a deal with them. I'm guessing she gets her revenge and he gets her magic at the end. The final vial to add to the group he's already amassed."

"The real question now," Bishop said, "is how he's choosing the vessel for all this magic he's amassed."

"And how he intends on remaining safe until then," Loretta added. "Without the halfies to protect him on all ends, he's left open."

Vera's head hurt from all the possibilities and what this psychopath wanted. She couldn't understand the greedy desire to have all that power. It felt like too much of a responsibility to her.

It was later than Camilla normally left the house. Much later.

So late that even with her magic and the ability to cast a spell around herself to keep predators—a.k.a. creepy men—away, she was on edge. All she knew was that she wanted to be at the astronomy tower, and even though it was one in the morning, she was going to make it happen.

The school was eerie at this time of night with not a single person walking its grounds. Camilla was so used to the packed quad and the noises coming from all directions that this almost felt like a dream and not like she was really there.

The best part of no one else being around was that Camilla didn't have to hide going up to the tower. The school had some cameras, but she'd already cast the spell around herself to make sure she didn't show up in them. She'd never been worried about that. It was always more a matter of students seeing her and following her up there. She wanted the astronomy tower only for herself.

She'd brought two blankets with her this time. One to lay on the ground so she didn't lie out on the cold ground of the tower, and another to lay on top of herself so she didn't freeze up there.

With the blankets snuggled around her, Camilla stared out at the sky and felt her heart relax as she thought back to their discussion.

Hunter had been quiet. He normally was, so that wasn't surprising, but it felt more like he was still trying to piece something together—something she assumed had to do with what Grandmama had told them—than because he didn't have anything to say. Camilla wanted to know what was bothering him, because if it was bothering him that much, then there was a large possibility it had to do with Maya. And she would do anything to save her sister.

But if it had to do with Maya, he'd mention it. His mating instinct and uncaring nature of what others thought of him would force him to say it so that anyone else could help. Even if he was a bit prideful in other parts of his life, he wouldn't allow pride to win out over Maya's safety. Which made Camilla believe he wasn't sure it had anything to do with Maya. He just wasn't sure at all.

His father had been quiet too, but that was because he was thinking about Maya and Hunter being in Hell's Gate. Camilla knew that much from the fact that he didn't seem to be paying attention at all to the rest of the conversation.

And Warren looked more in thought about how his theory had been right and what that could mean. Overall, the most helpful of the Delvauxs.

But none of it made sense yet. Why take Bella and Vincent?

A figure stood over her, and Camilla jumped from the sudden appearance.

"Is this spot taken?" Kai nodded to the spot on the blanket beside her.

"*What* are you doing here?" she grit out. This was *her* private spot.

"I've wondered where you run off to," he said while taking

the spot next to her. His hands rested on his chest, but he didn't try to take some of the blanket Camilla had over herself.

"Didn't you consider that I run off because I want to be alone?"

It wasn't a rhetorical question, but he seemed to take it as one. "It's beautiful up here."

She took in a large breath. "I know."

"What were you thinking about?"

"Don't you think I should be the one asking questions, Mr. Secrets?" She shot him a dark glare.

His eyes didn't waver from the sky, but his lips twitched up. "What secrets?"

"Why won't you tell anyone your coven name? You go by Kai Nothing."

Camilla couldn't really tell from her lying angle, but his smile looked to turn...sad.

"I'm not keeping it a secret, princess. I don't have a coven name."

"How could you not have a coven name? Warlocks are far and few. There's no way a coven wouldn't want you." She looked back up to the sky because she did not want to get riled up at the moment.

"I don't know if your warlock told you—I'm sure he did, but if not, then you should know—that I used to be best friends with a halfie demon. It was around the time I first passed my warlocking. He was half human and more my brother than best friend."

Camilla looked over to him, shocked. No wonder he was hostile toward her. She'd broken up with a halfie demon-human for what he was.

"I'd protect him over anyone else and vice versa. My brother." His tone sounded like he still grieved his friend. Camilla assumed he was dead since Kai was about a hundred years old. "One of the witches from my coven, she asked if we wanted to go on a double date. Nico, he was..." His lips widened into a grin, and Camilla's heart began to ache with how much he must be missing his friend. "He was excited. I was excited. We did double dates a lot. Fucked around a lot, but we were good guys. Never played with girls."

He looked lost in thought as he lay there, and Camilla didn't know what it was, but something compelled her to open her blanket and throw part of it over him. Maybe it was the comforting instincts in her, but instead of wrapping her arms around him, he'd get a blanket.

Finally, he continued, "We were good guys. *He* was a good guy. The best, most standup, decent person. But most creatures didn't see that, still don't see that. All they saw was that his mother was a demon, so he was a demon, and everyone hates demons." He scoffed. "I can't believe they still do."

Camilla's gaze drifted back up to the sky. She was part of that group, and she felt the guilt eating up around her.

"Had I known my coven still felt like that, I would've never agreed to the date. That's why they kept their thoughts hidden. They needed me."

Camilla couldn't help it, she looked back over at him.

"We were on a rooftop at the end of the date, just fooling around. Nico and I especially were just fooling around." He swallowed hard. "Then everything changed. My date, Liza," he said the name in disgust, "she cast a spell around me. She wasn't too powerful, but shields were her thing. I couldn't get out, couldn't do anything. Then the other one, Elle." More disgust. More loathing. "Elle had this dagger strapped beneath her dress that she took out and walked right up to Nico with. Her power was petrification. He couldn't move, couldn't do anything to stop her, and I couldn't get out of that *fucking* shield. So he just gave up, looked at me because we both knew where this was leading and that we couldn't do anything about it. I didn't want to give up, though. He was my brother. I couldn't leave him like that. But he looked okay, like he had run his life with me and that was it." A tear fell down his face. "She didn't hesitate, not for a second. But Nico's eyes were on me the entire time the dagger ripped through his chest. The entire time the blood spilled down his form until the life finally left him, he didn't break his eye contact with me. Because he was my brother, and he was all I cared about."

Camilla moved in closer. She wouldn't coddle him, but she needed to comfort as the tears strolled down her face.

"When he was *gone* and there was nothing my healing could do for him, Liza let me out of my shield, but I was already on my knees. She said *she was sorry it hurt, but she was doing the best thing for me.* That the coven believed this the best thing. That I shouldn't be associating with a demon." He swallowed back. "My rage grew so deep that I turned on them. I knew a spell that could freeze them. It's an old one and is difficult to do, but with the amount of rage that was in me, I didn't even feel it. I took my time killing them, letting them cry out. Then I cut them up into pieces and sent the pieces back to the coven. I took Nico's body and buried him in Scotland, by a shack that we used to go to all the time, that I still go to all the time."

Kai didn't move, but Camilla ran a soothing hand over his arm. He looked so far off into time as he looked up at the sky, like he was searching for his brother.

"I wanted to end myself, but we'd promised each other that we wouldn't do it. That if something happened to one, the other would go on. And I wasn't going to break my promise to my brother. So I went on. And I made revenge my livelihood. It's part of the reason I understand Grandmama, but I went after those actually responsible, not the decedents of those people. It's why I haven't been added to another coven. Everyone's too scared to have me."

"What'd you do?" she asked softly even though she thought she knew the answer.

"I killed the entire coven. One by one. Started from the bottom so that the leaders knew what they'd caused. Sent each person back, some in pieces, others whole, until it was me and

Bethany, the leader. Hers was the slowest of tortures, but finally within the year, the entire coven was gone."

"Then no one else wanted you? Even though they needed you?" she asked.

"No." He breathed out calmly. "And I didn't want them. For years, I just moved along doing whatever I pleased. Then I started getting into the business of helping people for favors like the demons do. I knew everything about everything so that creatures needed me, then made sure they paid for it. People started calling me the Demon Warlock. Funny, because it's not possible, even if I was a halfie. Any male born of a witch and demon, or warlock and demon, couldn't be both. Only the females can be both. I think that's why I was given the name. *The Demon Warlock.* I take great pride in that name."

Camilla let out a breathy laugh. After a moment, she turned to her back once again and stared at the sky. "That's why you hate me so much."

"Yes." He didn't sugarcoat. Just like a demon. "Parts of Warren remind me of Nico too, so it's even harder. But I can also see you're coming around. Plus, you'd never be as bad as them. You didn't necessarily hate Warren for what he was, you just couldn't date him for it. Still don't like you for it, but it's better than *those* witches."

"I still don't like you either," she said as she tasted the tears running down her cheeks.

She felt him finally look over at her. "Liar."

She met his gaze and felt a small quirk of her lips.

Maya hadn't been on a jog around the route she used to take in a while. Now that she lived at Delvaux Manor, she jogged one of the estate's paths, but she'd missed this old route of hers.

She moved through it without paying too much attention, though she had to go slower than normal. Her stomach was giving her one of those calm-down-or-I'll-throw-everything-up days.

She finally stopped when she felt her breakfast try to make its way up her throat. At least the chill that still lingered in the air helped stay her stomach's protests.

The walk was still a nice one even though she couldn't do her usual exercise.

She was a little over half-way through her route when she heard her name called out from the right. And it sounded familiar in a good way.

But her brows furrowed because why would she be hearing that sound?

"Maya," the voice called again, and Maya followed it to a clearing a little way's off of her route.

"Vikki," she breathed out.

The girl was standing before her calmly, but Maya swore she saw fear in her eyes. But it was gone in the matter of seconds.

"Vikki, what're you doing out here?" she asked.

"Looking for you." Something about the way she spoke didn't sound like Vikki. But this was Vikki. Right?

Maya's brows furrowed deeper. "What are the names I had picked out?"

"Myles and Esther."

So this was Vikki.

But why did talking to her feel so different? Was it because the last time Maya had seen the girl, she'd been cowering at the edge of the couch?

Maya stepped up to her. "Vikki, what's going on?"

"I need your help." She reached out for Maya's hand, and Maya offered it without hesitation.

Then there was a cuff around her hand.

And before she could process it, another around her other hand.

Maya stared down at the cuffs in disbelief. Power repellents.

She looked back to Vikki, and again, saw the flash of fear and sorrow in her eyes before they were gone. This *was* Vikki. But Maya knew the little girl wasn't the one in control of her body.

Vikki had a grasp of Maya's arm and a marble thrown on the ground quickly so that Maya couldn't question what was happening. Then they were through the portal.

And in an...other warehouse?

It looked like one of those large industrial places, but with only the lights in the middle of the room on. And with the power repellent cuffs, Maya couldn't manipulate the darkness to see past where she and Vikki stood.

Now that they were there, Maya turned to her little friend. "Okay you got me here. Now tell me who's controlling you."

The fear flashed in her eyes again, and Maya felt a sense of familiarity. This was the real Vikki now. "Help me, Maya. I can't…stand in the middle, don't touch me." Her tone changed when she lost control, but Maya saw the way she fought to win it back. "Help me. The mark. I can't…"

She pushed Maya on her back and stepped back and away from her, candles lining a circle around where Maya now lay. But that didn't matter because Vikki had told her everything she needed to know.

The mark was controlling her.

The mark that Colette Delvaux had placed on her.

The mark that gave that halfie sister of hers the control over this little girl's body, including the ability to make her do things she wanted to fight against.

The flames on the candles surrounding her flickered, but didn't dance like they would if any magic was being used. So it wasn't a shield. Then what was the point?

Then Maya saw Vikki pull out a dagger from the back of her pants and scream for help. Maya too screamed as she lunged up and after her, but it was too late. Vikki turned the dagger around and pierced it straight through her own heart.

She dropped to the ground as Maya reached her. Maya fell beside her, tears already staining her cheeks, and took Vikki's head into her lap. They were outside the circle of candles, but Maya still didn't know what they were for. And she didn't care at the moment.

Vikki was dead, taken using the mark that Maya hadn't been able to help her with. The girl had so much ahead of her, had children whose names Maya couldn't wait to hear, had powers still waiting to show themselves. She had love and friendship and every part of life waiting for her. And it was all gone now.

Maya looked back up at the warehouse surrounding her, tears blurring her vision. She pulled out her phone, no service. Unsurprising.

She was cuffed, so she wouldn't be able to shadow out, and there was no way for her to let Hunter know through the rings that she needed him. But he should be able to feel her distress the way he had when Bella had gone missing because the rings didn't work on magic, so the cuffs wouldn't be able to eliminate that factor.

Then it all clicked to her.

The candles weren't set out to do anything to her. They were set out to control emotion within the building. If her emotions seemed normal, then Hunter wouldn't be able to feel how much she needed him at the moment. Because though she felt the trauma in her mind and the tears rolling down her face, Maya realized in that instant that her heart beat in a steady rhythm.

She swallowed hard and pulled out the pocket watch she'd taken from Hunter's room all those weeks ago. Ever since Hunter refused to take it back, Maya had carried it around with her for comfort.

She held the watch in her shaky hand as she smoothed back Vikki's hair, hoping that holding the piece would help Maya calm down and find a way out of there and back to her mate.

***

The only negative part of the whole killing spree they'd went on in that warehouse with the halfies was that Colette hadn't been there. Or she'd been smart enough to bolt before they got to her. She would be smart enough to know she wouldn't be able to take on that many of them.

But Warren had wanted to know where she was.

And sometimes, those wishes came true in ways he didn't like.

They'd been in their usual family meetings in his father's office—just Warren, Hunter, and Augustine—when Loki interrupted to let them know they had a visitor at the gates. A quick glance through the cameras Augustine had set up showed Colette.

Augustine had thanked Loki, then the three of them had stepped out of the house and walked the long path to the gates,

Hunter in the middle. It was weird that Hunter being in the middle would be the case, given Augustine was the patriarch, but Colette had a fear of Hunter that even their father recognized as an advantage.

When they stopped on the other side of the gates, Warren saw the shimmer around his sister. He'd guess something to make sure they didn't just attack her right then and there.

"Well, if it isn't the men of my life." She smiled with a glint in her eyes.

"What do you want, Witch?" their father asked, and Warren saw the stiffening of his sister's spine. He'd always referred to her as her other half, something he didn't do to Warren. Maybe that was another reason she despised Warren so much.

"Hm." Her eyes grew dark like she was going to enjoy the next part. "Nice to see you, Father. Though I've heard you've replaced me with another witch. Is she better because she's full blooded, or just because she gets on her knees for your pride and joy?"

Hunter growled so deep, Warren knew Colette felt the threat in the vibrations. And he saw the way she stiffened too. As much bravado as she'd like to play off, she was terrified of him.

"Don't you find it a waste of time to threaten your own kind?" Augustine sounded bored.

Colette scowled. "My own kind are half-blood demon-witches. I would never hurt one of them. The rest of you can burn for all I care."

Warren was tired of standing there. "What do you want, Colette?"

She brought the smile back onto her lips, though it was more forced now. "I just came to inform you that Grandmama has her last victim. And she's given me full range on *her* matters." She turned to stare Hunter in the eyes as the next words left her lips. "The candles should be flickering out soon enough. You'll feel it through the rings, I suspect."

Warren's heart stopped.

He just about had time to meet his father's gaze as the ground rumbled with Hunter's growl, and the two reached for the man in the middle. Warren's fingers bit into his brother's shoulder and arm as his father's fingers dug into the opposite side, but they needed to keep him there. If he shadowed away, he'd be giving Colette exactly what she wanted and them with no way to help. Currently, Hunter was the only one able to find Maya, and he couldn't go in alone.

A sweat broke down Warren's neck as he and his father fought to keep Hunter restrained. Warren looked back to his sister to find the satisfaction before she threw a marble to the ground and portalled out of there.

One glance toward his father told Warren they were both thinking the same thing—they needed to get to the Whittles for backup and stabilize Hunter.

Like when Maya and Camilla had wanted to run after their sister when Melusine had captured her, Hunter wasn't thinking straight at the moment, and he couldn't go in there distracted. Especially considering this entire ploy was to get Hunter too. Because there's no way Colette would give up torturing Hunter if she could.

Warren didn't think about it, just nodded to his father as his arms burned with the strength it took to hold Hunter from shadowing, and together, Augustine and Warren shadowed the three of them to Whittle House.

3 8

Warren, Hunter, and Augustine shadowed into the living room. And from the looks of it, the middle man wasn't there voluntarily. *What the hell?*

Camilla watched as Augustine muttered the spell she'd only heard used against Colette in this household. The one Maya had used the moment she'd walked into the house and seen the Delvaux daughter standing amongst them. But why would they be using that spell on Hunter?

Warren and Augustine bent at the hips and caught their breaths, sweat lightly trickling down their necks. *Seriously, what the fuck?*

She was about to question it when Hunter interrupted her. "Let me out!" His gaze shot from his father to his brother. "Let me out." He banged against the shield. "After I kill Colette, I'm coming after you." He hit the shield again, and Camilla was convinced that if it weren't a shield made of magic, it would've shattered with the intensity of his fists. "Let me out!" he roared.

"What the hell is going on?" Loretta demanded in that authoritative, motherly tone of hers.

Hunter looked crazed as he continued beating on the shield and cursing at his father and brother.

Warren finally looked at them. "Colette just came by." His gaze met Loretta's and turned soft. "Apparently they have that final person Grandmama needs."

Camilla's heart stopped.

Stopped.

Completely.

It was only Kai's hand on her shoulder that reminded her to breathe. Because if Grandmama had the final person she needed and Hunter was reacting like *that*, then the final person was Maya.

Now that Camilla was breathing, it felt like too much.

Too much air.

Too much for her lungs to handle.

Again, it was Kai's hands on her arms that calmed her back down as the ringing in her ears subsided, and she looked around to find the conclusion on everyone else's features.

"We figured," Augustine continued after his son, "that it would be wiser for all of us to go in, and currently, Hunter is the only one with a location since he can track her through the rings."

"Wait a minute." Bishop's tone was hard, demanding, a little scary. "They have Maya. What the fuck do they have her for? How is our line part of those responsible?"

"We don't know." Warren looked to his brother like it pained him to see Hunter struggling so much. "But if I had to guess, the portal line is what makes her special, what makes her like that ancestor."

"Well, there you go. We all know everything. Hunter doesn't have to wait any longer, let's go," Loretta said as she tried to keep her cool.

Augustine slammed his fists into the fireplace mantel before any of them could move. "Fuck. Fuck! That's it!"

Camilla's heart was still racing, because what could be it now?

"What?" Kai asked from behind her.

"If we all go, we're all bound to be options for the vessel that boss wants." He looked back at them as he strained against the fireplace like he was really struggling with what decision to make. "The real question is, will we all be targets now or was Hunter it? Because taking Maya guaranteed at least Hunter would run after her. But now we'll all be there."

"I don't care," Camilla hissed. "I'm going after my sister."

"I know." He stood up straight and turned back to them. His gaze was hard, like he was telling her there was no way he'd leave Maya behind, and Camilla couldn't tell if that was just because Maya was an 'asset' to his family, because she was his son's mate, or because he actually cared—even slightly—for Maya's well-being. "I'm just trying to figure out which one of us they'll go after in the end."

Camilla looked back to Hunter in his shield. There was a sheen of sweat on his skin from all he exerted fighting the spell keeping him locked in place, but he'd calmed down when he'd heard everyone ready to immediately leave rather than wait around.

"We can't wait around." Vera stepped up. "This isn't like the Bridgers. We have no line of attack, and they aren't like that sick coven. They could kill Maya at any moment. Let's go." Authoritative Vera was sort of a scary Vera. "Now!"

Everyone nodded as Harry looked to Hunter. "We need the location."

That would be more difficult, considering he felt Maya's location, but he still bit out the name of a warehouse. "It's at the edge of town, in the middle of nowhere," he said like he knew the exact location.

Then Camilla remembered Hunter's sister had taken his mate, so maybe he did know the location. Maybe it was part of their past.

Augustine dropped the spell holding Hunter in, and Hunter was gone. He didn't wait around, just shadowed out. Then his brother and father were out. Then everyone paired off and was gone. Vera with Harry. Loretta with Bishop. Camilla with Kai. Tamire alone since Lila had to stay with Aurelia.

Hunter had told them the inside of a warehouse, but when they landed, Vera was looking out at the behemoth of a building.

Harry's brows were furrowing, then he muttered, "I can't port into the building."

A glance around told Vera everyone else was having the same problem. Hunter did not look happy about the matter.

Her mother muttered under her breath, then a shimmer came from around the building and Vera realized why they hadn't been able to make their way inside. There was a shield put up around the warehouse, and close inspection showed salt lining the edges all around with a candle every twenty feet or so. But even with the help of the salt and candles, that was a lot of work to shield an *entire* warehouse.

Then there were two figures stepping out—but still within the protective efforts of the shield—and Vera recognized one as Grandmama. The other, who she guessed was T.J., wore an ivy cap that did an excellent job covering his face.

And when he removed it, Vera felt a flutter of recognition travel through her. Standing before her group, as the enemy that they've been fighting this entire time, was the man she'd bumped into at the antique shop she'd found her family book in. The man who had clutched onto a storybook like his life depended on it. And Vera realized then that the storybook had been the one of Grandmama.

The same bald head. The same goatee. The same handsome features.

"You," she breathed at the same moment Kai muttered a "Fuck" and both Warren and Camilla exclaimed, "Professor Jenkins?"

Professor Jenkins?

The cute Professor Timothy Jenkins Camilla had told her all about?

Timothy Jenkins. T.J.. It was all coming together.

He grinned at them like he'd just fabricated the best mystery of all time and the audience was in awe. Except this was real life and not a movie, and Vera was far from awed.

They stopped in a mini circle of candles Vera hadn't noticed before. Their own form of extra protection.

"Hello, friends." His eyes glittered in the way that Hunter's had the first time they'd met in the church when he was pulling a staff out of a priest's chest—cold and cruel.

Harry turned to her. "You recognize him?"

Vera was still struck. "I—barely. We bumped into each other the day I found the family Book."

Her mother stepped up so she was directly between both of her daughters. "Another of the Book's warnings."

Vera scoffed. To think she could've stopped all of this by taking the storybook from the man who had clutched it tight to his chest. Timothy Jenkins.

Timothy looked to Hunter. "You look displeased, friend."

He was goading the demon. And in Hunter's current state, it would work.

"She is a pretty girl." His hands rested in the pockets of his trench coat lazily. "Too bad Selin needs her dead."

The growl that escaped Hunter rumbled the ground so badly, it felt like a portal was going to open.

But Vera had caught that—Selin. Was that Grandmama's true name? One so similar to the human they were friends with?

Timothy looked pleased.

No. More than pleased. It looked like this was exactly the response he was looking for. "I wonder, what will become of you when the girl is gone?"

Hunter was up against their shield, but they stood so far

back from it, the amusement never left them as Hunter beat into the force. "I will kill you!" he roared.

Grandmama's smile was still warm. She truly didn't care for the events before her. This was her final retribution, and she didn't care what harm it caused.

Timothy, on the other hand, tilted his head slightly as his lips quirked up. "Is that so? Because I was told that mates cannot live without one another. That they give up when their other half is gone. Am I mistaken to believe you two are mates?"

Hunter didn't respond. He didn't move away from the force, but he wasn't fighting against it anymore. He likely knew there was nothing he could do to break through it. And anyone looking into that man's eyes could see he would without a doubt give up his life if something happened to Maya.

Again, Timothy looked more than pleased.

"You are quite powerful," Timothy changed the subject.

Vera glanced around their little group. Augustine and Warren stood the closest to Hunter, and they both looked on edge. And now it was clear as day that Augustine didn't just want to save Maya because she could be an advantage to his family, but that he'd grown to care for her too.

His features didn't give that away, but his stance was too rigid.

And Warren looked as concerned as Vera would've expected. She'd seen the way he'd looked at Maya recently. Like he really considered her a sister.

"And without a mate, you'd be a body without a soul. Useless."

Tamire looked pained, like he needed to save Maya for his family's sake. For Lila and Aurelia's sake. For his own sake. Because they'd grown close in the last month.

Kai looked analyzing, always taking in the situation around him.

Camilla beside him, horrified. It was probably killing her the most after Hunter. They'd grown up together.

And their parents? They looked almost as ready to give up their lives. Except they wouldn't be able to since they had more kids so they'd have to live with the pain.

"But that body would be most useful to me. From what I hear, it holds the most stolen powers of any demon—though I must say, your sister was quite adamant that half of the powers aren't strong."

The tight squeeze on her hand told Vera how Harry felt. He'd grown closest to Maya first out of the three of them. Become her brother. His instincts always fired up to protect her the way a brother would.

"How your stolen powers affect you does not matter to me. I will have everything currently in your body, plus all that I have garnered. And after dear Selin here finishes this final step of her revenge, I will have her faerie dust as well. I will possess it all and it will all work. I will be indestructible."

And Vera herself? She'd just met Maya a few months prior. Had been scared of the girl at first, but now she adored the middle Whittle.

Or Delvaux now. A small smile escaped her thoughts.

Vera couldn't fathom a life without her dark witch of a sister.

"*I* will be the true magic."

Hunter was no longer paying attention to him, his gaze now off in the distance of a particular section of the warehouse. Vera guessed that's where he felt Maya.

"What about you?" Kai nodded to Grandmama—Selin—his tone inquisitive. "What does Maya have that makes her your last victim? How is it not any of the other Whittles?"

Selin's smile never wavered. She looked like an old woman ready to go. Like her life's work would finally be complete and she could rest in peace beside her family. "It was not a Whittle I was after."

What?

So why was Maya in the middle of this?

"Warlocks take the name of their covens. Bishop Whittle, that is not your true name. But even your true name is not what I am in search of. Because long back in your ancestors lies the witch Miradora. She was another dark witch."

"There are plenty of dark witches!" Vera seethed, though she realized those plenty of dark witches didn't hold her father's blood.

"But only one with her capabilities." Grandmama—Selin's— hands rested together at her front. It was almost relaxing, watching the way she stood there. Her serene features completely opposite to Timothy's greed.

"What capability?" her father bit out harsher than Vera had ever heard from him. The protective father.

Selin smiled. "Miradora was looking for a way to save her love, her soulmate. Mates. He was a demon as well." She looked to Hunter for the first time. "He was stuck in Hell's Gate, the demon Adramalech." Warren and Camilla both stiffened, unsurprising as the two most into stories within their group. "So she made it her mission to get him out. Without the key. She was the one who found out about my existence. The one who figured out that my kids each carried a bit of me. The one who stoked the flames that led to my family's despise. All to get enough power to get her mate out."

Vera's breath held. Maya's portal control.

"But she was never able to hold the power." Selin never broke her gaze from Hunter, and Hunter never looked away from that edge of the warehouse. "She killed my entire family for just enough power to pull her mate out. And now her descendant has that power too. Except it is a true power now. It was my family that created that girl, and it will be my family that takes her out."

A part of that story stuck with Vera.

Her descendant.

Miradora's descendant.

Miradora and Adramalech's descendant.

That meant far up in his line, Bishop had a demon.

"So what are you doing out here?" Camilla growled.

She was interrupted when Grandmama's smile grew, yet still somehow remained soft. "There is no need to keep this warehouse either."

Hunter's entire form froze.

Vera's form froze.

Everyone froze.

The Eight had a thing for bombs. And if this warehouse didn't need to stay…

Hunter was no longer sane about it, he banged against the shield, the attempts he continued to make to shadow through it obvious. He looked deranged, and Timothy had been right—Hunter would not be able to survive a world without his mate.

39

"You look cozy next to the dead."

Maya glanced up at the sound of Colette's voice as she walked into the light of the room. Maya had tried leaving using the light from her phone, but she hadn't been able to find a single entrance or exit. She'd guessed it was one of those doors that laid flat against the wall when closed—basically impossible to find with only the little flashlight on her phone. So she'd gone back and sat beside Vikki's body, which she'd laid nicely out in the middle of the circle of candles.

Candles that had stopped burning.

Maya shot to her feet, turning on guard against the halfie who still held all of her magic.

Colette smiled something cruel and delighted. "You're cuffed, Witch. I don't think it would be any fun to fight you. It'd be pathetic how easily you'd go down. Like a human. It wouldn't even be worth the expenditure of my powers."

Maya didn't make the mistake of believing she was safe. She moved slowly around the circle of the only light in the room, Colette walking opposite her. "Then what's the point of keeping me here?"

"Grandmama asked to specifically hold you here, her most anticipated ending."

If Grandmama wanted her here, then she was the last person on the list. How was *she* the last person on that list? How was her family involved at all?

"Plus," Colette smirked as they continued their advances around the circle, "it's killing my brother to have you in here."

"And you hate your brother oh so dearly?" She really shouldn't be goading the one with a full range of powers.

"I hate most everyone oh so dearly." Colette didn't look too bothered. "But let me ask you something, what is it in my brother that you *like*? You're bred to be the complete opposite of him. You *care*. I do not understand how you've lulled yourself into the falsehood that he is good."

He's my mate.

"I haven't," Maya answered. "Lulled myself. I know he's not good."

"Isn't that sacrilege?" Colette mimicked impropriety. "Witches who don't prosper from purity?"

Maya shrugged. "I'm a defective witch."

"And a soon to be dead one."

Colette stopped in her spot across the circle of light, causing Maya to stop and watch. It was like Colette was analyzing her for something.

"You feel different."

"Excuse me?" Maya wasn't offended, just confused. "What do you mean *feel*?"

Colette watched her curiously. "I can detect energies. It's how I knew Hunter wasn't around every time I attacked."

And her energy felt different?

"Wouldn't you wager my energy is off because you just made a little girl kill herself in front of me and have me trapped here as your fucking dead woman's sacrifice?"

"No," Colette spoke calmly, her eyes drinking in every aspect of Maya.

"Then what?" Maya was more annoyed now.

Colette didn't answer, her gaze slowly traveling back up and meeting Maya's chocolate browns. Her eyes narrowed on her, then dropped again.

Then her breathing hitched, and they were on Maya's again. Disbelieving.

"What the fuck are you doing, Colette?"

Colette glanced down to where Maya hands rested before her stomach. To the ring.

Fuck. If she hadn't figured it out before, Colette definitely knew now.

Her brother was mated.

And the best way to get back at a man you hate is to hurt—or worse, kill—said mate.

Colette froze, her gaze frozen to Maya's hands. *Fuck, fuck, fuck.*

Maya shot her right hand to cover her left, like there was any semblance of covering the ring now. The halfie had definitely seen it.

Her gaze slowly moved up until they met with Maya's and narrowed. But she didn't say anything.

Maya gave an ironic smile. "Guess figuring out I'm Hunter's mate and not just the woman he's fucking is going to make killing me all the more fun."

"I never thought he was just fucking you." She still looked half distracted, like she was processing something in her mind.

Maya almost rolled her eyes—only barely restraining herself at the last moment—and watched Colette closely. "Whatever. The point is you see the mating ring. I know that vindictive mind of yours is already coming up with the best way to elongate Hunter's torture."

Colette's eyes were on her, analyzing her. "I already knew about the rings."

Then they were back to where Maya still held her right hand covering her left. If she'd already known they were mated, then what was happening with the halfie? "Then what the hell is captivating you right now?"

Colette's eyes glowed, and Maya's heart rate sped up.

The candles were completely burnt out. Hunter would be able to feel her. Meaning, the only reason he wasn't beside her in that moment was because he couldn't be.

That fact scared Maya.

It meant something may have happened to him, but with Colette right in front of her, Maya doubted it. More likely, he was barred from wherever Maya was at the moment.

Then, like she'd made a decision, Colette simply replied, "I do not hurt my own kind."

<hr>

Hunter needed to get into that warehouse. If anything was going to happen, it was happening to the both of them.

But he couldn't *fucking* get through. He couldn't even walk through the shield. He needed to get to her.

He needed to get to her.

He needed to get to her.

He needed her.

He needed his family.

The ring was flaring up, telling him Maya was exerting plenty of energy. It only ever did that when they trained. And if she was exerting that much, she was fighting. Or trying desperately to escape because she saw the bomb.

Because it had to be a bomb. These fuckers loved bombs.

A growl vibrated through him as he focused on Timothy, who looked amused. He looked worse than greedy. He looked on the verge on an orgasm.

He was a dead man. Hunter would rip him apart before offing himself.

The shadows wrapped around him again and again and

again, but no matter what he did, Hunter couldn't get them to find their way through the shield and into the warehouse.

"Tick, tick, tick…" Timothy's grin was wider than the Cheshire Cat's.

Pain shot through the ring and up his arm. Somehow, he could tell that it was both physical and emotional.

"Tick…"

He needed to be there with her. To calm her worries. To kiss the pain away. To end with her. With his family.

"Tick…"

His body numbed to any feeling as he ravaged the shield that kept him so far back from the warehouse he doubted he'd feel the true force of the explosion.

The rushing feeling was gone from the ring.

Timothy breathed out in ecstasy. "Boom."

Hunter's heart stopped. No.

The warehouse blew up in a cacophony of steel, the flames exploding in a mix of acids Maya's fire wouldn't be able to protect her from.

He couldn't feel her through the ring.

He couldn't feel her.

He couldn't…

A roar tore from his throat as he banged against the shield, his gaze glued to the spot he'd felt her last, right in the warehouse. The world shook around him, but the cry wouldn't stop.

His mate.

His mate.

She was his mate.

Without her, he had no reason to be there.

40

The shield dropped with the force of the explosion, but he couldn't focus on that. He was so numb, he wasn't sure if he was still standing as he stared at the last spot she'd been.

The acid filled his scenting power so strongly, he knew there was almost no chance a body would survive it. No chance any remains would be found. No chance for his body to lay forever beside hers.

His ears rang, and the only voice his mind filled with was Maya's. Her laughs. Her cries. Her threats. Her moans. *Every piece of her.*

His fingers tingled, and the only thing he felt was Maya. Her hair. Her hips. Her legs. Her cunt. *Every piece of her.*

His vision blurred, and all he saw was Maya. Her chocolate browns. Her brilliant smile. Her flowing waves. Her luscious curves. *Every piece of her.*

His tongue dried, and all he tasted was Maya. Her tongue on his. Her pulse pounding under his lips. Her breaths mixing with his. Her cunt wet and ready for him. *Every piece of her.*

His scent picked through the acid and smelled the need

Maya always had around him. Her arousal filling his every thought. He needed her.

He had nothing without her.

He was death incarnate.

He felt savage ferocity rush him and turned on Timothy and Selin still hidden in that little shield of theirs that had protected them from the blast. Selin, who finally looked content. And Timothy, who looked like his wishes were all finally lining up.

But they wouldn't line up.

Never.

Because Hunter was going to rip him apart now or kill himself so he couldn't abuse Maya anymore. Because doing anything to him would be like doing it to Maya. Hunter couldn't allow any more harm on his mate.

His fire.

His everything.

His Maya.

His…

"Maya?" He heard from behind him.

"Maya?"

"Maya!"

What the fuck?

He turned and realized he was hallucinating. Because there she was. Running straight for him.

He grimaced and turned vengeful eyes back on the two responsible. And froze.

They were struck in awe. Which meant they were seeing the same thing he was, and they most definitely hadn't expected her to survive that explosion.

Then it was like his ears unclogged and the entire world came crashing in around him. His family was screaming for her. Her family was screaming for her.

A portal opened behind Timothy and Grandmama through a marble Hunter couldn't see, and they were gone, but he couldn't focus on that.

He turned and saw the family moving in her direction.

So he wasn't hallucinating. She was really there. And she was running right for him.

His breath caught in his throat, refusing to come back out until she was in his arms.

He finally pushed himself toward her and in seconds felt the warmth of her body crashing into his. Felt her fingers diggings into his back. Felt her legs wrapping around him so tightly his hips might break from the force. Felt her breath hit his neck. Felt her heart beating against his.

He fell to his knees as the relief hit him so hard, he was shocked he'd stayed on his feet so long.

Finally, he could breathe again.

Because she was in his arms.

Alive.

Breathing.

She was in his arms again.

M aya would never let go, couldn't fathom the thought. She'd felt him through the rings before she'd had to peel hers off. She'd felt the terror run through him and had known it was for fear that she would be gone.

She knew that fear, but couldn't imagine a time of knowing that fear and being completely helpless to do anything about it. She would never let go of him. Couldn't.

His lips pressed into her neck, into her pulse. Kissed the spot repeatedly, like the feeling of her pulse beating beneath his lips was a life-force in it of itself.

She kissed his neck, his pulse, because she, too, needed this reassurance. Then she pulled away just enough so their noses brushed together, and she could see the tears staining his cheeks. She'd never seen him cry before. She kissed him hard because she needed to.

When she pulled away, her hands cradling his face moved slowly so her thumbs could brush away the tears. "You're crying," she whispered softly, feeling her own eyes watering.

"Am I?" he asked as his eyes drank her in.

Her lips tipped up as she leaned back into him, pressing her lips to his, her tongue slipping through to taste all of him. While one of his hands remained at the small of her back as she sat on his lap, the other slipped up and into her hair, mussing into her tangles and angling her for his tongue.

Lords, she'd never let go.

"We understand you two are mates, but share, please." Her father's lively voice came from her side.

She pulled away and caught Hunter's stare. He didn't want to share. And the selfish part of her wanted to give him what he wanted and just shadow home and be the two of them.

But this was her family, and they deserved their own relief. Their own peace.

She pulled away a little bit more, and he understood that he had to release her. But the way his eyes darkened at the understanding told her how much he didn't like it.

Maya wiped the last stains of his tears away, then unwrapped herself from him and they rose to their feet. She turned so that her back still pressed into him and faced her family. The tears in her parents eyes, in her sisters', in Harry's and Warren's and Tamire's. The peace in Kai and Augustine.

She smiled at them, her parents the first to break and peel her away from Hunter to hug her between them. It'd been so long since she'd felt this from a parent, and never since she'd felt it from both.

The love and fear that comes with being a parent. She couldn't fathom that amount of stress, but if Hunter had his way, she'd find out soon enough.

She hugged them back tight because sometimes even Maya needed this warmth from her parents.

When they finally peeled away, Camilla and Vera were on

her. Harry didn't wait long before joining in. It was the four of them again, the way it had been at the beginning of finding out about the supernatural world.

Her sisters and brother. She couldn't imagine a life without them.

And when they peeled away, tears freely slipping down both of her sister's faces, Tamire brought her in for a hug. "Can you imagine what Aurelia would have done to us if something happened to your mate?"

Maya laughed. "So that's where the concern stems from."

He furrowed his brows jokingly at her. "Well of course. Why else?"

She pushed away and gave Kai a short hug before turning to Warren. Her little brother.

She stepped up to him. "You crying there, little bro?"

A grin broke through the couple of tears that still slipped down his cheeks, and he pulled her in tight. She hugged him back fiercely. Her brotherhood with Warren was different than Harry's. Warren was younger, and she had a sense of older sibling around him that she didn't feel with Harry, the need to protect him. And the way he embraced her told her how much he felt the need to protect her.

She could feel the irritation radiating off of Hunter when they finally peeled apart. Warren looked past her shoulder with a smirk. "One more hug, big sis?"

Hunter's growl grew and they laughed.

Finally, she turned to the patriarch of her new family. Her new father. Augustine Delvaux. "Scared something happened to your asset, old man?"

He smirked. "Terrified."

Maya's eyes warmed as she grinned up at the man and walked into his embrace. It took him a moment, but he finally gave in and wrapped his arms around her, holding her a little tighter before releasing.

"That's enough," Hunter barked.

To be fair, Maya also felt the incessant need to get back into his arms.

She pulled away from Augustine and moved back to Hunter, wrapping her arms around his waist. "Best for last?"

His arms circled around her shoulders and pulled her in so their bodies were flush. "Always." He kissed her again, then pulled away suddenly. "Why can't I feel you through the rings?"

She sighed and pulled her hand free to show him. "I hurt my fingers on our way out. I had to take it off." She'd refused to leave the warehouse without Vikki when Colette had surprisingly insisted that she follow her out. Maya still wasn't sure why the halfie had changed her mind so suddenly. But because Maya had refused to leave without Vikki's body, they'd carried her out. And moments before the explosion, they'd tripped and Maya had scraped her entire hand so harshly she'd needed to take the ring off to relieve some of the pain. She'd had just enough left in her to take Vikki far enough away before the warehouse blew up. "Don't worry, it's in my pocket, and when one of these warlocks fix me, it'll be back on my little finger."

"Warlock," he growled demandingly, obviously uncaring which one answered. "Heal her."

She laughed as her father stepped up. Hunter didn't release his hold on her as she turned so her father could reach her hand.

It was healed in the matter of seconds and she was glad for it. She'd become too used to having the ring on and Hunter beating through her system that she felt empty without it.

She didn't wait to take out the ring and slip it back on, Hunter's emotions immediately slipping through and a rush of need filling her. She turned admonishing eyes on him. "Behave."

"No." He grinned mischievously as his lips met hers.

Warren interrupted with a growl, "What the fuck is she doing here?"

Hunter looked up, and Maya turned in time to see Colette

walking toward them. Maya had wondered if she'd just leave, but apparently not.

Hunter moved on instinct, shoving her behind him, a hand settling over her stomach as she tried to step around him. The entire family stood on the defensive, Warren and Augustine stepping up on either side of them a little more than the others. They had experience with the halfie and knew how to control her better.

"Hunter. Hunt." She tried to calm him. "Baby, relax. She's the one that helped me get out."

"Why?" he growled possessively. He was smart to doubt said sister doing anything kind for him.

Colette smirked with a shrug, saying the same thing she'd said in the warehouse before offering Maya an out. "I do not hurt my own kind."

"What the fuck are you talking about?" Warren sounded ready to attack her himself.

"Nice to know I'm not the only lost one," Maya muttered.

But Hunter's breath hitched beside her, his hand tightening around Maya, and his eyes growing darker.

"I won't be on their nice list, so I'll be off. I think I've pissed off enough people in this territory," Colette spoke matter-of-factly, but Maya swore there was a bit more emotion behind it all.

Hunter stood rigidly staring at his sister. But the same hate wasn't there.

Colette's eyes were still hard as she stared back—they'd never grow warm for her brother—but her lips tipped up an inch. She nodded to him like they were in agreement and stepped back. "Take care of her." She took another step back. "Brother."

Then she turned and walked away.

Augustine's voice broke the silence that carried behind her. "Should I stop her?"

It dawned on Maya that he was asking his son, rather than

making this one decision on his own. Like he could see there was an agreement between the two even though he didn't understand it.

"No." Hunter watched his sister walk away for long minutes until she was gone from view entirely.

41

"*I* cannot believe I ever thought that man was attractive," Camilla muttered as she snuggled into the edge of the couch, pillows snuggled in her lap.

Kai sat right beside her and threw his arms over the couch's back. Like, so close her crisscrossed leg fell over his. "Now aren't you glad I didn't let him take you on a date?"

Camilla glared at him as her mother turned on her. "He asked you on a date? I don't care if he wasn't the psychopath we just met, he's closer to my age *and* your professor. That's inappropriate, Camilla."

Camilla curled in on herself. It'd been a while since she'd been reprimanded by her mother. "I didn't go," she argued meekly.

"Thanks to Kai," Loretta grumbled as she moved to the ottoman by the fireplace. Now that Maya's permanent seat was Hunter's lap, the ottoman was left open for anyone's taking. Her parents had made it their new spot.

Bishop sat beside his wife and calmly looked to Kai. "I think she means to say *thank you*." His tone gave off much more appreciation.

Kai winked, and Camilla felt an indescribable need to punch him in his smug little face.

"I *hate* you," she grumbled under her breath so only he could hear.

He didn't turn to her, but flicked the back of her neck. Her need to punch him only grew.

Harry, as always, brought the conversation to the important matter at hand, "We need to focus. That *man*—I loathe to give him that title—looked determined. Like he didn't care for the choosing. He had his mind set on Hunter."

Augustine shrugged from his usual spot next to said son. "He made a fair point. Hunter *has* always been able to steal as much as he wants."

Camilla's brows furrowed. "But can't all demons do that?"

"No," her father answered. "Most demons, and witches," he turned a knowing look to his middle daughter, "can steal powers, but there are limits to how much can be taken at different intervals. Most need time between taking one power and the next."

Augustine nodded. "I can take up to three if they're weaker powers, but the stronger the power, the less I'm capable of taking at once. I would assume Warren's the same, but he's never stolen, so I don't know. But Hunt," he clasped his son on the shoulder, "he's always been able to take as many as he likes."

Said son hardly looked to be paying attention. He only looked interested in taking his mate home.

"Is it like eating?" Vera asked. "Like when your stomach tells you you're full?"

"Almost," Augustine answered. "But more intense. It's more like a warning that you can't refuse even if you want to."

"So he knows that." Her mother looked upset, but Camilla figured it was for the safety of her newest son rather than because she had almost gone on a date with the literal villain. "This Timothy man, he figured that out. And he needs someone who can take as much power as possible so that all the vessels can be emptied at once."

"And I'm guessing taking Maya was his way of getting Hunter to go to him." Tamire played with his wife's hand like he needed the physical contact. "And killing her would have been his way of weakening Hunter to a point where he wouldn't fight so that he could take control of his body."

Kai tsked. "He wouldn't stop there. That man wants all the power. He's not going to risk putting it in another person. If he's using Hunter's body, he's going to want to be in Hunter's body. Become Hunter. Like he said, once Maya was gone, Hunter's soul would leave with her. He'd be useless, dead. It really just worked out for him that it turned out that the demon who *could* take that many powers at once is also mated."

"And his plan failed," Lila said softly.

"Which only means he'll still be after Hunt," Loretta said—and she'd used Hunt, a nickname Camilla had only ever heard come from the Delvauxs. "And Grandmama—Selin—saw Maya running out. She won't rest until Maya's taken care of too."

"Great," Camilla bitterly mumbled under her breath.

She looked to the couple in question, but neither looked like they had any input. They honestly only seemed interested in one another. And Camilla was glad to not feel the envy she once had when looking at them. Instead, it was like seeing a role model, something she could look to as the example of her future.

She just loved their love.

Hunter shadowed them back to the manor. He'd said it was about damn time they had their alone time. And Maya couldn't argue that she agreed.

He landed them in the hallway leading to their bedroom.

She narrowed her gaze on him. "You couldn't shadow the extra ten feet to the room?"

He pulled away from her with a crooked grin and turned to a door that did not lead to their room.

It was a small room, something Maya had always considered putting a few lounge chairs and chaises and candles into for when she wanted a *different* type of room to draw in.

She followed him in.

She'd made the progress to her little drawing room with a single chaise ottoman. "Why are we here?"

"I've been thinking," he moved to hold her from behind, pressing her back into his chest as he breathed her in, "this could make a pretty nice nursery."

Her breathing stilled as she imagined it. A crib in the middle, a soft plush rug, a thick reading chair in the corner, and a rocking chair in the opposite corner. Curtains that hugged the window, but never hid the beauty of the moon. And a mess of framed photos. It was a beautiful picture.

She relaxed into him and tilted her head back so that she could kiss his jaw as her gaze settled on the chaise ottoman. Right where the crib would be.

"I love the sound of that," she whispered almost inaudibly. Her heart ached so deeply with the need to have that picture become a reality that it was all she could muster.

His arms tightened around her waist as he dipped to the crook of her neck, leaving light kisses down her neck and over her shoulder.

"Then you're ready?" he asked, and she swore there was a hint of anticipation in his voice, like he needed to hear her say it. Like it was more important to him that she be ready than anything else.

She looked out at the small room, reimagining it all, and scoffed. "Not ready." A small smile tipped her lips upward as he froze behind her. "I'm...excited. I can't wait for...it all. The room, the keeping us up all night, the too tired for sex, the havoc the manor'll turn into. All of it. I want it more than I ever thought possible."

Her heart fluttered when his forehead dropped to the back of her head in relief, and small breath-filled chuckles left his body.

He turned her around and took her face softly into his hands. "You scared me, love."

She grinned wickedly up at him. "I know."

He kissed her slowly. "I hate you, Witch."

Her heart jumped. "Good."

His thumb played with her bottom lip as he stared into her eyes, and in those black depths, Maya saw her entire future. Saw not only the family they would make, but life beyond that. Life as they grew old together. Life as they waddled around on nimble limbs but still teased each other. Still fought for one another. Still lived and breathed only because their mate was in this world with them.

He leaned down and whispered against her lips, "By the way, we could never be too tired for sex." He kissed her before she could rebut his claim.

Her demon really did have a way with words.

<hr>

She'd insisted they go back to her parents house the next night. Hunter wanted to stay in and ravage her until the new year, but Maya knew her family wanted to see her. As much as they'd smiled at her warmly when Hunter had insisted it was time for them to leave the night before—all of them knowing how much they needed to be together—Maya also understood that the explosion had scared them too. They had almost lost her too.

Why Augustine had been in his usual spot when they arrived, Maya didn't know. She couldn't fathom why he'd be there without them around. Maybe he knew she wouldn't be able to stay away.

Warren, on the other hand, looked to be getting on quite well with Kai. The two laughed in the corner as they whispered to one another, and Camilla did not look happy about it. From what Maya had heard from Harry, Kai's best friend had been a half human-demon, so she could understand where the sentimentality came for Warren.

By night's end, Maya was glad she'd decided to come that night, and she knew—even if he'd never admit it—that Hunter had enjoyed himself too.

And her heart had pounded out extra hard when he'd reached for Aurelia the moment she'd made any sound, not even allowing a cry to escape her. The way he rested her on his shoulder and rocked her to sleep as he walked around the house. It was a deciding factor in that very moment, even though she'd agreed already in the nursery, that she didn't care what troubles they had, she wanted to have his babies.

And when the group moved from the kitchen to the living room and she'd had final sight of him passed out on the couch with little Aurelia on his chest? She'd literally felt her eyes water.

"He's getting better with her," Tamire said with a grin in her direction.

"And grumbling less." Lila's smirk was a bit mischievous.

Maya smiled at them. "He's never going to admit that he cares for her, so you could forget about that."

They laughed, and Lila said earnestly, "But he's going to make a great father."

Maya's heart beat with such adoration and love, she didn't think it was possible for the little organ to hold it all as she settled in beside her mate. She tossed a leg over his and settled a hand over the one he had stabilized on Aurelia's back.

"The best," she whispered as she snuggled into them.

Hunter's arm reached out around her instinctively, always bringing her closer, even in the depths of slumber.

Aurelia wasn't asleep, but she looked content to lie there on Hunter's chest. Maya smiled at the little girl and got the most beautiful grin in return.

This would be them with their little one. Soon. Because Maya didn't want to wait any longer. She didn't just want this family, she needed it.

But before she could settle on starting their family, she needed to make sure her baby daddy remained perfectly unharmed.

DON'T FORGET TO REVIEW!

Thank you so much for finishing your read! Don't forget to leave a review or rating on all platforms as it helps me as an author more than you can ever imagine!

Amazon and Goodreads ratings help the most but feel free to talk about it everywhere else too—including social medias, blogs, Youtube reviews, and most importantly—word of mouth, and more.

JOIN MY AUTHOR NEWSLETTER

Sign up for Nelly Alikyan's newsletter to be the first to know about new releases and cover reveals, receive exclusive content—like a special scene or two—and be up to date about any other exciting news, i.e. events, signed copies, etc.

www.nellyalikyan.com

ABOUT THE AUTHOR

Nelly Alikyan is a girl from the Los Angeles Valley who moved to Boston for school and found she prefers the East Coast. But really, London is where she'd like to be since it's her favorite city ever. She's the only reader in her family—not her only cause as the black sheep—and has dreamt of being a writer for as long as she can remember.

When she's not working on her books or in the real world, she's on Youtube at Nelly Alikyan!

For more books and updates:
www.nellyalikyan.com

instagram.com/authornellyalikyan

tiktok.com/@authornalikyan

youtube.com/NellyAlikyan

amazon.com/author/nellyalikyan

goodreads.com/nellyalikyan

facebook.com/authornellyalikyan

pinterest.com/insinpublishing

ACKNOWLEDGMENTS

I don't think we give enough credit to the fact that that it's hard to write sequels. Or the fact that they get so much better the more invested we are with characters.

This story is almost done and I have enjoyed so much of my time here. I couldn't put the book down these last hundred or so pages which is saying a lot since reading draft one, I had never hated a book more. I genuinely cringed reading it.

So, thanks to editing. As a writer, I think I need to give thanks to the process more. So, thanks process.

To anyone who's stuck around to book three, thanks for coming on the journey and I hope this book was worth it for you! And I cannot wait for you to get to the finale! Our characters are almost at the end of their problems!

This series is such a guilty pleasure for me—I know I'm much better at full contemporary and full fantasy—but I've had fun. And I'm glad you've enjoyed reading along.

To my family, as per usual, for supporting my starving artist ways and not judging me for it. For never once insisting that what I want to do with my life is a waste of time, but rather being in awe that I could write a whole book. Multiple times!

Thanks for the support, familia.

9 781956 847031